Montero por
Cavallero
de Doña Ana
Sarmiento de la
del Cap. Don Gaspar
en la Ciudad de Santi

Greatest Works of
OSCAR WILDE

CLASSICS

Reprint 2024

FiNGERPRINT! CLASSiCS
An imprint of Prakash Books India Pvt. Ltd

113/A, Darya Ganj,
New Delhi-110 002
Email: info@prakashbooks.com/sales@prakashbooks.com

Fingerprint Publishing
@FingerprintP
@fingerprintpublishingbooks
www.fingerprintpublishing.com

ISBN: 978 93 8993 144 0

"Yes, death. Death must be so beautiful. To lie in the soft brown earth, with the grasses waving above one's head, and listen to silence. To have no yesterday, and no tomorrow. To forget time, to forget life, to be at peace. You can help me. You can open for me the portals of death's house, for love is always with you, and love is stronger than death is."

– The Canterville Ghost

Born in Dublin in 1854 as Oscar Fingal O'Flahertie Wills Wilde, Oscar Wilde was educated at home till the age of nine. He attended the Portora Royal School, Enniskillen from 1864 to 1871. In 1874, he graduated from Trinity College, Dublin where he won many prizes including the Berkley Gold Medal for Greek. In the same year, with a scholarship, he entered the Magdalen College, Oxford. He became well known for his role in the aesthetic and decadent movements.

In 1878, Wilde won the Newdigate Prize for his poem *Ravenna.* His first play, *Vera: or the Nihilists,* printed privately in 1880, did not meet much success. *Poems* was published in 1881. He spent the next few years on lecture tours in U.S., Canada, and London. He came to be known for his glittering conversations, biting wit, and flamboyant attires. In early 1883, while he was in Paris, Wilde wrote *The Duchess of Padua*—a five-act melodramatic tragedy in blank verse—for the actress Mary Anderson who turned it down. It was first performed after years under the title *Guido Ferranti,* at the Broadway Theatre, New York in 1891. In mid-1887 he became the editor of *The Lady's World* magazine, renaming it *The Woman's World.*

Oscar Wilde was known for promoting art for art's sake. But, contrary to this, he published a collection of fairy tales that was didactic in form in 1888. *The Happy Prince and Other Tales* consists of nine tales that touch upon varied topics, from friendship to selfless love and sacrifice. They are tragic in an absolute sense since the main characters of the stories often suffer and die in vain. Wilde garnered both praise and criticism for these fairy tales from many readers. The esteemed poet W B Yeats found them 'charming and amusing', whereas one reviewer scoffed at the use of satire in the tales, stressing that children do not care for such things.

Wilde refined his ideas about art, its purpose and supremacy, and incorporated themes of decadence, duplicity,

and beauty into his only novel, *The Picture of Dorian Gray* (1890). Continuing his interest in theatre he wrote *Salome,* a play in one act, in 1891. Originally written in French it tells the Biblical story of Salome, the stepdaughter of the tetrarch Herod Antipas. Published jointly in Paris and London in 1893, it was not performed until 1896. Wilde became one of the most successful playwrights of the late Victorian London after producing four comedies—*Lady Windermere's Fan, A Woman of No Importance, An Ideal Husband,* and *The Importance of Being Earnest.* First performed in 1895 in collaboration with George Alexander at St. James's Theater, London, *The Importance of Being Earnest* was considered Wilde's masterpiece and continues to remain his most popular play.

In 1895, Wilde sued Queensberry for libel but evidences unearthed in the trial led to his own imprisonment. He was convicted and imprisoned for two years. In 1897, he wrote a long letter to Douglas, which was published in 1905 as *De Profundis.* After his release from the reading gaol in 1897, he lived abroad in exile. *The Ballad of Reading Gaol,* published in 1898, was his last work. In this long poem, he commemorates the prison life and narrates the execution of Wooldridge who murdered his wife for infidelity. Wilde died in 1900 at the age of 46, in Paris.

The celebrated playwright's life and his works continue to fascinate the literary and non-literary world. Since his death a number of biographies have been published, the earliest being memoirs by those known to him. Many of his plays and his only novel have also been adapted into movies.

About this Edition

From criticism, essays, reviews, to poetry, short stories, plays, and even children's fiction, the witty and versatile Oscar Wilde wrote a lot. Amongst all these are two of his masterstrokes, works that earned him laurels and established his fame as a writer. This beautiful edition holds these critically acclaimed pieces—*The Importance of Being Earnest*, a play that has been revived many times and adapted for radio, television, film, operas, musicals, and *The Picture of Dorian Gray*, Wilde's only novel that became his most-read and well-known work.

Contents

The Picture of Dorian Gray

The Preface

The artist is the creator of beautiful things. To reveal art and conceal the artist is art's aim. The critic is he who can translate into another manner or a new material his impression of beautiful things.

The highest as the lowest form of criticism is a mode of autobiography. Those who find ugly meanings in beautiful things are corrupt without being charming. This is a fault.

Those who find beautiful meanings in beautiful things are the cultivated. For these there is hope. They are the elect to whom beautiful things mean only beauty.

There is no such thing as a moral or an immoral book. Books are well written, or badly written. That is all.

The nineteenth century dislike of realism is the rage of Caliban* seeing his own face in a glass.

The nineteenth century dislike of romanticism is the rage of Caliban not seeing his own face in a glass. The moral life of man forms part of the subject-matter of the artist, but the morality of art consists in the perfect use of an imperfect medium. No artist desires to prove anything. Even things that are true can be proved. No artist has ethical sympathies. An ethical sympathy in an artist is an unpardonable mannerism of style. No artist is ever morbid. The artist can express

* A boorish, ignorant slave.

everything. Thought and language are to the artist instruments of an art. Vice and virtue are to the artist materials for an art. From the point of view of form, the type of all the arts is the art of the musician. From the point of view of feeling, the actor's craft is the type. All art is at once surface and symbol. Those who go beneath the surface do so at their peril. Those who read the symbol do so at their peril. It is the spectator, and not life, that art really mirrors. Diversity of opinion about a work of art shows that the work is new, complex, and vital. When critics disagree, the artist is in accord with himself. We can forgive a man for making a useful thing as long as he does not admire it. The only excuse for making a useless thing is that one admires it intensely.

All art is quite useless.
OSCAR WILDE

CHAPTER

1

The studio was filled with the rich odour of roses, and when the light summer wind stirred amidst the trees of the garden, there came through the open door the heavy scent of the lilac, or the more delicate perfume of the pink-flowering thorn.

From the corner of the divan of Persian saddle-bags on which he was lying, smoking, as was his custom, innumerable cigarettes, Lord Henry Wotton could just catch the gleam of the honey-sweet and honey-coloured blossoms of a laburnum, whose tremulous branches seemed hardly able to bear the burden of a beauty so flamelike as theirs; and now and then the fantastic shadows of birds in flight flitted across the long tussore-silk curtains that were stretched in front of the huge window, producing a kind of momentary Japanese effect, and making him think of those pallid, jade-faced painters of Tokyo who, through the medium of an art that is necessarily immobile, seek to convey the sense of swiftness and motion. The sullen murmur of the bees shouldering their way through the long unmown grass, or circling with monotonous insistence round the dusty gilt horns of the straggling woodbine, seemed to make the stillness more oppressive. The dim roar of London was like the bourdon note of a distant organ.

In the centre of the room, clamped to an upright easel, stood the full-length portrait of a young man of extraordinary personal beauty, and in front of it, some little distance away, was sitting the artist himself, Basil Hallward, whose sudden disappearance some years ago caused, at the time, such public excitement and gave rise to so many strange conjectures.

As the painter looked at the gracious and comely form he had so skilfully mirrored in his art, a smile of pleasure passed across his face, and seemed about to linger there. But he suddenly started up, and closing his eyes, placed his fingers upon the lids, as though he sought to imprison within his brain some curious dream from which he feared he might awake.

"It is your best work, Basil, the best thing you have ever done," said Lord Henry languidly. "You must certainly send it next year to the Grosvenor.* The Academy is too large and too vulgar. Whenever I have gone there, there have been either so many people that I have not been able to see the pictures, which was dreadful, or so many pictures that I have not been able to see the people, which was worse. The Grosvenor is really the only place."

"I don't think I shall send it anywhere," he answered, tossing his head back in that odd way that used to make his friends laugh at him at Oxford. "No, I won't send it anywhere."

Lord Henry elevated his eyebrows and looked at him in amazement through the thin blue wreaths of smoke that curled up in such fanciful whorls from his heavy, opium-tainted cigarette. "Not send it anywhere? My dear fellow, why? Have you any reason? What odd chaps you painters are! You do anything in the world to gain a reputation. As soon as you have one, you seem to want to throw it away. It is silly of you, for there is only one thing in the world worse than being talked about, and that is not being talked about. A portrait like this would set you far above all the young men in England, and make the old men quite jealous, if old men are ever capable of any emotion."

"I know you will laugh at me," he replied, "but I really can't exhibit it. I have put too much of myself into it."

* Located on New Bond Street in London, Grosvenor Art Gallery was opened in the year 1877.

Lord Henry stretched himself out on the divan and laughed.

"Yes, I knew you would; but it is quite true, all the same."

"Too much of yourself in it! Upon my word, Basil, I didn't know you were so vain; and I really can't see any resemblance between you, with your rugged strong face and your coal-black hair, and this young Adonis,* who looks as if he was made out of ivory and rose-leaves. Why, my dear Basil, he is a Narcissus,† and you—well, of course you have an intellectual expression and all that. But beauty, real beauty, ends where an intellectual expression begins. Intellect is in itself a mode of exaggeration, and destroys the harmony of any face. The moment one sits down to think, one becomes all nose, or all forehead, or something horrid. Look at the successful men in any of the learned professions. How perfectly hideous they are! Except, of course, in the Church. But then in the Church they don't think. A bishop keeps on saying at the age of eighty what he was told to say when he was a boy of eighteen, and as a natural consequence he always looks absolutely delightful. Your mysterious young friend, whose name you have never told me, but whose picture really fascinates me, never thinks. I feel quite sure of that. He is some brainless beautiful creature who should be always here in winter when we have no flowers to look at, and always here in summer when we want something to chill our intelligence. Don't flatter yourself, Basil: you are not in the least like him."

"You don't understand me, Harry," answered the artist. "Of course I am not like him. I know that perfectly well. Indeed, I should be sorry to look like him. You shrug your shoulders? I am telling you the truth. There is a fatality about all physical and intellectual distinction, the sort of fatality that seems to dog through history the faltering steps of kings. It is better not to be different from one's fellows. The ugly and the stupid have the best of it in this world. They can sit at their ease and gape at the play. If they know nothing of victory, they are at least spared the knowledge of defeat. They live as we all should live—undisturbed,

* In classical myth he is a beautiful young man, killed by a boar. He turns into a purple flower as per poets Shakespeare and Ovid.

† Another beautiful young man who fell in love with his own reflection in a fountain.

indifferent, and without disquiet. They neither bring ruin upon others, nor ever receive it from alien hands. Your rank and wealth, Harry; my brains, such as they are—my art, whatever it may be worth; Dorian Gray's good looks—we shall all suffer for what the gods have given us, suffer terribly."

"Dorian Gray? Is that his name?" asked Lord Henry, walking across the studio towards Basil Hallward.

"Yes, that is his name. I didn't intend to tell it to you."

"But why not?"

"Oh, I can't explain. When I like people immensely, I never tell their names to any one. It is like surrendering a part of them. I have grown to love secrecy. It seems to be the one thing that can make modern life mysterious or marvellous to us. The commonest thing is delightful if one only hides it. When I leave town now I never tell my people where I am going. If I did, I would lose all my pleasure. It is a silly habit, I dare say, but somehow it seems to bring a great deal of romance into one's life. I suppose you think me awfully foolish about it?"

"Not at all," answered Lord Henry, "not at all, my dear Basil. You seem to forget that I am married, and the one charm of marriage is that it makes a life of deception absolutely necessary for both parties. I never know where my wife is, and my wife never knows what I am doing. When we meet—we do meet occasionally, when we dine out together, or go down to the Duke's—we tell each other the most absurd stories with the most serious faces. My wife is very good at it—much better, in fact, than I am. She never gets confused over her dates, and I always do. But when she does find me out, she makes no row at all. I sometimes wish she would; but she merely laughs at me."

"I hate the way you talk about your married life, Harry," said Basil Hallward, strolling towards the door that led into the garden. "I believe that you are really a very good husband, but that you are thoroughly ashamed of your own virtues. You are an extraordinary fellow. You never say a moral thing, and you never do a wrong thing. Your cynicism is simply a pose."

"Being natural is simply a pose, and the most irritating pose I know," cried Lord Henry, laughing; and the two young men went out into the garden together and ensconced themselves on a

long bamboo seat that stood in the shade of a tall laurel bush. The sunlight slipped over the polished leaves. In the grass, white daisies were tremulous.

After a pause, Lord Henry pulled out his watch. "I am afraid I must be going, Basil," he murmured, "and before I go, I insist on your answering a question I put to you some time ago."

"What is that?" said the painter, keeping his eyes fixed on the ground.

"You know quite well."

"I do not, Harry."

"Well, I will tell you what it is. I want you to explain to me why you won't exhibit Dorian Gray's picture. I want the real reason."

"I told you the real reason."

"No, you did not. You said it was because there was too much of yourself in it. Now, that is childish."

"Harry," said Basil Hallward, looking him straight in the face, "every portrait that is painted with feeling is a portrait of the artist, not of the sitter. The sitter is merely the accident, the occasion. It is not he who is revealed by the painter; it is rather the painter who, on the coloured canvas, reveals himself. The reason I will not exhibit this picture is that I am afraid that I have shown in it the secret of my own soul."

Lord Henry laughed. "And what is that?" he asked.

"I will tell you," said Hallward; but an expression of perplexity came over his face.

"I am all expectation, Basil," continued his companion, glancing at him.

"Oh, there is really very little to tell, Harry," answered the painter; "and I am afraid you will hardly understand it. Perhaps you will hardly believe it."

Lord Henry smiled, and leaning down, plucked a pink-petalled daisy from the grass and examined it. "I am quite sure I shall understand it," he replied, gazing intently at the little golden, white-feathered disk, "and as for believing things, I can believe anything, provided that it is quite incredible."

The wind shook some blossoms from the trees, and the heavy lilac-blooms, with their clustering stars, moved to and fro in the

languid air. A grasshopper began to chirrup by the wall, and like a blue thread a long thin dragon-fly floated past on its brown gauze wings. Lord Henry felt as if he could hear Basil Hallward's heart beating, and wondered what was coming.

"The story is simply this," said the painter after some time. "Two months ago I went to a crush at Lady Brandon's. You know we poor artists have to show ourselves in society from time to time, just to remind the public that we are not savages. With an evening coat and a white tie, as you told me once, anybody, even a stock-broker, can gain a reputation for being civilized. Well, after I had been in the room about ten minutes, talking to huge overdressed dowagers and tedious academicians, I suddenly became conscious that some one was looking at me. I turned half-way round and saw Dorian Gray for the first time. When our eyes met, I felt that I was growing pale. A curious sensation of terror came over me. I knew that I had come face to face with some one whose mere personality was so fascinating that, if I allowed it to do so, it would absorb my whole nature, my whole soul, my very art itself. I did not want any external influence in my life. You know yourself, Harry, how independent I am by nature. I have always been my own master; had at least always been so, till I met Dorian Gray. Then—but I don't know how to explain it to you. Something seemed to tell me that I was on the verge of a terrible crisis in my life. I had a strange feeling that fate had in store for me exquisite joys and exquisite sorrows. I grew afraid and turned to quit the room. It was not conscience that made me do so: it was a sort of cowardice. I take no credit to myself for trying to escape."

"Conscience and cowardice are really the same things, Basil. Conscience is the trade-name of the firm. That is all."

"I don't believe that, Harry, and I don't believe you do either. However, whatever was my motive—and it may have been pride, for I used to be very proud—I certainly struggled to the door. There, of course, I stumbled against Lady Brandon. 'You are not going to run away so soon, Mr. Hallward?' she screamed out. You know her curiously shrill voice?"

"Yes; she is a peacock in everything but beauty," said Lord Henry, pulling the daisy to bits with his long nervous fingers.

"I could not get rid of her. She brought me up to royalties, and people with stars and garters,* and elderly ladies with gigantic tiaras and parrot noses. She spoke of me as her dearest friend. I had only met her once before, but she took it into her head to lionize me. I believe some picture of mine had made a great success at the time, at least had been chattered about in the penny newspapers, which is the nineteenth-century standard of immortality. Suddenly I found myself face to face with the young man whose personality had so strangely stirred me. We were quite close, almost touching. Our eyes met again. It was reckless of me, but I asked Lady Brandon to introduce me to him. Perhaps it was not so reckless, after all. It was simply inevitable. We would have spoken to each other without any introduction. I am sure of that. Dorian told me so afterwards. He, too, felt that we were destined to know each other."

"And how did Lady Brandon describe this wonderful young man?" asked his companion. "I know she goes in for giving a rapid *precis* of all her guests. I remember her bringing me up to a truculent and red-faced old gentleman covered all over with orders and ribbons, and hissing into my ear, in a tragic whisper which must have been perfectly audible to everybody in the room, the most astounding details. I simply fled. I like to find out people for myself. But Lady Brandon treats her guests exactly as an auctioneer treats his goods. She either explains them entirely away, or tells one everything about them except what one wants to know."

"Poor Lady Brandon! You are hard on her, Harry!" said Hallward listlessly.

"My dear fellow, she tried to found a *salon*, and only succeeded in opening a restaurant. How could I admire her? But tell me, what did she say about Mr. Dorian Gray?"

"Oh, something like, 'Charming boy—poor dear mother and I absolutely inseparable. Quite forget what he does—afraid he—doesn't do anything—oh, yes, plays the piano—or is it the violin, dear Mr. Gray?' Neither of us could help laughing, and we became friends at once."

---

* Badges of knighthood.

"Laughter is not at all a bad beginning for a friendship, and it is far the best ending for one," said the young lord, plucking another daisy.

Hallward shook his head. "You don't understand what friendship is, Harry," he murmured—"or what enmity is, for that matter. You like every one; that is to say, you are indifferent to every one."

"How horribly unjust of you!" cried Lord Henry, tilting his hat back and looking up at the little clouds that, like ravelled skeins of glossy white silk, were drifting across the hollowed turquoise of the summer sky. "Yes; horribly unjust of you. I make a great difference between people. I choose my friends for their good looks, my acquaintances for their good characters, and my enemies for their good intellects. A man cannot be too careful in the choice of his enemies. I have not got one who is a fool. They are all men of some intellectual power, and consequently they all appreciate me. Is that very vain of me? I think it is rather vain."

"I should think it was, Harry. But according to your category I must be merely an acquaintance."

"My dear old Basil, you are much more than an acquaintance."

"And much less than a friend. A sort of brother, I suppose?"

"Oh, brothers! I don't care for brothers. My elder brother won't die, and my younger brothers seem never to do anything else."

"Harry!" exclaimed Hallward, frowning.

"My dear fellow, I am not quite serious. But I can't help detesting my relations. I suppose it comes from the fact that none of us can stand other people having the same faults as ourselves. I quite sympathize with the rage of the English democracy against what they call the vices of the upper orders. The masses feel that drunkenness, stupidity, and immorality should be their own special property, and that if any one of us makes an ass of himself, he is poaching on their preserves. When poor Southwark got into the divorce court, their indignation was quite magnificent. And yet I don't suppose that ten per cent of the proletariat live correctly."

"I don't agree with a single word that you have said, and, what is more, Harry, I feel sure you don't either."

Lord Henry stroked his pointed brown beard and tapped the toe of his patent-leather boot with a tasselled ebony cane. "How

English you are Basil! That is the second time you have made that observation. If one puts forward an idea to a true Englishman—always a rash thing to do—he never dreams of considering whether the idea is right or wrong. The only thing he considers of any importance is whether one believes it oneself. Now, the value of an idea has nothing whatsoever to do with the sincerity of the man who expresses it. Indeed, the probabilities are that the more insincere the man is, the more purely intellectual will the idea be, as in that case it will not be coloured by either his wants, his desires, or his prejudices. However, I don't propose to discuss politics, sociology, or metaphysics with you. I like persons better than principles, and I like persons with no principles better than anything else in the world. Tell me more about Mr. Dorian Gray. How often do you see him?"

"Every day. I couldn't be happy if I didn't see him every day. He is absolutely necessary to me."

"How extraordinary! I thought you would never care for anything but your art."

"He is all my art to me now," said the painter gravely. "I sometimes think, Harry, that there are only two eras of any importance in the world's history. The first is the appearance of a new medium for art, and the second is the appearance of a new personality for art also. What the invention of oil-painting was to the Venetians, the face of Antinous* was to late Greek sculpture, and the face of Dorian Gray will some day be to me. It is not merely that I paint from him, draw from him, sketch from him. Of course, I have done all that. But he is much more to me than a model or a sitter. I won't tell you that I am dissatisfied with what I have done of him, or that his beauty is such that art cannot express it. There is nothing that art cannot express, and I know that the work I have done, since I met Dorian Gray, is good work, is the best work of my life. But in some curious way—I wonder will you understand me?—his personality has suggested to me an entirely new manner in art, an entirely new mode of style. I see things differently, I think of them differently. I can now recreate life in a way that was hidden from me before. 'A dream of form in days of thought'—who is it who says that? I forget; but it is what

* Favourite page boy of the Roman emperor Hadrian (AD 76-138).

Dorian Gray has been to me. The merely visible presence of this lad—for he seems to me little more than a lad, though he is really over twenty—his merely visible presence—ah! I wonder can you realize all that that means? Unconsciously he defines for me the lines of a fresh school, a school that is to have in it all the passion of the romantic spirit, all the perfection of the spirit that is Greek. The harmony of soul and body—how much that is! We in our madness have separated the two, and have invented a realism that is vulgar, an ideality that is void. Harry! if you only knew what Dorian Gray is to me! You remember that landscape of mine, for which Agnew* offered me such a huge price but which I would not part with? It is one of the best things I have ever done. And why is it so? Because, while I was painting it, Dorian Gray sat beside me. Some subtle influence passed from him to me, and for the first time in my life I saw in the plain woodland the wonder I had always looked for and always missed."

"Basil, this is extraordinary! I must see Dorian Gray."

Hallward got up from the seat and walked up and down the garden. After some time he came back. "Harry," he said, "Dorian Gray is to me simply a motive in art. You might see nothing in him. I see everything in him. He is never more present in my work than when no image of him is there. He is a suggestion, as I have said, of a new manner. I find him in the curves of certain lines, in the loveliness and subtleties of certain colours. That is all."

"Then why won't you exhibit his portrait?" asked Lord Henry.

"Because, without intending it, I have put into it some expression of all this curious artistic idolatry, of which, of course, I have never cared to speak to him. He knows nothing about it. He shall never know anything about it. But the world might guess it, and I will not bare my soul to their shallow prying eyes. My heart shall never be put under their microscope. There is too much of myself in the thing, Harry—too much of myself!"

"Poets are not so scrupulous as you are. They know how useful passion is for publication. Nowadays a broken heart will run to many editions."

---

* Erstwhile London art dealer and adviser Sir William Agnew (1825-1910).

"I hate them for it," cried Hallward. "An artist should create beautiful things, but should put nothing of his own life into them. We live in an age when men treat art as if it were meant to be a form of autobiography. We have lost the abstract sense of beauty. Some day I will show the world what it is; and for that reason the world shall never see my portrait of Dorian Gray."

"I think you are wrong, Basil, but I won't argue with you. It is only the intellectually lost who ever argue. Tell me, is Dorian Gray very fond of you?"

The painter considered for a few moments. "He likes me," he answered after a pause; "I know he likes me. Of course I flatter him dreadfully. I find a strange pleasure in saying things to him that I know I shall be sorry for having said. As a rule, he is charming to me, and we sit in the studio and talk of a thousand things. Now and then, however, he is horribly thoughtless, and seems to take a real delight in giving me pain. Then I feel, Harry, that I have given away my whole soul to some one who treats it as if it were a flower to put in his coat, a bit of decoration to charm his vanity, an ornament for a summer's day."

"Days in summer, Basil, are apt to linger," murmured Lord Henry. "Perhaps you will tire sooner than he will. It is a sad thing to think of, but there is no doubt that genius lasts longer than beauty. That accounts for the fact that we all take such pains to over-educate ourselves. In the wild struggle for existence, we want to have something that endures, and so we fill our minds with rubbish and facts, in the silly hope of keeping our place. The thoroughly well-informed man—that is the modern ideal. And the mind of the thoroughly well-informed man is a dreadful thing. It is like a *bric-a-brac* shop, all monsters and dust, with everything priced above its proper value. I think you will tire first, all the same. Some day you will look at your friend, and he will seem to you to be a little out of drawing, or you won't like his tone of colour, or something. You will bitterly reproach him in your own heart, and seriously think that he has behaved very badly to you. The next time he calls, you will be perfectly cold and indifferent. It will be a great pity, for it will alter you. What you have told me is quite a romance, a romance of art one might call it, and the worst of having a romance of any kind is that it leaves one so unromantic."

"Harry, don't talk like that. As long as I live, the personality of Dorian Gray will dominate me. You can't feel what I feel. You change too often."

"Ah, my dear Basil, that is exactly why I can feel it. Those who are faithful know only the trivial side of love: it is the faithless who know love's tragedies." And Lord Henry struck a light on a dainty silver case and began to smoke a cigarette with a self-conscious and satisfied air, as if he had summed up the world in a phrase. There was a rustle of chirruping sparrows in the green lacquer leaves of the ivy, and the blue cloud-shadows chased themselves across the grass like swallows. How pleasant it was in the garden! And how delightful other people's emotions were!—much more delightful than their ideas, it seemed to him. One's own soul, and the passions of one's friends—those were the fascinating things in life. He pictured to himself with silent amusement the tedious luncheon that he had missed by staying so long with Basil Hallward. Had he gone to his aunt's, he would have been sure to have met Lord Goodbody there, and the whole conversation would have been about the feeding of the poor and the necessity for model lodging-houses. Each class would have preached the importance of those virtues, for whose exercise there was no necessity in their own lives. The rich would have spoken on the value of thrift, and the idle grown eloquent over the dignity of labour. It was charming to have escaped all that! As he thought of his aunt, an idea seemed to strike him. He turned to Hallward and said, "My dear fellow, I have just remembered."

"Remembered what, Harry?"

"Where I heard the name of Dorian Gray."

"Where was it?" asked Hallward, with a slight frown.

"Don't look so angry, Basil. It was at my aunt, Lady Agatha's. She told me she had discovered a wonderful young man who was going to help her in the East End, and that his name was Dorian Gray. I am bound to state that she never told me he was good-looking. Women have no appreciation of good looks; at least, good women have not. She said that he was very earnest and had a beautiful nature. I at once pictured to myself a creature with spectacles and lank hair, horribly freckled, and tramping about on huge feet. I wish I had known it was your friend."

"I am very glad you didn't, Harry."

"Why?"

"I don't want you to meet him."

"You don't want me to meet him?"

"No."

"Mr. Dorian Gray is in the studio, sir," said the butler, coming into the garden.

"You must introduce me now," cried Lord Henry, laughing.

The painter turned to his servant, who stood blinking in the sunlight. "Ask Mr. Gray to wait, Parker: I shall be in in a few moments." The man bowed and went up the walk.

Then he looked at Lord Henry. "Dorian Gray is my dearest friend," he said. "He has a simple and a beautiful nature. Your aunt was quite right in what she said of him. Don't spoil him. Don't try to influence him. Your influence would be bad. The world is wide, and has many marvellous people in it. Don't take away from me the one person who gives to my art whatever charm it possesses: my life as an artist depends on him. Mind, Harry, I trust you." He spoke very slowly, and the words seemed wrung out of him almost against his will.

"What nonsense you talk!" said Lord Henry, smiling, and taking Hallward by the arm, he almost led him into the house.

CHAPTER

2

As they entered they saw Dorian Gray. He was seated at the piano, with his back to them, turning over the pages of a volume of Schumann's "Forest Scenes."* "You must lend me these, Basil," he cried. "I want to learn them. They are perfectly charming."

"That entirely depends on how you sit to-day, Dorian."

"Oh, I am tired of sitting, and I don't want a life-sized portrait of myself," answered the lad, swinging round on the music-stool in a wilful, petulant manner. When he caught sight of Lord Henry, a faint blush coloured his cheeks for a moment, and he started up. "I beg your pardon, Basil, but I didn't know you had any one with you."

"This is Lord Henry Wotton, Dorian, an old Oxford friend of mine. I have just been telling him what a capital sitter you were, and now you have spoiled everything."

"You have not spoiled my pleasure in meeting you, Mr. Gray," said Lord Henry, stepping forward and extending his hand. "My aunt has often spoken to me about you. You are one of her favourites, and, I am afraid, one of her victims also."

---

* German Romantic composer Robert A. Schumann whose 'Forest Scenes' date from 1848-9.

"I am in Lady Agatha's black books at present," answered Dorian with a funny look of penitence. "I promised to go to a club in Whitechapel with her last Tuesday, and I really forgot all about it. We were to have played a duet together—three duets, I believe. I don't know what she will say to me. I am far too frightened to call."

"Oh, I will make your peace with my aunt. She is quite devoted to you. And I don't think it really matters about your not being there. The audience probably thought it was a duet. When Aunt Agatha sits down to the piano, she makes quite enough noise for two people."

"That is very horrid to her, and not very nice to me," answered Dorian, laughing.

Lord Henry looked at him. Yes, he was certainly wonderfully handsome, with his finely curved scarlet lips, his frank blue eyes, his crisp gold hair. There was something in his face that made one trust him at once. All the candour of youth was there, as well as all youth's passionate purity. One felt that he had kept himself unspotted from the world.* No wonder Basil Hallward worshipped him.

"You are too charming to go in for philanthropy, Mr. Gray—far too charming." And Lord Henry flung himself down on the divan and opened his cigarette-case.

The painter had been busy mixing his colours and getting his brushes ready. He was looking worried, and when he heard Lord Henry's last remark, he glanced at him, hesitated for a moment, and then said, "Harry, I want to finish this picture to-day. Would you think it awfully rude of me if I asked you to go away?"

Lord Henry smiled and looked at Dorian Gray. "Am I to go, Mr. Gray?" he asked.

"Oh, please don't, Lord Henry. I see that Basil is in one of his sulky moods, and I can't bear him when he sulks. Besides, I want you to tell me why I should not go in for philanthropy."

"I don't know that I shall tell you that, Mr. Gray. It is so tedious a subject that one would have to talk seriously about it. But I certainly shall not run away, now that you have asked me to stop. You don't really mind, Basil, do you? You have often told me that you liked your sitters to have some one to chat to."

---

* As in *James* 1: 27.

Hallward bit his lip. "If Dorian wishes it, of course you must stay. Dorian's whims are laws to everybody, except himself."

Lord Henry took up his hat and gloves. "You are very pressing, Basil, but I am afraid I must go. I have promised to meet a man at the Orleans.* Good-bye, Mr. Gray. Come and see me some afternoon in Curzon Street. I am nearly always at home at five o'clock. Write to me when you are coming. I should be sorry to miss you."

"Basil," cried Dorian Gray, "if Lord Henry Wotton goes, I shall go, too. You never open your lips while you are painting, and it is horribly dull standing on a platform and trying to look pleasant. Ask him to stay. I insist upon it."

"Stay, Harry, to oblige Dorian, and to oblige me," said Hallward, gazing intently at his picture. "It is quite true, I never talk when I am working, and never listen either, and it must be dreadfully tedious for my unfortunate sitters. I beg you to stay."

"But what about my man at the Orleans?"

The painter laughed. "I don't think there will be any difficulty about that. Sit down again, Harry. And now, Dorian, get up on the platform, and don't move about too much, or pay any attention to what Lord Henry says. He has a very bad influence over all his friends, with the single exception of myself."

Dorian Gray stepped up on the dais with the air of a young Greek martyr, and made a little *moue*† of discontent to Lord Henry, to whom he had rather taken a fancy. He was so unlike Basil. They made a delightful contrast. And he had such a beautiful voice. After a few moments he said to him, "Have you really a very bad influence, Lord Henry? As bad as Basil says?"

"There is no such thing as a good influence, Mr. Gray. All influence is immoral—immoral from the scientific point of view."

"Why?"

"Because to influence a person is to give him one's own soul. He does not think his natural thoughts, or burn with his natural passions. His virtues are not real to him. His sins, if there are such things as sins, are borrowed. He becomes an echo of some one else's

---

* A High-end club in London.

† A grimace or pout.

music, an actor of a part that has not been written for him. The aim of life is self-development. To realize one's nature perfectly—that is what each of us is here for. People are afraid of themselves, nowadays. They have forgotten the highest of all duties, the duty that one owes to one's self. Of course, they are charitable. They feed the hungry and clothe the beggar. But their own souls starve, and are naked. Courage has gone out of our race. Perhaps we never really had it. The terror of society, which is the basis of morals, the terror of God, which is the secret of religion—these are the two things that govern us. And yet—"

"Just turn your head a little more to the right, Dorian, like a good boy," said the painter, deep in his work and conscious only that a look had come into the lad's face that he had never seen there before.

"And yet," continued Lord Henry, in his low, musical voice, and with that graceful wave of the hand that was always so characteristic of him, and that he had even in his Eton days, "I believe that if one man were to live out his life fully and completely, were to give form to every feeling, expression to every thought, reality to every dream—I believe that the world would gain such a fresh impulse of joy that we would forget all the maladies of mediaevalism, and return to the Hellenic ideal—to something finer, richer than the Hellenic ideal, it may be. But the bravest man amongst us is afraid of himself. The mutilation of the savage has its tragic survival in the self-denial that mars our lives. We are punished for our refusals. Every impulse that we strive to strangle broods in the mind and poisons us. The body sins once, and has done with its sin, for action is a mode of purification. Nothing remains then but the recollection of a pleasure, or the luxury of a regret. The only way to get rid of a temptation is to yield to it. Resist it, and your soul grows sick with longing for the things it has forbidden to itself, with desire for what its monstrous laws have made monstrous and unlawful. It has been said that the great events of the world take place in the brain. It is in the brain, and the brain only, that the great sins of the world take place also. You, Mr. Gray, you yourself, with your rose-red youth and your rose-white boyhood, you have had passions that have made you afraid, thoughts that have filled you with terror, day-

dreams and sleeping dreams whose mere memory might stain your cheek with shame—"

"Stop!" faltered Dorian Gray, "stop! you bewilder me. I don't know what to say. There is some answer to you, but I cannot find it. Don't speak. Let me think. Or, rather, let me try not to think."

For nearly ten minutes he stood there, motionless, with parted lips and eyes strangely bright. He was dimly conscious that entirely fresh influences were at work within him. Yet they seemed to him to have come really from himself. The few words that Basil's friend had said to him—words spoken by chance, no doubt, and with wilful paradox in them—had touched some secret chord that had never been touched before, but that he felt was now vibrating and throbbing to curious pulses.

Music had stirred him like that. Music had troubled him many times. But music was not articulate. It was not a new world, but rather another chaos, that it created in us. Words! Mere words! How terrible they were! How clear, and vivid, and cruel! One could not escape from them. And yet what a subtle magic there was in them! They seemed to be able to give a plastic form to formless things, and to have a music of their own as sweet as that of viol or of lute. Mere words! Was there anything so real as words?

Yes; there had been things in his boyhood that he had not understood. He understood them now. Life suddenly became fiery-coloured to him. It seemed to him that he had been walking in fire. Why had he not known it?

With his subtle smile, Lord Henry watched him. He knew the precise psychological moment when to say nothing. He felt intensely interested. He was amazed at the sudden impression that his words had produced, and, remembering a book that he had read when he was sixteen, a book which had revealed to him much that he had not known before, he wondered whether Dorian Gray was passing through a similar experience. He had merely shot an arrow into the air. Had it hit the mark? How fascinating the lad was!

Hallward painted away with that marvellous bold touch of his, that had the true refinement and perfect delicacy that in art, at any rate comes only from strength. He was unconscious of the silence.

"Basil, I am tired of standing," cried Dorian Gray suddenly. "I must go out and sit in the garden. The air is stifling here."

"My dear fellow, I am so sorry. When I am painting, I can't think of anything else. But you never sat better. You were perfectly still. And I have caught the effect I wanted—the half-parted lips and the bright look in the eyes. I don't know what Harry has been saying to you, but he has certainly made you have the most wonderful expression. I suppose he has been paying you compliments. You mustn't believe a word that he says."

"He has certainly not been paying me compliments. Perhaps that is the reason that I don't believe anything he has told me."

"You know you believe it all," said Lord Henry, looking at him with his dreamy languorous eyes. "I will go out to the garden with you. It is horribly hot in the studio. Basil, let us have something iced to drink, something with strawberries in it."

"Certainly, Harry. Just touch the bell, and when Parker comes I will tell him what you want. I have got to work up this background, so I will join you later on. Don't keep Dorian too long. I have never been in better form for painting than I am to-day. This is going to be my masterpiece. It is my masterpiece as it stands."

Lord Henry went out to the garden and found Dorian Gray burying his face in the great cool lilac-blossoms, feverishly drinking in their perfume as if it had been wine. He came close to him and put his hand upon his shoulder. "You are quite right to do that," he murmured. "Nothing can cure the soul but the senses, just as nothing can cure the senses but the soul."

The lad started and drew back. He was bareheaded, and the leaves had tossed his rebellious curls and tangled all their gilded threads. There was a look of fear in his eyes, such as people have when they are suddenly awakened. His finely chiselled nostrils quivered, and some hidden nerve shook the scarlet of his lips and left them trembling.

"Yes," continued Lord Henry, "that is one of the great secrets of life—to cure the soul by means of the senses, and the senses by means of the soul. You are a wonderful creation. You know more than you think you know, just as you know less than you want to know."

Dorian Gray frowned and turned his head away. He could not help liking the tall, graceful young man who was standing by him. His romantic, olive-coloured face and worn expression interested him. There was something in his low languid voice that was absolutely fascinating. His cool, white, flowerlike hands, even, had a curious charm. They moved, as he spoke, like music, and seemed to have a language of their own. But he felt afraid of him, and ashamed of being afraid. Why had it been left for a stranger to reveal him to himself? He had known Basil Hallward for months, but the friendship between them had never altered him. Suddenly there had come some one across his life who seemed to have disclosed to him life's mystery. And, yet, what was there to be afraid of? He was not a schoolboy or a girl. It was absurd to be frightened.

"Let us go and sit in the shade," said Lord Henry. "Parker has brought out the drinks, and if you stay any longer in this glare, you will be quite spoiled, and Basil will never paint you again. You really must not allow yourself to become sunburnt. It would be unbecoming."

"What can it matter?" cried Dorian Gray, laughing, as he sat down on the seat at the end of the garden.

"It should matter everything to you, Mr. Gray."

"Why?"

"Because you have the most marvellous youth, and youth is the one thing worth having."

"I don't feel that, Lord Henry."

"No, you don't feel it now. Some day, when you are old and wrinkled and ugly, when thought has seared your forehead with its lines, and passion branded your lips with its hideous fires, you will feel it, you will feel it terribly. Now, wherever you go, you charm the world. Will it always be so? . . . You have a wonderfully beautiful face, Mr. Gray. Don't frown. You have. And beauty is a form of genius—is higher, indeed, than genius, as it needs no explanation. It is of the great facts of the world, like sunlight, or spring-time, or the reflection in dark waters of that silver shell we call the moon. It cannot be questioned. It has its divine right of sovereignty. It makes princes of those who have it. You smile? Ah! when you have lost it you won't smile . . . People say sometimes that beauty is only superficial.

That may be so, but at least it is not so superficial as thought is. To me, beauty is the wonder of wonders. It is only shallow people who do not judge by appearances. The true mystery of the world is the visible, not the invisible . . . Yes, Mr. Gray, the gods have been good to you. But what the gods give they quickly take away. You have only a few years in which to live really, perfectly, and fully. When your youth goes, your beauty will go with it, and then you will suddenly discover that there are no triumphs left for you, or have to content yourself with those mean triumphs that the memory of your past will make more bitter than defeats. Every month as it wanes brings you nearer to something dreadful. Time is jealous of you, and wars against your lilies and your roses. You will become sallow, and hollow-cheeked, and dull-eyed. You will suffer horribly . . . Ah! realize your youth while you have it. Don't squander the gold of your days, listening to the tedious, trying to improve the hopeless failure, or giving away your life to the ignorant, the common, and the vulgar. These are the sickly aims, the false ideals, of our age. Live! Live the wonderful life that is in you! Let nothing be lost upon you. Be always searching for new sensations. Be afraid of nothing . . . A new Hedonism*—that is what our century wants. You might be its visible symbol. With your personality there is nothing you could not do. The world belongs to you for a season . . . The moment I met you I saw that you were quite unconscious of what you really are, of what you really might be. There was so much in you that charmed me that I felt I must tell you something about yourself. I thought how tragic it would be if you were wasted. For there is such a little time that your youth will last—such a little time. The common hill-flowers wither, but they blossom again. The laburnum will be as yellow next June as it is now. In a month there will be purple stars on the clematis, and year after year the green night of its leaves will hold its purple stars. But we never get back our youth. The pulse of joy that beats in us at twenty becomes sluggish. Our limbs fail, our senses rot. We degenerate into hideous puppets, haunted by the memory of the passions of which we were too much afraid, and the

* A fourth century doctrine by Aristippus (435-366 BC) in which the life's proper aim should be *pursuit of pleasure.*

exquisite temptations that we had not the courage to yield to. Youth! Youth! There is absolutely nothing in the world but youth!"

Dorian Gray listened, open-eyed and wondering. The spray of lilac fell from his hand upon the gravel. A furry bee came and buzzed round it for a moment. Then it began to scramble all over the oval stellated globe of the tiny blossoms. He watched it with that strange interest in trivial things that we try to develop when things of high import make us afraid, or when we are stirred by some new emotion for which we cannot find expression, or when some thought that terrifies us lays sudden siege to the brain and calls on us to yield. After a time the bee flew away. He saw it creeping into the stained trumpet of a Tyrian convolvulus.* The flower seemed to quiver, and then swayed gently to and fro.

Suddenly the painter appeared at the door of the studio and made staccato signs for them to come in. They turned to each other and smiled.

"I am waiting," he cried. "Do come in. The light is quite perfect, and you can bring your drinks."

They rose up and sauntered down the walk together. Two green-and-white butterflies fluttered past them, and in the pear-tree at the corner of the garden a thrush began to sing.

"You are glad you have met me, Mr. Gray," said Lord Henry, looking at him.

"Yes, I am glad now. I wonder shall I always be glad?"

"Always! That is a dreadful word. It makes me shudder when I hear it. Women are so fond of using it. They spoil every romance by trying to make it last for ever. It is a meaningless word, too. The only difference between a caprice and a lifelong passion is that the caprice lasts a little longer."

As they entered the studio, Dorian Gray put his hand upon Lord Henry's arm. "In that case, let our friendship be a caprice," he murmured, flushing at his own boldness, then stepped up on the platform and resumed his pose.

Lord Henry flung himself into a large wicker armchair and watched him. The sweep and dash of the brush on the canvas made

* Related to *genera Convolvulus* and *Calystegia*, mostly twining, often weedy.

the only sound that broke the stillness, except when, now and then, Hallward stepped back to look at his work from a distance. In the slanting beams that streamed through the open doorway the dust danced and was golden. The heavy scent of the roses seemed to brood over everything.

After about a quarter of an hour Hallward stopped painting, looked for a long time at Dorian Gray, and then for a long time at the picture, biting the end of one of his huge brushes and frowning. "It is quite finished," he cried at last, and stooping down he wrote his name in long vermilion letters on the left-hand corner of the canvas.

Lord Henry came over and examined the picture. It was certainly a wonderful work of art, and a wonderful likeness as well.

"My dear fellow, I congratulate you most warmly," he said. "It is the finest portrait of modern times. Mr. Gray, come over and look at yourself."

The lad started, as if awakened from some dream.

"Is it really finished?" he murmured, stepping down from the platform.

"Quite finished," said the painter. "And you have sat splendidly to-day. I am awfully obliged to you."

"That is entirely due to me," broke in Lord Henry. "Isn't it, Mr. Gray?"

Dorian made no answer, but passed listlessly in front of his picture and turned towards it. When he saw it he drew back, and his cheeks flushed for a moment with pleasure. A look of joy came into his eyes, as if he had recognized himself for the first time. He stood there motionless and in wonder, dimly conscious that Hallward was speaking to him, but not catching the meaning of his words. The sense of his own beauty came on him like a revelation. He had never felt it before. Basil Hallward's compliments had seemed to him to be merely the charming exaggeration of friendship. He had listened to them, laughed at them, forgotten them. They had not influenced his nature. Then had come Lord Henry Wotton with his strange panegyric on youth, his terrible warning of its brevity. That had stirred him at the time, and now, as he stood gazing at the shadow of his own loveliness, the full reality of the description flashed across

him. Yes, there would be a day when his face would be wrinkled and wizen, his eyes dim and colourless, the grace of his figure broken and deformed. The scarlet would pass away from his lips and the gold steal from his hair. The life that was to make his soul would mar his body. He would become dreadful, hideous, and uncouth.

As he thought of it, a sharp pang of pain struck through him like a knife and made each delicate fibre of his nature quiver. His eyes deepened into amethyst, and across them came a mist of tears. He felt as if a hand of ice had been laid upon his heart.

"Don't you like it?" cried Hallward at last, stung a little by the lad's silence, not understanding what it meant.

"Of course he likes it," said Lord Henry. "Who wouldn't like it? It is one of the greatest things in modern art. I will give you anything you like to ask for it. I must have it."

"It is not my property, Harry."

"Whose property is it?"

"Dorian's, of course," answered the painter.

"He is a very lucky fellow."

"How sad it is!" murmured Dorian Gray with his eyes still fixed upon his own portrait. "How sad it is! I shall grow old, and horrible, and dreadful. But this picture will remain always young. It will never be older than this particular day of June . . . If it were only the other way! If it were I who was to be always young, and the picture that was to grow old! For that—for that—I would give everything! Yes, there is nothing in the whole world I would not give! I would give my soul for that!"

"You would hardly care for such an arrangement, Basil," cried Lord Henry, laughing. "It would be rather hard lines on your work."

"I should object very strongly, Harry," said Hallward.

Dorian Gray turned and looked at him. "I believe you would, Basil. You like your art better than your friends. I am no more to you than a green bronze figure. Hardly as much, I dare say."

The painter stared in amazement. It was so unlike Dorian to speak like that. What had happened? He seemed quite angry. His face was flushed and his cheeks burning.

"Yes," he continued, "I am less to you than your ivory Hermes or your silver Faun. You will like them always. How long will you

like me? Till I have my first wrinkle, I suppose. I know, now, that when one loses one's good looks, whatever they may be, one loses everything. Your picture has taught me that. Lord Henry Wotton is perfectly right. Youth is the only thing worth having. When I find that I am growing old, I shall kill myself."

Hallward turned pale and caught his hand. "Dorian! Dorian!" he cried, "don't talk like that. I have never had such a friend as you, and I shall never have such another. You are not jealous of material things, are you?—you who are finer than any of them!"

"I am jealous of everything whose beauty does not die. I am jealous of the portrait you have painted of me. Why should it keep what I must lose? Every moment that passes takes something from me and gives something to it. Oh, if it were only the other way! If the picture could change, and I could be always what I am now! Why did you paint it? It will mock me some day—mock me horribly!" The hot tears welled into his eyes; he tore his hand away and, flinging himself on the divan, he buried his face in the cushions, as though he was praying.

"This is your doing, Harry," said the painter bitterly.

Lord Henry shrugged his shoulders. "It is the real Dorian Gray—that is all."

"It is not."

"If it is not, what have I to do with it?"

"You should have gone away when I asked you," he muttered.

"I stayed when you asked me," was Lord Henry's answer.

"Harry, I can't quarrel with my two best friends at once, but between you both you have made me hate the finest piece of work I have ever done, and I will destroy it. What is it but canvas and colour? I will not let it come across our three lives and mar them."

Dorian Gray lifted his golden head from the pillow, and with pallid face and tear-stained eyes, looked at him as he walked over to the deal painting-table that was set beneath the high curtained window. What was he doing there? His fingers were straying about among the litter of tin tubes and dry brushes, seeking for something. Yes, it was for the long palette-knife, with its thin blade of lithe steel. He had found it at last. He was going to rip up the canvas.

With a stifled sob the lad leaped from the couch, and, rushing over to Hallward, tore the knife out of his hand, and flung it to the end of the studio. "Don't, Basil, don't!" he cried. "It would be murder!"

"I am glad you appreciate my work at last, Dorian," said the painter coldly when he had recovered from his surprise. "I never thought you would."

"Appreciate it? I am in love with it, Basil. It is part of myself. I feel that."

"Well, as soon as you are dry, you shall be varnished, and framed, and sent home. Then you can do what you like with yourself." And he walked across the room and rang the bell for tea. "You will have tea, of course, Dorian? And so will you, Harry? Or do you object to such simple pleasures?"

"I adore simple pleasures," said Lord Henry. "They are the last refuge of the complex. But I don't like scenes, except on the stage. What absurd fellows you are, both of you! I wonder who it was defined man as a rational animal. It was the most premature definition ever given. Man is many things, but he is not rational. I am glad he is not, after all—though I wish you chaps would not squabble over the picture. You had much better let me have it, Basil. This silly boy doesn't really want it, and I really do."

"If you let any one have it but me, Basil, I shall never forgive you!" cried Dorian Gray; "and I don't allow people to call me a silly boy."

"You know the picture is yours, Dorian. I gave it to you before it existed."

"And you know you have been a little silly, Mr. Gray, and that you don't really object to being reminded that you are extremely young."

"I should have objected very strongly this morning, Lord Henry."

"Ah! this morning! You have lived since then."

There came a knock at the door, and the butler entered with a laden tea-tray and set it down upon a small Japanese table. There was a rattle of cups and saucers and the hissing of a fluted Georgian urn. Two globe-shaped china dishes were brought in by a page. Dorian

Gray went over and poured out the tea. The two men sauntered languidly to the table and examined what was under the covers.

"Let us go to the theatre to-night," said Lord Henry. "There is sure to be something on, somewhere. I have promised to dine at White's,* but it is only with an old friend, so I can send him a wire to say that I am ill, or that I am prevented from coming in consequence of a subsequent engagement. I think that would be a rather nice excuse: it would have all the surprise of candour."

"It is such a bore putting on one's dress-clothes," muttered Hallward. "And, when one has them on, they are so horrid."

"Yes," answered Lord Henry dreamily, "the costume of the nineteenth century is detestable. It is so sombre, so depressing. Sin is the only real colour-element left in modern life."

"You really must not say things like that before Dorian, Harry."

"Before which Dorian? The one who is pouring out tea for us, or the one in the picture?"

"Before either."

"I should like to come to the theatre with you, Lord Henry," said the lad.

"Then you shall come; and you will come, too, Basil, won't you?"

"I can't, really. I would sooner not. I have a lot of work to do."

"Well, then, you and I will go alone, Mr. Gray."

"I should like that awfully."

The painter bit his lip and walked over, cup in hand, to the picture. "I shall stay with the real Dorian," he said, sadly.

"Is it the real Dorian?" cried the original of the portrait, strolling across to him. "Am I really like that?"

"Yes; you are just like that."

"How wonderful, Basil!"

"At least you are like it in appearance. But it will never alter," sighed Hallward. "That is something."

"What a fuss people make about fidelity!" exclaimed Lord Henry. "Why, even in love it is purely a question for physiology. It has nothing to do with our own will. Young men want to be faithful, and are not; old men want to be faithless, and cannot: that is all one can say."

---

* An exclusive men's club in St. James's Street in London.

"Don't go to the theatre to-night, Dorian," said Hallward. "Stop and dine with me."

"I can't, Basil."

"Why?"

"Because I have promised Lord Henry Wotton to go with him."

"He won't like you the better for keeping your promises. He always breaks his own. I beg you not to go."

Dorian Gray laughed and shook his head.

"I entreat you."

The lad hesitated, and looked over at Lord Henry, who was watching them from the tea-table with an amused smile.

"I must go, Basil," he answered.

"Very well," said Hallward, and he went over and laid down his cup on the tray. "It is rather late, and, as you have to dress, you had better lose no time. Good-bye, Harry. Good-bye, Dorian. Come and see me soon. Come to-morrow."

"Certainly."

"You won't forget?"

"No, of course not," cried Dorian.

"And . . . Harry!"

"Yes, Basil?"

"Remember what I asked you, when we were in the garden this morning."

"I have forgotten it."

"I trust you."

"I wish I could trust myself," said Lord Henry, laughing. "Come, Mr. Gray, my hansom is outside, and I can drop you at your own place. Good-bye, Basil. It has been a most interesting afternoon."

As the door closed behind them, the painter flung himself down on a sofa, and a look of pain came into his face.

CHAPTER

3

At half-past twelve next day Lord Henry Wotton strolled from Curzon Street over to the Albany to call on his uncle, Lord Fermor, a genial if somewhat rough-mannered old bachelor, whom the outside world called selfish because it derived no particular benefit from him, but who was considered generous by Society as he fed the people who amused him. His father had been our ambassador at Madrid when Isabella was young and Prim* unthought of, but had retired from the diplomatic service in a capricious moment of annoyance on not being offered the Embassy at Paris, a post to which he considered that he was fully entitled by reason of his birth, his indolence, the good English of his dispatches, and his inordinate passion for pleasure. The son, who had been his father's secretary, had resigned along with his chief, somewhat foolishly as was thought at the time, and on succeeding some months later to the title, had set himself to the serious study of the great aristocratic art of doing absolutely nothing. He had two large town houses, but preferred to live in chambers as it was less trouble, and took most of his meals at his club. He paid some attention to the management of his collieries in

---

* Spanish soldier Juan Prim y Prats (1814-1870) who overthrew Queen Isabella in a coup in 1868.

the Midland counties, excusing himself for this taint of industry on the ground that the one advantage of having coal was that it enabled a gentleman to afford the decency of burning wood on his own hearth. In politics he was a Tory, except when the Tories were in office, during which period he roundly abused them for being a pack of Radicals. He was a hero to his valet, who bullied him, and a terror to most of his relations, whom he bullied in turn. Only England could have produced him, and he always said that the country was going to the dogs. His principles were out of date, but there was a good deal to be said for his prejudices.

When Lord Henry entered the room, he found his uncle sitting in a rough shooting-coat, smoking a cheroot and grumbling over *The Times*. "Well, Harry," said the old gentleman, "what brings you out so early? I thought you dandies never got up till two, and were not visible till five."

"Pure family affection, I assure you, Uncle George. I want to get something out of you."

"Money, I suppose," said Lord Fermor, making a wry face. "Well, sit down and tell me all about it. Young people, nowadays, imagine that money is everything."

"Yes," murmured Lord Henry, settling his button-hole in his coat; "and when they grow older they know it. But I don't want money. It is only people who pay their bills who want that, Uncle George, and I never pay mine. Credit is the capital of a younger son, and one lives charmingly upon it. Besides, I always deal with Dartmoor's tradesmen, and consequently they never bother me. What I want is information: not useful information, of course; useless information."

"Well, I can tell you anything that is in an English Blue Book,* Harry, although those fellows nowadays write a lot of nonsense. When I was in the Diplomatic, things were much better. But I hear they let them in now by examination.† What can you expect? Examinations, sir, are pure humbug from beginning to end. If a man

* The statistical reports of Parliamentary and Royal Commissions inquiring into various aspects of British society.

† Entry to the British Civil Service was opened through competitive examination in 1817.

is a gentleman, he knows quite enough, and if he is not a gentleman, whatever he knows is bad for him."

"Mr. Dorian Gray does not belong to Blue Books, Uncle George," said Lord Henry languidly.

"Mr. Dorian Gray? Who is he?" asked Lord Fermor, knitting his bushy white eyebrows.

"That is what I have come to learn, Uncle George. Or rather, I know who he is. He is the last Lord Kelso's grandson. His mother was a Devereux, Lady Margaret Devereux. I want you to tell me about his mother. What was she like? Whom did she marry? You have known nearly everybody in your time, so you might have known her. I am very much interested in Mr. Gray at present. I have only just met him."

"Kelso's grandson!" echoed the old gentleman. "Kelso's grandson! . . . Of course . . . I knew his mother intimately. I believe I was at her christening. She was an extraordinarily beautiful girl, Margaret Devereux, and made all the men frantic by running away with a penniless young fellow—a mere nobody, sir, a subaltern in a foot regiment, or something of that kind. Certainly. I remember the whole thing as if it happened yesterday. The poor chap was killed in a duel at Spa a few months after the marriage. There was an ugly story about it. They said Kelso got some rascally adventurer, some Belgian brute, to insult his son-in-law in public—paid him, sir, to do it, paid him—and that the fellow spitted his man as if he had been a pigeon. The thing was hushed up, but, egad, Kelso ate his chop alone at the club for some time afterwards. He brought his daughter back with him, I was told, and she never spoke to him again. Oh, yes; it was a bad business. The girl died, too, died within a year. So she left a son, did she? I had forgotten that. What sort of boy is he? If he is like his mother, he must be a good-looking chap."

"He is very good-looking," assented Lord Henry.

"I hope he will fall into proper hands," continued the old man. "He should have a pot of money waiting for him if Kelso did the right thing by him. His mother had money, too. All the Selby property came to her, through her grandfather. Her grandfather hated Kelso, thought him a mean dog. He was, too. Came to Madrid once when I was there. Egad, I was ashamed of him. The Queen used to ask

me about the English noble who was always quarrelling with the cabmen about their fares. They made quite a story of it. I didn't dare show my face at Court for a month. I hope he treated his grandson better than he did the jarvies."*

"I don't know," answered Lord Henry. "I fancy that the boy will be well off. He is not of age yet. He has Selby, I know. He told me so. And . . . his mother was very beautiful?"

"Margaret Devereux was one of the loveliest creatures I ever saw, Harry. What on earth induced her to behave as she did, I never could understand. She could have married anybody she chose. Carlington was mad after her. She was romantic, though. All the women of that family were. The men were a poor lot, but, egad! the women were wonderful. Carlington went on his knees to her. Told me so himself. She laughed at him, and there wasn't a girl in London at the time who wasn't after him. And by the way, Harry, talking about silly marriages, what is this humbug your father tells me about Dartmoor wanting to marry an American? Ain't English girls good enough for him?"

"It is rather fashionable to marry Americans just now, Uncle George."

"I'll back English women against the world, Harry," said Lord Fermor, striking the table with his fist.

"The betting is on the Americans."

"They don't last, I am told," muttered his uncle.

"A long engagement exhausts them, but they are capital at a steeplechase. They take things flying. I don't think Dartmoor has a chance."

"Who are her people?" grumbled the old gentleman. "Has she got any?"

Lord Henry shook his head. "American girls are as clever at concealing their parents, as English women are at concealing their past," he said, rising to go.

"They are pork-packers, I suppose?"

"I hope so, Uncle George, for Dartmoor's sake. I am told that pork-packing is the most lucrative profession in America, after politics."

---

* A coachman.

"Is she pretty?"

"She behaves as if she was beautiful. Most American women do. It is the secret of their charm."

"Why can't these American women stay in their own country? They are always telling us that it is the paradise for women."

"It is. That is the reason why, like Eve, they are so excessively anxious to get out of it," said Lord Henry. "Good-bye, Uncle George. I shall be late for lunch, if I stop any longer. Thanks for giving me the information I wanted. I always like to know everything about my new friends, and nothing about my old ones."

"Where are you lunching, Harry?"

"At Aunt Agatha's. I have asked myself and Mr. Gray. He is her latest *protege*."

"Humph! tell your Aunt Agatha, Harry, not to bother me any more with her charity appeals. I am sick of them. Why, the good woman thinks that I have nothing to do but to write cheques for her silly fads."

"All right, Uncle George, I'll tell her, but it won't have any effect. Philanthropic people lose all sense of humanity. It is their distinguishing characteristic."

The old gentleman growled approvingly and rang the bell for his servant. Lord Henry passed up the low arcade into Burlington Street and turned his steps in the direction of Berkeley Square.

So that was the story of Dorian Gray's parentage. Crudely as it had been told to him, it had yet stirred him by its suggestion of a strange, almost modern romance. A beautiful woman risking everything for a mad passion. A few wild weeks of happiness cut short by a hideous, treacherous crime. Months of voiceless agony, and then a child born in pain. The mother snatched away by death, the boy left to solitude and the tyranny of an old and loveless man. Yes; it was an interesting background. It posed the lad, made him more perfect, as it were. Behind every exquisite thing that existed, there was something tragic. Worlds had to be in travail, that the meanest flower might blow . . . And how charming he had been at dinner the night before, as with startled eyes and lips parted in frightened pleasure he had sat opposite to him at the club, the red candleshades staining to a richer rose the

wakening wonder of his face. Talking to him was like playing upon an exquisite violin. He answered to every touch and thrill of the bow . . . There was something terribly enthralling in the exercise of influence. No other activity was like it. To project one's soul into some gracious form, and let it tarry there for a moment; to hear one's own intellectual views echoed back to one with all the added music of passion and youth; to convey one's temperament into another as though it were a subtle fluid or a strange perfume: there was a real joy in that—perhaps the most satisfying joy left to us in an age so limited and vulgar as our own, an age grossly carnal in its pleasures, and grossly common in its aims . . . He was a marvellous type, too, this lad, whom by so curious a chance he had met in Basil's studio, or could be fashioned into a marvellous type, at any rate. Grace was his, and the white purity of boyhood, and beauty such as old Greek marbles kept for us. There was nothing that one could not do with him. He could be made a Titan* or a toy. What a pity it was that such beauty was destined to fade! . . . And Basil? From a psychological point of view, how interesting he was! The new manner in art, the fresh mode of looking at life, suggested so strangely by the merely visible presence of one who was unconscious of it all; the silent spirit that dwelt in dim woodland, and walked unseen in open field, suddenly showing herself, Dryadlike† and not afraid, because in his soul who sought for her there had been wakened that wonderful vision to which alone are wonderful things revealed; the mere shapes and patterns of things becoming, as it were, refined, and gaining a kind of symbolical value, as though they were themselves patterns of some other and more perfect form whose shadow they made real: how strange it all was! He remembered something like it in history. Was it not Plato, that artist in thought, who had first analyzed it?‡ Was it not Buonarotti§ who had carved it in the coloured marbles of

* One of the giant gods in Greek mythology, son of Heaven (Uranus) and Earth (Gaia).

† Like the wood-nymphs in Classical mythology.

‡ Plato's doctrine of Ideal Forms to which all perceived ideas are mere shadows, seen on the walls of a cave, is elucidated in *The Republic and other Dialogues.*

§ Italian poet, sculptor and painter Michelagniolo de Lodovico Buonarotti (1475-1564), popularly known as Michelangelo.

a sonnet-sequence? But in our own century it was strange . . . Yes; he would try to be to Dorian Gray what, without knowing it, the lad was to the painter who had fashioned the wonderful portrait. He would seek to dominate him—had already, indeed, half done so. He would make that wonderful spirit his own. There was something fascinating in this son of love and death.

Suddenly he stopped and glanced up at the houses. He found that he had passed his aunt's some distance, and, smiling to himself, turned back. When he entered the somewhat sombre hall, the butler told him that they had gone in to lunch. He gave one of the footmen his hat and stick and passed into the dining room.

"Late as usual, Harry," cried his aunt, shaking her head at him.

He invented a facile excuse, and having taken the vacant seat next to her, looked round to see who was there. Dorian bowed to him shyly from the end of the table, a flush of pleasure stealing into his cheek. Opposite was the Duchess of Harley, a lady of admirable good-nature and good temper, much liked by every one who knew her, and of those ample architectural proportions that in women who are not duchesses are described by contemporary historians as stoutness. Next to her sat, on her right, Sir Thomas Burdon, a Radical member of Parliament, who followed his leader in public life and in private life followed the best cooks, dining with the Tories and thinking with the Liberals, in accordance with a wise and well-known rule.* The post on her left was occupied by Mr. Erskine of Treadley, an old gentleman of considerable charm and culture, who had fallen, however, into bad habits of silence, having, as he explained once to Lady Agatha, said everything that he had to say before he was thirty. His own neighbour was Mrs. Vandeleur, one of his aunt's oldest friends, a perfect saint amongst women, but so dreadfully dowdy that she reminded one of a badly bound hymn-book. Fortunately for him she had on the other side Lord Faudel, a most intelligent middle-aged mediocrity, as bald as a ministerial statement in the House of Commons, with whom she was conversing in that intensely earnest manner which is the one unpardonable

* *i.e.* 'Running with the hare and hunting with the hounds', usually with a negative connotation, as being double-dealing and deceitful.

error, as he remarked once himself, that all really good people fall into, and from which none of them ever quite escape.

"We are talking about poor Dartmoor, Lord Henry," cried the duchess, nodding pleasantly to him across the table. "Do you think he will really marry this fascinating young person?"

"I believe she has made up her mind to propose to him, Duchess."

"How dreadful!" exclaimed Lady Agatha. "Really, some one should interfere."

"I am told, on excellent authority, that her father keeps an American dry-goods store," said Sir Thomas Burdon, looking supercilious.

"My uncle has already suggested pork-packing, Sir Thomas."

"Dry-goods! What are American dry-goods?" asked the duchess, raising her large hands in wonder and accentuating the verb.

"American novels," answered Lord Henry, helping himself to some quail.

The duchess looked puzzled.

"Don't mind him, my dear," whispered Lady Agatha. "He never means anything that he says."

"When America was discovered," said the Radical member—and he began to give some wearisome facts. Like all people who try to exhaust a subject, he exhausted his listeners. The duchess sighed and exercised her privilege of interruption. "I wish to goodness it never had been discovered at all!" she exclaimed. "Really, our girls have no chance nowadays. It is most unfair."

"Perhaps, after all, America never has been discovered," said Mr. Erskine; "I myself would say that it had merely been detected."

"Oh! but I have seen specimens of the inhabitants," answered the duchess vaguely. "I must confess that most of them are extremely pretty. And they dress well, too. They get all their dresses in Paris. I wish I could afford to do the same."

"They say that when good Americans die they go to Paris," chuckled Sir Thomas, who had a large wardrobe of Humour's cast-off clothes.

"Really! And where do bad Americans go to when they die?" inquired the duchess.

"They go to America," murmured Lord Henry.

Sir Thomas frowned. "I am afraid that your nephew is prejudiced against that great country," he said to Lady Agatha. "I have travelled all over it in cars provided by the directors, who, in such matters, are extremely civil. I assure you that it is an education to visit it."

"But must we really see Chicago in order to be educated?" asked Mr. Erskine plaintively. "I don't feel up to the journey."

Sir Thomas waved his hand. "Mr. Erskine of Treadley has the world on his shelves. We practical men like to see things, not to read about them. The Americans are an extremely interesting people. They are absolutely reasonable. I think that is their distinguishing characteristic. Yes, Mr. Erskine, an absolutely reasonable people. I assure you there is no nonsense about the Americans."

"How dreadful!" cried Lord Henry. "I can stand brute force, but brute reason is quite unbearable. There is something unfair about its use. It is hitting below the intellect."

"I do not understand you," said Sir Thomas, growing rather red.

"I do, Lord Henry," murmured Mr. Erskine, with a smile.

"Paradoxes are all very well in their way. . . ." rejoined the baronet.

"Was that a paradox?" asked Mr. Erskine. "I did not think so. Perhaps it was. Well, the way of paradoxes is the way of truth. To test reality we must see it on the tight rope. When the verities become acrobats, we can judge them."

"Dear me!" said Lady Agatha, "how you men argue! I am sure I never can make out what you are talking about. Oh! Harry, I am quite vexed with you. Why do you try to persuade our nice Mr. Dorian Gray to give up the East End? I assure you he would be quite invaluable. They would love his playing."

"I want him to play to me," cried Lord Henry, smiling, and he looked down the table and caught a bright answering glance.

"But they are so unhappy in Whitechapel," continued Lady Agatha.

"I can sympathize with everything except suffering," said Lord Henry, shrugging his shoulders. "I cannot sympathize with that. It is too ugly, too horrible, too distressing. There is something terribly

morbid in the modern sympathy with pain. One should sympathize with the colour, the beauty, the joy of life. The less said about life's sores, the better."

"Still, the East End is a very important problem," remarked Sir Thomas with a grave shake of the head.

"Quite so," answered the young lord. "It is the problem of slavery, and we try to solve it by amusing the slaves."

The politician looked at him keenly. "What change do you propose, then?" he asked.

Lord Henry laughed. "I don't desire to change anything in England except the weather," he answered. "I am quite content with philosophic contemplation. But, as the nineteenth century has gone bankrupt through an over-expenditure of sympathy, I would suggest that we should appeal to science to put us straight. The advantage of the emotions is that they lead us astray, and the advantage of science is that it is not emotional."

"But we have such grave responsibilities," ventured Mrs. Vandeleur timidly.

"Terribly grave," echoed Lady Agatha.

Lord Henry looked over at Mr. Erskine. "Humanity takes itself too seriously. It is the world's original sin. If the caveman had known how to laugh, history would have been different."

"You are really very comforting," warbled the duchess. "I have always felt rather guilty when I came to see your dear aunt, for I take no interest at all in the East End. For the future I shall be able to look her in the face without a blush."

"A blush is very becoming, Duchess," remarked Lord Henry.
"Only when one is young," she answered. "When an old woman like myself blushes, it is a very bad sign. Ah! Lord Henry, I wish you would tell me how to become young again."

He thought for a moment. "Can you remember any great error that you committed in your early days, Duchess?" he asked, looking at her across the table.

"A great many, I fear," she cried.

"Then commit them over again," he said gravely. "To get back one's youth, one has merely to repeat one's follies."

"A delightful theory!" she exclaimed. "I must put it into practice."

"A dangerous theory!" came from Sir Thomas's tight lips. Lady Agatha shook her head, but could not help being amused. Mr. Erskine listened.

"Yes," he continued, "that is one of the great secrets of life. Nowadays most people die of a sort of creeping common sense, and discover when it is too late that the only things one never regrets are one's mistakes."

A laugh ran round the table.

He played with the idea and grew wilful; tossed it into the air and transformed it; let it escape and recaptured it; made it iridescent with fancy and winged it with paradox. The praise of folly, as he went on, soared into a philosophy, and philosophy herself became young, and catching the mad music of pleasure, wearing, one might fancy, her wine-stained robe and wreath of ivy, danced like a Bacchante* over the hills of life, and mocked the slow Silenus† for being sober. Facts fled before her like frightened forest things. Her white feet trod the huge press at which wise Omar‡ sits, till the seething grape-juice rose round her bare limbs in waves of purple bubbles, or crawled in red foam over the vat's black, dripping, sloping sides. It was an extraordinary improvisation. He felt that the eyes of Dorian Gray were fixed on him, and the consciousness that amongst his audience there was one whose temperament he wished to fascinate seemed to give his wit keenness and to lend colour to his imagination. He was brilliant, fantastic, irresponsible. He charmed his listeners out of themselves, and they followed his pipe, laughing. Dorian Gray never took his gaze off him, but sat like one under a spell, smiles chasing each other over his lips and wonder growing grave in his darkening eyes.

At last, liveried in the costume of the age, reality entered the room in the shape of a servant to tell the duchess that her carriage was waiting. She wrung her hands in mock despair. "How annoying!" she cried. "I must go. I have to call for my husband at the club, to take him to some absurd meeting at Willis's Rooms, where he is going to be in the chair. If I am late he is sure to be furious, and

* A wine-spirited priestess of the Roman god of wine Bacchus.

† The foster father of Bacchus who was lazy and debauched.

‡ Persian poet Omar Khayyám (1048-1131).

I couldn't have a scene in this bonnet. It is far too fragile. A harsh word would ruin it. No, I must go, dear Agatha. Good-bye, Lord Henry, you are quite delightful and dreadfully demoralizing. I am sure I don't know what to say about your views. You must come and dine with us some night. Tuesday? Are you disengaged Tuesday?"

"For you I would throw over anybody, Duchess," said Lord Henry with a bow.

"Ah! that is very nice, and very wrong of you," she cried; "so mind you come"; and she swept out of the room, followed by Lady Agatha and the other ladies.

When Lord Henry had sat down again, Mr. Erskine moved round, and taking a chair close to him, placed his hand upon his arm.

"You talk books away," he said; "why don't you write one?"

"I am too fond of reading books to care to write them, Mr. Erskine. I should like to write a novel certainly, a novel that would be as lovely as a Persian carpet and as unreal. But there is no literary public in England for anything except newspapers, primers, and encyclopaedias. Of all people in the world the English have the least sense of the beauty of literature."

"I fear you are right," answered Mr. Erskine. "I myself used to have literary ambitions, but I gave them up long ago. And now, my dear young friend, if you will allow me to call you so, may I ask if you really meant all that you said to us at lunch?"

"I quite forget what I said," smiled Lord Henry. "Was it all very bad?"

"Very bad indeed. In fact I consider you extremely dangerous, and if anything happens to our good duchess, we shall all look on you as being primarily responsible. But I should like to talk to you about life. The generation into which I was born was tedious. Some day, when you are tired of London, come down to Treadley and expound to me your philosophy of pleasure over some admirable Burgundy I am fortunate enough to possess."

"I shall be charmed. A visit to Treadley would be a great privilege. It has a perfect host, and a perfect library."

"You will complete it," answered the old gentleman with a courteous bow. "And now I must bid good-bye to your excellent

aunt. I am due at the Athenaeum.* It is the hour when we sleep there."

"All of you, Mr. Erskine?"

"Forty of us, in forty armchairs. We are practising for an English Academy of Letters."

Lord Henry laughed and rose. "I am going to the park," he cried.

As he was passing out of the door, Dorian Gray touched him on the arm. "Let me come with you," he murmured.

"But I thought you had promised Basil Hallward to go and see him," answered Lord Henry.

"I would sooner come with you; yes, I feel I must come with you. Do let me. And you will promise to talk to me all the time? No one talks so wonderfully as you do."

"Ah! I have talked quite enough for to-day," said Lord Henry, smiling. "All I want now is to look at life. You may come and look at it with me, if you care to."

* An elite club for artists and intellectuals.

CHAPTER

4

One afternoon, a month later, Dorian Gray was reclining in a luxurious armchair, in the little library of Lord Henry's house in Mayfair. It was, in its way, a very charming room, with its high panelled wainscoting of olive-stained oak, its cream-coloured frieze and ceiling of raised plasterwork, and its brickdust felt carpet strewn with silk, long-fringed Persian rugs. On a tiny satinwood table stood a statuette by Clodion,* and beside it lay a copy of *Les Cent Nouvelles*, bound for Margaret of Valois by Clovis Eve and powdered with the gilt daisies that Queen had selected for her device. Some large blue china jars and parrot-tulips were ranged on the mantelshelf, and through the small leaded panes of the window streamed the apricot-coloured light of a summer day in London.

Lord Henry had not yet come in. He was always late on principle, his principle being that punctuality is the thief of time. So the lad was looking rather sulky, as with listless fingers he turned over the pages of an elaborately illustrated edition of *Manon Lescaut* that he had found in one of the book-cases. The formal monotonous ticking of the Louis Quatorze clock annoyed him. Once or twice he thought of going away.

* French sculptor Claude Michel Clodion (1738-1814).

At last he heard a step outside, and the door opened. "How late you are, Harry!" he murmured.

"I am afraid it is not Harry, Mr. Gray," answered a shrill voice.

He glanced quickly round and rose to his feet. "I beg your pardon. I thought—"

"You thought it was my husband. It is only his wife. You must let me introduce myself. I know you quite well by your photographs. I think my husband has got seventeen of them."

"Not seventeen, Lady Henry?"

"Well, eighteen, then. And I saw you with him the other night at the opera." She laughed nervously as she spoke, and watched him with her vague forget-me-not eyes. She was a curious woman, whose dresses always looked as if they had been designed in a rage and put on in a tempest. She was usually in love with somebody, and, as her passion was never returned, she had kept all her illusions. She tried to look picturesque, but only succeeded in being untidy. Her name was Victoria, and she had a perfect mania for going to church.

"That was at *Lohengrin*,* Lady Henry, I think?"

"Yes; it was at dear Lohengrin. I like Wagner's music better than anybody's. It is so loud that one can talk the whole time without other people hearing what one says. That is a great advantage, don't you think so, Mr. Gray?"

The same nervous staccato laugh broke from her thin lips, and her fingers began to play with a long tortoise-shell paper-knife.

Dorian smiled and shook his head: "I am afraid I don't think so, Lady Henry. I never talk during music—at least, during good music. If one hears bad music, it is one's duty to drown it in conversation."

"Ah! that is one of Harry's views, isn't it, Mr. Gray? I always hear Harry's views from his friends. It is the only way I get to know of them. But you must not think I don't like good music. I adore it, but I am afraid of it. It makes me too romantic. I have simply worshipped pianists—two at a time, sometimes, Harry tells me. I don't know what it is about them. Perhaps it is that they are foreigners. They all are, ain't they? Even those that are born in England become foreigners after a time, don't they? It is so clever of them, and such a compliment to

* A German opera by famous composer Richard Wagner (1813-1883).

art. Makes it quite cosmopolitan, doesn't it? You have never been to any of my parties, have you, Mr. Gray? You must come. I can't afford orchids, but I spare no expense in foreigners. They make one's rooms look so picturesque. But here is Harry! Harry, I came in to look for you, to ask you something—I forget what it was—and I found Mr. Gray here. We have had such a pleasant chat about music. We have quite the same ideas. No; I think our ideas are quite different. But he has been most pleasant. I am so glad I've seen him."

"I am charmed, my love, quite charmed," said Lord Henry, elevating his dark, crescent-shaped eyebrows and looking at them both with an amused smile. "So sorry I am late, Dorian. I went to look after a piece of old brocade in Wardour Street* and had to bargain for hours for it. Nowadays people know the price of everything and the value of nothing."

"I am afraid I must be going," exclaimed Lady Henry, breaking an awkward silence with her silly sudden laugh. "I have promised to drive with the duchess. Good-bye, Mr. Gray. Good-bye, Harry. You are dining out, I suppose? So am I. Perhaps I shall see you at Lady Thornbury's."

"I dare say, my dear," said Lord Henry, shutting the door behind her as, looking like a bird of paradise that had been out all night in the rain, she flitted out of the room, leaving a faint odour of frangipanni.† Then he lit a cigarette and flung himself down on the sofa.

"Never marry a woman with straw-coloured hair, Dorian," he said after a few puffs.

"Why, Harry?"

"Because they are so sentimental."

"But I like sentimental people."

"Never marry at all, Dorian. Men marry because they are tired; women, because they are curious: both are disappointed."

"I don't think I am likely to marry, Harry. I am too much in love. That is one of your aphorisms. I am putting it into practice, as I do everything that you say."

---

* Famous for its antique shops.

† A popular Jasmine perfume named after its Italian inventor.

"Who are you in love with?" asked Lord Henry after a pause.

"With an actress," said Dorian Gray, blushing.

Lord Henry shrugged his shoulders. "That is a rather commonplace *debut*."

"You would not say so if you saw her, Harry."

"Who is she?"

"Her name is Sibyl Vane."

"Never heard of her."

"No one has. People will some day, however. She is a genius."

"My dear boy, no woman is a genius. Women are a decorative sex. They never have anything to say, but they say it charmingly. Women represent the triumph of matter over mind, just as men represent the triumph of mind over morals."

"Harry, how can you?"

"My dear Dorian, it is quite true. I am analysing women at present, so I ought to know. The subject is not so abstruse as I thought it was. I find that, ultimately, there are only two kinds of women, the plain and the coloured. The plain women are very useful. If you want to gain a reputation for respectability, you have merely to take them down to supper. The other women are very charming. They commit one mistake, however. They paint in order to try and look young. Our grandmothers painted in order to try and talk brilliantly. *Rouge* and *esprit* used to go together. That is all over now. As long as a woman can look ten years younger than her own daughter, she is perfectly satisfied. As for conversation, there are only five women in London worth talking to, and two of these can't be admitted into decent society. However, tell me about your genius. How long have you known her?"

"Ah! Harry, your views terrify me."

"Never mind that. How long have you known her?"

"About three weeks."

"And where did you come across her?"

"I will tell you, Harry, but you mustn't be unsympathetic about it. After all, it never would have happened if I had not met you. You filled me with a wild desire to know everything about life. For days after I met you, something seemed to throb in my veins. As I lounged in the park, or strolled down Piccadilly, I used to look at

every one who passed me and wonder, with a mad curiosity, what sort of lives they led. Some of them fascinated me. Others filled me with terror. There was an exquisite poison in the air. I had a passion for sensations . . . Well, one evening about seven o'clock, I determined to go out in search of some adventure. I felt that this grey monstrous London of ours, with its myriads of people, its sordid sinners, and its splendid sins, as you once phrased it, must have something in store for me. I fancied a thousand things. The mere danger gave me a sense of delight. I remembered what you had said to me on that wonderful evening when we first dined together, about the search for beauty being the real secret of life. I don't know what I expected, but I went out and wandered eastward, soon losing my way in a labyrinth of grimy streets and black grassless squares. About half-past eight I passed by an absurd little theatre, with great flaring gas-jets and gaudy play-bills. A hideous Jew, in the most amazing waistcoat I ever beheld in my life, was standing at the entrance, smoking a vile cigar. He had greasy ringlets, and an enormous diamond blazed in the centre of a soiled shirt. 'Have a box, my Lord?' he said, when he saw me, and he took off his hat with an air of gorgeous servility. There was something about him, Harry, that amused me. He was such a monster. You will laugh at me, I know, but I really went in and paid a whole guinea for the stage-box. To the present day I can't make out why I did so; and yet if I hadn't—my dear Harry, if I hadn't—I should have missed the greatest romance of my life. I see you are laughing. It is horrid of you!"

"I am not laughing, Dorian; at least I am not laughing at you. But you should not say the greatest romance of your life. You should say the first romance of your life. You will always be loved, and you will always be in love with love. A *grande passion* is the privilege of people who have nothing to do. That is the one use of the idle classes of a country. Don't be afraid. There are exquisite things in store for you. This is merely the beginning."

"Do you think my nature so shallow?" cried Dorian Gray angrily.

"No; I think your nature so deep."

"How do you mean?"

"My dear boy, the people who love only once in their lives are really the shallow people. What they call their loyalty, and their

fidelity, I call either the lethargy of custom or their lack of imagination. Faithfulness is to the emotional life what consistency is to the life of the intellect—simply a confession of failure. Faithfulness! I must analyse it some day. The passion for property is in it. There are many things that we would throw away if we were not afraid that others might pick them up. But I don't want to interrupt you. Go on with your story."

"Well, I found myself seated in a horrid little private box, with a vulgar drop-scene staring me in the face. I looked out from behind the curtain and surveyed the house. It was a tawdry affair, all Cupids and cornucopias, like a third-rate wedding-cake. The gallery and pit were fairly full, but the two rows of dingy stalls were quite empty, and there was hardly a person in what I suppose they called the dress-circle. Women went about with oranges and ginger-beer, and there was a terrible consumption of nuts going on."

"It must have been just like the palmy days of the British drama."

"Just like, I should fancy, and very depressing. I began to wonder what on earth I should do when I caught sight of the play-bill. What do you think the play was, Harry?"

"I should think '*The Idiot Boy*', or '*Dumb but Innocent*'. Our fathers used to like that sort of piece, I believe. The longer I live, Dorian, the more keenly I feel that whatever was good enough for our fathers is not good enough for us. In art, as in politics, *les grandperes ont toujours tort.*"*

"This play was good enough for us, Harry. It was *Romeo and Juliet.* I must admit that I was rather annoyed at the idea of seeing Shakespeare done in such a wretched hole of a place. Still, I felt interested, in a sort of way. At any rate, I determined to wait for the first act. There was a dreadful orchestra, presided over by a young Hebrew who sat at a cracked piano, that nearly drove me away, but at last the drop-scene was drawn up and the play began. Romeo was a stout elderly gentleman, with corked eyebrows, a husky tragedy voice, and a figure like a beer-barrel. Mercutio was almost as bad. He was played by the low-comedian, who had introduced gags of his own and was on most friendly terms with the pit. They were

* (Fr.) 'Our grandparents are always wrong.'

both as grotesque as the scenery, and that looked as if it had come out of a country-booth. But Juliet! Harry, imagine a girl, hardly seventeen years of age, with a little, flowerlike face, a small Greek head with plaited coils of dark-brown hair, eyes that were violet wells of passion, lips that were like the petals of a rose. She was the loveliest thing I had ever seen in my life. You said to me once that pathos left you unmoved, but that beauty, mere beauty, could fill your eyes with tears. I tell you, Harry, I could hardly see this girl for the mist of tears that came across me. And her voice—I never heard such a voice. It was very low at first, with deep mellow notes that seemed to fall singly upon one's ear. Then it became a little louder, and sounded like a flute or a distant hautboy.* In the garden-scene it had all the tremulous ecstasy that one hears just before dawn when nightingales are singing. There were moments, later on, when it had the wild passion of violins. You know how a voice can stir one. Your voice and the voice of Sibyl Vane are two things that I shall never forget. When I close my eyes, I hear them, and each of them says something different. I don't know which to follow. Why should I not love her? Harry, I do love her. She is everything to me in life. Night after night I go to see her play. One evening she is Rosalind, and the next evening she is Imogen. I have seen her die in the gloom of an Italian tomb, sucking the poison from her lover's lips. I have watched her wandering through the forest of Arden, disguised as a pretty boy in hose and doublet and dainty cap. She has been mad, and has come into the presence of a guilty king, and given him rue to wear and bitter herbs to taste of. She has been innocent, and the black hands of jealousy have crushed her reedlike throat. I have seen her in every age and in every costume. Ordinary women never appeal to one's imagination. They are limited to their century. No glamour ever transfigures them. One knows their minds as easily as one knows their bonnets. One can always find them. There is no mystery in any of them. They ride in the park in the morning and chatter at tea-parties in the afternoon. They have their stereotyped smile and their fashionable manner. They are quite obvious. But an

* A double-reed woodwind instrument having a conical tube and a brilliant penetrating tone.

actress! How different an actress is! Harry! why didn't you tell me that the only thing worth loving is an actress?"

"Because I have loved so many of them, Dorian."

"Oh, yes, horrid people with dyed hair and painted faces."

"Don't run down dyed hair and painted faces. There is an extraordinary charm in them, sometimes," said Lord Henry.

"I wish now I had not told you about Sibyl Vane."

"You could not have helped telling me, Dorian. All through your life you will tell me everything you do."

"Yes, Harry, I believe that is true. I cannot help telling you things. You have a curious influence over me. If I ever did a crime, I would come and confess it to you. You would understand me."

"People like you—the wilful sunbeams of life—don't commit crimes, Dorian. But I am much obliged for the compliment, all the same. And now tell me—reach me the matches, like a good boy—thanks—what are your actual relations with Sibyl Vane?"

Dorian Gray leaped to his feet, with flushed cheeks and burning eyes. "Harry! Sibyl Vane is sacred!"

"It is only the sacred things that are worth touching, Dorian," said Lord Henry, with a strange touch of pathos in his voice. "But why should you be annoyed? I suppose she will belong to you some day. When one is in love, one always begins by deceiving one's self, and one always ends by deceiving others. That is what the world calls a romance. You know her, at any rate, I suppose?"

"Of course I know her. On the first night I was at the theatre, the horrid old Jew came round to the box after the performance was over and offered to take me behind the scenes and introduce me to her. I was furious with him, and told him that Juliet had been dead for hundreds of years and that her body was lying in a marble tomb in Verona. I think, from his blank look of amazement, that he was under the impression that I had taken too much champagne, or something."

"I am not surprised."

"Then he asked me if I wrote for any of the newspapers. I told him I never even read them. He seemed terribly disappointed at that, and confided to me that all the dramatic critics were in a conspiracy against him, and that they were every one of them to be bought."

"I should not wonder if he was quite right there. But, on the other hand, judging from their appearance, most of them cannot be at all expensive."

"Well, he seemed to think they were beyond his means," laughed Dorian. "By this time, however, the lights were being put out in the theatre, and I had to go. He wanted me to try some cigars that he strongly recommended. I declined. The next night, of course, I arrived at the place again. When he saw me, he made me a low bow and assured me that I was a munificent patron of art. He was a most offensive brute, though he had an extraordinary passion for Shakespeare. He told me once, with an air of pride, that his five bankruptcies were entirely due to 'The Bard,' as he insisted on calling him. He seemed to think it a distinction."

"It was a distinction, my dear Dorian—a great distinction. Most people become bankrupt through having invested too heavily in the prose of life. To have ruined one's self over poetry is an honour. But when did you first speak to Miss Sibyl Vane?"

"The third night. She had been playing Rosalind. I could not help going round. I had thrown her some flowers, and she had looked at me—at least I fancied that she had. The old Jew was persistent. He seemed determined to take me behind, so I consented. It was curious my not wanting to know her, wasn't it?"

"No; I don't think so."

"My dear Harry, why?"

"I will tell you some other time. Now I want to know about the girl."

"Sibyl? Oh, she was so shy and so gentle. There is something of a child about her. Her eyes opened wide in exquisite wonder when I told her what I thought of her performance, and she seemed quite unconscious of her power. I think we were both rather nervous. The old Jew stood grinning at the doorway of the dusty greenroom, making elaborate speeches about us both, while we stood looking at each other like children. He would insist on calling me 'My Lord,' so I had to assure Sibyl that I was not anything of the kind. She said quite simply to me, 'You look more like a prince. I must call you Prince Charming.'"

"Upon my word, Dorian, Miss Sibyl knows how to pay compliments."

"You don't understand her, Harry. She regarded me merely as a person in a play. She knows nothing of life. She lives with her mother, a faded tired woman who played Lady Capulet in a sort of magenta dressing-wrapper on the first night, and looks as if she had seen better days."

"I know that look. It depresses me," murmured Lord Henry, examining his rings.

"The Jew wanted to tell me her history, but I said it did not interest me."

"You were quite right. There is always something infinitely mean about other people's tragedies."

"Sibyl is the only thing I care about. What is it to me where she came from? From her little head to her little feet, she is absolutely and entirely divine. Every night of my life I go to see her act, and every night she is more marvellous."

"That is the reason, I suppose, that you never dine with me now. I thought you must have some curious romance on hand. You have; but it is not quite what I expected."

"My dear Harry, we either lunch or sup together every day, and I have been to the opera with you several times," said Dorian, opening his blue eyes in wonder.

"You always come dreadfully late."

"Well, I can't help going to see Sibyl play," he cried, "even if it is only for a single act. I get hungry for her presence; and when I think of the wonderful soul that is hidden away in that little ivory body, I am filled with awe."

"You can dine with me to-night, Dorian, can't you?"

He shook his head. "To-night she is Imogen," he answered, "and to-morrow night she will be Juliet."

"When is she Sibyl Vane?"

"Never."

"I congratulate you."

"How horrid you are! She is all the great heroines of the world in one. She is more than an individual. You laugh, but I tell you she has genius. I love her, and I must make her love me. You, who know all the secrets of life, tell me how to charm Sibyl Vane to love me! I want to make Romeo jealous. I want the dead lovers of the world

to hear our laughter and grow sad. I want a breath of our passion to stir their dust into consciousness, to wake their ashes into pain. My God, Harry, how I worship her!" He was walking up and down the room as he spoke. Hectic spots of red burned on his cheeks. He was terribly excited.

Lord Henry watched him with a subtle sense of pleasure. How different he was now from the shy frightened boy he had met in Basil Hallward's studio! His nature had developed like a flower, had borne blossoms of scarlet flame. Out of its secret hiding-place had crept his soul, and desire had come to meet it on the way.

"And what do you propose to do?" said Lord Henry at last.

"I want you and Basil to come with me some night and see her act. I have not the slightest fear of the result. You are certain to acknowledge her genius. Then we must get her out of the Jew's hands. She is bound to him for three years—at least for two years and eight months—from the present time. I shall have to pay him something, of course. When all that is settled, I shall take a West End theatre and bring her out properly. She will make the world as mad as she has made me."

"That would be impossible, my dear boy."

"Yes, she will. She has not merely art, consummate art-instinct, in her, but she has personality also; and you have often told me that it is personalities, not principles, that move the age."

"Well, what night shall we go?"

"Let me see. To-day is Tuesday. Let us fix to-morrow. She plays Juliet to-morrow."

"All right. The Bristol at eight o'clock; and I will get Basil."

"Not eight, Harry, please. Half-past six. We must be there before the curtain rises. You must see her in the first act, where she meets Romeo."

"Half-past six! What an hour! It will be like having a meat-tea, or reading an English novel. It must be seven. No gentleman dines before seven. Shall you see Basil between this and then? Or shall I write to him?"

"Dear Basil! I have not laid eyes on him for a week. It is rather horrid of me, as he has sent me my portrait in the most wonderful frame, specially designed by himself, and, though I am a little jealous

of the picture for being a whole month younger than I am, I must admit that I delight in it. Perhaps you had better write to him. I don't want to see him alone. He says things that annoy me. He gives me good advice."

Lord Henry smiled. "People are very fond of giving away what they need most themselves. It is what I call the depth of generosity."

"Oh, Basil is the best of fellows, but he seems to me to be just a bit of a Philistine. Since I have known you, Harry, I have discovered that."

"Basil, my dear boy, puts everything that is charming in him into his work. The consequence is that he has nothing left for life but his prejudices, his principles, and his common sense. The only artists I have ever known who are personally delightful are bad artists. Good artists exist simply in what they make, and consequently are perfectly uninteresting in what they are. A great poet, a really great poet, is the most unpoetical of all creatures. But inferior poets are absolutely fascinating. The worse their rhymes are, the more picturesque they look. The mere fact of having published a book of second-rate sonnets makes a man quite irresistible. He lives the poetry that he cannot write. The others write the poetry that they dare not realize."

"I wonder is that really so, Harry?" said Dorian Gray, putting some perfume on his handkerchief out of a large, gold-topped bottle that stood on the table. "It must be, if you say it. And now I am off. Imogen is waiting for me. Don't forget about to-morrow. Good-bye."

As he left the room, Lord Henry's heavy eyelids drooped, and he began to think. Certainly few people had ever interested him so much as Dorian Gray, and yet the lad's mad adoration of some one else caused him not the slightest pang of annoyance or jealousy. He was pleased by it. It made him a more interesting study. He had been always enthralled by the methods of natural science, but the ordinary subject-matter of that science had seemed to him trivial and of no import. And so he had begun by vivisecting himself, as he had ended by vivisecting others. Human life—that appeared to him the one thing worth investigating. Compared to it there was nothing else of any value. It was true that as one watched life in its curious crucible of pain and pleasure, one could not wear over one's face a

mask of glass, nor keep the sulphurous fumes from troubling the brain and making the imagination turbid with monstrous fancies and misshapen dreams. There were poisons so subtle that to know their properties one had to sicken of them. There were maladies so strange that one had to pass through them if one sought to understand their nature. And, yet, what a great reward one received! How wonderful the whole world became to one! To note the curious hard logic of passion, and the emotional coloured life of the intellect—to observe where they met, and where they separated, at what point they were in unison, and at what point they were at discord—there was a delight in that! What matter what the cost was? One could never pay too high a price for any sensation.

He was conscious—and the thought brought a gleam of pleasure into his brown agate eyes—that it was through certain words of his, musical words said with musical utterance, that Dorian Gray's soul had turned to this white girl and bowed in worship before her. To a large extent the lad was his own creation. He had made him premature. That was something. Ordinary people waited till life disclosed to them its secrets, but to the few, to the elect, the mysteries of life were revealed before the veil was drawn away. Sometimes this was the effect of art, and chiefly of the art of literature, which dealt immediately with the passions and the intellect. But now and then a complex personality took the place and assumed the office of art, was indeed, in its way, a real work of art, life having its elaborate masterpieces, just as poetry has, or sculpture, or painting.

Yes, the lad was premature. He was gathering his harvest while it was yet spring. The pulse and passion of youth were in him, but he was becoming self-conscious. It was delightful to watch him. With his beautiful face, and his beautiful soul, he was a thing to wonder at. It was no matter how it all ended, or was destined to end. He was like one of those gracious figures in a pageant or a play, whose joys seem to be remote from one, but whose sorrows stir one's sense of beauty, and whose wounds are like red roses.

Soul and body, body and soul—how mysterious they were! There was animalism in the soul, and the body had its moments of spirituality. The senses could refine, and the intellect could degrade. Who could say where the fleshly impulse ceased, or the psychical

impulse began? How shallow were the arbitrary definitions of ordinary psychologists! And yet how difficult to decide between the claims of the various schools! Was the soul a shadow seated in the house of sin? Or was the body really in the soul, as Giordano Bruno* thought? The separation of spirit from matter was a mystery, and the union of spirit with matter was a mystery also.

He began to wonder whether we could ever make psychology so absolute a science that each little spring of life would be revealed to us. As it was, we always misunderstood ourselves and rarely understood others. Experience was of no ethical value. It was merely the name men gave to their mistakes. Moralists had, as a rule, regarded it as a mode of warning, had claimed for it a certain ethical efficacy in the formation of character, had praised it as something that taught us what to follow and showed us what to avoid. But there was no motive power in experience. It was as little of an active cause as conscience itself. All that it really demonstrated was that our future would be the same as our past, and that the sin we had done once, and with loathing, we would do many times, and with joy.

It was clear to him that the experimental method was the only method by which one could arrive at any scientific analysis of the passions; and certainly Dorian Gray was a subject made to his hand, and seemed to promise rich and fruitful results. His sudden mad love for Sibyl Vane was a psychological phenomenon of no small interest. There was no doubt that curiosity had much to do with it, curiosity and the desire for new experiences, yet it was not a simple, but rather a very complex passion. What there was in it of the purely sensuous instinct of boyhood had been transformed by the workings of the imagination, changed into something that seemed to the lad himself to be remote from sense, and was for that very reason all the more dangerous. It was the passions about whose origin we deceived ourselves that tyrannized most strongly over us. Our weakest motives were those of whose nature we were conscious.

It often happened that when we thought we were experimenting on others we were really experimenting on ourselves.

---

* Italian philosopher and scientist Giordano Bruno (1548-1600) whose radical views led to his execution.

While Lord Henry sat dreaming on these things, a knock came to the door, and his valet entered and reminded him it was time to dress for dinner. He got up and looked out into the street. The sunset had smitten into scarlet gold the upper windows of the houses opposite. The panes glowed like plates of heated metal. The sky above was like a faded rose. He thought of his friend's young fiery-coloured life and wondered how it was all going to end.

When he arrived home, about half-past twelve o'clock, he saw a telegram lying on the hall table. He opened it and found it was from Dorian Gray. It was to tell him that he was engaged to be married to Sibyl Vane.

CHAPTER

5

"Mother, Mother, I am so happy!" whispered the girl, burying her face in the lap of the faded, tired-looking woman who, with back turned to the shrill intrusive light, was sitting in the one armchair that their dingy sitting room contained. "I am so happy!" she repeated, "and you must be happy, too!"

Mrs. Vane winced and put her thin, bismuth-whitened* hands on her daughter's head. "Happy!" she echoed, "I am only happy, Sibyl, when I see you act. You must not think of anything but your acting. Mr. Isaacs has been very good to us, and we owe him money."

The girl looked up and pouted. "Money, Mother?" she cried, "what does money matter? Love is more than money."

"Mr. Isaacs has advanced us fifty pounds to pay off our debts and to get a proper outfit for James. You must not forget that, Sibyl. Fifty pounds is a very large sum. Mr. Isaacs has been most considerate."

"He is not a gentleman, Mother, and I hate the way he talks to me," said the girl, rising to her feet and going over to the window.

---

* This metal-based whitener is used in cosmetics and stage paints.

"I don't know how we could manage without him," answered the elder woman querulously.

Sibyl Vane tossed her head and laughed. "We don't want him any more, Mother. Prince Charming rules life for us now." Then she paused. A rose shook in her blood and shadowed her cheeks. Quick breath parted the petals of her lips. They trembled. Some southern wind of passion swept over her and stirred the dainty folds of her dress. "I love him," she said simply.

"Foolish child! foolish child!" was the parrot-phrase flung in answer. The waving of crooked, false-jewelled fingers gave grotesqueness to the words.

The girl laughed again. The joy of a caged bird was in her voice. Her eyes caught the melody and echoed it in radiance, then closed for a moment, as though to hide their secret. When they opened, the mist of a dream had passed across them.

Thin-lipped wisdom spoke at her from the worn chair, hinted at prudence, quoted from that book of cowardice whose author apes the name of common sense. She did not listen. She was free in her prison of passion. Her prince, Prince Charming, was with her. She had called on memory to remake him. She had sent her soul to search for him, and it had brought him back. His kiss burned again upon her mouth. Her eyelids were warm with his breath.

Then wisdom altered its method and spoke of espial and discovery. This young man might be rich. If so, marriage should be thought of. Against the shell of her ear broke the waves of worldly cunning. The arrows of craft shot by her. She saw the thin lips moving, and smiled.

Suddenly she felt the need to speak. The wordy silence troubled her. "Mother, Mother," she cried, "why does he love me so much? I know why I love him. I love him because he is like what love himself should be. But what does he see in me? I am not worthy of him. And yet—why, I cannot tell—though I feel so much beneath him, I don't feel humble. I feel proud, terribly proud. Mother, did you love my father as I love Prince Charming?"

The elder woman grew pale beneath the coarse powder that daubed her cheeks, and her dry lips twitched with a spasm of pain. Sybil rushed to her, flung her arms round her neck, and kissed her.

"Forgive me, Mother. I know it pains you to talk about our father. But it only pains you because you loved him so much. Don't look so sad. I am as happy to-day as you were twenty years ago. Ah! let me be happy for ever!"

"My child, you are far too young to think of falling in love. Besides, what do you know of this young man? You don't even know his name. The whole thing is most inconvenient, and really, when James is going away to Australia, and I have so much to think of, I must say that you should have shown more consideration. However, as I said before, if he is rich . . ."

"Ah! Mother, Mother, let me be happy!"

Mrs. Vane glanced at her, and with one of those false theatrical gestures that so often become a mode of second nature to a stage-player, clasped her in her arms. At this moment, the door opened and a young lad with rough brown hair came into the room. He was thick-set of figure, and his hands and feet were large and somewhat clumsy in movement. He was not so finely bred as his sister. One would hardly have guessed the close relationship that existed between them. Mrs. Vane fixed her eyes on him and intensified her smile. She mentally elevated her son to the dignity of an audience. She felt sure that the *tableau* was interesting.

"You might keep some of your kisses for me, Sibyl, I think," said the lad with a good-natured grumble.

"Ah! but you don't like being kissed, Jim," she cried. "You are a dreadful old bear." And she ran across the room and hugged him.

James Vane looked into his sister's face with tenderness. "I want you to come out with me for a walk, Sibyl. I don't suppose I shall ever see this horrid London again. I am sure I don't want to."

"My son, don't say such dreadful things," murmured Mrs. Vane, taking up a tawdry theatrical dress, with a sigh, and beginning to patch it. She felt a little disappointed that he had not joined the group. It would have increased the theatrical picturesqueness of the situation.

"Why not, Mother? I mean it."

"You pain me, my son. I trust you will return from Australia in a position of affluence. I believe there is no society of any kind in the Colonies—nothing that I would call society—so when you

have made your fortune, you must come back and assert yourself in London."

"Society!" muttered the lad. "I don't want to know anything about that. I should like to make some money to take you and Sibyl off the stage. I hate it."

"Oh, Jim!" said Sibyl, laughing, "how unkind of you! But are you really going for a walk with me? That will be nice! I was afraid you were going to say good-bye to some of your friends—to Tom Hardy, who gave you that hideous pipe, or Ned Langton, who makes fun of you for smoking it. It is very sweet of you to let me have your last afternoon. Where shall we go? Let us go to the park."

"I am too shabby," he answered, frowning. "Only swell people go to the park."

"Nonsense, Jim," she whispered, stroking the sleeve of his coat.

He hesitated for a moment. "Very well," he said at last, "but don't be too long dressing." She danced out of the door. One could hear her singing as she ran upstairs. Her little feet pattered overhead.

He walked up and down the room two or three times. Then he turned to the still figure in the chair. "Mother, are my things ready?" he asked.

"Quite ready, James," she answered, keeping her eyes on her work. For some months past she had felt ill at ease when she was alone with this rough stern son of hers. Her shallow secret nature was troubled when their eyes met. She used to wonder if he suspected anything. The silence, for he made no other observation, became intolerable to her. She began to complain. Women defend themselves by attacking, just as they attack by sudden and strange surrenders. "I hope you will be contented, James, with your sea-faring life," she said. "You must remember that it is your own choice. You might have entered a solicitor's office. Solicitors are a very respectable class, and in the country often dine with the best families."

"I hate offices, and I hate clerks," he replied. "But you are quite right. I have chosen my own life. All I say is, watch over Sibyl. Don't let her come to any harm. Mother, you must watch over her."

"James, you really talk very strangely. Of course I watch over Sibyl."

"I hear a gentleman comes every night to the theatre and goes behind to talk to her. Is that right? What about that?"

"You are speaking about things you don't understand, James. In the profession we are accustomed to receive a great deal of most gratifying attention. I myself used to receive many bouquets at one time. That was when acting was really understood. As for Sibyl, I do not know at present whether her attachment is serious or not. But there is no doubt that the young man in question is a perfect gentleman. He is always most polite to me. Besides, he has the appearance of being rich, and the flowers he sends are lovely."

"You don't know his name, though," said the lad harshly.

"No," answered his mother with a placid expression in her face. "He has not yet revealed his real name. I think it is quite romantic of him. He is probably a member of the aristocracy."

James Vane bit his lip. "Watch over Sibyl, Mother," he cried, "watch over her."

"My son, you distress me very much. Sibyl is always under my special care. Of course, if this gentleman is wealthy, there is no reason why she should not contract an alliance with him. I trust he is one of the aristocracy. He has all the appearance of it, I must say. It might be a most brilliant marriage for Sibyl. They would make a charming couple. His good looks are really quite remarkable; everybody notices them."

The lad muttered something to himself and drummed on the window-pane with his coarse fingers. He had just turned round to say something when the door opened and Sibyl ran in.

"How serious you both are!" she cried. "What is the matter?"

"Nothing," he answered. "I suppose one must be serious sometimes. Good-bye, Mother; I will have my dinner at five o'clock. Everything is packed, except my shirts, so you need not trouble."

"Good-bye, my son," she answered with a bow of strained stateliness.

She was extremely annoyed at the tone he had adopted with her, and there was something in his look that had made her feel afraid.

"Kiss me, Mother," said the girl. Her flowerlike lips touched the withered cheek and warmed its frost.

"My child! my child!" cried Mrs. Vane, looking up to the ceiling in search of an imaginary gallery.

"Come, Sibyl," said her brother impatiently. He hated his mother's affectations.

They went out into the flickering, wind-blown sunlight and strolled down the dreary Euston Road. The passersby glanced in wonder at the sullen heavy youth who, in coarse, ill-fitting clothes, was in the company of such a graceful, refined-looking girl. He was like a common gardener walking with a rose.

Jim frowned from time to time when he caught the inquisitive glance of some stranger. He had that dislike of being stared at, which comes on geniuses late in life and never leaves the commonplace. Sibyl, however, was quite unconscious of the effect she was producing. Her love was trembling in laughter on her lips. She was thinking of Prince Charming, and, that she might think of him all the more, she did not talk of him, but prattled on about the ship in which Jim was going to sail, about the gold he was certain to find, about the wonderful heiress whose life he was to save from the wicked, red-shirted bushrangers. For he was not to remain a sailor, or a supercargo, or whatever he was going to be. Oh, no! A sailor's existence was dreadful. Fancy being cooped up in a horrid ship, with the hoarse, hump-backed waves trying to get in, and a black wind blowing the masts down and tearing the sails into long screaming ribands! He was to leave the vessel at Melbourne, bid a polite good-bye to the captain, and go off at once to the gold-fields. Before a week was over he was to come across a large nugget of pure gold, the largest nugget that had ever been discovered, and bring it down to the coast in a waggon guarded by six mounted policemen. The bushrangers were to attack them three times, and be defeated with immense slaughter. Or, no. He was not to go to the gold-fields at all. They were horrid places, where men got intoxicated, and shot each other in bar-rooms, and used bad language. He was to be a nice sheep-farmer, and one evening, as he was riding home, he was to see the beautiful heiress being carried off by a robber on a black horse, and give chase, and rescue her. Of course, she would fall in love with him, and he with her, and they would get married, and come home, and live in an immense house in London. Yes, there were delightful

things in store for him. But he must be very good, and not lose his temper, or spend his money foolishly. She was only a year older than he was, but she knew so much more of life. He must be sure, also, to write to her by every mail, and to say his prayers each night before he went to sleep. God was very good, and would watch over him. She would pray for him, too, and in a few years he would come back quite rich and happy.

The lad listened sulkily to her and made no answer. He was heart-sick at leaving home.

Yet it was not this alone that made him gloomy and morose. Inexperienced though he was, he had still a strong sense of the danger of Sibyl's position. This young dandy who was making love to her could mean her no good. He was a gentleman, and he hated him for that, hated him through some curious race-instinct for which he could not account, and which for that reason was all the more dominant within him. He was conscious also of the shallowness and vanity of his mother's nature, and in that saw infinite peril for Sibyl and Sibyl's happiness. Children begin by loving their parents; as they grow older they judge them; sometimes they forgive them.

His mother! He had something on his mind to ask of her, something that he had brooded on for many months of silence. A chance phrase that he had heard at the theatre, a whispered sneer that had reached his ears one night as he waited at the stage-door, had set loose a train of horrible thoughts. He remembered it as if it had been the lash of a hunting-crop across his face. His brows knit together into a wedge-like furrow, and with a twitch of pain he bit his underlip.

"You are not listening to a word I am saying, Jim," cried Sibyl, "and I am making the most delightful plans for your future. Do say something."

"What do you want me to say?"

"Oh! that you will be a good boy and not forget us," she answered, smiling at him.

He shrugged his shoulders. "You are more likely to forget me than I am to forget you, Sibyl."

She flushed. "What do you mean, Jim?" she asked.

"You have a new friend, I hear. Who is he? Why have you not told me about him? He means you no good."

"Stop, Jim!" she exclaimed. "You must not say anything against him. I love him."

"Why, you don't even know his name," answered the lad. "Who is he? I have a right to know."

"He is called Prince Charming. Don't you like the name. Oh! you silly boy! you should never forget it. If you only saw him, you would think him the most wonderful person in the world. Some day you will meet him—when you come back from Australia. You will like him so much. Everybody likes him, and I . . . love him. I wish you could come to the theatre to-night. He is going to be there, and I am to play Juliet. Oh! how I shall play it! Fancy, Jim, to be in love and play Juliet! To have him sitting there! To play for his delight! I am afraid I may frighten the company, frighten or enthrall them. To be in love is to surpass one's self. Poor dreadful Mr. Isaacs will be shouting 'genius' to his loafers at the bar. He has preached me as a dogma; to-night he will announce me as a revelation. I feel it. And it is all his, his only, Prince Charming, my wonderful lover, my god of graces. But I am poor beside him. Poor? What does that matter? When poverty creeps in at the door, love flies in through the window. Our proverbs want rewriting. They were made in winter, and it is summer now; spring-time for me, I think, a very dance of blossoms in blue skies."

"He is a gentleman," said the lad sullenly.

"A prince!" she cried musically. "What more do you want?"

"He wants to enslave you."

"I shudder at the thought of being free."

"I want you to beware of him."

"To see him is to worship him; to know him is to trust him."

"Sibyl, you are mad about him."

She laughed and took his arm. "You dear old Jim, you talk as if you were a hundred. Some day you will be in love yourself. Then you will know what it is. Don't look so sulky. Surely you should be glad to think that, though you are going away, you leave me happier than I have ever been before. Life has been hard for us both, terribly hard and difficult. But it will be different now. You are going to a new

world, and I have found one. Here are two chairs; let us sit down and see the smart people go by."

They took their seats amidst a crowd of watchers. The tulip-beds across the road flamed like throbbing rings of fire. A white dust—tremulous cloud of orris-root* it seemed—hung in the panting air. The brightly coloured parasols danced and dipped like monstrous butterflies.

She made her brother talk of himself, his hopes, his prospects. He spoke slowly and with effort. They passed words to each other as players at a game pass counters. Sibyl felt oppressed. She could not communicate her joy. A faint smile curving that sullen mouth was all the echo she could win. After some time she became silent. Suddenly she caught a glimpse of golden hair and laughing lips, and in an open carriage with two ladies Dorian Gray drove past.

She started to her feet. "There he is!" she cried.

"Who?" said Jim Vane.

"Prince Charming," she answered, looking after the victoria.

He jumped up and seized her roughly by the arm. "Show him to me. Which is he? Point him out. I must see him!" he exclaimed; but at that moment the Duke of Berwick's four-in-hand came between, and when it had left the space clear, the carriage had swept out of the park.

"He is gone," murmured Sibyl sadly. "I wish you had seen him."

"I wish I had, for as sure as there is a God in heaven, if he ever does you any wrong, I shall kill him."

She looked at him in horror. He repeated his words. They cut the air like a dagger. The people round began to gape. A lady standing close to her tittered.

"Come away, Jim; come away," she whispered. He followed her doggedly as she passed through the crowd. He felt glad at what he had said.

When they reached the Achilles Statue,† she turned round. There was pity in her eyes that became laughter on her lips. She shook her head at him. "You are foolish, Jim, utterly foolish; a bad-

---

* Powdered root of the iris flower, used in perfumery.

† A huge statue of a Greek hero by sculptor Richard Westmacott that was erected in London (1822), in tribute to the Duke of Wellington and his soldiers.

tempered boy, that is all. How can you say such horrible things? You don't know what you are talking about. You are simply jealous and unkind. Ah! I wish you would fall in love. Love makes people good, and what you said was wicked."

"I am sixteen," he answered, "and I know what I am about. Mother is no help to you. She doesn't understand how to look after you. I wish now that I was not going to Australia at all. I have a great mind to chuck the whole thing up. I would, if my articles hadn't been signed."

"Oh, don't be so serious, Jim. You are like one of the heroes of those silly melodramas Mother used to be so fond of acting in. I am not going to quarrel with you. I have seen him, and oh! to see him is perfect happiness. We won't quarrel. I know you would never harm any one I love, would you?"

"Not as long as you love him, I suppose," was the sullen answer.

"I shall love him for ever!" she cried.

"And he?"

"For ever, too!"

"He had better."

She shrank from him. Then she laughed and put her hand on his arm. He was merely a boy.

At the Marble Arch they hailed an omnibus, which left them close to their shabby home in the Euston Road. It was after five o'clock, and Sibyl had to lie down for a couple of hours before acting. Jim insisted that she should do so. He said that he would sooner part with her when their mother was not present. She would be sure to make a scene, and he detested scenes of every kind.

In Sybil's own room they parted. There was jealousy in the lad's heart, and a fierce murderous hatred of the stranger who, as it seemed to him, had come between them. Yet, when her arms were flung round his neck, and her fingers strayed through his hair, he softened and kissed her with real affection. There were tears in his eyes as he went downstairs.

His mother was waiting for him below. She grumbled at his unpunctuality, as he entered. He made no answer, but sat down to his meagre meal. The flies buzzed round the table and crawled over the stained cloth. Through the rumble of omnibuses, and the clatter

of street-cabs, he could hear the droning voice devouring each minute that was left to him.

After some time, he thrust away his plate and put his head in his hands. He felt that he had a right to know. It should have been told to him before, if it was as he suspected. Leaden with fear, his mother watched him. Words dropped mechanically from her lips. A tattered lace handkerchief twitched in her fingers. When the clock struck six, he got up and went to the door. Then he turned back and looked at her. Their eyes met. In hers he saw a wild appeal for mercy. It enraged him.

"Mother, I have something to ask you," he said. Her eyes wandered vaguely about the room. She made no answer. "Tell me the truth. I have a right to know. Were you married to my father?"

She heaved a deep sigh. It was a sigh of relief. The terrible moment, the moment that night and day, for weeks and months, she had dreaded, had come at last, and yet she felt no terror. Indeed, in some measure it was a disappointment to her. The vulgar directness of the question called for a direct answer. The situation had not been gradually led up to. It was crude. It reminded her of a bad rehearsal.

"No," she answered, wondering at the harsh simplicity of life.

"My father was a scoundrel then!" cried the lad, clenching his fists.

She shook her head. "I knew he was not free. We loved each other very much. If he had lived, he would have made provision for us. Don't speak against him, my son. He was your father, and a gentleman. Indeed, he was highly connected."

An oath broke from his lips. "I don't care for myself," he exclaimed, "but don't let Sibyl . . . It is a gentleman, isn't it, who is in love with her, or says he is? Highly connected, too, I suppose."

For a moment a hideous sense of humiliation came over the woman. Her head drooped. She wiped her eyes with shaking hands. "Sibyl has a mother," she murmured; "I had none."

The lad was touched. He went towards her, and stooping down, he kissed her. "I am sorry if I have pained you by asking about my father," he said, "but I could not help it. I must go now. Good-bye. Don't forget that you will have only one child now to look after, and

believe me that if this man wrongs my sister, I will find out who he is, track him down, and kill him like a dog. I swear it."

The exaggerated folly of the threat, the passionate gesture that accompanied it, the mad melodramatic words, made life seem more vivid to her. She was familiar with the atmosphere. She breathed more freely, and for the first time for many months she really admired her son. She would have liked to have continued the scene on the same emotional scale, but he cut her short. Trunks had to be carried down and mufflers looked for. The lodging-house drudge bustled in and out. There was the bargaining with the cabman. The moment was lost in vulgar details. It was with a renewed feeling of disappointment that she waved the tattered lace handkerchief from the window, as her son drove away. She was conscious that a great opportunity had been wasted. She consoled herself by telling Sibyl how desolate she felt her life would be, now that she had only one child to look after. She remembered the phrase. It had pleased her. Of the threat she said nothing. It was vividly and dramatically expressed. She felt that they would all laugh at it some day.

CHAPTER

6

"I suppose you have heard the news, Basil?" said Lord Henry that evening as Hallward was shown into a little private room at the Bristol where dinner had been laid for three.

"No, Harry," answered the artist, giving his hat and coat to the bowing waiter. "What is it? Nothing about politics, I hope! They don't interest me. There is hardly a single person in the House of Commons worth painting, though many of them would be the better for a little whitewashing."

"Dorian Gray is engaged to be married," said Lord Henry, watching him as he spoke.

Hallward started and then frowned. "Dorian engaged to be married!" he cried. "Impossible!"

"It is perfectly true."

"To whom?"

"To some little actress or other."

"I can't believe it. Dorian is far too sensible."

"Dorian is far too wise not to do foolish things now and then, my dear Basil."

"Marriage is hardly a thing that one can do now and then, Harry."

"Except in America," rejoined Lord Henry languidly. "But I didn't say he was married. I said he was engaged to be married. There is a great difference. I have a distinct remembrance of being married, but I have no recollection at all of being engaged. I am inclined to think that I never was engaged."

"But think of Dorian's birth, and position, and wealth. It would be absurd for him to marry so much beneath him."

"If you want to make him marry this girl, tell him that, Basil. He is sure to do it, then. Whenever a man does a thoroughly stupid thing, it is always from the noblest motives."

"I hope the girl is good, Harry. I don't want to see Dorian tied to some vile creature, who might degrade his nature and ruin his intellect."

"Oh, she is better than good—she is beautiful," murmured Lord Henry, sipping a glass of vermouth and orange-bitters. "Dorian says she is beautiful, and he is not often wrong about things of that kind. Your portrait of him has quickened his appreciation of the personal appearance of other people. It has had that excellent effect, amongst others. We are to see her to-night, if that boy doesn't forget his appointment."

"Are you serious?"

"Quite serious, Basil. I should be miserable if I thought I should ever be more serious than I am at the present moment."

"But do you approve of it, Harry?" asked the painter, walking up and down the room and biting his lip. "You can't approve of it, possibly. It is some silly infatuation."

"I never approve, or disapprove, of anything now. It is an absurd attitude to take towards life. We are not sent into the world to air our moral prejudices. I never take any notice of what common people say, and I never interfere with what charming people do. If a personality fascinates me, whatever mode of expression that personality selects is absolutely delightful to me. Dorian Gray falls in love with a beautiful girl who acts Juliet, and proposes to marry her. Why not? If he wedded Messalina,* he would be none

* Scandalously unfaithful and cleverly calculating young wife of Roman emperor Claudius, executed subsequently for plotting against her husband.

the less interesting. You know I am not a champion of marriage. The real drawback to marriage is that it makes one unselfish. And unselfish people are colourless. They lack individuality. Still, there are certain temperaments that marriage makes more complex. They retain their egotism, and add to it many other egos. They are forced to have more than one life. They become more highly organized, and to be highly organized is, I should fancy, the object of man's existence. Besides, every experience is of value, and whatever one may say against marriage, it is certainly an experience. I hope that Dorian Gray will make this girl his wife, passionately adore her for six months, and then suddenly become fascinated by some one else. He would be a wonderful study."

"You don't mean a single word of all that, Harry; you know you don't. If Dorian Gray's life were spoiled, no one would be sorrier than yourself. You are much better than you pretend to be."

Lord Henry laughed. "The reason we all like to think so well of others is that we are all afraid for ourselves. The basis of optimism is sheer terror. We think that we are generous because we credit our neighbour with the possession of those virtues that are likely to be a benefit to us. We praise the banker that we may overdraw our account, and find good qualities in the highwayman in the hope that he may spare our pockets. I mean everything that I have said. I have the greatest contempt for optimism. As for a spoiled life, no life is spoiled but one whose growth is arrested. If you want to mar a nature, you have merely to reform it. As for marriage, of course that would be silly, but there are other and more interesting bonds between men and women. I will certainly encourage them. They have the charm of being fashionable. But here is Dorian himself. He will tell you more than I can."

"My dear Harry, my dear Basil, you must both congratulate me!" said the lad, throwing off his evening cape with its satin-lined wings and shaking each of his friends by the hand in turn. "I have never been so happy. Of course, it is sudden—all really delightful things are. And yet it seems to me to be the one thing I have been looking for all my life." He was flushed with excitement and pleasure, and looked extraordinarily handsome.

"I hope you will always be very happy, Dorian," said Hallward,

"but I don't quite forgive you for not having let me know of your engagement. You let Harry know."

"And I don't forgive you for being late for dinner," broke in Lord Henry, putting his hand on the lad's shoulder and smiling as he spoke. "Come, let us sit down and try what the new *chef* here is like, and then you will tell us how it all came about."

"There is really not much to tell," cried Dorian as they took their seats at the small round table. "What happened was simply this. After I left you yesterday evening, Harry, I dressed, had some dinner at that little Italian restaurant in Rupert Street you introduced me to, and went down at eight o'clock to the theatre. Sibyl was playing Rosalind. Of course, the scenery was dreadful and the Orlando absurd. But Sibyl! You should have seen her! When she came on in her boy's clothes, she was perfectly wonderful. She wore a moss-coloured velvet jerkin with cinnamon sleeves, slim, brown, cross-gartered hose, a dainty little green cap with a hawk's feather caught in a jewel, and a hooded cloak lined with dull red. She had never seemed to me more exquisite. She had all the delicate grace of that Tanagra figurine* that you have in your studio, Basil. Her hair clustered round her face like dark leaves round a pale rose. As for her acting—well, you shall see her to-night. She is simply a born artist. I sat in the dingy box absolutely enthralled. I forgot that I was in London and in the nineteenth century. I was away with my love in a forest that no man had ever seen. After the performance was over, I went behind and spoke to her. As we were sitting together, suddenly there came into her eyes a look that I had never seen there before. My lips moved towards hers. We kissed each other. I can't describe to you what I felt at that moment. It seemed to me that all my life had been narrowed to one perfect point of rose-coloured joy. She trembled all over and shook like a white narcissus. Then she flung herself on her knees and kissed my hands. I feel that I should not tell you all this, but I can't help it. Of course, our engagement is a dead secret. She has not even told her own mother. I don't know what my guardians will say. Lord Radley is sure to be furious. I don't care. I

* Small statues of red clay found in the tombs near the ancient city of Tanagra in Boeotia (in eastern-central Greece).

shall be of age in less than a year, and then I can do what I like. I have been right, Basil, haven't I, to take my love out of poetry and to find my wife in Shakespeare's plays? Lips that Shakespeare taught to speak have whispered their secret in my ear. I have had the arms of Rosalind around me, and kissed Juliet on the mouth."

"Yes, Dorian, I suppose you were right," said Hallward slowly.

"Have you seen her to-day?" asked Lord Henry.

Dorian Gray shook his head. "I left her in the forest of Arden; I shall find her in an orchard in Verona."

Lord Henry sipped his champagne in a meditative manner. "At what particular point did you mention the word marriage, Dorian? And what did she say in answer? Perhaps you forgot all about it."

"My dear Harry, I did not treat it as a business transaction, and I did not make any formal proposal. I told her that I loved her, and she said she was not worthy to be my wife. Not worthy! Why, the whole world is nothing to me compared with her."

"Women are wonderfully practical," murmured Lord Henry, "much more practical than we are. In situations of that kind we often forget to say anything about marriage, and they always remind us."

Hallward laid his hand upon his arm. "Don't, Harry. You have annoyed Dorian. He is not like other men. He would never bring misery upon any one. His nature is too fine for that."

Lord Henry looked across the table. "Dorian is never annoyed with me," he answered. "I asked the question for the best reason possible, for the only reason, indeed, that excuses one for asking any question—simple curiosity. I have a theory that it is always the women who propose to us, and not we who propose to the women. Except, of course, in middle-class life. But then the middle classes are not modern."

Dorian Gray laughed, and tossed his head. "You are quite incorrigible, Harry; but I don't mind. It is impossible to be angry with you. When you see Sibyl Vane, you will feel that the man who could wrong her would be a beast, a beast without a heart. I cannot understand how any one can wish to shame the thing he loves. I love Sibyl Vane. I want to place her on a pedestal of gold and to see the world worship the woman who is mine. What is marriage? An

irrevocable vow. You mock at it for that. Ah! don't mock. It is an irrevocable vow that I want to take. Her trust makes me faithful, her belief makes me good. When I am with her, I regret all that you have taught me. I become different from what you have known me to be. I am changed, and the mere touch of Sibyl Vane's hand makes me forget you and all your wrong, fascinating, poisonous, delightful theories."

"And those are . . .?" asked Lord Henry, helping himself to some salad.

"Oh, your theories about life, your theories about love, your theories about pleasure. All your theories, in fact, Harry."

"Pleasure is the only thing worth having a theory about," he answered in his slow melodious voice. "But I am afraid I cannot claim my theory as my own. It belongs to Nature, not to me. Pleasure is Nature's test, her sign of approval. When we are happy, we are always good, but when we are good, we are not always happy."

"Ah! but what do you mean by good?" cried Basil Hallward.

"Yes," echoed Dorian, leaning back in his chair and looking at Lord Henry over the heavy clusters of purple-lipped irises that stood in the centre of the table, "what do you mean by good, Harry?"

"To be good is to be in harmony with one's self," he replied, touching the thin stem of his glass with his pale, fine-pointed fingers. "Discord is to be forced to be in harmony with others. One's own life—that is the important thing. As for the lives of one's neighbours, if one wishes to be a prig or a Puritan, one can flaunt one's moral views about them, but they are not one's concern. Besides, individualism has really the higher aim. Modern morality consists in accepting the standard of one's age. I consider that for any man of culture to accept the standard of his age is a form of the grossest immorality."

"But, surely, if one lives merely for one's self, Harry, one pays a terrible price for doing so?" suggested the painter.

"Yes, we are overcharged for everything nowadays. I should fancy that the real tragedy of the poor is that they can afford nothing but self-denial. Beautiful sins, like beautiful things, are the privilege of the rich."

"One has to pay in other ways but money."

"What sort of ways, Basil?"

"Oh! I should fancy in remorse, in suffering, in . . . well, in the consciousness of degradation."

Lord Henry shrugged his shoulders. "My dear fellow, mediaeval art is charming, but mediaeval emotions are out of date. One can use them in fiction, of course. But then the only things that one can use in fiction are the things that one has ceased to use in fact. Believe me, no civilized man ever regrets a pleasure, and no uncivilized man ever knows what a pleasure is."

"I know what pleasure is," cried Dorian Gray. "It is to adore some one."

"That is certainly better than being adored," he answered, toying with some fruits. "Being adored is a nuisance. Women treat us just as humanity treats its gods. They worship us, and are always bothering us to do something for them."

"I should have said that whatever they ask for they had first given to us," murmured the lad gravely. "They create love in our natures. They have a right to demand it back."

"That is quite true, Dorian," cried Hallward.

"Nothing is ever quite true," said Lord Henry.

"This is," interrupted Dorian. "You must admit, Harry, that women give to men the very gold of their lives."

"Possibly," he sighed, "but they invariably want it back in such very small change. That is the worry. Women, as some witty Frenchman once put it, inspire us with the desire to do masterpieces and always prevent us from carrying them out."

"Harry, you are dreadful! I don't know why I like you so much."

"You will always like me, Dorian," he replied. "Will you have some coffee, you fellows? Waiter, bring coffee, and *fine-champagne*, and some cigarettes. No, don't mind the cigarettes—I have some. Basil, I can't allow you to smoke cigars. You must have a cigarette. A cigarette is the perfect type of a perfect pleasure. It is exquisite, and it leaves one unsatisfied. What more can one want? Yes, Dorian, you will always be fond of me. I represent to you all the sins you have never had the courage to commit."

"What nonsense you talk, Harry!" cried the lad, taking a light from a fire-breathing silver dragon that the waiter had placed on the

table. "Let us go down to the theatre. When Sibyl comes on the stage you will have a new ideal of life. She will represent something to you that you have never known."

"I have known everything," said Lord Henry, with a tired look in his eyes, "but I am always ready for a new emotion. I am afraid, however, that, for me at any rate, there is no such thing. Still, your wonderful girl may thrill me. I love acting. It is so much more real than life. Let us go. Dorian, you will come with me. I am so sorry, Basil, but there is only room for two in the brougham. You must follow us in a hansom."

They got up and put on their coats, sipping their coffee standing. The painter was silent and preoccupied. There was a gloom over him. He could not bear this marriage, and yet it seemed to him to be better than many other things that might have happened. After a few minutes, they all passed downstairs. He drove off by himself, as had been arranged, and watched the flashing lights of the little brougham in front of him. A strange sense of loss came over him. He felt that Dorian Gray would never again be to him all that he had been in the past. Life had come between them . . . His eyes darkened, and the crowded flaring streets became blurred to his eyes. When the cab drew up at the theatre, it seemed to him that he had grown years older.

CHAPTER 7

For some reason or other, the house was crowded that night, and the fat Jew manager who met them at the door was beaming from ear to ear with an oily tremulous smile. He escorted them to their box with a sort of pompous humility, waving his fat jewelled hands and talking at the top of his voice. Dorian Gray loathed him more than ever. He felt as if he had come to look for Miranda and had been met by Caliban. Lord Henry, upon the other hand, rather liked him. At least he declared he did, and insisted on shaking him by the hand and assuring him that he was proud to meet a man who had discovered a real genius and gone bankrupt over a poet. Hallward amused himself with watching the faces in the pit. The heat was terribly oppressive, and the huge sunlight flamed like a monstrous dahlia with petals of yellow fire. The youths in the gallery had taken off their coats and waistcoats and hung them over the side. They talked to each other across the theatre and shared their oranges with the tawdry girls who sat beside them. Some women were laughing in the pit. Their voices were horribly shrill and discordant. The sound of the popping of corks came from the bar.

"What a place to find one's divinity in!" said Lord Henry.

"Yes!" answered Dorian Gray. "It was here I found her, and she is divine beyond all living things. When she acts, you will forget everything. These common rough people, with their coarse faces and brutal gestures, become quite different when she is on the stage. They sit silently and watch her. They weep and laugh as she wills them to do. She makes them as responsive as a violin. She spiritualizes them, and one feels that they are of the same flesh and blood as one's self."

"The same flesh and blood as one's self! Oh, I hope not!" exclaimed Lord Henry, who was scanning the occupants of the gallery through his opera-glass.

"Don't pay any attention to him, Dorian," said the painter. "I understand what you mean, and I believe in this girl. Any one you love must be marvellous, and any girl who has the effect you describe must be fine and noble. To spiritualize one's age—that is something worth doing. If this girl can give a soul to those who have lived without one, if she can create the sense of beauty in people whose lives have been sordid and ugly, if she can strip them of their selfishness and lend them tears for sorrows that are not their own, she is worthy of all your adoration, worthy of the adoration of the world. This marriage is quite right. I did not think so at first, but I admit it now. The gods made Sibyl Vane for you. Without her you would have been incomplete."

"Thanks, Basil," answered Dorian Gray, pressing his hand. "I knew that you would understand me. Harry is so cynical, he terrifies me. But here is the orchestra. It is quite dreadful, but it only lasts for about five minutes. Then the curtain rises, and you will see the girl to whom I am going to give all my life, to whom I have given everything that is good in me."

A quarter of an hour afterwards, amidst an extraordinary turmoil of applause, Sibyl Vane stepped on to the stage. Yes, she was certainly lovely to look at—one of the loveliest creatures, Lord Henry thought, that he had ever seen. There was something of the fawn in her shy grace and startled eyes. A faint blush, like the shadow of a rose in a mirror of silver, came to her cheeks as she glanced at the crowded enthusiastic house. She stepped back a few paces and her lips seemed to tremble. Basil Hallward leaped to his

feet and began to applaud. Motionless, and as one in a dream, sat Dorian Gray, gazing at her. Lord Henry peered through his glasses, murmuring, "Charming! charming!"

The scene was the hall of Capulet's house, and Romeo in his pilgrim's dress had entered with Mercutio and his other friends. The band, such as it was, struck up a few bars of music, and the dance began. Through the crowd of ungainly, shabbily dressed actors, Sibyl Vane moved like a creature from a finer world. Her body swayed, while she danced, as a plant sways in the water. The curves of her throat were the curves of a white lily. Her hands seemed to be made of cool ivory.

Yet she was curiously listless. She showed no sign of joy when her eyes rested on Romeo. The few words she had to speak—

> Good pilgrim, you do wrong your hand too much,
> Which mannerly devotion shows in this;
> For saints have hands that pilgrims' hands do touch,
> And palm to palm is holy palmers' kiss—

with the brief dialogue that follows, were spoken in a thoroughly artificial manner. The voice was exquisite, but from the point of view of tone it was absolutely false. It was wrong in colour. It took away all the life from the verse. It made the passion unreal.

Dorian Gray grew pale as he watched her. He was puzzled and anxious. Neither of his friends dared to say anything to him. She seemed to them to be absolutely incompetent. They were horribly disappointed.

Yet they felt that the true test of any Juliet is the balcony scene of the second act. They waited for that. If she failed there, there was nothing in her.

She looked charming as she came out in the moonlight. That could not be denied. But the staginess of her acting was unbearable, and grew worse as she went on. Her gestures became absurdly artificial. She overemphasized everything that she had to say. The beautiful passage—

> Thou knowest the mask of night is on my face,

Else would a maiden blush bepaint my cheek
For that which thou hast heard me speak to-night—

was declaimed with the painful precision of a schoolgirl who has been taught to recite by some second-rate professor of elocution. When she leaned over the balcony and came to those wonderful lines—

Although I joy in thee,
I have no joy of this contract to-night:
It is too rash, too unadvised, too sudden;
Too like the lightning, which doth cease to be
Ere one can say, "It lightens." Sweet, good-night!
This bud of love by summer's ripening breath
May prove a beauteous flower when next we meet—

she spoke the words as though they conveyed no meaning to her. It was not nervousness. Indeed, so far from being nervous, she was absolutely self-contained. It was simply bad art. She was a complete failure.

Even the common uneducated audience of the pit and gallery lost their interest in the play. They got restless, and began to talk loudly and to whistle. The Jew manager, who was standing at the back of the dress-circle, stamped and swore with rage. The only person unmoved was the girl herself.

When the second act was over, there came a storm of hisses, and Lord Henry got up from his chair and put on his coat. "She is quite beautiful, Dorian," he said, "but she can't act. Let us go."

"I am going to see the play through," answered the lad, in a hard bitter voice. "I am awfully sorry that I have made you waste an evening, Harry. I apologize to you both."

"My dear Dorian, I should think Miss Vane was ill," interrupted Hallward. "We will come some other night."

"I wish she were ill," he rejoined. "But she seems to me to be simply callous and cold. She has entirely altered. Last night she was a great artist. This evening she is merely a commonplace mediocre actress."

"Don't talk like that about any one you love, Dorian. Love is a more wonderful thing than art."

"They are both simply forms of imitation," remarked Lord Henry. "But do let us go. Dorian, you must not stay here any longer. It is not good for one's morals to see bad acting. Besides, I don't suppose you will want your wife to act, so what does it matter if she plays Juliet like a wooden doll? She is very lovely, and if she knows as little about life as she does about acting, she will be a delightful experience. There are only two kinds of people who are really fascinating—people who know absolutely everything, and people who know absolutely nothing. Good heavens, my dear boy, don't look so tragic! The secret of remaining young is never to have an emotion that is unbecoming. Come to the club with Basil and myself. We will smoke cigarettes and drink to the beauty of Sibyl Vane. She is beautiful. What more can you want?"

"Go away, Harry," cried the lad. "I want to be alone. Basil, you must go. Ah! can't you see that my heart is breaking?" The hot tears came to his eyes. His lips trembled, and rushing to the back of the box, he leaned up against the wall, hiding his face in his hands.

"Let us go, Basil," said Lord Henry with a strange tenderness in his voice, and the two young men passed out together.

A few moments afterwards the footlights flared up and the curtain rose on the third act. Dorian Gray went back to his seat. He looked pale, and proud, and indifferent. The play dragged on, and seemed interminable. Half of the audience went out, tramping in heavy boots and laughing. The whole thing was a *fiasco*. The last act was played to almost empty benches. The curtain went down on a titter and some groans.

As soon as it was over, Dorian Gray rushed behind the scenes into the greenroom. The girl was standing there alone, with a look of triumph on her face. Her eyes were lit with an exquisite fire. There was a radiance about her. Her parted lips were smiling over some secret of their own.

When he entered, she looked at him, and an expression of infinite joy came over her. "How badly I acted to-night, Dorian!" she cried.

"Horribly!" he answered, gazing at her in amazement. "Horribly!

It was dreadful. Are you ill? You have no idea what it was. You have no idea what I suffered."

The girl smiled. "Dorian," she answered, lingering over his name with long-drawn music in her voice, as though it were sweeter than honey to the red petals of her mouth. "Dorian, you should have understood. But you understand now, don't you?"

"Understand what?" he asked, angrily.

"Why I was so bad to-night. Why I shall always be bad. Why I shall never act well again."

He shrugged his shoulders. "You are ill, I suppose. When you are ill you shouldn't act. You make yourself ridiculous. My friends were bored. I was bored."

She seemed not to listen to him. She was transfigured with joy. An ecstasy of happiness dominated her.

"Dorian, Dorian," she cried, "before I knew you, acting was the one reality of my life. It was only in the theatre that I lived. I thought that it was all true. I was Rosalind one night and Portia the other. The joy of Beatrice was my joy, and the sorrows of Cordelia were mine also. I believed in everything. The common people who acted with me seemed to me to be godlike. The painted scenes were my world. I knew nothing but shadows, and I thought them real. You came—oh, my beautiful love!—and you freed my soul from prison. You taught me what reality really is. To-night, for the first time in my life, I saw through the hollowness, the sham, the silliness of the empty pageant in which I had always played. To-night, for the first time, I became conscious that the Romeo was hideous, and old, and painted, that the moonlight in the orchard was false, that the scenery was vulgar, and that the words I had to speak were unreal, were not my words, were not what I wanted to say. You had brought me something higher, something of which all art is but a reflection. You had made me understand what love really is. My love! My love! Prince Charming! Prince of life! I have grown sick of shadows. You are more to me than all art can ever be. What have I to do with the puppets of a play? When I came on to-night, I could not understand how it was that everything had gone from me. I thought that I was going to be wonderful. I found that I could do nothing. Suddenly it dawned on my soul

what it all meant. The knowledge was exquisite to me. I heard them hissing, and I smiled. What could they know of love such as ours? Take me away, Dorian—take me away with you, where we can be quite alone. I hate the stage. I might mimic a passion that I do not feel, but I cannot mimic one that burns me like fire. Oh, Dorian, Dorian, you understand now what it signifies? Even if I could do it, it would be profanation for me to play at being in love. You have made me see that."

He flung himself down on the sofa and turned away his face. "You have killed my love," he muttered.

She looked at him in wonder and laughed. He made no answer. She came across to him, and with her little fingers stroked his hair. She knelt down and pressed his hands to her lips. He drew them away, and a shudder ran through him.

Then he leaped up and went to the door. "Yes," he cried, "you have killed my love. You used to stir my imagination. Now you don't even stir my curiosity. You simply produce no effect. I loved you because you were marvellous, because you had genius and intellect, because you realized the dreams of great poets and gave shape and substance to the shadows of art. You have thrown it all away. You are shallow and stupid. My God! how mad I was to love you! What a fool I have been! You are nothing to me now. I will never see you again. I will never think of you. I will never mention your name. You don't know what you were to me, once. Why, once . . . Oh, I can't bear to think of it! I wish I had never laid eyes upon you! You have spoiled the romance of my life. How little you can know of love, if you say it mars your art! Without your art, you are nothing. I would have made you famous, splendid, magnificent. The world would have worshipped you, and you would have borne my name. What are you now? A third-rate actress with a pretty face."

The girl grew white, and trembled. She clenched her hands together, and her voice seemed to catch in her throat. "You are not serious, Dorian?" she murmured. "You are acting."

"Acting! I leave that to you. You do it so well," he answered bitterly.

She rose from her knees and, with a piteous expression of pain in her face, came across the room to him. She put her hand upon

his arm and looked into his eyes. He thrust her back. "Don't touch me!" he cried.

A low moan broke from her, and she flung herself at his feet and lay there like a trampled flower. "Dorian, Dorian, don't leave me!" she whispered. "I am so sorry I didn't act well. I was thinking of you all the time. But I will try—indeed, I will try. It came so suddenly across me, my love for you. I think I should never have known it if you had not kissed me—if we had not kissed each other. Kiss me again, my love. Don't go away from me. I couldn't bear it. Oh! don't go away from me. My brother . . . No; never mind. He didn't mean it. He was in jest . . . But you, oh! can't you forgive me for to-night? I will work so hard and try to improve. Don't be cruel to me, because I love you better than anything in the world. After all, it is only once that I have not pleased you. But you are quite right, Dorian. I should have shown myself more of an artist. It was foolish of me, and yet I couldn't help it. Oh, don't leave me, don't leave me." A fit of passionate sobbing choked her. She crouched on the floor like a wounded thing, and Dorian Gray, with his beautiful eyes, looked down at her, and his chiselled lips curled in exquisite disdain. There is always something ridiculous about the emotions of people whom one has ceased to love. Sibyl Vane seemed to him to be absurdly melodramatic. Her tears and sobs annoyed him.

"I am going," he said at last in his calm clear voice. "I don't wish to be unkind, but I can't see you again. You have disappointed me."

She wept silently, and made no answer, but crept nearer. Her little hands stretched blindly out, and appeared to be seeking for him. He turned on his heel and left the room. In a few moments he was out of the theatre.

Where he went to he hardly knew. He remembered wandering through dimly lit streets, past gaunt, black-shadowed archways and evil-looking houses. Women with hoarse voices and harsh laughter had called after him. Drunkards had reeled by, cursing and chattering to themselves like monstrous apes. He had seen grotesque children huddled upon door-steps, and heard shrieks and oaths from gloomy courts.

As the dawn was just breaking, he found himself close to Covent

Garden.* The darkness lifted, and, flushed with faint fires, the sky hollowed itself into a perfect pearl. Huge carts filled with nodding lilies rumbled slowly down the polished empty street. The air was heavy with the perfume of the flowers, and their beauty seemed to bring him an anodyne for his pain. He followed into the market and watched the men unloading their waggons. A white-smocked carter offered him some cherries. He thanked him, wondered why he refused to accept any money for them, and began to eat them listlessly. They had been plucked at midnight, and the coldness of the moon had entered into them. A long line of boys carrying crates of striped tulips, and of yellow and red roses, defiled in front of him, threading their way through the huge, jade-green piles of vegetables. Under the portico, with its grey, sun-bleached pillars, loitered a troop of draggled bareheaded girls, waiting for the auction to be over. Others crowded round the swinging doors of the coffee-house in the piazza. The heavy cart-horses slipped and stamped upon the rough stones, shaking their bells and trappings. Some of the drivers were lying asleep on a pile of sacks. Iris-necked and pink-footed, the pigeons ran about picking up seeds.

After a little while, he hailed a hansom and drove home. For a few moments he loitered upon the doorstep, looking round at the silent square, with its blank, close-shuttered windows and its staring blinds. The sky was pure opal now, and the roofs of the houses glistened like silver against it. From some chimney opposite a thin wreath of smoke was rising. It curled, a violet riband, through the nacre-coloured air.

In the huge gilt Venetian lantern, spoil of some Doge's† barge, that hung from the ceiling of the great, oak-panelled hall of entrance, lights were still burning from three flickering jets: thin blue petals of flame they seemed, rimmed with white fire. He turned them out and, having thrown his hat and cape on the table, passed through the library towards the door of his bedroom, a large octagonal chamber on the ground floor that, in his new-born feeling for luxury, he had just had decorated for himself and hung with some curious

---

* A busy market of fruit, flowers and vegetables.

† Italian Doge was the principle magistrate of Venice.

Renaissance tapestries that had been discovered stored in a disused attic at Selby Royal. As he was turning the handle of the door, his eye fell upon the portrait Basil Hallward had painted of him. He started back as if in surprise. Then he went on into his own room, looking somewhat puzzled. After he had taken the button-hole out of his coat, he seemed to hesitate. Finally, he came back, went over to the picture, and examined it. In the dim arrested light that struggled through the cream-coloured silk blinds, the face appeared to him to be a little changed. The expression looked different. One would have said that there was a touch of cruelty in the mouth. It was certainly strange.

He turned round and, walking to the window, drew up the blind. The bright dawn flooded the room and swept the fantastic shadows into dusky corners, where they lay shuddering. But the strange expression that he had noticed in the face of the portrait seemed to linger there, to be more intensified even. The quivering ardent sunlight showed him the lines of cruelty round the mouth as clearly as if he had been looking into a mirror after he had done some dreadful thing.

He winced and, taking up from the table an oval glass framed in ivory Cupids, one of Lord Henry's many presents to him, glanced hurriedly into its polished depths. No line like that warped his red lips. What did it mean?

He rubbed his eyes, and came close to the picture, and examined it again. There were no signs of any change when he looked into the actual painting, and yet there was no doubt that the whole expression had altered. It was not a mere fancy of his own. The thing was horribly apparent.

He threw himself into a chair and began to think. Suddenly there flashed across his mind what he had said in Basil Hallward's studio the day the picture had been finished. Yes, he remembered it perfectly.

He had uttered a mad wish that he himself might remain young, and the portrait grow old; that his own beauty might be untarnished, and the face on the canvas bear the burden of his passions and his sins; that the painted image might be seared with the lines of suffering and thought, and that he might keep all the delicate bloom

and loveliness of his then just conscious boyhood. Surely his wish had not been fulfilled? Such things were impossible. It seemed monstrous even to think of them. And, yet, there was the picture before him, with the touch of cruelty in the mouth.

Cruelty! Had he been cruel? It was the girl's fault, not his. He had dreamed of her as a great artist, had given his love to her because he had thought her great. Then she had disappointed him. She had been shallow and unworthy. And, yet, a feeling of infinite regret came over him, as he thought of her lying at his feet sobbing like a little child. He remembered with what callousness he had watched her. Why had he been made like that? Why had such a soul been given to him? But he had suffered also. During the three terrible hours that the play had lasted, he had lived centuries of pain, aeon upon aeon of torture. His life was well worth hers. She had marred him for a moment, if he had wounded her for an age. Besides, women were better suited to bear sorrow than men. They lived on their emotions. They only thought of their emotions. When they took lovers, it was merely to have some one with whom they could have scenes. Lord Henry had told him that, and Lord Henry knew what women were. Why should he trouble about Sibyl Vane? She was nothing to him now.

But the picture? What was he to say of that? It held the secret of his life, and told his story. It had taught him to love his own beauty. Would it teach him to loathe his own soul? Would he ever look at it again?

No; it was merely an illusion wrought on the troubled senses. The horrible night that he had passed had left phantoms behind it. Suddenly there had fallen upon his brain that tiny scarlet speck that makes men mad. The picture had not changed. It was folly to think so.

Yet it was watching him, with its beautiful marred face and its cruel smile. Its bright hair gleamed in the early sunlight. Its blue eyes met his own. A sense of infinite pity, not for himself, but for the painted image of himself, came over him. It had altered already, and would alter more. Its gold would wither into grey. Its red and white roses would die. For every sin that he committed, a stain would fleck and wreck its fairness. But he would not sin. The picture, changed or

unchanged, would be to him the visible emblem of conscience. He would resist temptation. He would not see Lord Henry any more—would not, at any rate, listen to those subtle poisonous theories that in Basil Hallward's garden had first stirred within him the passion for impossible things. He would go back to Sibyl Vane, make her amends, marry her, try to love her again. Yes, it was his duty to do so. She must have suffered more than he had. Poor child! He had been selfish and cruel to her. The fascination that she had exercised over him would return. They would be happy together. His life with her would be beautiful and pure.

He got up from his chair and drew a large screen right in front of the portrait, shuddering as he glanced at it. "How horrible!" he murmured to himself, and he walked across to the window and opened it. When he stepped out on to the grass, he drew a deep breath. The fresh morning air seemed to drive away all his sombre passions. He thought only of Sibyl. A faint echo of his love came back to him. He repeated her name over and over again. The birds that were singing in the dew-drenched garden seemed to be telling the flowers about her.

CHAPTER

8

It was long past noon when he awoke. His valet had crept several times on tiptoe into the room to see if he was stirring, and had wondered what made his young master sleep so late. Finally his bell sounded, and Victor came in softly with a cup of tea, and a pile of letters, on a small tray of old Sevres china,* and drew back the olive-satin curtains, with their shimmering blue lining, that hung in front of the three tall windows.

"Monsieur has well slept this morning," he said, smiling.

"What o'clock is it, Victor?" asked Dorian Gray drowsily.

"One hour and a quarter, Monsieur."

How late it was! He sat up, and having sipped some tea, turned over his letters. One of them was from Lord Henry, and had been brought by hand that morning. He hesitated for a moment, and then put it aside. The others he opened listlessly. They contained the usual collection of cards, invitations to dinner, tickets for private views, programmes of charity concerts, and the like that are showered on fashionable young men every morning during the season. There was a rather heavy bill for a chased silver Louis-

* A fine porcelain from Sèrves near Paris.

Quinze toilet-set that he had not yet had the courage to send on to his guardians, who were extremely old-fashioned people and did not realize that we live in an age when unnecessary things are our only necessities; and there were several very courteously worded communications from Jermyn Street money-lenders offering to advance any sum of money at a moment's notice and at the most reasonable rates of interest.

After about ten minutes he got up, and throwing on an elaborate dressing-gown of silk-embroidered cashmere wool, passed into the onyx paved bathroom. The cool water refreshed him after his long sleep. He seemed to have forgotten all that he had gone through. A dim sense of having taken part in some strange tragedy came to him once or twice, but there was the unreality of a dream about it.

As soon as he was dressed, he went into the library and sat down to a light French breakfast that had been laid out for him on a small round table close to the open window. It was an exquisite day. The warm air seemed laden with spices. A bee flew in and buzzed round the blue-dragon bowl that, filled with sulphur-yellow roses, stood before him. He felt perfectly happy.

Suddenly his eye fell on the screen that he had placed in front of the portrait, and he started.

"Too cold for Monsieur?" asked his valet, putting an omelette on the table. "I shut the window?"

Dorian shook his head. "I am not cold," he murmured.

Was it all true? Had the portrait really changed? Or had it been simply his own imagination that had made him see a look of evil where there had been a look of joy? Surely a painted canvas could not alter? The thing was absurd. It would serve as a tale to tell Basil some day. It would make him smile.

And, yet, how vivid was his recollection of the whole thing! First in the dim twilight, and then in the bright dawn, he had seen the touch of cruelty round the warped lips. He almost dreaded his valet leaving the room. He knew that when he was alone he would have to examine the portrait. He was afraid of certainty. When the coffee and cigarettes had been brought and the man turned to go, he felt a wild desire to tell him to remain. As the door was closing behind him, he called him back. The man stood waiting for his orders.

Dorian looked at him for a moment. "I am not at home to any one, Victor," he said with a sigh. The man bowed and retired.

Then he rose from the table, lit a cigarette, and flung himself down on a luxuriously cushioned couch that stood facing the screen. The screen was an old one, of gilt Spanish leather, stamped and wrought with a rather florid Louis-Quatorze pattern. He scanned it curiously, wondering if ever before it had concealed the secret of a man's life.

Should he move it aside, after all? Why not let it stay there? What was the use of knowing? If the thing was true, it was terrible. If it was not true, why trouble about it? But what if, by some fate or deadlier chance, eyes other than his spied behind and saw the horrible change? What should he do if Basil Hallward came and asked to look at his own picture? Basil would be sure to do that. No; the thing had to be examined, and at once. Anything would be better than this dreadful state of doubt.

He got up and locked both doors. At least he would be alone when he looked upon the mask of his shame. Then he drew the screen aside and saw himself face to face. It was perfectly true. The portrait had altered.

As he often remembered afterwards, and always with no small wonder, he found himself at first gazing at the portrait with a feeling of almost scientific interest. That such a change should have taken place was incredible to him. And yet it was a fact. Was there some subtle affinity between the chemical atoms that shaped themselves into form and colour on the canvas and the soul that was within him? Could it be that what that soul thought, they realized?—that what it dreamed, they made true? Or was there some other, more terrible reason? He shuddered, and felt afraid, and, going back to the couch, lay there, gazing at the picture in sickened horror.

One thing, however, he felt that it had done for him. It had made him conscious how unjust, how cruel, he had been to Sibyl Vane. It was not too late to make reparation for that. She could still be his wife. His unreal and selfish love would yield to some higher influence, would be transformed into some nobler passion, and the portrait that Basil Hallward had painted of him would be a guide to him through life, would be to him what holiness is to some, and

conscience to others, and the fear of God to us all. There were opiates for remorse, drugs that could lull the moral sense to sleep. But here was a visible symbol of the degradation of sin. Here was an ever-present sign of the ruin men brought upon their souls.

Three o'clock struck, and four, and the half-hour rang its double chime, but Dorian Gray did not stir. He was trying to gather up the scarlet threads of life and to weave them into a pattern; to find his way through the sanguine labyrinth of passion through which he was wandering. He did not know what to do, or what to think. Finally, he went over to the table and wrote a passionate letter to the girl he had loved, imploring her forgiveness and accusing himself of madness. He covered page after page with wild words of sorrow and wilder words of pain. There is a luxury in self-reproach. When we blame ourselves, we feel that no one else has a right to blame us. It is the confession, not the priest, that gives us absolution. When Dorian had finished the letter, he felt that he had been forgiven.

Suddenly there came a knock to the door, and he heard Lord Henry's voice outside. "My dear boy, I must see you. Let me in at once. I can't bear your shutting yourself up like this."

He made no answer at first, but remained quite still. The knocking still continued and grew louder. Yes, it was better to let Lord Henry in, and to explain to him the new life he was going to lead, to quarrel with him if it became necessary to quarrel, to part if parting was inevitable. He jumped up, drew the screen hastily across the picture, and unlocked the door.

"I am so sorry for it all, Dorian," said Lord Henry as he entered. "But you must not think too much about it."

"Do you mean about Sibyl Vane?" asked the lad.

"Yes, of course," answered Lord Henry, sinking into a chair and slowly pulling off his yellow gloves. "It is dreadful, from one point of view, but it was not your fault. Tell me, did you go behind and see her, after the play was over?"

"Yes."

"I felt sure you had. Did you make a scene with her?"

"I was brutal, Harry—perfectly brutal. But it is all right now. I am not sorry for anything that has happened. It has taught me to know myself better."

"Ah, Dorian, I am so glad you take it in that way! I was afraid I would find you plunged in remorse and tearing that nice curly hair of yours."

"I have got through all that," said Dorian, shaking his head and smiling. "I am perfectly happy now. I know what conscience is, to begin with. It is not what you told me it was. It is the divinest thing in us. Don't sneer at it, Harry, any more—at least not before me. I want to be good. I can't bear the idea of my soul being hideous."

"A very charming artistic basis for ethics, Dorian! I congratulate you on it. But how are you going to begin?"

"By marrying Sibyl Vane."

"Marrying Sibyl Vane!" cried Lord Henry, standing up and looking at him in perplexed amazement. "But, my dear Dorian—"

"Yes, Harry, I know what you are going to say. Something dreadful about marriage. Don't say it. Don't ever say things of that kind to me again. Two days ago I asked Sibyl to marry me. I am not going to break my word to her. She is to be my wife."

"Your wife! Dorian! . . . Didn't you get my letter? I wrote to you this morning, and sent the note down by my own man."

"Your letter? Oh, yes, I remember. I have not read it yet, Harry. I was afraid there might be something in it that I wouldn't like. You cut life to pieces with your epigrams."

"You know nothing then?"

"What do you mean?"

Lord Henry walked across the room, and sitting down by Dorian Gray, took both his hands in his own and held them tightly. "Dorian," he said, "my letter—don't be frightened—was to tell you that Sibyl Vane is dead."

A cry of pain broke from the lad's lips, and he leaped to his feet, tearing his hands away from Lord Henry's grasp. "Dead! Sibyl dead! It is not true! It is a horrible lie! How dare you say it?"

"It is quite true, Dorian," said Lord Henry, gravely. "It is in all the morning papers. I wrote down to you to ask you not to see any one till I came. There will have to be an inquest, of course, and you must not be mixed up in it. Things like that make a man fashionable in Paris. But in London people are so prejudiced. Here, one should never make one's *debut* with a scandal. One should reserve that to

give an interest to one's old age. I suppose they don't know your name at the theatre? If they don't, it is all right. Did any one see you going round to her room? That is an important point."

Dorian did not answer for a few moments. He was dazed with horror. Finally he stammered, in a stifled voice, "Harry, did you say an inquest? What did you mean by that? Did Sibyl—? Oh, Harry, I can't bear it! But be quick. Tell me everything at once."

"I have no doubt it was not an accident, Dorian, though it must be put in that way to the public. It seems that as she was leaving the theatre with her mother, about half-past twelve or so, she said she had forgotten something upstairs. They waited some time for her, but she did not come down again. They ultimately found her lying dead on the floor of her dressing room. She had swallowed something by mistake, some dreadful thing they use at theatres. I don't know what it was, but it had either prussic acid or white lead in it. I should fancy it was prussic acid, as she seems to have died instantaneously."

"Harry, Harry, it is terrible!" cried the lad.

"Yes; it is very tragic, of course, but you must not get yourself mixed up in it. I see by *The Standard* that she was seventeen. I should have thought she was almost younger than that. She looked such a child, and seemed to know so little about acting. Dorian, you mustn't let this thing get on your nerves. You must come and dine with me, and afterwards we will look in at the opera. It is a Patti* night, and everybody will be there. You can come to my sister's box. She has got some smart women with her."

"So I have murdered Sibyl Vane," said Dorian Gray, half to himself, "murdered her as surely as if I had cut her little throat with a knife. Yet the roses are not less lovely for all that. The birds sing just as happily in my garden. And to-night I am to dine with you, and then go on to the opera, and sup somewhere, I suppose, afterwards. How extraordinarily dramatic life is! If I had read all this in a book, Harry, I think I would have wept over it. Somehow, now that it has happened actually, and to me, it seems far too wonderful for tears. Here is the first passionate love-letter I have ever written in

* British soprano of Italian origin Adelina Patti (1843-1919).

my life. Strange, that my first passionate love-letter should have been addressed to a dead girl. Can they feel, I wonder, those white silent people we call the dead? Sibyl! Can she feel, or know, or listen? Oh, Harry, how I loved her once! It seems years ago to me now. She was everything to me. Then came that dreadful night—was it really only last night?—when she played so badly, and my heart almost broke. She explained it all to me. It was terribly pathetic. But I was not moved a bit. I thought her shallow. Suddenly something happened that made me afraid. I can't tell you what it was, but it was terrible. I said I would go back to her. I felt I had done wrong. And now she is dead. My God! My God! Harry, what shall I do? You don't know the danger I am in, and there is nothing to keep me straight. She would have done that for me. She had no right to kill herself. It was selfish of her."

"My dear Dorian," answered Lord Henry, taking a cigarette from his case and producing a gold-latten matchbox, "the only way a woman can ever reform a man is by boring him so completely that he loses all possible interest in life. If you had married this girl, you would have been wretched. Of course, you would have treated her kindly. One can always be kind to people about whom one cares nothing. But she would have soon found out that you were absolutely indifferent to her. And when a woman finds that out about her husband, she either becomes dreadfully dowdy, or wears very smart bonnets that some other woman's husband has to pay for. I say nothing about the social mistake, which would have been abject—which, of course, I would not have allowed—but I assure you that in any case the whole thing would have been an absolute failure."

"I suppose it would," muttered the lad, walking up and down the room and looking horribly pale. "But I thought it was my duty. It is not my fault that this terrible tragedy has prevented my doing what was right. I remember your saying once that there is a fatality about good resolutions—that they are always made too late. Mine certainly were."

"Good resolutions are useless attempts to interfere with scientific laws. Their origin is pure vanity. Their result is absolutely *nil.* They give us, now and then, some of those luxurious sterile

emotions that have a certain charm for the weak. That is all that can be said for them. They are simply cheques that men draw on a bank where they have no account."

"Harry," cried Dorian Gray, coming over and sitting down beside him, "why is it that I cannot feel this tragedy as much as I want to? I don't think I am heartless. Do you?"

"You have done too many foolish things during the last fortnight to be entitled to give yourself that name, Dorian," answered Lord Henry with his sweet melancholy smile.

The lad frowned. "I don't like that explanation, Harry," he rejoined, "but I am glad you don't think I am heartless. I am nothing of the kind. I know I am not. And yet I must admit that this thing that has happened does not affect me as it should. It seems to me to be simply like a wonderful ending to a wonderful play. It has all the terrible beauty of a Greek tragedy, a tragedy in which I took a great part, but by which I have not been wounded."

"It is an interesting question," said Lord Henry, who found an exquisite pleasure in playing on the lad's unconscious egotism, "an extremely interesting question. I fancy that the true explanation is this: It often happens that the real tragedies of life occur in such an inartistic manner that they hurt us by their crude violence, their absolute incoherence, their absurd want of meaning, their entire lack of style. They affect us just as vulgarity affects us. They give us an impression of sheer brute force, and we revolt against that. Sometimes, however, a tragedy that possesses artistic elements of beauty crosses our lives. If these elements of beauty are real, the whole thing simply appeals to our sense of dramatic effect. Suddenly we find that we are no longer the actors, but the spectators of the play. Or rather we are both. We watch ourselves, and the mere wonder of the spectacle enthralls us. In the present case, what is it that has really happened? Some one has killed herself for love of you. I wish that I had ever had such an experience. It would have made me in love with love for the rest of my life. The people who have adored me—there have not been very many, but there have been some—have always insisted on living on, long after I had ceased to care for them, or they to care for me. They have become stout and tedious, and when I meet them, they go in at once for

reminiscences. That awful memory of woman! What a fearful thing it is! And what an utter intellectual stagnation it reveals! One should absorb the colour of life, but one should never remember its details. Details are always vulgar."

"I must sow poppies in my garden," sighed Dorian.

"There is no necessity," rejoined his companion. "Life has always poppies in her hands. Of course, now and then things linger. I once wore nothing but violets all through one season, as a form of artistic mourning for a romance that would not die. Ultimately, however, it did die. I forget what killed it. I think it was her proposing to sacrifice the whole world for me. That is always a dreadful moment. It fills one with the terror of eternity. Well—would you believe it?—a week ago, at Lady Hampshire's, I found myself seated at dinner next the lady in question, and she insisted on going over the whole thing again, and digging up the past, and raking up the future. I had buried my romance in a bed of asphodel.* She dragged it out again and assured me that I had spoiled her life. I am bound to state that she ate an enormous dinner, so I did not feel any anxiety. But what a lack of taste she showed! The one charm of the past is that it is the past. But women never know when the curtain has fallen. They always want a sixth act, and as soon as the interest of the play is entirely over, they propose to continue it. If they were allowed their own way, every comedy would have a tragic ending, and every tragedy would culminate in a farce. They are charmingly artificial, but they have no sense of art. You are more fortunate than I am. I assure you, Dorian, that not one of the women I have known would have done for me what Sibyl Vane did for you. Ordinary women always console themselves. Some of them do it by going in for sentimental colours. Never trust a woman who wears mauve, whatever her age may be, or a woman over thirty-five who is fond of pink ribbons. It always means that they have a history. Others find a great consolation in suddenly discovering the good qualities of their husbands. They flaunt their conjugal felicity in one's face, as if it were the most fascinating of sins. Religion consoles some. Its

* A Mediterranean lily, widely grown on Elysian Fields, symbolising death and immortality.

mysteries have all the charm of a flirtation, a woman once told me, and I can quite understand it. Besides, nothing makes one so vain as being told that one is a sinner. Conscience makes egotists of us all. Yes; there is really no end to the consolations that women find in modern life. Indeed, I have not mentioned the most important one."

"What is that, Harry?" said the lad listlessly.

"Oh, the obvious consolation. Taking some one else's admirer when one loses one's own. In good society that always whitewashes a woman. But really, Dorian, how different Sibyl Vane must have been from all the women one meets! There is something to me quite beautiful about her death. I am glad I am living in a century when such wonders happen. They make one believe in the reality of the things we all play with, such as romance, passion, and love."

"I was terribly cruel to her. You forget that."

"I am afraid that women appreciate cruelty, downright cruelty, more than anything else. They have wonderfully primitive instincts. We have emancipated them, but they remain slaves looking for their masters, all the same. They love being dominated. I am sure you were splendid. I have never seen you really and absolutely angry, but I can fancy how delightful you looked. And, after all, you said something to me the day before yesterday that seemed to me at the time to be merely fanciful, but that I see now was absolutely true, and it holds the key to everything."

"What was that, Harry?"

"You said to me that Sibyl Vane represented to you all the heroines of romance—that she was Desdemona one night, and Ophelia the other; that if she died as Juliet, she came to life as Imogen."

"She will never come to life again now," muttered the lad, burying his face in his hands.

"No, she will never come to life. She has played her last part. But you must think of that lonely death in the tawdry dressing room simply as a strange lurid fragment from some Jacobean tragedy, as a wonderful scene from Webster, or Ford, or Cyril Tourneur.* The girl never really lived, and so she has never really

* All three were Jacobean dramatists whose tragedies dealt with love, revenge and murder.

died. To you at least she was always a dream, a phantom that flitted through Shakespeare's plays and left them lovelier for its presence, a reed through which Shakespeare's music sounded richer and more full of joy. The moment she touched actual life, she marred it, and it marred her, and so she passed away. Mourn for Ophelia, if you like. Put ashes on your head because Cordelia was strangled. Cry out against Heaven because the daughter of Brabantio died. But don't waste your tears over Sibyl Vane. She was less real than they are."

There was a silence. The evening darkened in the room. Noiselessly, and with silver feet, the shadows crept in from the garden. The colours faded wearily out of things.

After some time Dorian Gray looked up. "You have explained me to myself, Harry," he murmured with something of a sigh of relief. "I felt all that you have said, but somehow I was afraid of it, and I could not express it to myself. How well you know me! But we will not talk again of what has happened. It has been a marvellous experience. That is all. I wonder if life has still in store for me anything as marvellous."

"Life has everything in store for you, Dorian. There is nothing that you, with your extraordinary good looks, will not be able to do."

"But suppose, Harry, I became haggard, and old, and wrinkled? What then?"

"Ah, then," said Lord Henry, rising to go, "then, my dear Dorian, you would have to fight for your victories. As it is, they are brought to you. No, you must keep your good looks. We live in an age that reads too much to be wise, and that thinks too much to be beautiful. We cannot spare you. And now you had better dress and drive down to the club. We are rather late, as it is."

"I think I shall join you at the opera, Harry. I feel too tired to eat anything. What is the number of your sister's box?"

"Twenty-seven, I believe. It is on the grand tier. You will see her name on the door. But I am sorry you won't come and dine."

"I don't feel up to it," said Dorian listlessly. "But I am awfully obliged to you for all that you have said to me. You are certainly my best friend. No one has ever understood me as you have."

"We are only at the beginning of our friendship, Dorian," answered Lord Henry, shaking him by the hand. "Good-bye. I shall see you before nine-thirty, I hope. Remember, Patti is singing."

As he closed the door behind him, Dorian Gray touched the bell, and in a few minutes Victor appeared with the lamps and drew the blinds down. He waited impatiently for him to go. The man seemed to take an interminable time over everything.

As soon as he had left, he rushed to the screen and drew it back. No; there was no further change in the picture. It had received the news of Sibyl Vane's death before he had known of it himself. It was conscious of the events of life as they occurred. The vicious cruelty that marred the fine lines of the mouth had, no doubt, appeared at the very moment that the girl had drunk the poison, whatever it was. Or was it indifferent to results? Did it merely take cognizance of what passed within the soul? He wondered, and hoped that some day he would see the change taking place before his very eyes, shuddering as he hoped it.

Poor Sibyl! What a romance it had all been! She had often mimicked death on the stage. Then Death himself had touched her and taken her with him. How had she played that dreadful last scene? Had she cursed him, as she died? No; she had died for love of him, and love would always be a sacrament to him now. She had atoned for everything by the sacrifice she had made of her life. He would not think any more of what she had made him go through, on that horrible night at the theatre. When he thought of her, it would be as a wonderful tragic figure sent on to the world's stage to show the supreme reality of love. A wonderful tragic figure? Tears came to his eyes as he remembered her childlike look, and winsome fanciful ways, and shy tremulous grace. He brushed them away hastily and looked again at the picture.

He felt that the time had really come for making his choice. Or had his choice already been made? Yes, life had decided that for him—life, and his own infinite curiosity about life. Eternal youth, infinite passion, pleasures subtle and secret, wild joys and wilder sins—he was to have all these things. The portrait was to bear the burden of his shame: that was all.

A feeling of pain crept over him as he thought of the

desecration that was in store for the fair face on the canvas. Once, in boyish mockery of Narcissus, he had kissed, or feigned to kiss, those painted lips that now smiled so cruelly at him. Morning after morning he had sat before the portrait wondering at its beauty, almost enamoured of it, as it seemed to him at times. Was it to alter now with every mood to which he yielded? Was it to become a monstrous and loathsome thing, to be hidden away in a locked room, to be shut out from the sunlight that had so often touched to brighter gold the waving wonder of its hair? The pity of it! the pity of it!

For a moment, he thought of praying that the horrible sympathy that existed between him and the picture might cease. It had changed in answer to a prayer; perhaps in answer to a prayer it might remain unchanged. And yet, who, that knew anything about life, would surrender the chance of remaining always young, however fantastic that chance might be, or with what fateful consequences it might be fraught? Besides, was it really under his control? Had it indeed been prayer that had produced the substitution? Might there not be some curious scientific reason for it all? If thought could exercise its influence upon a living organism, might not thought exercise an influence upon dead and inorganic things? Nay, without thought or conscious desire, might not things external to ourselves vibrate in unison with our moods and passions, atom calling to atom in secret love or strange affinity? But the reason was of no importance. He would never again tempt by a prayer any terrible power. If the picture was to alter, it was to alter. That was all. Why inquire too closely into it?

For there would be a real pleasure in watching it. He would be able to follow his mind into its secret places. This portrait would be to him the most magical of mirrors. As it had revealed to him his own body, so it would reveal to him his own soul. And when winter came upon it, he would still be standing where spring trembles on the verge of summer. When the blood crept from its face, and left behind a pallid mask of chalk with leaden eyes, he would keep the glamour of boyhood. Not one blossom of his loveliness would ever fade. Not one pulse of his life would ever weaken. Like the gods of the Greeks, he would be strong, and fleet, and joyous. What did

it matter what happened to the coloured image on the canvas? He would be safe. That was everything.

He drew the screen back into its former place in front of the picture, smiling as he did so, and passed into his bedroom, where his valet was already waiting for him. An hour later he was at the opera, and Lord Henry was leaning over his chair.

CHAPTER

9

As he was sitting at breakfast next morning, Basil Hallward was shown into the room.

"I am so glad I have found you, Dorian," he said gravely. "I called last night, and they told me you were at the opera. Of course, I knew that was impossible. But I wish you had left word where you had really gone to. I passed a dreadful evening, half afraid that one tragedy might be followed by another. I think you might have telegraphed for me when you heard of it first. I read of it quite by chance in a late edition of *The Globe* that I picked up at the club. I came here at once and was miserable at not finding you. I can't tell you how heart-broken I am about the whole thing. I know what you must suffer. But where were you? Did you go down and see the girl's mother? For a moment I thought of following you there. They gave the address in the paper. Somewhere in the Euston Road, isn't it? But I was afraid of intruding upon a sorrow that I could not lighten. Poor woman! What a state she must be in! And her only child, too! What did she say about it all?"

"My dear Basil, how do I know?" murmured Dorian Gray, sipping some pale-yellow wine from a delicate, gold-beaded bubble of Venetian glass and looking dreadfully

bored. "I was at the opera. You should have come on there. I met Lady Gwendolen, Harry's sister, for the first time. We were in her box. She is perfectly charming; and Patti sang divinely. Don't talk about horrid subjects. If one doesn't talk about a thing, it has never happened. It is simply expression, as Harry says, that gives reality to things. I may mention that she was not the woman's only child. There is a son, a charming fellow, I believe. But he is not on the stage. He is a sailor, or something. And now, tell me about yourself and what you are painting."

"You went to the opera?" said Hallward, speaking very slowly and with a strained touch of pain in his voice. "You went to the opera while Sibyl Vane was lying dead in some sordid lodging? You can talk to me of other women being charming, and of Patti singing divinely, before the girl you loved has even the quiet of a grave to sleep in? Why, man, there are horrors in store for that little white body of hers!"

"Stop, Basil! I won't hear it!" cried Dorian, leaping to his feet. "You must not tell me about things. What is done is done. What is past is past."

"You call yesterday the past?"

"What has the actual lapse of time got to do with it? It is only shallow people who require years to get rid of an emotion. A man who is master of himself can end a sorrow as easily as he can invent a pleasure. I don't want to be at the mercy of my emotions. I want to use them, to enjoy them, and to dominate them."

"Dorian, this is horrible! Something has changed you completely. You look exactly the same wonderful boy who, day after day, used to come down to my studio to sit for his picture. But you were simple, natural, and affectionate then. You were the most unspoiled creature in the whole world. Now, I don't know what has come over you. You talk as if you had no heart, no pity in you. It is all Harry's influence. I see that."

The lad flushed up and, going to the window, looked out for a few moments on the green, flickering, sun-lashed garden. "I owe a great deal to Harry, Basil," he said at last, "more than I owe to you. You only taught me to be vain."

"Well, I am punished for that, Dorian—or shall be some day."

"I don't know what you mean, Basil," he exclaimed, turning round. "I don't know what you want. What do you want?"

"I want the Dorian Gray I used to paint," said the artist sadly.

"Basil," said the lad, going over to him and putting his hand on his shoulder, "you have come too late. Yesterday, when I heard that Sibyl Vane had killed herself—"

"Killed herself! Good heavens! is there no doubt about that?" cried Hallward, looking up at him with an expression of horror.

"My dear Basil! Surely you don't think it was a vulgar accident? Of course she killed herself."

The elder man buried his face in his hands. "How fearful," he muttered, and a shudder ran through him.

"No," said Dorian Gray, "there is nothing fearful about it. It is one of the great romantic tragedies of the age. As a rule, people who act lead the most commonplace lives. They are good husbands, or faithful wives, or something tedious. You know what I mean—middle-class virtue and all that kind of thing. How different Sibyl was! She lived her finest tragedy. She was always a heroine. The last night she played—the night you saw her—she acted badly because she had known the reality of love. When she knew its unreality, she died, as Juliet might have died. She passed again into the sphere of art. There is something of the martyr about her. Her death has all the pathetic uselessness of martyrdom, all its wasted beauty. But, as I was saying, you must not think I have not suffered. If you had come in yesterday at a particular moment—about half-past five, perhaps, or a quarter to six—you would have found me in tears. Even Harry, who was here, who brought me the news, in fact, had no idea what I was going through. I suffered immensely. Then it passed away. I cannot repeat an emotion. No one can, except sentimentalists. And you are awfully unjust, Basil. You come down here to console me. That is charming of you. You find me consoled, and you are furious. How like a sympathetic person! You remind me of a story Harry told me about a certain philanthropist who spent twenty years of his life in trying to get some grievance redressed, or some unjust law altered—I forget exactly what it was. Finally he succeeded, and nothing could exceed his disappointment. He had absolutely nothing to do, almost died of *ennui*, and became a

confirmed misanthrope.* And besides, my dear old Basil, if you really want to console me, teach me rather to forget what has happened, or to see it from a proper artistic point of view. Was it not Gautier† who used to write about *la consolation des arts*? I remember picking up a little vellum-covered book in your studio one day and chancing on that delightful phrase. Well, I am not like that young man you told me of when we were down at Marlow together, the young man who used to say that yellow satin could console one for all the miseries of life. I love beautiful things that one can touch and handle. Old brocades, green bronzes, lacquer-work, carved ivories, exquisite surroundings, luxury, pomp—there is much to be got from all these. But the artistic temperament that they create, or at any rate reveal, is still more to me. To become the spectator of one's own life, as Harry says, is to escape the suffering of life. I know you are surprised at my talking to you like this. You have not realized how I have developed. I was a schoolboy when you knew me. I am a man now. I have new passions, new thoughts, new ideas. I am different, but you must not like me less. I am changed, but you must always be my friend. Of course, I am very fond of Harry. But I know that you are better than he is. You are not stronger—you are too much afraid of life—but you are better. And how happy we used to be together! Don't leave me, Basil, and don't quarrel with me. I am what I am. There is nothing more to be said."

The painter felt strangely moved. The lad was infinitely dear to him, and his personality had been the great turning point in his art. He could not bear the idea of reproaching him any more. After all, his indifference was probably merely a mood that would pass away. There was so much in him that was good, so much in him that was noble.

"Well, Dorian," he said at length, with a sad smile, "I won't speak to you again about this horrible thing, after to-day. I only trust your name won't be mentioned in connection with it. The inquest is to take place this afternoon. Have they summoned you?"

Dorian shook his head, and a look of annoyance passed over his

* A person who hates or distrusts mankind.

† French novelist and poet Théophile Gautier (1811-1872).

face at the mention of the word "inquest." There was something so crude and vulgar about everything of the kind. "They don't know my name," he answered.

"But surely she did?"

"Only my Christian name, and that I am quite sure she never mentioned to any one. She told me once that they were all rather curious to learn who I was, and that she invariably told them my name was Prince Charming. It was pretty of her. You must do me a drawing of Sibyl, Basil. I should like to have something more of her than the memory of a few kisses and some broken pathetic words."

"I will try and do something, Dorian, if it would please you. But you must come and sit to me yourself again. I can't get on without you."

"I can never sit to you again, Basil. It is impossible!" he exclaimed, starting back.

The painter stared at him. "My dear boy, what nonsense!" he cried. "Do you mean to say you don't like what I did of you? Where is it? Why have you pulled the screen in front of it? Let me look at it. It is the best thing I have ever done. Do take the screen away, Dorian. It is simply disgraceful of your servant hiding my work like that. I felt the room looked different as I came in."

"My servant has nothing to do with it, Basil. You don't imagine I let him arrange my room for me? He settles my flowers for me sometimes—that is all. No; I did it myself. The light was too strong on the portrait."

"Too strong! Surely not, my dear fellow? It is an admirable place for it. Let me see it." And Hallward walked towards the corner of the room.

A cry of terror broke from Dorian Gray's lips, and he rushed between the painter and the screen. "Basil," he said, looking very pale, "you must not look at it. I don't wish you to."

"Not look at my own work! You are not serious. Why shouldn't I look at it?" exclaimed Hallward, laughing.

"If you try to look at it, Basil, on my word of honour I will never speak to you again as long as I live. I am quite serious. I don't offer any explanation, and you are not to ask for any. But, remember, if you touch this screen, everything is over between us."

Hallward was thunderstruck. He looked at Dorian Gray in absolute amazement. He had never seen him like this before. The lad was actually pallid with rage. His hands were clenched, and the pupils of his eyes were like disks of blue fire. He was trembling all over.

"Dorian!"

"Don't speak!"

"But what is the matter? Of course I won't look at it if you don't want me to," he said, rather coldly, turning on his heel and going over towards the window. "But, really, it seems rather absurd that I shouldn't see my own work, especially as I am going to exhibit it in Paris in the autumn. I shall probably have to give it another coat of varnish before that, so I must see it some day, and why not to-day?"

"To exhibit it! You want to exhibit it?" exclaimed Dorian Gray, a strange sense of terror creeping over him. Was the world going to be shown his secret? Were people to gape at the mystery of his life? That was impossible. Something—he did not know what—had to be done at once.

"Yes; I don't suppose you will object to that. Georges Petit is going to collect all my best pictures for a special exhibition in the Rue de Seze,* which will open the first week in October. The portrait will only be away a month. I should think you could easily spare it for that time. In fact, you are sure to be out of town. And if you keep it always behind a screen, you can't care much about it."

Dorian Gray passed his hand over his forehead. There were beads of perspiration there. He felt that he was on the brink of a horrible danger. "You told me a month ago that you would never exhibit it," he cried. "Why have you changed your mind? You people who go in for being consistent have just as many moods as others have. The only difference is that your moods are rather meaningless. You can't have forgotten that you assured me most solemnly that nothing in the world would induce you to send it to any exhibition. You told Harry exactly the same thing." He stopped suddenly, and a gleam of light came into his eyes. He remembered that Lord Henry had said to him once, half seriously and half in jest, "If you want

* An art gallery in Paris.

to have a strange quarter of an hour, get Basil to tell you why he won't exhibit your picture. He told me why he wouldn't, and it was a revelation to me." Yes, perhaps Basil, too, had his secret. He would ask him and try.

"Basil," he said, coming over quite close and looking him straight in the face, "we have each of us a secret. Let me know yours, and I shall tell you mine. What was your reason for refusing to exhibit my picture?"

The painter shuddered in spite of himself. "Dorian, if I told you, you might like me less than you do, and you would certainly laugh at me. I could not bear your doing either of those two things. If you wish me never to look at your picture again, I am content. I have always you to look at. If you wish the best work I have ever done to be hidden from the world, I am satisfied. Your friendship is dearer to me than any fame or reputation."

"No, Basil, you must tell me," insisted Dorian Gray. "I think I have a right to know." His feeling of terror had passed away, and curiosity had taken its place. He was determined to find out Basil Hallward's mystery.

"Let us sit down, Dorian," said the painter, looking troubled. "Let us sit down. And just answer me one question. Have you noticed in the picture something curious?—something that probably at first did not strike you, but that revealed itself to you suddenly?"

"Basil!" cried the lad, clutching the arms of his chair with trembling hands and gazing at him with wild startled eyes.

"I see you did. Don't speak. Wait till you hear what I have to say. Dorian, from the moment I met you, your personality had the most extraordinary influence over me. I was dominated, soul, brain, and power, by you. You became to me the visible incarnation of that unseen ideal whose memory haunts us artists like an exquisite dream. I worshipped you. I grew jealous of every one to whom you spoke. I wanted to have you all to myself. I was only happy when I was with you. When you were away from me, you were still present in my art . . . Of course, I never let you know anything about this. It would have been impossible. You would not have understood it. I hardly understood it myself. I only knew that I had seen perfection

face to face, and that the world had become wonderful to my eyes—too wonderful, perhaps, for in such mad worships there is peril, the peril of losing them, no less than the peril of keeping them . . . Weeks and weeks went on, and I grew more and more absorbed in you. Then came a new development. I had drawn you as Paris* in dainty armour, and as Adonis with huntsman's cloak and polished boar-spear. Crowned with heavy lotus-blossoms you had sat on the prow of Adrian's barge, gazing across the green turbid Nile. You had leaned over the still pool of some Greek woodland and seen in the water's silent silver the marvel of your own face. And it had all been what art should be—unconscious, ideal, and remote. One day, a fatal day I sometimes think, I determined to paint a wonderful portrait of you as you actually are, not in the costume of dead ages, but in your own dress and in your own time. Whether it was the realism of the method, or the mere wonder of your own personality, thus directly presented to me without mist or veil, I cannot tell. But I know that as I worked at it, every flake and film of colour seemed to me to reveal my secret. I grew afraid that others would know of my idolatry. I felt, Dorian, that I had told too much, that I had put too much of myself into it. Then it was that I resolved never to allow the picture to be exhibited. You were a little annoyed; but then you did not realize all that it meant to me. Harry, to whom I talked about it, laughed at me. But I did not mind that. When the picture was finished, and I sat alone with it, I felt that I was right . . . Well, after a few days the thing left my studio, and as soon as I had got rid of the intolerable fascination of its presence, it seemed to me that I had been foolish in imagining that I had seen anything in it, more than that you were extremely good-looking and that I could paint. Even now I cannot help feeling that it is a mistake to think that the passion one feels in creation is ever really shown in the work one creates. Art is always more abstract than we fancy. Form and colour tell us of form and colour—that is all. It often seems to me that art conceals the artist far more completely than it ever reveals him. And so when I got this offer from Paris, I determined

* Trojan king Priam's handsome son who abducted Helen, causing the Siege of Troy.

to make your portrait the principal thing in my exhibition. It never occurred to me that you would refuse. I see now that you were right. The picture cannot be shown. You must not be angry with me, Dorian, for what I have told you. As I said to Harry, once, you are made to be worshipped."

Dorian Gray drew a long breath. The colour came back to his cheeks, and a smile played about his lips. The peril was over. He was safe for the time. Yet he could not help feeling infinite pity for the painter who had just made this strange confession to him, and wondered if he himself would ever be so dominated by the personality of a friend. Lord Henry had the charm of being very dangerous. But that was all. He was too clever and too cynical to be really fond of. Would there ever be some one who would fill him with a strange idolatry? Was that one of the things that life had in store?

"It is extraordinary to me, Dorian," said Hallward, "that you should have seen this in the portrait. Did you really see it?"

"I saw something in it," he answered, "something that seemed to me very curious."

"Well, you don't mind my looking at the thing now?"

Dorian shook his head. "You must not ask me that, Basil. I could not possibly let you stand in front of that picture."

"You will some day, surely?"

"Never."

"Well, perhaps you are right. And now good-bye, Dorian. You have been the one person in my life who has really influenced my art. Whatever I have done that is good, I owe to you. Ah! you don't know what it cost me to tell you all that I have told you."

"My dear Basil," said Dorian, "what have you told me? Simply that you felt that you admired me too much. That is not even a compliment."

"It was not intended as a compliment. It was a confession. Now that I have made it, something seems to have gone out of me. Perhaps one should never put one's worship into words."

"It was a very disappointing confession."

"Why, what did you expect, Dorian? You didn't see anything else in the picture, did you? There was nothing else to see?"

"No; there was nothing else to see. Why do you ask? But you mustn't talk about worship. It is foolish. You and I are friends, Basil, and we must always remain so."

"You have got Harry," said the painter sadly.

"Oh, Harry!" cried the lad, with a ripple of laughter. "Harry spends his days in saying what is incredible and his evenings in doing what is improbable. Just the sort of life I would like to lead. But still I don't think I would go to Harry if I were in trouble. I would sooner go to you, Basil."

"You will sit to me again?"

"Impossible!"

"You spoil my life as an artist by refusing, Dorian. No man comes across two ideal things. Few come across one."

"I can't explain it to you, Basil, but I must never sit to you again. There is something fatal about a portrait. It has a life of its own. I will come and have tea with you. That will be just as pleasant."

"Pleasanter for you, I am afraid," murmured Hallward regretfully. "And now good-bye. I am sorry you won't let me look at the picture once again. But that can't be helped. I quite understand what you feel about it."

As he left the room, Dorian Gray smiled to himself. Poor Basil! How little he knew of the true reason! And how strange it was that, instead of having been forced to reveal his own secret, he had succeeded, almost by chance, in wresting a secret from his friend! How much that strange confession explained to him! The painter's absurd fits of jealousy, his wild devotion, his extravagant panegyrics, his curious reticences—he understood them all now, and he felt sorry. There seemed to him to be something tragic in a friendship so coloured by romance.

He sighed and touched the bell. The portrait must be hidden away at all costs. He could not run such a risk of discovery again. It had been mad of him to have allowed the thing to remain, even for an hour, in a room to which any of his friends had access.

CHAPTER

10

When his servant entered, he looked at him steadfastly and wondered if he had thought of peering behind the screen. The man was quite impassive and waited for his orders. Dorian lit a cigarette and walked over to the glass and glanced into it. He could see the reflection of Victor's face perfectly. It was like a placid mask of servility. There was nothing to be afraid of, there. Yet he thought it best to be on his guard.

Speaking very slowly, he told him to tell the house-keeper that he wanted to see her, and then to go to the frame-maker and ask him to send two of his men round at once. It seemed to him that as the man left the room his eyes wandered in the direction of the screen. Or was that merely his own fancy?

After a few moments, in her black silk dress, with old-fashioned thread mittens on her wrinkled hands, Mrs. Leaf bustled into the library. He asked her for the key of the schoolroom.

"The old schoolroom, Mr. Dorian?" she exclaimed. "Why, it is full of dust. I must get it arranged and put straight before you go into it. It is not fit for you to see, sir. It is not, indeed."

"I don't want it put straight, Leaf. I only want the key."

"Well, sir, you'll be covered with cobwebs if you go into it. Why, it hasn't been opened for nearly five years—not since his lordship died."

He winced at the mention of his grandfather. He had hateful memories of him. "That does not matter," he answered. "I simply want to see the place—that is all. Give me the key."

"And here is the key, sir," said the old lady, going over the contents of her bunch with tremulously uncertain hands. "Here is the key. I'll have it off the bunch in a moment. But you don't think of living up there, sir, and you so comfortable here?"

"No, no," he cried petulantly. "Thank you, Leaf. That will do."

She lingered for a few moments, and was garrulous over some detail of the household. He sighed and told her to manage things as she thought best. She left the room, wreathed in smiles.

As the door closed, Dorian put the key in his pocket and looked round the room. His eye fell on a large, purple satin coverlet heavily embroidered with gold, a splendid piece of late seventeenth-century Venetian work that his grandfather had found in a convent near Bologna. Yes, that would serve to wrap the dreadful thing in. It had perhaps served often as a pall for the dead. Now it was to hide something that had a corruption of its own, worse than the corruption of death itself—something that would breed horrors and yet would never die. What the worm was to the corpse, his sins would be to the painted image on the canvas. They would mar its beauty and eat away its grace. They would defile it and make it shameful. And yet the thing would still live on. It would be always alive.

He shuddered, and for a moment he regretted that he had not told Basil the true reason why he had wished to hide the picture away. Basil would have helped him to resist Lord Henry's influence, and the still more poisonous influences that came from his own temperament. The love that he bore him—for it was really love—had nothing in it that was not noble and intellectual. It was not that mere physical admiration of beauty that is born of the senses and that dies when the senses tire. It was such love as Michelangelo had known, and Montaigne, and Winckelmann, and Shakespeare himself. Yes, Basil could have saved him. But it was too late now. The past could

always be annihilated. Regret, denial, or forgetfulness could do that. But the future was inevitable. There were passions in him that would find their terrible outlet, dreams that would make the shadow of their evil real.

He took up from the couch the great purple-and-gold texture that covered it, and, holding it in his hands, passed behind the screen. Was the face on the canvas viler than before? It seemed to him that it was unchanged, and yet his loathing of it was intensified. Gold hair, blue eyes, and rose-red lips—they all were there. It was simply the expression that had altered. That was horrible in its cruelty. Compared to what he saw in it of censure or rebuke, how shallow Basil's reproaches about Sibyl Vane had been!—how shallow, and of what little account! His own soul was looking out at him from the canvas and calling him to judgement. A look of pain came across him, and he flung the rich pall over the picture. As he did so, a knock came to the door. He passed out as his servant entered.

"The persons are here, Monsieur."

He felt that the man must be got rid of at once. He must not be allowed to know where the picture was being taken to. There was something sly about him, and he had thoughtful, treacherous eyes. Sitting down at the writing-table he scribbled a note to Lord Henry, asking him to send him round something to read and reminding him that they were to meet at eight-fifteen that evening.

"Wait for an answer," he said, handing it to him, "and show the men in here."

In two or three minutes there was another knock, and Mr. Hubbard himself, the celebrated frame-maker of South Audley Street, came in with a somewhat rough-looking young assistant. Mr. Hubbard was a florid, red-whiskered little man, whose admiration for art was considerably tempered by the inveterate impecuniosity of most of the artists who dealt with him. As a rule, he never left his shop. He waited for people to come to him. But he always made an exception in favour of Dorian Gray. There was something about Dorian that charmed everybody. It was a pleasure even to see him.

"What can I do for you, Mr. Gray?" he said, rubbing his fat freckled hands. "I thought I would do myself the honour of coming round in person. I have just got a beauty of a frame, sir. Picked it up

at a sale. Old Florentine. Came from Fonthill, I believe. Admirably suited for a religious subject, Mr. Gray."

"I am so sorry you have given yourself the trouble of coming round, Mr. Hubbard. I shall certainly drop in and look at the frame—though I don't go in much at present for religious art—but to-day I only want a picture carried to the top of the house for me. It is rather heavy, so I thought I would ask you to lend me a couple of your men."

"No trouble at all, Mr. Gray. I am delighted to be of any service to you. Which is the work of art, sir?"

"This," replied Dorian, moving the screen back. "Can you move it, covering and all, just as it is? I don't want it to get scratched going upstairs."

"There will be no difficulty, sir," said the genial frame-maker, beginning, with the aid of his assistant, to unhook the picture from the long brass chains by which it was suspended. "And, now, where shall we carry it to, Mr. Gray?"

"I will show you the way, Mr. Hubbard, if you will kindly follow me. Or perhaps you had better go in front. I am afraid it is right at the top of the house. We will go up by the front staircase, as it is wider."

He held the door open for them, and they passed out into the hall and began the ascent. The elaborate character of the frame had made the picture extremely bulky, and now and then, in spite of the obsequious protests of Mr. Hubbard, who had the true tradesman's spirited dislike of seeing a gentleman doing anything useful, Dorian put his hand to it so as to help them.

"Something of a load to carry, sir," gasped the little man when they reached the top landing. And he wiped his shiny forehead.

"I am afraid it is rather heavy," murmured Dorian as he unlocked the door that opened into the room that was to keep for him the curious secret of his life and hide his soul from the eyes of men.

He had not entered the place for more than four years—not, indeed, since he had used it first as a playroom when he was a child, and then as a study when he grew somewhat older. It was a large, well-proportioned room, which had been specially built by the last Lord Kelso for the use of the little grandson whom, for his strange

likeness to his mother, and also for other reasons, he had always hated and desired to keep at a distance. It appeared to Dorian to have but little changed. There was the huge Italian *cassone*,* with its fantastically painted panels and its tarnished gilt mouldings, in which he had so often hidden himself as a boy. There the satinwood bookcase filled with his dog-eared schoolbooks. On the wall behind it was hanging the same ragged Flemish tapestry where a faded king and queen were playing chess in a garden, while a company of hawkers rode by, carrying hooded birds on their gauntleted wrists. How well he remembered it all! Every moment of his lonely childhood came back to him as he looked round. He recalled the stainless purity of his boyish life, and it seemed horrible to him that it was here the fatal portrait was to be hidden away. How little he had thought, in those dead days, of all that was in store for him!

But there was no other place in the house so secure from prying eyes as this. He had the key, and no one else could enter it. Beneath its purple pall, the face painted on the canvas could grow bestial, sodden, and unclean. What did it matter? No one could see it. He himself would not see it. Why should he watch the hideous corruption of his soul? He kept his youth—that was enough. And, besides, might not his nature grow finer, after all? There was no reason that the future should be so full of shame. Some love might come across his life, and purify him, and shield him from those sins that seemed to be already stirring in spirit and in flesh—those curious unpictured sins whose very mystery lent them their subtlety and their charm. Perhaps, some day, the cruel look would have passed away from the scarlet sensitive mouth, and he might show to the world Basil Hallward's masterpiece.

No; that was impossible. Hour by hour, and week by week, the thing upon the canvas was growing old. It might escape the hideousness of sin, but the hideousness of age was in store for it. The cheeks would become hollow or flaccid. Yellow crow's feet would creep round the fading eyes and make them horrible. The hair would lose its brightness, the mouth would gape or droop, would be foolish or gross, as the mouths of old men are. There

* A chest or a coffer.

would be the wrinkled throat, the cold, blue-veined hands, the twisted body, that he remembered in the grandfather who had been so stern to him in his boyhood. The picture had to be concealed. There was no help for it.

"Bring it in, Mr. Hubbard, please," he said, wearily, turning round. "I am sorry I kept you so long. I was thinking of something else."

"Always glad to have a rest, Mr. Gray," answered the frame-maker, who was still gasping for breath. "Where shall we put it, sir?"

"Oh, anywhere. Here: this will do. I don't want to have it hung up. Just lean it against the wall. Thanks."

"Might one look at the work of art, sir?"

Dorian started. "It would not interest you, Mr. Hubbard," he said, keeping his eye on the man. He felt ready to leap upon him and fling him to the ground if he dared to lift the gorgeous hanging that concealed the secret of his life. "I shan't trouble you any more now. I am much obliged for your kindness in coming round."

"Not at all, not at all, Mr. Gray. Ever ready to do anything for you, sir." And Mr. Hubbard tramped downstairs, followed by the assistant, who glanced back at Dorian with a look of shy wonder in his rough uncomely face. He had never seen any one so marvellous.

When the sound of their footsteps had died away, Dorian locked the door and put the key in his pocket. He felt safe now. No one would ever look upon the horrible thing. No eye but his would ever see his shame.

On reaching the library, he found that it was just after five o'clock and that the tea had been already brought up. On a little table of dark perfumed wood thickly incrusted with nacre,* a present from Lady Radley, his guardian's wife, a pretty professional invalid who had spent the preceding winter in Cairo, was lying a note from Lord Henry, and beside it was a book bound in yellow paper, the cover slightly torn and the edges soiled. A copy of the third edition of *The St. James's Gazette* had been placed on the tea-tray. It was evident that Victor had returned. He wondered if he had met the men in the hall as they were leaving the house and had

* Mother-of-pearl.

wormed out of them what they had been doing. He would be sure to miss the picture—had no doubt missed it already, while he had been laying the tea-things. The screen had not been set back, and a blank space was visible on the wall. Perhaps some night he might find him creeping upstairs and trying to force the door of the room. It was a horrible thing to have a spy in one's house. He had heard of rich men who had been blackmailed all their lives by some servant who had read a letter, or overheard a conversation, or picked up a card with an address, or found beneath a pillow a withered flower or a shred of crumpled lace.

He sighed, and having poured himself out some tea, opened Lord Henry's note. It was simply to say that he sent him round the evening paper, and a book that might interest him, and that he would be at the club at eight-fifteen. He opened *The St. James's* languidly, and looked through it. A red pencil-mark on the fifth page caught his eye. It drew attention to the following paragraph:

INQUEST ON AN ACTRESS

> An inquest was held this morning at the Bell Tavern, Hoxton Road, by Mr. Danby, the District Coroner, on the body of Sibyl Vane, a young actress recently engaged at the Royal Theatre, Holborn. A verdict of death by misadventure was returned. Considerable sympathy was expressed for the mother of the deceased, who was greatly affected during the giving of her own evidence, and that of Dr. Birrell, who had made the post-mortem examination of the deceased.

He frowned, and tearing the paper in two, went across the room and flung the pieces away. How ugly it all was! And how horribly real ugliness made things! He felt a little annoyed with Lord Henry for having sent him the report. And it was certainly stupid of him to have marked it with red pencil. Victor might have read it. The man knew more than enough English for that.

Perhaps he had read it and had begun to suspect something. And, yet, what did it matter? What had Dorian Gray to do with

Sibyl Vane's death? There was nothing to fear. Dorian Gray had not killed her.

His eye fell on the yellow book that Lord Henry had sent him. What was it, he wondered. He went towards the little, pearl-coloured octagonal stand that had always looked to him like the work of some strange Egyptian bees that wrought in silver, and taking up the volume, flung himself into an armchair and began to turn over the leaves. After a few minutes he became absorbed. It was the strangest book that he had ever read. It seemed to him that in exquisite raiment, and to the delicate sound of flutes, the sins of the world were passing in dumb show before him. Things that he had dimly dreamed of were suddenly made real to him. Things of which he had never dreamed were gradually revealed.

It was a novel without a plot and with only one character, being, indeed, simply a psychological study of a certain young Parisian who spent his life trying to realize in the nineteenth century all the passions and modes of thought that belonged to every century except his own, and to sum up, as it were, in himself the various moods through which the world-spirit had ever passed, loving for their mere artificiality those renunciations that men have unwisely called virtue, as much as those natural rebellions that wise men still call sin. The style in which it was written was that curious jewelled style, vivid and obscure at once, full of *argot** and of archaisms, of technical expressions and of elaborate paraphrases, that characterizes the work of some of the finest artists of the French school of *Symbolistes.* There were in it metaphors as monstrous as orchids and as subtle in colour. The life of the senses was described in the terms of mystical philosophy. One hardly knew at times whether one was reading the spiritual ecstasies of some mediaeval saint or the morbid confessions of a modern sinner. It was a poisonous book. The heavy odour of incense seemed to cling about its pages and to trouble the brain. The mere cadence of the sentences, the subtle monotony of their music, so full as it was of complex refrains and movements elaborately repeated, produced in the mind of the lad, as he passed from chapter to chapter, a form of

---

* Slang of rogues.

reverie, a malady of dreaming, that made him unconscious of the falling day and creeping shadows.

Cloudless, and pierced by one solitary star, a copper-green sky gleamed through the windows. He read on by its wan light till he could read no more. Then, after his valet had reminded him several times of the lateness of the hour, he got up, and going into the next room, placed the book on the little Florentine table that always stood at his bedside and began to dress for dinner.

It was almost nine o'clock before he reached the club, where he found Lord Henry sitting alone, in the morning room, looking very much bored.

"I am so sorry, Harry," he cried, "but really it is entirely your fault. That book you sent me so fascinated me that I forgot how the time was going."

"Yes, I thought you would like it," replied his host, rising from his chair.

"I didn't say I liked it, Harry. I said it fascinated me. There is a great difference."

"Ah, you have discovered that?" murmured Lord Henry. And they passed into the dining room.

CHAPTER

11

For years, Dorian Gray could not free himself from the influence of this book. Or perhaps it would be more accurate to say that he never sought to free himself from it. He procured from Paris no less than nine large-paper copies of the first edition, and had them bound in different colours, so that they might suit his various moods and the changing fancies of a nature over which he seemed, at times, to have almost entirely lost control. The hero, the wonderful young Parisian in whom the romantic and the scientific temperaments were so strangely blended, became to him a kind of prefiguring type of himself. And, indeed, the whole book seemed to him to contain the story of his own life, written before he had lived it.

In one point he was more fortunate than the novel's fantastic hero. He never knew—never, indeed, had any cause to know—that somewhat grotesque dread of mirrors, and polished metal surfaces, and still water which came upon the young Parisian so early in his life, and was occasioned by the sudden decay of a beau that had once, apparently, been so remarkable. It was with an almost cruel joy—and perhaps in nearly every joy, as certainly in every pleasure, cruelty has its place—that he used to read the latter part of the book, with

its really tragic, if somewhat overemphasized, account of the sorrow and despair of one who had himself lost what in others, and the world, he had most dearly valued.

For the wonderful beauty that had so fascinated Basil Hallward, and many others besides him, seemed never to leave him. Even those who had heard the most evil things against him—and from time to time strange rumours about his mode of life crept through London and became the chatter of the clubs—could not believe anything to his dishonour when they saw him. He had always the look of one who had kept himself unspotted from the world. Men who talked grossly became silent when Dorian Gray entered the room. There was something in the purity of his face that rebuked them. His mere presence seemed to recall to them the memory of the innocence that they had tarnished. They wondered how one so charming and graceful as he was could have escaped the stain of an age that was at once sordid and sensual.

Often, on returning home from one of those mysterious and prolonged absences that gave rise to such strange conjecture among those who were his friends, or thought that they were so, he himself would creep upstairs to the locked room, open the door with the key that never left him now, and stand, with a mirror, in front of the portrait that Basil Hallward had painted of him, looking now at the evil and aging face on the canvas, and now at the fair young face that laughed back at him from the polished glass. The very sharpness of the contrast used to quicken his sense of pleasure. He grew more and more enamoured of his own beauty, more and more interested in the corruption of his own soul. He would examine with minute care, and sometimes with a monstrous and terrible delight, the hideous lines that seared the wrinkling forehead or crawled around the heavy sensual mouth, wondering sometimes which were the more horrible, the signs of sin or the signs of age. He would place his white hands beside the coarse bloated hands of the picture, and smile. He mocked the misshapen body and the failing limbs.

There were moments, indeed, at night, when, lying sleepless in his own delicately scented chamber, or in the sordid room of the little ill-famed tavern near the docks which, under an assumed name and in disguise, it was his habit to frequent, he would think

of the ruin he had brought upon his soul with a pity that was all the more poignant because it was purely selfish. But moments such as these were rare. That curiosity about life which Lord Henry had first stirred in him, as they sat together in the garden of their friend, seemed to increase with gratification. The more he knew, the more he desired to know. He had mad hungers that grew more ravenous as he fed them.

Yet he was not really reckless, at any rate in his relations to society. Once or twice every month during the winter, and on each Wednesday evening while the season lasted, he would throw open to the world his beautiful house and have the most celebrated musicians of the day to charm his guests with the wonders of their art. His little dinners, in the settling of which Lord Henry always assisted him, were noted as much for the careful selection and placing of those invited, as for the exquisite taste shown in the decoration of the table, with its subtle symphonic arrangements of exotic flowers, and embroidered cloths, and antique plate of gold and silver. Indeed, there were many, especially among the very young men, who saw, or fancied that they saw, in Dorian Gray the true realization of a type of which they had often dreamed in Eton or Oxford days, a type that was to combine something of the real culture of the scholar with all the grace and distinction and perfect manner of a citizen of the world. To them he seemed to be of the company of those whom Dante describes as having sought to "make themselves perfect by the worship of beauty." Like Gautier, he was one for whom "the visible world existed."

And, certainly, to him life itself was the first, the greatest, of the arts, and for it all the other arts seemed to be but a preparation. Fashion, by which what is really fantastic becomes for a moment universal, and dandyism, which, in its own way, is an attempt to assert the absolute modernity of beauty, had, of course, their fascination for him. His mode of dressing, and the particular styles that from time to time he affected, had their marked influence on the young exquisites of the Mayfair balls and Pall Mall club windows, who copied him in everything that he did, and tried to reproduce the accidental charm of his graceful, though to him only half-serious, fopperies.

For, while he was but too ready to accept the position that was almost immediately offered to him on his coming of age, and found, indeed, a subtle pleasure in the thought that he might really become to the London of his own day what to imperial Neronian Rome the author of the Satyricon once had been, yet in his inmost heart he desired to be something more than a mere *arbiter elegantiarum*,* to be consulted on the wearing of a jewel, or the knotting of a necktie, or the conduct of a cane. He sought to elaborate some new scheme of life that would have its reasoned philosophy and its ordered principles, and find in the spiritualizing of the senses its highest realization.

The worship of the senses has often, and with much justice, been decried, men feeling a natural instinct of terror about passions and sensations that seem stronger than themselves, and that they are conscious of sharing with the less highly organized forms of existence. But it appeared to Dorian Gray that the true nature of the senses had never been understood, and that they had remained savage and animal merely because the world had sought to starve them into submission or to kill them by pain, instead of aiming at making them elements of a new spirituality, of which a fine instinct for beauty was to be the dominant characteristic. As he looked back upon man moving through history, he was haunted by a feeling of loss. So much had been surrendered! and to such little purpose! There had been mad wilful rejections, monstrous forms of self-torture and self-denial, whose origin was fear and whose result was a degradation infinitely more terrible than that fancied degradation from which, in their ignorance, they had sought to escape; Nature, in her wonderful irony, driving out the anchorite to feed with the wild animals of the desert and giving to the hermit the beasts of the field as his companions.

Yes: there was to be, as Lord Henry had prophesied, a new Hedonism that was to recreate life and to save it from that harsh uncomely puritanism that is having, in our own day, its curious revival. It was to have its service of the intellect, certainly, yet it was

* Gaius Petronius Arbiter was considered a judge of tasteful things at the court of emperor Nero.

never to accept any theory or system that would involve the sacrifice of any mode of passionate experience. Its aim, indeed, was to be experience itself, and not the fruits of experience, sweet or bitter as they might be. Of the asceticism that deadens the senses, as of the vulgar profligacy that dulls them, it was to know nothing. But it was to teach man to concentrate himself upon the moments of a life that is itself but a moment.

There are few of us who have not sometimes wakened before dawn, either after one of those dreamless nights that make us almost enamoured of death, or one of those nights of horror and misshapen joy, when through the chambers of the brain sweep phantoms more terrible than reality itself, and instinct with that vivid life that lurks in all grotesques, and that lends to Gothic art its enduring vitality, this art being, one might fancy, especially the art of those whose minds have been troubled with the malady of reverie. Gradually white fingers creep through the curtains, and they appear to tremble. In black fantastic shapes, dumb shadows crawl into the corners of the room and crouch there. Outside, there is the stirring of birds among the leaves, or the sound of men going forth to their work, or the sigh and sob of the wind coming down from the hills and wandering round the silent house, as though it feared to wake the sleepers and yet must needs call forth sleep from her purple cave. Veil after veil of thin dusky gauze is lifted, and by degrees the forms and colours of things are restored to them, and we watch the dawn remaking the world in its antique pattern. The wan mirrors get back their mimic life. The flameless tapers stand where we had left them, and beside them lies the half-cut book that we had been studying, or the wired flower that we had worn at the ball, or the letter that we had been afraid to read, or that we had read too often. Nothing seems to us changed. Out of the unreal shadows of the night comes back the real life that we had known. We have to resume it where we had left off, and there steals over us a terrible sense of the necessity for the continuance of energy in the same wearisome round of stereotyped habits, or a wild longing, it may be, that our eyelids might open some morning upon a world that had been refashioned anew in the darkness for our pleasure, a world in which things would have fresh shapes and colours, and be changed, or have other secrets, a world in

which the past would have little or no place, or survive, at any rate, in no conscious form of obligation or regret, the remembrance even of joy having its bitterness and the memories of pleasure their pain.

It was the creation of such worlds as these that seemed to Dorian Gray to be the true object, or amongst the true objects, of life; and in his search for sensations that would be at once new and delightful, and possess that element of strangeness that is so essential to romance, he would often adopt certain modes of thought that he knew to be really alien to his nature, abandon himself to their subtle influences, and then, having, as it were, caught their colour and satisfied his intellectual curiosity, leave them with that curious indifference that is not incompatible with a real ardour of temperament, and that, indeed, according to certain modern psychologists, is often a condition of it.

It was rumoured of him once that he was about to join the Roman Catholic communion, and certainly the Roman ritual had always a great attraction for him. The daily sacrifice, more awful really than all the sacrifices of the antique world, stirred him as much by its superb rejection of the evidence of the senses as by the primitive simplicity of its elements and the eternal pathos of the human tragedy that it sought to symbolize. He loved to kneel down on the cold marble pavement and watch the priest, in his stiff flowered dalmatic,* slowly and with white hands moving aside the veil of the tabernacle, or raising aloft the jewelled, lantern-shaped monstrance with that pallid wafer that at times, one would fain think, is indeed the "*panis caelestis*," the bread of angels, or, robed in the garments of the Passion of Christ, breaking the Host into the chalice and smiting his breast for his sins. The fuming censers that the grave boys, in their lace and scarlet, tossed into the air like great gilt flowers had their subtle fascination for him. As he passed out, he used to look with wonder at the black confessionals and long to sit in the dim shadow of one of them and listen to men and women whispering through the worn grating the true story of their lives.

But he never fell into the error of arresting his intellectual development by any formal acceptance of creed or system, or of

---

* A ceremonial garment made of Dalmatian wool.

mistaking, for a house in which to live, an inn that is but suitable for the sojourn of a night, or for a few hours of a night in which there are no stars and the moon is in travail. Mysticism, with its marvellous power of making common things strange to us, and the subtle antinomianism* that always seems to accompany it, moved him for a season; and for a season he inclined to the materialistic doctrines of the *Darwinismus* movement in Germany,† and found a curious pleasure in tracing the thoughts and passions of men to some pearly cell in the brain, or some white nerve in the body, delighting in the conception of the absolute dependence of the spirit on certain physical conditions, morbid or healthy, normal or diseased. Yet, as has been said of him before, no theory of life seemed to him to be of any importance compared with life itself. He felt keenly conscious of how barren all intellectual speculation is when separated from action and experiment. He knew that the senses, no less than the soul, have their spiritual mysteries to reveal.

And so he would now study perfumes and the secrets of their manufacture, distilling heavily scented oils and burning odorous gums from the East. He saw that there was no mood of the mind that had not its counterpart in the sensuous life, and set himself to discover their true relations, wondering what there was in frankincense that made one mystical, and in ambergris that stirred one's passions, and in violets that woke the memory of dead romances, and in musk that troubled the brain, and in champak that stained the imagination; and seeking often to elaborate a real psychology of perfumes, and to estimate the several influences of sweet-smelling roots and scented, pollen-laden flowers; of aromatic balms and of dark and fragrant woods; of spikenard, that sickens; of hovenia, that makes men mad; and of aloes, that are said to be able to expel melancholy from the soul.

At another time he devoted himself entirely to music, and in a long latticed room, with a vermilion-and-gold ceiling and walls of olive-green lacquer, he used to give curious concerts in which

* Certain Christians, especially those in the 16th century Germany, felt free from moral restraints through pre-destination and refused to be bound by them.

† The Theory of Evolution by Charles Darwin (1809-1882) was quite influential in Germany.

mad gipsies tore wild music from little zithers, or grave, yellow-shawled Tunisians plucked at the strained strings of monstrous lutes, while grinning Negroes beat monotonously upon copper drums and, crouching upon scarlet mats, slim turbaned Indians blew through long pipes of reed or brass and charmed—or feigned to charm—great hooded snakes and horrible horned adders. The harsh intervals and shrill discords of barbaric music stirred him at times when Schubert's grace, and Chopin's beautiful sorrows, and the mighty harmonies of Beethoven himself,* fell unheeded on his ear. He collected together from all parts of the world the strangest instruments that could be found, either in the tombs of dead nations or among the few savage tribes that have survived contact with Western civilizations, and loved to touch and try them. He had the mysterious *juruparis* of the Rio Negro Indians, that women are not allowed to look at and that even youths may not see till they have been subjected to fasting and scourging, and the earthen jars of the Peruvians that have the shrill cries of birds, and flutes of human bones such as Alfonso de Ovalle heard in Chile, and the sonorous green jaspers that are found near Cuzco and give forth a note of singular sweetness. He had painted gourds filled with pebbles that rattled when they were shaken; the long *clarin* of the Mexicans, into which the performer does not blow, but through which he inhales the air; the harsh *ture* of the Amazon tribes, that is sounded by the sentinels who sit all day long in high trees, and can be heard, it is said, at a distance of three leagues; the *teponaztli*, that has two vibrating tongues of wood and is beaten with sticks that are smeared with an elastic gum obtained from the milky juice of plants; the *yotl*-bells of the Aztecs, that are hung in clusters like grapes; and a huge cylindrical drum, covered with the skins of great serpents, like the one that Bernal Diaz saw when he went with Cortes† into the Mexican temple, and of whose doleful sound he has left us so vivid a description. The fantastic character

* Austrian composer Franz Schubert (1797-1828); Polish composer of Romantic piano music Frédéric Chopin (1810-1849); and German Romantic of great creativity Ludwig van Beethoven (1770-1827).

† In 1519 Mexico was conquered by Bernal Díaz del Castillo (1492-1581) and Hernando Cortés.

of these instruments fascinated him, and he felt a curious delight in the thought that art, like Nature, has her monsters, things of bestial shape and with hideous voices. Yet, after some time, he wearied of them, and would sit in his box at the opera, either alone or with Lord Henry, listening in rapt pleasure to "Tannhauser"* and seeing in the prelude to that great work of art a presentation of the tragedy of his own soul.

On one occasion he took up the study of jewels, and appeared at a costume ball as Anne de Joyeuse, Admiral of France, in a dress covered with five hundred and sixty pearls. This taste enthralled him for years, and, indeed, may be said never to have left him. He would often spend a whole day settling and resettling in their cases the various stones that he had collected, such as the olive-green chrysoberyl that turns red by lamplight, the cymophane with its wirelike line of silver, the pistachio-coloured peridot, rose-pink and wine-yellow topazes, carbuncles of fiery scarlet with tremulous, four-rayed stars, flame-red cinnamon-stones, orange and violet spinels, and amethysts with their alternate layers of ruby and sapphire. He loved the red gold of the sunstone, and the moonstone's pearly whiteness, and the broken rainbow of the milky opal. He procured from Amsterdam three emeralds of extraordinary size and richness of colour, and had a turquoise *de la vieille roche* that was the envy of all the connoisseurs.

He discovered wonderful stories, also, about jewels. In Alphonso's *Clericalis Disciplina* a serpent was mentioned with eyes of real jacinth, and in the romantic history of Alexander, the Conqueror of Emathia was said to have found in the vale of Jordan snakes "with collars of real emeralds growing on their backs." There was a gem in the brain of the dragon, Philostratus† told us, and "by the exhibition of golden letters and a scarlet robe" the monster could be thrown into a magical sleep and slain. According to the great alchemist, Pierre de Boniface, the diamond rendered a man invisible, and the agate of India made him eloquent. The cornelian appeased anger, and the hyacinth provoked sleep, and the amethyst drove away the fumes of

* An opera by Richard Wagner.
† Greek sophist Philostratus Flavius (A.D. 170-245).

wine. The garnet cast out demons, and the hydropicus deprived the moon of her colour. The selenite waxed and waned with the moon, and the meloceus, that discovers thieves, could be affected only by the blood of kids. Leonardus Camillus had seen a white stone taken from the brain of a newly killed toad, that was a certain antidote against poison. The bezoar, that was found in the heart of the Arabian deer, was a charm that could cure the plague. In the nests of Arabian birds was the aspilates, that, according to Democritus,* kept the wearer from any danger by fire.

The King of Ceilan rode through his city with a large ruby in his hand, as the ceremony of his coronation. The gates of the palace of John the Priest were "made of sardius, with the horn of the horned snake inwrought, so that no man might bring poison within." Over the gable were "two golden apples, in which were two carbuncles," so that the gold might shine by day and the carbuncles by night. In Lodge's strange romance *'A Margarite of America'*,† it was stated that in the chamber of the queen one could behold "all the chaste ladies of the world, inchased out of silver, looking through fair mirrours of chrysolites, carbuncles, sapphires, and greene emeraults." Marco Polo‡ had seen the inhabitants of Zipangu place rose-coloured pearls in the mouths of the dead. A sea-monster had been enamoured of the pearl that the diver brought to King Perozes, and had slain the thief, and mourned for seven moons over its loss. When the Huns lured the king into the great pit, he flung it away—Procopius§ tells the story—nor was it ever found again, though the Emperor Anastasius offered five hundred-weight of gold pieces for it. The King of Malabar had shown to a certain Venetian a rosary of three hundred and four pearls, one for every god that he worshipped.

When the Duke de Valentinois, son of Alexander VI, visited Louis XII of France, his horse was loaded with gold leaves, according to Brantôme,¶ and his cap had double rows of rubies that

* Greek philosopher of science (400 B.C.).

† A romance in elegant Elizabethan literary style by Thomas Lodge (1558-1625).

‡ Venetian explorer Marco Polo (1254-1324).

§ Byzantine historian Procopius (499-565).

¶ Pierre de Bourdeille Brantôme (1530-1614), soldier and author of *Vies des dames galantes* containing lively and often scurrilous tales of the French court.

threw out a great light. Charles of England had ridden in stirrups hung with four hundred and twenty-one diamonds. Richard II had a coat, valued at thirty thousand marks, which was covered with balas rubies. Hall* described Henry VIII, on his way to the Tower previous to his coronation, as wearing "a jacket of raised gold, the placard embroidered with diamonds and other rich stones, and a great bauderike about his neck of large balasses." The favourites of James I wore ear-rings of emeralds set in gold filigrane. Edward II gave to Piers Gaveston a suit of red-gold armour studded with jacinths, a collar of gold roses set with turquoise-stones, and a skull-cap *parseme*† with pearls. Henry II wore jewelled gloves reaching to the elbow, and had a hawk-glove sewn with twelve rubies and fifty-two great orients. The ducal hat of Charles the Rash,‡ the last Duke of Burgundy of his race, was hung with pear-shaped pearls and studded with sapphires.

How exquisite life had once been! How gorgeous in its pomp and decoration! Even to read of the luxury of the dead was wonderful.

Then he turned his attention to embroideries and to the tapestries that performed the office of frescoes in the chill rooms of the northern nations of Europe. As he investigated the subject—and he always had an extraordinary faculty of becoming absolutely absorbed for the moment in whatever he took up—he was almost saddened by the reflection of the ruin that time brought on beautiful and wonderful things. He, at any rate, had escaped that. Summer followed summer, and the yellow jonquils bloomed and died many times, and nights of horror repeated the story of their shame, but he was unchanged. No winter marred his face or stained his flowerlike bloom. How different it was with material things! Where had they passed to? Where was the great crocus-coloured robe, on which the gods fought against the giants, that had been worked by brown girls

---

* Edward Hall (d. 1547), historian and author of the first part of the Union of the Noble and Illustre Famelies of Lancastre and York known as Hall's Chronicle which was used by Shakespeare as a source.

† (Fr.) Spangled.

‡ Duke of Burgundy, Charles (1433-77), known as the 'Bold' for his reckless feats in war.

for the pleasure of Athena?* Where the huge velarium that Nero† had stretched across the Colosseum at Rome, that Titan sail of purple on which was represented the starry sky, and Apollo‡ driving a chariot drawn by white, gilt-reined steeds? He longed to see the curious table-napkins wrought for the Priest of the Sun, on which were displayed all the dainties and viands that could be wanted for a feast; the mortuary cloth of King Chilperic,§ with its three hundred golden bees; the fantastic robes that excited the indignation of the Bishop of Pontus and were figured with "lions, panthers, bears, dogs, forests, rocks, hunters—all, in fact, that a painter can copy from nature"; and the coat that Charles of Orleans once wore, on the sleeves of which were embroidered the verses of a song beginning "*Madame, je suis tout joyeux*,"¶ the musical accompaniment of the words being wrought in gold thread, and each note, of square shape in those days, formed with four pearls. He read of the room that was prepared at the palace at Rheims for the use of Queen Joan of Burgundy and was decorated with "thirteen hundred and twenty-one parrots, made in broidery, and blazoned with the king's arms, and five hundred and sixty-one butterflies, whose wings were similarly ornamented with the arms of the queen, the whole worked in gold." Catherine de Medicis had a mourning-bed made for her of black velvet powdered with crescents and suns. Its curtains were of damask, with leafy wreaths and garlands, figured upon a gold and silver ground, and fringed along the edges with broideries of pearls, and it stood in a room hung with rows of the queen's devices in cut black velvet upon cloth of silver. Louis XIV had gold embroidered caryatides fifteen feet high in his apartment. The state bed of Sobieski, King of Poland, was made of Smyrna gold brocade embroidered in turquoises with verses from the Koran. Its supports were of silver gilt, beautifully chased, and profusely set with enamelled and jewelled medallions. It had been taken from the Turkish camp before Vienna, and the standard of Mohammed had stood beneath the tremulous gilt of its canopy.

---

* Greek goddess of wisdom, war and peace: Pallas Athene.

† Decadent Roman emperor (AD 37-68).

‡ The sun god, associated with music, medicine and reason.

§ Merovingian king (A.D. 539-84).

¶ (Fr.) 'Madam I'm wholly happy.'

And so, for a whole year, he sought to accumulate the most exquisite specimens that he could find of textile and embroidered work, getting the dainty Delhi muslins, finely wrought with gold-thread palmates and stitched over with iridescent beetles' wings; the Dacca gauzes, that from their transparency are known in the East as "woven air," and "running water," and "evening dew"; strange figured cloths from Java; elaborate yellow Chinese hangings; books bound in tawny satins or fair blue silks and wrought with *fleurs-de-lis*,* birds and images; veils of *lacis* worked in Hungary point; Sicilian brocades and stiff Spanish velvets; Georgian work, with its gilt coins, and Japanese *Foukousas*,† with their green-toned golds and their marvellously plumaged birds.

He had a special passion, also, for ecclesiastical vestments, as indeed he had for everything connected with the service of the Church. In the long cedar chests that lined the west gallery of his house, he had stored away many rare and beautiful specimens of what is really the raiment of the Bride of Christ, who must wear purple and jewels and fine linen that she may hide the pallid macerated body that is worn by the suffering that she seeks for and wounded by self-inflicted pain. He possessed a gorgeous cope‡ of crimson silk and gold-thread damask, figured with a repeating pattern of golden pomegranates set in six-petalled formal blossoms, beyond which on either side was the pine-apple device wrought in seed-pearls. The orphreys were divided into panels representing scenes from the life of the Virgin, and the coronation of the Virgin was figured in coloured silks upon the hood. This was Italian work of the fifteenth century. Another cope was of green velvet, embroidered with heart-shaped groups of acanthus-leaves, from which spread long-stemmed white blossoms, the details of which were picked out with silver thread and coloured crystals. The morse bore a seraph's head in gold-thread raised work. The orphreys were woven in a diaper of red and gold silk, and were starred with medallions of many saints and martyrs, among whom was St. Sebastian. He had chasubles, also, of amber-coloured silk, and blue silk and gold brocade, and yellow silk damask

---

* The iris flower emblem of the French aristocracy.

† (Jap.) A decorated silk cloth used as a cover for gifts.

‡ A cloak worn in church processions.

and cloth of gold, figured with representations of the Passion and Crucifixion of Christ, and embroidered with lions and peacocks and other emblems; dalmatics of white satin and pink silk damask, decorated with tulips and dolphins and *fleurs-de-lis*; altar frontals of crimson velvet and blue linen; and many corporals, chalice-veils, and sudaria.* In the mystic offices to which such things were put, there was something that quickened his imagination.

For these treasures, and everything that he collected in his lovely house, were to be to him means of forgetfulness, modes by which he could escape, for a season, from the fear that seemed to him at times to be almost too great to be borne. Upon the walls of the lonely locked room where he had spent so much of his boyhood, he had hung with his own hands the terrible portrait whose changing features showed him the real degradation of his life, and in front of it had draped the purple-and-gold pall as a curtain. For weeks he would not go there, would forget the hideous painted thing, and get back his light heart, his wonderful joyousness, his passionate absorption in mere existence. Then, suddenly, some night he would creep out of the house, go down to dreadful places near Blue Gate Fields, and stay there, day after day, until he was driven away. On his return he would sit in front of the picture, sometimes loathing it and himself, but filled, at other times, with that pride of individualism that is half the fascination of sin, and smiling with secret pleasure at the misshapen shadow that had to bear the burden that should have been his own.

After a few years he could not endure to be long out of England, and gave up the villa that he had shared at Trouville with Lord Henry, as well as the little white walled-in house at Algiers where they had more than once spent the winter. He hated to be separated from the picture that was such a part of his life, and was also afraid that during his absence some one might gain access to the room, in spite of the elaborate bars that he had caused to be placed upon the door.

He was quite conscious that this would tell them nothing. It was true that the portrait still preserved, under all the foulness and

* (Lat.) Ceremonial cloths.

ugliness of the face, its marked likeness to himself; but what could they learn from that? He would laugh at any one who tried to taunt him. He had not painted it. What was it to him how vile and full of shame it looked? Even if he told them, would they believe it?

Yet he was afraid. Sometimes when he was down at his great house in Nottinghamshire, entertaining the fashionable young men of his own rank who were his chief companions, and astounding the county by the wanton luxury and gorgeous splendour of his mode of life, he would suddenly leave his guests and rush back to town to see that the door had not been tampered with and that the picture was still there. What if it should be stolen? The mere thought made him cold with horror. Surely the world would know his secret then. Perhaps the world already suspected it.

For, while he fascinated many, there were not a few who distrusted him. He was very nearly blackballed at a West End club of which his birth and social position fully entitled him to become a member, and it was said that on one occasion, when he was brought by a friend into the smoking room of the Churchill, the Duke of Berwick and another gentleman got up in a marked manner and went out. Curious stories became current about him after he had passed his twenty-fifth year. It was rumoured that he had been seen brawling with foreign sailors in a low den in the distant parts of Whitechapel, and that he consorted with thieves and coiners and knew the mysteries of their trade. His extraordinary absences became notorious, and, when he used to reappear again in society, men would whisper to each other in corners, or pass him with a sneer, or look at him with cold searching eyes, as though they were determined to discover his secret.

Of such insolences and attempted slights he, of course, took no notice, and in the opinion of most people his frank debonair manner, his charming boyish smile, and the infinite grace of that wonderful youth that seemed never to leave him, were in themselves a sufficient answer to the calumnies, for so they termed them, that were circulated about him. It was remarked, however, that some of those who had been most intimate with him appeared, after a time, to shun him. Women who had wildly adored him, and for his sake had braved all social censure and set convention at defiance, were

seen to grow pallid with shame or horror if Dorian Gray entered the room.

Yet these whispered scandals only increased in the eyes of many his strange and dangerous charm. His great wealth was a certain element of security. Society—civilized society, at least—is never very ready to believe anything to the detriment of those who are both rich and fascinating. It feels instinctively that manners are of more importance than morals, and, in its opinion, the highest respectability is of much less value than the possession of a good *chef*. And, after all, it is a very poor consolation to be told that the man who has given one a bad dinner, or poor wine, is irreproachable in his private life. Even the cardinal virtues cannot atone for half-cold *entrees*, as Lord Henry remarked once, in a discussion on the subject, and there is possibly a good deal to be said for his view. For the canons of good society are, or should be, the same as the canons of art. Form is absolutely essential to it. It should have the dignity of a ceremony, as well as its unreality, and should combine the insincere character of a romantic play with the wit and beauty that make such plays delightful to us. Is insincerity such a terrible thing? I think not. It is merely a method by which we can multiply our personalities.

Such, at any rate, was Dorian Gray's opinion. He used to wonder at the shallow psychology of those who conceive the ego in man as a thing simple, permanent, reliable, and of one essence. To him, man was a being with myriad lives and myriad sensations, a complex multiform creature that bore within itself strange legacies of thought and passion, and whose very flesh was tainted with the monstrous maladies of the dead. He loved to stroll through the gaunt cold picture-gallery of his country house and look at the various portraits of those whose blood flowed in his veins. Here was Philip Herbert, described by Francis Osborne, in his Memoires on the *Reigns of Queen Elizabeth and King James,* as one who was "caressed by the Court for his handsome face, which kept him not long company." Was it young Herbert's life that he sometimes led? Had some strange poisonous germ crept from body to body till it had reached his own? Was it some dim sense of that ruined grace that had made him so suddenly, and almost without cause, give utterance, in

Basil Hallward's studio, to the mad prayer that had so changed his life? Here, in gold-embroidered red doublet, jewelled surcoat, and gilt-edged ruff and wristbands, stood Sir Anthony Sherard, with his silver-and-black armour piled at his feet. What had this man's legacy been? Had the lover of Giovanna of Naples bequeathed him some inheritance of sin and shame? Were his own actions merely the dreams that the dead man had not dared to realize? Here, from the fading canvas, smiled Lady Elizabeth Devereux, in her gauze hood, pearl stomacher, and pink slashed sleeves. A flower was in her right hand, and her left clasped an enamelled collar of white and damask roses. On a table by her side lay a mandolin and an apple. There were large green rosettes upon her little pointed shoes. He knew her life, and the strange stories that were told about her lovers. Had he something of her temperament in him? These oval, heavy-lidded eyes seemed to look curiously at him. What of George Willoughby, with his powdered hair and fantastic patches? How evil he looked! The face was saturnine and swarthy, and the sensual lips seemed to be twisted with disdain. Delicate lace ruffles fell over the lean yellow hands that were so overladen with rings. He had been a macaroni of the eighteenth century, and the friend, in his youth, of Lord Ferrars. What of the second Lord Beckenham, the companion of the Prince Regent in his wildest days, and one of the witnesses at the secret marriage with Mrs. Fitzherbert? How proud and handsome he was, with his chestnut curls and insolent pose! What passions had he bequeathed? The world had looked upon him as infamous. He had led the orgies at Carlton House. The star of the Garter glittered upon his breast. Beside him hung the portrait of his wife, a pallid, thin-lipped woman in black. Her blood, also, stirred within him. How curious it all seemed! And his mother with her Lady Hamilton face and her moist, wine-dashed lips—he knew what he had got from her. He had got from her his beauty, and his passion for the beauty of others. She laughed at him in her loose Bacchante dress. There were vine leaves in her hair. The purple spilled from the cup she was holding. The carnations of the painting had withered, but the eyes were still wonderful in their depth and brilliancy of colour. They seemed to follow him wherever he went.

Yet one had ancestors in literature as well as in one's own race, nearer perhaps in type and temperament, many of them, and certainly with an influence of which one was more absolutely conscious. There were times when it appeared to Dorian Gray that the whole of history was merely the record of his own life, not as he had lived it in act and circumstance, but as his imagination had created it for him, as it had been in his brain and in his passions. He felt that he had known them all, those strange terrible figures that had passed across the stage of the world and made sin so marvellous and evil so full of subtlety. It seemed to him that in some mysterious way their lives had been his own.

The hero of the wonderful novel that had so influenced his life had himself known this curious fancy. In the seventh chapter he tells how, crowned with laurel, lest lightning might strike him, he had sat, as Tiberius, in a garden at Capri, reading the shameful books of Elephantis, while dwarfs and peacocks strutted round him and the flute-player mocked the swinger of the censer; and, as Caligula, had caroused with the green-shirted jockeys in their stables and supped in an ivory manger with a jewel-frontleted horse; and, as Domitian,* had wandered through a corridor lined with marble mirrors, looking round with haggard eyes for the reflection of the dagger that was to end his days, and sick with that ennui, that terrible *taedium vitae*,† that comes on those to whom life denies nothing; and had peered through a clear emerald at the red shambles of the circus and then, in a litter of pearl and purple drawn by silver-shod mules, been carried through the Street of Pomegranates to a House of Gold and heard men cry on Nero Caesar as he passed by; and, as Elagabalus,‡ had painted his face with colours, and plied the distaff among the women, and brought the Moon from Carthage and given her in mystic marriage to the Sun.

Over and over again Dorian used to read this fantastic chapter, and the two chapters immediately following, in which, as in some curious tapestries or cunningly wrought enamels, were pictured the awful and beautiful forms of those whom vice and blood and

* Tiberius, Caligula and Domitian were violent Roman emperors.

† (Lat.) Weariness of life.

‡ Roman emperor Heliogabalus (A.D. 200)

weariness had made monstrous or mad: Filippo, Duke of Milan, who slew his wife and painted her lips with a scarlet poison that her lover might suck death from the dead thing he fondled; Pietro Barbi, the Venetian, known as Paul the Second,* who sought in his vanity to assume the title of Formosus, and whose tiara, valued at two hundred thousand florins, was bought at the price of a terrible sin; Gian Maria Visconti,† who used hounds to chase living men and whose murdered body was covered with roses by a harlot who had loved him; the Borgia‡ on his white horse, with Fratricide riding beside him and his mantle stained with the blood of Perotto; Pietro Riario, the young Cardinal Archbishop of Florence, child and minion of Sixtus IV, whose beauty was equalled only by his debauchery, and who received Leonora of Aragon in a pavilion of white and crimson silk, filled with nymphs and centaurs, and gilded a boy that he might serve at the feast as Ganymede or Hylas; Ezzelin, whose melancholy could be cured only by the spectacle of death, and who had a passion for red blood, as other men have for red wine—the son of the Fiend, as was reported, and one who had cheated his father at dice when gambling with him for his own soul; Giambattista Cibo, who in mockery took the name of Innocent and into whose torpid veins the blood of three lads was infused by a Jewish doctor; Sigismondo Malatesta, the lover of Isotta and the lord of Rimini, whose effigy was burned at Rome as the enemy of God and man, who strangled Polyssena with a napkin, and gave poison to Ginevra d'Este in a cup of emerald, and in honour of a shameful passion built a pagan church for Christian worship; Charles VI, who had so wildly adored his brother's wife that a leper had warned him of the insanity that was coming on him, and who, when his brain had sickened and grown strange, could only be soothed by Saracen cards painted with the images of love and death and madness; and, in his trimmed jerkin and jewelled cap and acanthuslike curls, Grifonetto Baglioni, who slew Astorre with his bride, and Simonetto with his page, and whose comeliness was such that, as he lay dying in the yellow piazza

* He was Pope from 1464-71.

† The bloodthirsty son of Duke of Milan (d. 1412).

‡ Cesare Borgia (1476-1507). illegitimate son of Pope Alexander VI who headed the papal armies.

of Perugia, those who had hated him could not choose but weep, and Atalanta,* who had cursed him, blessed him.

There was a horrible fascination in them all. He saw them at night, and they troubled his imagination in the day. The Renaissance knew of strange manners of poisoning—poisoning by a helmet and a lighted torch, by an embroidered glove and a jewelled fan, by a gilded pomander and by an amber chain. Dorian Gray had been poisoned by a book. There were moments when he looked on evil simply as a mode through which he could realize his conception of the beautiful.

* Members of Baglioni family which governed the city of Perugia in Italy around 1500.

CHAPTER 12

It was on the ninth of November, the eve of his own thirty-eighth birthday, as he often remembered afterwards.

He was walking home about eleven o'clock from Lord Henry's, where he had been dining, and was wrapped in heavy furs, as the night was cold and foggy. At the corner of Grosvenor Square and South Audley Street, a man passed him in the mist, walking very fast and with the collar of his grey ulster turned up. He had a bag in his hand. Dorian recognized him. It was Basil Hallward. A strange sense of fear, for which he could not account, came over him. He made no sign of recognition and went on quickly in the direction of his own house.

But Hallward had seen him. Dorian heard him first stopping on the pavement and then hurrying after him. In a few moments, his hand was on his arm.

"Dorian! What an extraordinary piece of luck! I have been waiting for you in your library ever since nine o'clock. Finally I took pity on your tired servant and told him to go to bed, as he let me out. I am off to Paris by the midnight train, and I particularly wanted to see you before I left. I thought it was you, or rather your fur coat, as you passed me. But I wasn't quite sure. Didn't you recognize me?"

"In this fog, my dear Basil? Why, I can't even recognize

Grosvenor Square. I believe my house is somewhere about here, but I don't feel at all certain about it. I am sorry you are going away, as I have not seen you for ages. But I suppose you will be back soon?"

"No: I am going to be out of England for six months. I intend to take a studio in Paris and shut myself up till I have finished a great picture I have in my head. However, it wasn't about myself I wanted to talk. Here we are at your door. Let me come in for a moment. I have something to say to you."

"I shall be charmed. But won't you miss your train?" said Dorian Gray languidly as he passed up the steps and opened the door with his latch-key.

The lamplight struggled out through the fog, and Hallward looked at his watch. "I have heaps of time," he answered. "The train doesn't go till twelve-fifteen, and it is only just eleven. In fact, I was on my way to the club to look for you, when I met you. You see, I shan't have any delay about luggage, as I have sent on my heavy things. All I have with me is in this bag, and I can easily get to Victoria in twenty minutes."

Dorian looked at him and smiled. "What a way for a fashionable painter to travel! A Gladstone bag and an ulster! Come in, or the fog will get into the house. And mind you don't talk about anything serious. Nothing is serious nowadays. At least nothing should be."

Hallward shook his head, as he entered, and followed Dorian into the library. There was a bright wood fire blazing in the large open hearth. The lamps were lit, and an open Dutch silver spirit-case stood, with some siphons of soda-water and large cut-glass tumblers, on a little marqueterie table.

"You see your servant made me quite at home, Dorian. He gave me everything I wanted, including your best gold-tipped cigarettes. He is a most hospitable creature. I like him much better than the Frenchman you used to have. What has become of the Frenchman, by the bye?"

Dorian shrugged his shoulders. "I believe he married Lady Radley's maid, and has established her in Paris as an English dressmaker. *Anglomania** is very fashionable over there now, I hear.

---

* Craving for everything English.

It seems silly of the French, doesn't it? But—do you know?—he was not at all a bad servant. I never liked him, but I had nothing to complain about. One often imagines things that are quite absurd. He was really very devoted to me and seemed quite sorry when he went away. Have another brandy-and-soda? Or would you like hock-and-seltzer? I always take hock-and-seltzer myself. There is sure to be some in the next room."

"Thanks, I won't have anything more," said the painter, taking his cap and coat off and throwing them on the bag that he had placed in the corner. "And now, my dear fellow, I want to speak to you seriously. Don't frown like that. You make it so much more difficult for me."

"What is it all about?" cried Dorian in his petulant way, flinging himself down on the sofa. "I hope it is not about myself. I am tired of myself to-night. I should like to be somebody else."

"It is about yourself," answered Hallward in his grave deep voice, "and I must say it to you. I shall only keep you half an hour."

Dorian sighed and lit a cigarette. "Half an hour!" he murmured.

"It is not much to ask of you, Dorian, and it is entirely for your own sake that I am speaking. I think it right that you should know that the most dreadful things are being said against you in London."

"I don't wish to know anything about them. I love scandals about other people, but scandals about myself don't interest me. They have not got the charm of novelty."

"They must interest you, Dorian. Every gentleman is interested in his good name. You don't want people to talk of you as something vile and degraded. Of course, you have your position, and your wealth, and all that kind of thing. But position and wealth are not everything. Mind you, I don't believe these rumours at all. At least, I can't believe them when I see you. Sin is a thing that writes itself across a man's face. It cannot be concealed. People talk sometimes of secret vices. There are no such things. If a wretched man has a vice, it shows itself in the lines of his mouth, the droop of his eyelids, the moulding of his hands even. Somebody—I won't mention his name, but you know him—came to me last year to have his portrait done. I had never seen him before, and had never heard anything about him at the time, though I have heard a good deal since. He

offered an extravagant price. I refused him. There was something in the shape of his fingers that I hated. I know now that I was quite right in what I fancied about him. His life is dreadful. But you, Dorian, with your pure, bright, innocent face, and your marvellous untroubled youth—I can't believe anything against you. And yet I see you very seldom, and you never come down to the studio now, and when I am away from you, and I hear all these hideous things that people are whispering about you, I don't know what to say. Why is it, Dorian, that a man like the Duke of Berwick leaves the room of a club when you enter it? Why is it that so many gentlemen in London will neither go to your house or invite you to theirs? You used to be a friend of Lord Staveley. I met him at dinner last week. Your name happened to come up in conversation, in connection with the miniatures you have lent to the exhibition at the Dudley. Staveley curled his lip and said that you might have the most artistic tastes, but that you were a man whom no pure-minded girl should be allowed to know, and whom no chaste woman should sit in the same room with. I reminded him that I was a friend of yours, and asked him what he meant. He told me. He told me right out before everybody. It was horrible! Why is your friendship so fatal to young men? There was that wretched boy in the Guards who committed suicide. You were his great friend. There was Sir Henry Ashton, who had to leave England with a tarnished name. You and he were inseparable. What about Adrian Singleton and his dreadful end? What about Lord Kent's only son and his career? I met his father yesterday in St. James's Street. He seemed broken with shame and sorrow. What about the young Duke of Perth? What sort of life has he got now? What gentleman would associate with him?"

"Stop, Basil. You are talking about things of which you know nothing," said Dorian Gray, biting his lip, and with a note of infinite contempt in his voice. "You ask me why Berwick leaves a room when I enter it. It is because I know everything about his life, not because he knows anything about mine. With such blood as he has in his veins, how could his record be clean? You ask me about Henry Ashton and young Perth. Did I teach the one his vices, and the other his debauchery? If Kent's silly son takes his wife from the streets, what is that to me? If Adrian Singleton writes his friend's

name across a bill, am I his keeper?* I know how people chatter in England. The middle classes air their moral prejudices over their gross dinner-tables, and whisper about what they call the profligacies of their betters in order to try and pretend that they are in smart society and on intimate terms with the people they slander. In this country, it is enough for a man to have distinction and brains for every common tongue to wag against him. And what sort of lives do these people, who pose as being moral, lead themselves? My dear fellow, you forget that we are in the native land of the hypocrite."

"Dorian," cried Hallward, "that is not the question. England is bad enough I know, and English society is all wrong. That is the reason why I want you to be fine. You have not been fine. One has a right to judge of a man by the effect he has over his friends. Yours seem to lose all sense of honour, of goodness, of purity. You have filled them with a madness for pleasure. They have gone down into the depths. You led them there. Yes: you led them there, and yet you can smile, as you are smiling now. And there is worse behind. I know you and Harry are inseparable. Surely for that reason, if for none other, you should not have made his sister's name a by-word."

"Take care, Basil. You go too far."

"I must speak, and you must listen. You shall listen. When you met Lady Gwendolen, not a breath of scandal had ever touched her. Is there a single decent woman in London now who would drive with her in the park? Why, even her children are not allowed to live with her. Then there are other stories—stories that you have been seen creeping at dawn out of dreadful houses and slinking in disguise into the foulest dens in London. Are they true? Can they be true? When I first heard them, I laughed. I hear them now, and they make me shudder. What about your country-house and the life that is led there? Dorian, you don't know what is said about you. I won't tell you that I don't want to preach to you. I remember Harry saying once that every man who turned himself into an amateur curate for the moment always began by saying that, and then proceeded to break his word. I do want to preach to you. I want you to lead such a life as will make the world respect you. I want you to have a

* As in Genesis 4: 9.

clean name and a fair record. I want you to get rid of the dreadful people you associate with. Don't shrug your shoulders like that. Don't be so indifferent. You have a wonderful influence. Let it be for good, not for evil. They say that you corrupt every one with whom you become intimate, and that it is quite sufficient for you to enter a house for shame of some kind to follow after. I don't know whether it is so or not. How should I know? But it is said of you. I am told things that it seems impossible to doubt. Lord Gloucester was one of my greatest friends at Oxford. He showed me a letter that his wife had written to him when she was dying alone in her villa at Mentone. Your name was implicated in the most terrible confession I ever read. I told him that it was absurd—that I knew you thoroughly and that you were incapable of anything of the kind. Know you? I wonder do I know you? Before I could answer that, I should have to see your soul."

"To see my soul!" muttered Dorian Gray, starting up from the sofa and turning almost white from fear.

"Yes," answered Hallward gravely, and with deep-toned sorrow in his voice, "to see your soul. But only God can do that."

A bitter laugh of mockery broke from the lips of the younger man. "You shall see it yourself, to-night!" he cried, seizing a lamp from the table. "Come: it is your own handiwork. Why shouldn't you look at it? You can tell the world all about it afterwards, if you choose. Nobody would believe you. If they did believe you, they would like me all the better for it. I know the age better than you do, though you will prate about it so tediously. Come, I tell you. You have chattered enough about corruption. Now you shall look on it face to face."

There was the madness of pride in every word he uttered. He stamped his foot upon the ground in his boyish insolent manner. He felt a terrible joy at the thought that some one else was to share his secret, and that the man who had painted the portrait that was the origin of all his shame was to be burdened for the rest of his life with the hideous memory of what he had done.

"Yes," he continued, coming closer to him and looking steadfastly into his stern eyes, "I shall show you my soul. You shall see the thing that you fancy only God can see."

Hallward started back. "This is blasphemy, Dorian!" he cried. "You must not say things like that. They are horrible, and they don't mean anything."

"You think so?" He laughed again.

"I know so. As for what I said to you to-night, I said it for your good. You know I have been always a stanch friend to you."

"Don't touch me. Finish what you have to say."

A twisted flash of pain shot across the painter's face. He paused for a moment, and a wild feeling of pity came over him. After all, what right had he to pry into the life of Dorian Gray? If he had done a tithe of what was rumoured about him, how much he must have suffered! Then he straightened himself up, and walked over to the fire-place, and stood there, looking at the burning logs with their frostlike ashes and their throbbing cores of flame.

"I am waiting, Basil," said the young man in a hard clear voice.

He turned round. "What I have to say is this," he cried. "You must give me some answer to these horrible charges that are made against you. If you tell me that they are absolutely untrue from beginning to end, I shall believe you. Deny them, Dorian, deny them! Can't you see what I am going through? My God! don't tell me that you are bad, and corrupt, and shameful."

Dorian Gray smiled. There was a curl of contempt in his lips. "Come upstairs, Basil," he said quietly. "I keep a diary of my life from day to day, and it never leaves the room in which it is written. I shall show it to you if you come with me."

"I shall come with you, Dorian, if you wish it. I see I have missed my train. That makes no matter. I can go to-morrow. But don't ask me to read anything to-night. All I want is a plain answer to my question."

"That shall be given to you upstairs. I could not give it here. You will not have to read long."

CHAPTER 13

He passed out of the room and began the ascent, Basil Hallward following close behind. They walked softly, as men do instinctively at night. The lamp cast fantastic shadows on the wall and staircase. A rising wind made some of the windows rattle.

When they reached the top landing, Dorian set the lamp down on the floor, and taking out the key, turned it in the lock. "You insist on knowing, Basil?" he asked in a low voice.

"Yes."

"I am delighted," he answered, smiling. Then he added, somewhat harshly, "You are the one man in the world who is entitled to know everything about me. You have had more to do with my life than you think"; and, taking up the lamp, he opened the door and went in. A cold current of air passed them, and the light shot up for a moment in a flame of murky orange. He shuddered. "Shut the door behind you," he whispered, as he placed the lamp on the table.

Hallward glanced round him with a puzzled expression. The room looked as if it had not been lived in for years. A faded Flemish tapestry, a curtained picture, an old Italian *cassone*, and an almost empty book-case—that was all that it seemed to contain, besides a chair and a table. As Dorian

Gray was lighting a half-burned candle that was standing on the mantelshelf, he saw that the whole place was covered with dust and that the carpet was in holes. A mouse ran scuffling behind the wainscoting. There was a damp odour of mildew.

"So you think that it is only God who sees the soul, Basil? Draw that curtain back, and you will see mine."

The voice that spoke was cold and cruel. "You are mad, Dorian, or playing a part," muttered Hallward, frowning.

"You won't? Then I must do it myself," said the young man, and he tore the curtain from its rod and flung it on the ground.

An exclamation of horror broke from the painter's lips as he saw in the dim light the hideous face on the canvas grinning at him. There was something in its expression that filled him with disgust and loathing. Good heavens! it was Dorian Gray's own face that he was looking at! The horror, whatever it was, had not yet entirely spoiled that marvellous beauty. There was still some gold in the thinning hair and some scarlet on the sensual mouth. The sodden eyes had kept something of the loveliness of their blue, the noble curves had not yet completely passed away from chiselled nostrils and from plastic throat. Yes, it was Dorian himself. But who had done it? He seemed to recognize his own brushwork, and the frame was his own design. The idea was monstrous, yet he felt afraid. He seized the lighted candle, and held it to the picture. In the left-hand corner was his own name, traced in long letters of bright vermilion.

It was some foul parody, some infamous ignoble satire. He had never done that. Still, it was his own picture. He knew it, and he felt as if his blood had changed in a moment from fire to sluggish ice. His own picture! What did it mean? Why had it altered? He turned and looked at Dorian Gray with the eyes of a sick man. His mouth twitched, and his parched tongue seemed unable to articulate. He passed his hand across his forehead. It was dank with clammy sweat.

The young man was leaning against the mantelshelf, watching him with that strange expression that one sees on the faces of those who are absorbed in a play when some great artist is acting. There was neither real sorrow in it nor real joy. There was simply the passion of the spectator, with perhaps a flicker of triumph in his

eyes. He had taken the flower out of his coat, and was smelling it, or pretending to do so.

"What does this mean?" cried Hallward, at last. His own voice sounded shrill and curious in his ears.

"Years ago, when I was a boy," said Dorian Gray, crushing the flower in his hand, "you met me, flattered me, and taught me to be vain of my good looks. One day you introduced me to a friend of yours, who explained to me the wonder of youth, and you finished a portrait of me that revealed to me the wonder of beauty. In a mad moment that, even now, I don't know whether I regret or not, I made a wish, perhaps you would call it a prayer. . . ."

"I remember it! Oh, how well I remember it! No! the thing is impossible. The room is damp. Mildew has got into the canvas. The paints I used had some wretched mineral poison in them. I tell you the thing is impossible."

"Ah, what is impossible?" murmured the young man, going over to the window and leaning his forehead against the cold, mist-stained glass.

"You told me you had destroyed it."

"I was wrong. It has destroyed me."

"I don't believe it is my picture."

"Can't you see your ideal in it?" said Dorian bitterly.

"My ideal, as you call it . . ."

"As you called it."

"There was nothing evil in it, nothing shameful. You were to me such an ideal as I shall never meet again. This is the face of a satyr."

"It is the face of my soul."

"Christ! what a thing I must have worshipped! It has the eyes of a devil."

"Each of us has heaven and hell in him, Basil," cried Dorian with a wild gesture of despair.

Hallward turned again to the portrait and gazed at it. "My God! If it is true," he exclaimed, "and this is what you have done with your life, why, you must be worse even than those who talk against you fancy you to be!" He held the light up again to the canvas and examined it. The surface seemed to be quite undisturbed and as he had left it. It was from within, apparently, that the foulness and

horror had come. Through some strange quickening of inner life the leprosies of sin were slowly eating the thing away. The rotting of a corpse in a watery grave was not so fearful.

His hand shook, and the candle fell from its socket on the floor and lay there sputtering. He placed his foot on it and put it out. Then he flung himself into the rickety chair that was standing by the table and buried his face in his hands.

"Good God, Dorian, what a lesson! What an awful lesson!" There was no answer, but he could hear the young man sobbing at the window. "Pray, Dorian, pray," he murmured. "What is it that one was taught to say in one's boyhood? 'Lead us not into temptation. Forgive us our sins. Wash away our iniquities.'* Let us say that together. The prayer of your pride has been answered. The prayer of your repentance will be answered also. I worshipped you too much. I am punished for it. You worshipped yourself too much. We are both punished."

Dorian Gray turned slowly around and looked at him with tear-dimmed eyes. "It is too late, Basil," he faltered.

"It is never too late, Dorian. Let us kneel down and try if we cannot remember a prayer. Isn't there a verse somewhere, 'Though your sins be as scarlet, yet I will make them as white as snow'?"†

"Those words mean nothing to me now."

"Hush! Don't say that. You have done enough evil in your life. My God! Don't you see that accursed thing leering at us?"

Dorian Gray glanced at the picture, and suddenly an uncontrollable feeling of hatred for Basil Hallward came over him, as though it had been suggested to him by the image on the canvas, whispered into his ear by those grinning lips. The mad passions of a hunted animal stirred within him, and he loathed the man who was seated at the table, more than in his whole life he had ever loathed anything. He glanced wildly around. Something glimmered on the top of the painted chest that faced him. His eye fell on it. He knew what it was. It was a knife that he had brought up, some days before, to cut a piece of cord, and had forgotten to take away with him. He

---

* Psalms 51: 2.

† *Isaiah* 1: 18.

moved slowly towards it, passing Hallward as he did so. As soon as he got behind him, he seized it and turned round. Hallward stirred in his chair as if he was going to rise. He rushed at him and dug the knife into the great vein that is behind the ear, crushing the man's head down on the table and stabbing again and again.

There was a stifled groan and the horrible sound of some one choking with blood. Three times the outstretched arms shot up convulsively, waving grotesque, stiff-fingered hands in the air. He stabbed him twice more, but the man did not move. Something began to trickle on the floor. He waited for a moment, still pressing the head down. Then he threw the knife on the table, and listened.

He could hear nothing, but the drip, drip on the threadbare carpet. He opened the door and went out on the landing. The house was absolutely quiet. No one was about. For a few seconds he stood bending over the balustrade and peering down into the black seething well of darkness. Then he took out the key and returned to the room, locking himself in as he did so.

The thing was still seated in the chair, straining over the table with bowed head, and humped back, and long fantastic arms. Had it not been for the red jagged tear in the neck and the clotted black pool that was slowly widening on the table, one would have said that the man was simply asleep.

How quickly it had all been done! He felt strangely calm, and walking over to the window, opened it and stepped out on the balcony. The wind had blown the fog away, and the sky was like a monstrous peacock's tail, starred with myriads of golden eyes. He looked down and saw the policeman going his rounds and flashing the long beam of his lantern on the doors of the silent houses. The crimson spot of a prowling hansom gleamed at the corner and then vanished. A woman in a fluttering shawl was creeping slowly by the railings, staggering as she went. Now and then she stopped and peered back. Once, she began to sing in a hoarse voice. The policeman strolled over and said something to her. She stumbled away, laughing. A bitter blast swept across the square. The gas-lamps flickered and became blue, and the leafless trees shook their black iron branches to and fro. He shivered and went back, closing the window behind him.

Having reached the door, he turned the key and opened it. He did not even glance at the murdered man. He felt that the secret of the whole thing was not to realize the situation. The friend who had painted the fatal portrait to which all his misery had been due had gone out of his life. That was enough.

Then he remembered the lamp. It was a rather curious one of Moorish workmanship, made of dull silver inlaid with arabesques of burnished steel, and studded with coarse turquoises. Perhaps it might be missed by his servant, and questions would be asked. He hesitated for a moment, then he turned back and took it from the table. He could not help seeing the dead thing. How still it was! How horribly white the long hands looked! It was like a dreadful wax image.

Having locked the door behind him, he crept quietly downstairs. The woodwork creaked and seemed to cry out as if in pain. He stopped several times and waited. No: everything was still. It was merely the sound of his own footsteps.

When he reached the library, he saw the bag and coat in the corner. They must be hidden away somewhere. He unlocked a secret press that was in the wainscoting, a press in which he kept his own curious disguises, and put them into it. He could easily burn them afterwards. Then he pulled out his watch. It was twenty minutes to two.

He sat down and began to think. Every year—every month, almost—men were strangled in England for what he had done. There had been a madness of murder in the air. Some red star had come too close to the earth . . . And yet, what evidence was there against him? Basil Hallward had left the house at eleven. No one had seen him come in again. Most of the servants were at Selby Royal. His valet had gone to bed . . . Paris! Yes. It was to Paris that Basil had gone, and by the midnight train, as he had intended. With his curious reserved habits, it would be months before any suspicions would be roused. Months! Everything could be destroyed long before then.

A sudden thought struck him. He put on his fur coat and hat and went out into the hall. There he paused, hearing the slow heavy tread of the policeman on the pavement outside and seeing the

flash of the bull's-eye reflected in the window. He waited and held his breath.

After a few moments he drew back the latch and slipped out, shutting the door very gently behind him. Then he began ringing the bell. In about five minutes his valet appeared, half-dressed and looking very drowsy.

"I am sorry to have had to wake you up, Francis," he said, stepping in; "but I had forgotten my latch-key. What time is it?"

"Ten minutes past two, sir," answered the man, looking at the clock and blinking.

"Ten minutes past two? How horribly late! You must wake me at nine to-morrow. I have some work to do."

"All right, sir."

"Did any one call this evening?"

"Mr. Hallward, sir. He stayed here till eleven, and then he went away to catch his train."

"Oh! I am sorry I didn't see him. Did he leave any message?"

"No, sir, except that he would write to you from Paris, if he did not find you at the club."

"That will do, Francis. Don't forget to call me at nine to-morrow."

"No, sir."

The man shambled down the passage in his slippers.

Dorian Gray threw his hat and coat upon the table and passed into the library. For a quarter of an hour he walked up and down the room, biting his lip and thinking. Then he took down the Blue Book from one of the shelves and began to turn over the leaves. "Alan Campbell, 152, Hertford Street, Mayfair." Yes; that was the man he wanted.

CHAPTER

14

At nine o'clock the next morning his servant came in with a cup of chocolate on a tray and opened the shutters. Dorian was sleeping quite peacefully, lying on his right side, with one hand underneath his cheek. He looked like a boy who had been tired out with play, or study.

The man had to touch him twice on the shoulder before he woke, and as he opened his eyes a faint smile passed across his lips, as though he had been lost in some delightful dream. Yet he had not dreamed at all. His night had been untroubled by any images of pleasure or of pain. But youth smiles without any reason. It is one of its chiefest charms.

He turned round, and leaning upon his elbow, began to sip his chocolate. The mellow November sun came streaming into the room. The sky was bright, and there was a genial warmth in the air. It was almost like a morning in May.

Gradually the events of the preceding night crept with silent, blood-stained feet into his brain and reconstructed themselves there with terrible distinctness. He winced at the memory of all that he had suffered, and for a moment the same curious feeling of loathing for Basil Hallward that had made him kill him as he sat in the chair came back to him, and he grew cold with passion. The dead man was still sitting

there, too, and in the sunlight now. How horrible that was! Such hideous things were for the darkness, not for the day.

He felt that if he brooded on what he had gone through he would sicken or grow mad. There were sins whose fascination was more in the memory than in the doing of them, strange triumphs that gratified the pride more than the passions, and gave to the intellect a quickened sense of joy, greater than any joy they brought, or could ever bring, to the senses. But this was not one of them. It was a thing to be driven out of the mind, to be drugged with poppies, to be strangled lest it might strangle one itself.

When the half-hour struck, he passed his hand across his forehead, and then got up hastily and dressed himself with even more than his usual care, giving a good deal of attention to the choice of his necktie and scarf-pin and changing his rings more than once. He spent a long time also over breakfast, tasting the various dishes, talking to his valet about some new liveries that he was thinking of getting made for the servants at Selby, and going through his correspondence. At some of the letters, he smiled. Three of them bored him. One he read several times over and then tore up with a slight look of annoyance in his face. "That awful thing, a woman's memory!" as Lord Henry had once said.

After he had drunk his cup of black coffee, he wiped his lips slowly with a napkin, motioned to his servant to wait, and going over to the table, sat down and wrote two letters. One he put in his pocket, the other he handed to the valet.

"Take this round to 152, Hertford Street, Francis, and if Mr. Campbell is out of town, get his address."

As soon as he was alone, he lit a cigarette and began sketching upon a piece of paper, drawing first flowers and bits of architecture, and then human faces. Suddenly he remarked that every face that he drew seemed to have a fantastic likeness to Basil Hallward. He frowned, and getting up, went over to the book-case and took out a volume at hazard. He was determined that he would not think about what had happened until it became absolutely necessary that he should do so.

When he had stretched himself on the sofa, he looked at the title-page of the book. It was Gautier's Emaux et Camees, Charpentier's

Japanese-paper edition, with the Jacquemart etching. The binding was of citron-green leather, with a design of gilt trellis-work and dotted pomegranates. It had been given to him by Adrian Singleton. As he turned over the pages, his eye fell on the poem about the hand of Lacenaire, the cold yellow hand "*du supplice encore mal lavee,*" with its downy red hairs and its "*doigts de faune.*" He glanced at his own white taper fingers, shuddering slightly in spite of himself, and passed on, till he came to those lovely stanzas upon Venice:

Sur une gamme chromatique,
Le sein de peries ruisselant,
La Venus de l'Adriatique
Sort de l'eau son corps rose et blanc.
Les domes, sur l'azur des ondes
Suivant la phrase au pur contour,
S'enflent comme des gorges rondes
Que souleve un soupir d'amour.
L'esquif aborde et me depose,
Jetant son amarre au pilier,
Devant une facade rose,
Sur le marbre d'un escalier.*

How exquisite they were! As one read them, one seemed to be floating down the green water-ways of the pink and pearl city, seated in a black gondola with silver prow and trailing curtains. The mere lines looked to him like those straight lines of turquoise-blue that follow one as one pushes out to the Lido. The sudden flashes of colour reminded him of the gleam of the opal-and-iris-throated birds that flutter round the tall honeycombed Campanile, or stalk, with such stately grace, through the dim, dust-stained arcades. Leaning back with half-closed eyes, he kept saying over and over to himself:

* Loosely translated: On the chromatic notes/gently dripping on her breasts/the Venus of Adriatic/Rose and White, rests;/Her domes follow above the blue waters/the contours of a phrase so pure/like the throats that bob and dip/raising a sigh of love;/a skiff comes and I alight/as it anchors flinging its rope/at the pink-facaded town/on the marbled-stairs.

"Devant une facade rose,
Sur le marbre d'un escalier."

The whole of Venice was in those two lines. He remembered the autumn that he had passed there, and a wonderful love that had stirred him to mad delightful follies. There was romance in every place. But Venice, like Oxford, had kept the background for romance, and, to the true romantic, background was everything, or almost everything. Basil had been with him part of the time, and had gone wild over Tintoret.* Poor Basil! What a horrible way for a man to die!

He sighed, and took up the volume again, and tried to forget. He read of the swallows that fly in and out of the little *cafe* at Smyrna where the Hadjis sit counting their amber beads and the turbaned merchants smoke their long tasselled pipes and talk gravely to each other; he read of the Obelisk in the Place de la Concorde that weeps tears of granite in its lonely sunless exile and longs to be back by the hot, lotus-covered Nile, where there are Sphinxes, and rose-red ibises, and white vultures with gilded claws, and crocodiles with small beryl eyes that crawl over the green steaming mud; he began to brood over those verses which, drawing music from kiss-stained marble, tell of that curious statue that Gautier compares to a contralto voice, the "*monstre charmant*"† that couches in the porphyry-room of the Louvre.‡ But after a time the book fell from his hand. He grew nervous, and a horrible fit of terror came over him. What if Alan Campbell should be out of England? Days would elapse before he could come back. Perhaps he might refuse to come. What could he do then? Every moment was of vital importance.

They had been great friends once, five years before—almost inseparable, indeed. Then the intimacy had come suddenly to an end. When they met in society now, it was only Dorian Gray who smiled: Alan Campbell never did.

He was an extremely clever young man, though he had no real appreciation of the visible arts, and whatever little sense of the beauty of poetry he possessed he had gained entirely from Dorian. His

* Venetian painter (known as Tintoretto) Jacopo Robusti (1518-1594).

† (Fr.) Charming monster.

‡ The museum and art gallery in Paris.

dominant intellectual passion was for science. At Cambridge he had spent a great deal of his time working in the laboratory, and had taken a good class in the Natural Science Tripos of his year. Indeed, he was still devoted to the study of chemistry, and had a laboratory of his own in which he used to shut himself up all day long, greatly to the annoyance of his mother, who had set her heart on his standing for Parliament and had a vague idea that a chemist was a person who made up prescriptions. He was an excellent musician, however, as well, and played both the violin and the piano better than most amateurs. In fact, it was music that had first brought him and Dorian Gray together—music and that indefinable attraction that Dorian seemed to be able to exercise whenever he wished—and, indeed, exercised often without being conscious of it. They had met at Lady Berkshire's the night that Rubinstein* played there, and after that used to be always seen together at the opera and wherever good music was going on. For eighteen months their intimacy lasted. Campbell was always either at Selby Royal or in Grosvenor Square. To him, as to many others, Dorian Gray was the type of everything that is wonderful and fascinating in life. Whether or not a quarrel had taken place between them no one ever knew. But suddenly people remarked that they scarcely spoke when they met and that Campbell seemed always to go away early from any party at which Dorian Gray was present. He had changed, too—was strangely melancholy at times, appeared almost to dislike hearing music, and would never himself play, giving as his excuse, when he was called upon, that he was so absorbed in science that he had no time left in which to practise. And this was certainly true. Every day he seemed to become more interested in biology, and his name appeared once or twice in some of the scientific reviews in connection with certain curious experiments.

This was the man Dorian Gray was waiting for. Every second he kept glancing at the clock. As the minutes went by he became horribly agitated. At last he got up and began to pace up and down the room, looking like a beautiful caged thing. He took long stealthy strides. His hands were curiously cold.

The suspense became unbearable. Time seemed to him to be

* Russian pianist and composer Anton Rubinstein (1829-1894).

crawling with feet of lead, while he by monstrous winds was being swept towards the jagged edge of some black cleft of precipice. He knew what was waiting for him there; saw it, indeed, and, shuddering, crushed with dank hands his burning lids as though he would have robbed the very brain of sight and driven the eyeballs back into their cave. It was useless. The brain had its own food on which it battened, and the imagination, made grotesque by terror, twisted and distorted as a living thing by pain, danced like some foul puppet on a stand and grinned through moving masks. Then, suddenly, time stopped for him. Yes: that blind, slow-breathing thing crawled no more, and horrible thoughts, time being dead, raced nimbly on in front, and dragged a hideous future from its grave, and showed it to him. He stared at it. Its very horror made him stone.

At last the door opened and his servant entered. He turned glazed eyes upon him.

"Mr. Campbell, sir," said the man.

A sigh of relief broke from his parched lips, and the colour came back to his cheeks.

"Ask him to come in at once, Francis." He felt that he was himself again. His mood of cowardice had passed away.

The man bowed and retired. In a few moments, Alan Campbell walked in, looking very stern and rather pale, his pallor being intensified by his coal-black hair and dark eyebrows.

"Alan! This is kind of you. I thank you for coming."

"I had intended never to enter your house again, Gray. But you said it was a matter of life and death." His voice was hard and cold. He spoke with slow deliberation. There was a look of contempt in the steady searching gaze that he turned on Dorian. He kept his hands in the pockets of his Astrakhan coat, and seemed not to have noticed the gesture with which he had been greeted.

"Yes: it is a matter of life and death, Alan, and to more than one person. Sit down."

Campbell took a chair by the table, and Dorian sat opposite to him. The two men's eyes met. In Dorian's there was infinite pity. He knew that what he was going to do was dreadful.

After a strained moment of silence, he leaned across and said, very quietly, but watching the effect of each word upon the face of

him he had sent for, "Alan, in a locked room at the top of this house, a room to which nobody but myself has access, a dead man is seated at a table. He has been dead ten hours now. Don't stir, and don't look at me like that. Who the man is, why he died, how he died, are matters that do not concern you. What you have to do is this—"

"Stop, Gray. I don't want to know anything further. Whether what you have told me is true or not true doesn't concern me. I entirely decline to be mixed up in your life. Keep your horrible secrets to yourself. They don't interest me any more."

"Alan, they will have to interest you. This one will have to interest you. I am awfully sorry for you, Alan. But I can't help myself. You are the one man who is able to save me. I am forced to bring you into the matter. I have no option. Alan, you are scientific. You know about chemistry and things of that kind. You have made experiments. What you have got to do is to destroy the thing that is upstairs—to destroy it so that not a vestige of it will be left. Nobody saw this person come into the house. Indeed, at the present moment he is supposed to be in Paris. He will not be missed for months. When he is missed, there must be no trace of him found here. You, Alan, you must change him, and everything that belongs to him, into a handful of ashes that I may scatter in the air."

"You are mad, Dorian."

"Ah! I was waiting for you to call me Dorian."

"You are mad, I tell you—mad to imagine that I would raise a finger to help you, mad to make this monstrous confession. I will have nothing to do with this matter, whatever it is. Do you think I am going to peril my reputation for you? What is it to me what devil's work you are up to?"

"It was suicide, Alan."

"I am glad of that. But who drove him to it? You, I should fancy."

"Do you still refuse to do this for me?"

"Of course I refuse. I will have absolutely nothing to do with it. I don't care what shame comes on you. You deserve it all. I should not be sorry to see you disgraced, publicly disgraced. How dare you ask me, of all men in the world, to mix myself up in this horror? I should have thought you knew more about people's characters. Your friend Lord Henry Wotton can't have taught you much about

psychology, whatever else he has taught you. Nothing will induce me to stir a step to help you. You have come to the wrong man. Go to some of your friends. Don't come to me."

"Alan, it was murder. I killed him. You don't know what he had made me suffer. Whatever my life is, he had more to do with the making or the marring of it than poor Harry has had. He may not have intended it, the result was the same."

"Murder! Good God, Dorian, is that what you have come to? I shall not inform upon you. It is not my business. Besides, without my stirring in the matter, you are certain to be arrested. Nobody ever commits a crime without doing something stupid. But I will have nothing to do with it."

"You must have something to do with it. Wait, wait a moment; listen to me. Only listen, Alan. All I ask of you is to perform a certain scientific experiment. You go to hospitals and dead-houses, and the horrors that you do there don't affect you. If in some hideous dissecting room or fetid laboratory you found this man lying on a leaden table with red gutters scooped out in it for the blood to flow through, you would simply look upon him as an admirable subject. You would not turn a hair. You would not believe that you were doing anything wrong. On the contrary, you would probably feel that you were benefiting the human race, or increasing the sum of knowledge in the world, or gratifying intellectual curiosity, or something of that kind. What I want you to do is merely what you have often done before. Indeed, to destroy a body must be far less horrible than what you are accustomed to work at. And, remember, it is the only piece of evidence against me. If it is discovered, I am lost; and it is sure to be discovered unless you help me."

"I have no desire to help you. You forget that. I am simply indifferent to the whole thing. It has nothing to do with me."

"Alan, I entreat you. Think of the position I am in. Just before you came I almost fainted with terror. You may know terror yourself some day. No! don't think of that. Look at the matter purely from the scientific point of view. You don't inquire where the dead things on which you experiment come from. Don't inquire now. I have told you too much as it is. But I beg of you to do this. We were friends once, Alan."

"Don't speak about those days, Dorian—they are dead."

"The dead linger sometimes. The man upstairs will not go away. He is sitting at the table with bowed head and outstretched arms. Alan! Alan! If you don't come to my assistance, I am ruined. Why, they will hang me, Alan! Don't you understand? They will hang me for what I have done."

"There is no good in prolonging this scene. I absolutely refuse to do anything in the matter. It is insane of you to ask me."

"You refuse?"

"Yes."

"I entreat you, Alan."

"It is useless."

The same look of pity came into Dorian Gray's eyes. Then he stretched out his hand, took a piece of paper, and wrote something on it. He read it over twice, folded it carefully, and pushed it across the table. Having done this, he got up and went over to the window.

Campbell looked at him in surprise, and then took up the paper, and opened it. As he read it, his face became ghastly pale and he fell back in his chair. A horrible sense of sickness came over him. He felt as if his heart was beating itself to death in some empty hollow.

After two or three minutes of terrible silence, Dorian turned round and came and stood behind him, putting his hand upon his shoulder.

"I am so sorry for you, Alan," he murmured, "but you leave me no alternative. I have a letter written already. Here it is. You see the address. If you don't help me, I must send it. If you don't help me, I will send it. You know what the result will be. But you are going to help me. It is impossible for you to refuse now. I tried to spare you. You will do me the justice to admit that. You were stern, harsh, offensive. You treated me as no man has ever dared to treat me—no living man, at any rate. I bore it all. Now it is for me to dictate terms."

Campbell buried his face in his hands, and a shudder passed through him.

"Yes, it is my turn to dictate terms, Alan. You know what they are. The thing is quite simple. Come, don't work yourself into this fever. The thing has to be done. Face it, and do it."

A groan broke from Campbell's lips and he shivered all over. The ticking of the clock on the mantelpiece seemed to him to be dividing

time into separate atoms of agony, each of which was too terrible to be borne. He felt as if an iron ring was being slowly tightened round his forehead, as if the disgrace with which he was threatened had already come upon him. The hand upon his shoulder weighed like a hand of lead. It was intolerable. It seemed to crush him.

"Come, Alan, you must decide at once."

"I cannot do it," he said, mechanically, as though words could alter things.

"You must. You have no choice. Don't delay."

He hesitated a moment. "Is there a fire in the room upstairs?"

"Yes, there is a gas-fire with asbestos."

"I shall have to go home and get some things from the laboratory."

"No, Alan, you must not leave the house. Write out on a sheet of notepaper what you want and my servant will take a cab and bring the things back to you."

Campbell scrawled a few lines, blotted them, and addressed an envelope to his assistant. Dorian took the note up and read it carefully. Then he rang the bell and gave it to his valet, with orders to return as soon as possible and to bring the things with him.

As the hall door shut, Campbell started nervously, and having got up from the chair, went over to the chimney-piece. He was shivering with a kind of ague. For nearly twenty minutes, neither of the men spoke. A fly buzzed noisily about the room, and the ticking of the clock was like the beat of a hammer.

As the chime struck one, Campbell turned round, and looking at Dorian Gray, saw that his eyes were filled with tears. There was something in the purity and refinement of that sad face that seemed to enrage him. "You are infamous, absolutely infamous!" he muttered.

"Hush, Alan. You have saved my life," said Dorian.

"Your life? Good heavens! what a life that is! You have gone from corruption to corruption, and now you have culminated in crime. In doing what I am going to do—what you force me to do—it is not of your life that I am thinking."

"Ah, Alan," murmured Dorian with a sigh, "I wish you had a thousandth part of the pity for me that I have for you." He turned

away as he spoke and stood looking out at the garden. Campbell made no answer.

After about ten minutes a knock came to the door, and the servant entered, carrying a large mahogany chest of chemicals, with a long coil of steel and platinum wire and two rather curiously shaped iron clamps.

"Shall I leave the things here, sir?" he asked Campbell.

"Yes," said Dorian. "And I am afraid, Francis, that I have another errand for you. What is the name of the man at Richmond who supplies Selby with orchids?"

"Harden, sir."

"Yes—Harden. You must go down to Richmond at once, see Harden personally, and tell him to send twice as many orchids as I ordered, and to have as few white ones as possible. In fact, I don't want any white ones. It is a lovely day, Francis, and Richmond is a very pretty place—otherwise I wouldn't bother you about it."

"No trouble, sir. At what time shall I be back?"

Dorian looked at Campbell. "How long will your experiment take, Alan?" he said in a calm indifferent voice. The presence of a third person in the room seemed to give him extraordinary courage.

Campbell frowned and bit his lip. "It will take about five hours," he answered.

"It will be time enough, then, if you are back at half-past seven, Francis. Or stay: just leave my things out for dressing. You can have the evening to yourself. I am not dining at home, so I shall not want you."

"Thank you, sir," said the man, leaving the room.

"Now, Alan, there is not a moment to be lost. How heavy this chest is! I'll take it for you. You bring the other things." He spoke rapidly and in an authoritative manner. Campbell felt dominated by him. They left the room together.

When they reached the top landing, Dorian took out the key and turned it in the lock. Then he stopped, and a troubled look came into his eyes. He shuddered. "I don't think I can go in, Alan," he murmured.

"It is nothing to me. I don't require you," said Campbell coldly.

Dorian half opened the door. As he did so, he saw the face of his portrait leering in the sunlight. On the floor in front of it the

torn curtain was lying. He remembered that the night before he had forgotten, for the first time in his life, to hide the fatal canvas, and was about to rush forward, when he drew back with a shudder.

What was that loathsome red dew that gleamed, wet and glistening, on one of the hands, as though the canvas had sweated blood? How horrible it was!—more horrible, it seemed to him for the moment, than the silent thing that he knew was stretched across the table, the thing whose grotesque misshapen shadow on the spotted carpet showed him that it had not stirred, but was still there, as he had left it.

He heaved a deep breath, opened the door a little wider, and with half-closed eyes and averted head, walked quickly in, determined that he would not look even once upon the dead man. Then, stooping down and taking up the gold-and-purple hanging, he flung it right over the picture.

There he stopped, feeling afraid to turn round, and his eyes fixed themselves on the intricacies of the pattern before him. He heard Campbell bringing in the heavy chest, and the irons, and the other things that he had required for his dreadful work. He began to wonder if he and Basil Hallward had ever met, and, if so, what they had thought of each other.

"Leave me now," said a stern voice behind him.

He turned and hurried out, just conscious that the dead man had been thrust back into the chair and that Campbell was gazing into a glistening yellow face. As he was going downstairs, he heard the key being turned in the lock.

It was long after seven when Campbell came back into the library. He was pale, but absolutely calm. "I have done what you asked me to do," he muttered. "And now, good-bye. Let us never see each other again."

"You have saved me from ruin, Alan. I cannot forget that," said Dorian simply.

As soon as Campbell had left, he went upstairs. There was a horrible smell of nitric acid in the room. But the thing that had been sitting at the table was gone.

CHAPTER

15

That evening, at eight-thirty, exquisitely dressed and wearing a large button-hole of Parma violets, Dorian Gray was ushered into Lady Narborough's drawing room by bowing servants. His forehead was throbbing with maddened nerves, and he felt wildly excited, but his manner as he bent over his hostess's hand was as easy and graceful as ever. Perhaps one never seems so much at one's ease as when one has to play a part. Certainly no one looking at Dorian Gray that night could have believed that he had passed through a tragedy as horrible as any tragedy of our age. Those finely shaped fingers could never have clutched a knife for sin, nor those smiling lips have cried out on God and goodness. He himself could not help wondering at the calm of his demeanour, and for a moment felt keenly the terrible pleasure of a double life.

It was a small party, got up rather in a hurry by Lady Narborough, who was a very clever woman with what Lord Henry used to describe as the remains of really remarkable ugliness. She had proved an excellent wife to one of our most tedious ambassadors, and having buried her husband properly in a marble mausoleum, which she had herself designed, and married off her daughters to some rich, rather elderly men,

she devoted herself now to the pleasures of French fiction, French cookery, and French *esprit* when she could get it.

Dorian was one of her especial favourites, and she always told him that she was extremely glad she had not met him in early life. "I know, my dear, I should have fallen madly in love with you," she used to say, "and thrown my bonnet right over the mills for your sake. It is most fortunate that you were not thought of at the time. As it was, our bonnets were so unbecoming, and the mills were so occupied in trying to raise the wind, that I never had even a flirtation with anybody. However, that was all Narborough's fault. He was dreadfully short-sighted, and there is no pleasure in taking in a husband who never sees anything."

Her guests this evening were rather tedious. The fact was, as she explained to Dorian, behind a very shabby fan, one of her married daughters had come up quite suddenly to stay with her, and, to make matters worse, had actually brought her husband with her. "I think it is most unkind of her, my dear," she whispered. "Of course I go and stay with them every summer after I come from Homburg, but then an old woman like me must have fresh air sometimes, and besides, I really wake them up. You don't know what an existence they lead down there. It is pure unadulterated country life. They get up early, because they have so much to do, and go to bed early, because they have so little to think about. There has not been a scandal in the neighbourhood since the time of Queen Elizabeth, and consequently they all fall asleep after dinner. You shan't sit next either of them. You shall sit by me and amuse me."

Dorian murmured a graceful compliment and looked round the room. Yes: it was certainly a tedious party. Two of the people he had never seen before, and the others consisted of Ernest Harrowden, one of those middle-aged mediocrities so common in London clubs who have no enemies, but are thoroughly disliked by their friends; Lady Ruxton, an overdressed woman of forty-seven, with a hooked nose, who was always trying to get herself compromised, but was so peculiarly plain that to her great disappointment no one would ever believe anything against her; Mrs. Erlynne, a pushing nobody, with a delightful lisp and Venetian-red hair; Lady Alice Chapman, his hostess's daughter, a dowdy dull girl, with one of those characteristic

British faces that, once seen, are never remembered; and her husband, a red-cheeked, white-whiskered creature who, like so many of his class, was under the impression that inordinate joviality can atone for an entire lack of ideas.

He was rather sorry he had come, till Lady Narborough, looking at the great ormolu* gilt clock that sprawled in gaudy curves on the mauve-draped mantelshelf, exclaimed: "How horrid of Henry Wotton to be so late! I sent round to him this morning on chance and he promised faithfully not to disappoint me."

It was some consolation that Harry was to be there, and when the door opened and he heard his slow musical voice lending charm to some insincere apology, he ceased to feel bored.

But at dinner he could not eat anything. Plate after plate went away untasted. Lady Narborough kept scolding him for what she called "an insult to poor Adolphe, who invented the *menu* specially for you," and now and then Lord Henry looked across at him, wondering at his silence and abstracted manner. From time to time the butler filled his glass with champagne. He drank eagerly, and his thirst seemed to increase.

"Dorian," said Lord Henry at last, as the *chaud-froid*† was being handed round, "what is the matter with you to-night? You are quite out of sorts."

"I believe he is in love," cried Lady Narborough, "and that he is afraid to tell me for fear I should be jealous. He is quite right. I certainly should."

"Dear Lady Narborough," murmured Dorian, smiling, "I have not been in love for a whole week—not, in fact, since Madame de Ferrol left town."

"How you men can fall in love with that woman!" exclaimed the old lady. "I really cannot understand it."

"It is simply because she remembers you when you were a little girl, Lady Narborough," said Lord Henry. "She is the one link between us and your short frocks."

"She does not remember my short frocks at all, Lord Henry.

---

* Golden or gilded brass or bronze used decoratively.

† (Fr.) A dish of jellied cold meat or fish.

But I remember her very well at Vienna thirty years ago, and how *decolletee** she was then."

"She is still *decolletee*," he answered, taking an olive in his long fingers; "and when she is in a very smart gown she looks like an *edition de luxe* of a bad French novel. She is really wonderful, and full of surprises. Her capacity for family affection is extraordinary. When her third husband died, her hair turned quite gold from grief."

"How can you, Harry!" cried Dorian.

"It is a most romantic explanation," laughed the hostess. "But her third husband, Lord Henry! You don't mean to say Ferrol is the fourth?"

"Certainly, Lady Narborough."

"I don't believe a word of it."

"Well, ask Mr. Gray. He is one of her most intimate friends."

"Is it true, Mr. Gray?"

"She assures me so, Lady Narborough," said Dorian. "I asked her whether, like Marguerite de Navarre, she had their hearts embalmed and hung at her girdle. She told me she didn't, because none of them had had any hearts at all."

"Four husbands! Upon my word that is *trop de zele*."

"*Trop d'audace*,† I tell her," said Dorian.

"Oh! she is audacious enough for anything, my dear. And what is Ferrol like? I don't know him."

"The husbands of very beautiful women belong to the criminal classes," said Lord Henry, sipping his wine.

Lady Narborough hit him with her fan. "Lord Henry, I am not at all surprised that the world says that you are extremely wicked."

"But what world says that?" asked Lord Henry, elevating his eyebrows. "It can only be the next world. This world and I are on excellent terms."

"Everybody I know says you are very wicked," cried the old lady, shaking her head.

Lord Henry looked serious for some moments. "It is perfectly monstrous," he said, at last, "the way people go about nowadays

* With a low-cut dress.

† To keen – too bold.

saying things against one behind one's back that are absolutely and entirely true."

"Isn't he incorrigible?" cried Dorian, leaning forward in his chair.

"I hope so," said his hostess, laughing. "But really, if you all worship Madame de Ferrol in this ridiculous way, I shall have to marry again so as to be in the fashion."

"You will never marry again, Lady Narborough," broke in Lord Henry. "You were far too happy. When a woman marries again, it is because she detested her first husband. When a man marries again, it is because he adored his first wife. Women try their luck; men risk theirs."

"Narborough wasn't perfect," cried the old lady.

"If he had been, you would not have loved him, my dear lady," was the rejoinder. "Women love us for our defects. If we have enough of them, they will forgive us everything, even our intellects. You will never ask me to dinner again after saying this, I am afraid, Lady Narborough, but it is quite true."

"Of course it is true, Lord Henry. If we women did not love you for your defects, where would you all be? Not one of you would ever be married. You would be a set of unfortunate bachelors. Not, however, that that would alter you much. Nowadays all the married men live like bachelors, and all the bachelors like married men."

"*Fin de siecle*," murmured Lord Henry.

"*Fin du globe*," answered his hostess.*

"I wish it were *fin du globe*," said Dorian with a sigh. "Life is a great disappointment."

"Ah, my dear," cried Lady Narborough, putting on her gloves, "don't tell me that you have exhausted life. When a man says that one knows that life has exhausted him. Lord Henry is very wicked, and I sometimes wish that I had been; but you are made to be good—you look so good. I must find you a nice wife. Lord Henry, don't you think that Mr. Gray should get married?"

"I am always telling him so, Lady Narborough," said Lord Henry with a bow.

---

* The end of the century – The end of the world.

"Well, we must look out for a suitable match for him. I shall go through Debrett carefully to-night and draw out a list of all the eligible young ladies."

"With their ages, Lady Narborough?" asked Dorian.

"Of course, with their ages, slightly edited. But nothing must be done in a hurry. I want it to be what *The Morning Post* calls a suitable alliance, and I want you both to be happy."

"What nonsense people talk about happy marriages!" exclaimed Lord Henry. "A man can be happy with any woman, as long as he does not love her."

"Ah! what a cynic you are!" cried the old lady, pushing back her chair and nodding to Lady Ruxton. "You must come and dine with me soon again. You are really an admirable tonic, much better than what Sir Andrew prescribes for me. You must tell me what people you would like to meet, though. I want it to be a delightful gathering."

"I like men who have a future and women who have a past," he answered. "Or do you think that would make it a petticoat party?"

"I fear so," she said, laughing, as she stood up. "A thousand pardons, my dear Lady Ruxton," she added, "I didn't see you hadn't finished your cigarette."

"Never mind, Lady Narborough. I smoke a great deal too much. I am going to limit myself, for the future."

"Pray don't, Lady Ruxton," said Lord Henry. "Moderation is a fatal thing. Enough is as bad as a meal. More than enough is as good as a feast."

Lady Ruxton glanced at him curiously. "You must come and explain that to me some afternoon, Lord Henry. It sounds a fascinating theory," she murmured, as she swept out of the room.

"Now, mind you don't stay too long over your politics and scandal," cried Lady Narborough from the door. "If you do, we are sure to squabble upstairs."

The men laughed, and Mr. Chapman got up solemnly from the foot of the table and came up to the top. Dorian Gray changed his seat and went and sat by Lord Henry. Mr. Chapman began to talk in a loud voice about the situation in the House of Commons. He guffawed at his adversaries. The word *doctrinaire*—word full of

terror to the British mind—reappeared from time to time between his explosions. An alliterative prefix served as an ornament of oratory. He hoisted the Union Jack on the pinnacles of thought. The inherited stupidity of the race—sound English common sense he jovially termed it—was shown to be the proper bulwark for society.

A smile curved Lord Henry's lips, and he turned round and looked at Dorian.

"Are you better, my dear fellow?" he asked. "You seemed rather out of sorts at dinner."

"I am quite well, Harry. I am tired. That is all."

"You were charming last night. The little duchess is quite devoted to you. She tells me she is going down to Selby."

"She has promised to come on the twentieth."

"Is Monmouth to be there, too?"

"Oh, yes, Harry."

"He bores me dreadfully, almost as much as he bores her. She is very clever, too clever for a woman. She lacks the indefinable charm of weakness. It is the feet of clay that make the gold of the image precious. Her feet are very pretty, but they are not feet of clay. White porcelain feet, if you like. They have been through the fire, and what fire does not destroy, it hardens. She has had experiences."

"How long has she been married?" asked Dorian.

"An eternity, she tells me. I believe, according to the peerage, it is ten years, but ten years with Monmouth must have been like eternity, with time thrown in. Who else is coming?"

"Oh, the Willoughbys, Lord Rugby and his wife, our hostess, Geoffrey Clouston, the usual set. I have asked Lord Grotrian."

"I like him," said Lord Henry. "A great many people don't, but I find him charming. He atones for being occasionally somewhat overdressed by being always absolutely over-educated. He is a very modern type."

"I don't know if he will be able to come, Harry. He may have to go to Monte Carlo with his father."

"Ah! what a nuisance people's people are! Try and make him come. By the way, Dorian, you ran off very early last night. You left before eleven. What did you do afterwards? Did you go straight home?"

Dorian glanced at him hurriedly and frowned.

"No, Harry," he said at last, "I did not get home till nearly three."

"Did you go to the club?"

"Yes," he answered. Then he bit his lip. "No, I don't mean that. I didn't go to the club. I walked about. I forget what I did . . . How inquisitive you are, Harry! You always want to know what one has been doing. I always want to forget what I have been doing. I came in at half-past two, if you wish to know the exact time. I had left my latch-key at home, and my servant had to let me in. If you want any corroborative evidence on the subject, you can ask him."

Lord Henry shrugged his shoulders. "My dear fellow, as if I cared! Let us go up to the drawing room. No sherry, thank you, Mr. Chapman. Something has happened to you, Dorian. Tell me what it is. You are not yourself to-night."

"Don't mind me, Harry. I am irritable, and out of temper. I shall come round and see you to-morrow, or next day. Make my excuses to Lady Narborough. I shan't go upstairs. I shall go home. I must go home."

"All right, Dorian. I dare say I shall see you to-morrow at tea-time. The duchess is coming."

"I will try to be there, Harry," he said, leaving the room. As he drove back to his own house, he was conscious that the sense of terror he thought he had strangled had come back to him. Lord Henry's casual questioning had made him lose his nerve for the moment, and he wanted his nerve still. Things that were dangerous had to be destroyed. He winced. He hated the idea of even touching them.

Yet it had to be done. He realized that, and when he had locked the door of his library, he opened the secret press into which he had thrust Basil Hallward's coat and bag. A huge fire was blazing. He piled another log on it. The smell of the singeing clothes and burning leather was horrible. It took him three-quarters of an hour to consume everything. At the end he felt faint and sick, and having lit some Algerian pastilles in a pierced copper brazier, he bathed his hands and forehead with a cool musk-scented vinegar.

Suddenly he started. His eyes grew strangely bright, and he gnawed nervously at his underlip. Between two of the windows stood a large Florentine cabinet, made out of ebony and inlaid with

ivory and blue lapis. He watched it as though it were a thing that could fascinate and make afraid, as though it held something that he longed for and yet almost loathed. His breath quickened. A mad craving came over him. He lit a cigarette and then threw it away. His eyelids drooped till the long fringed lashes almost touched his cheek. But he still watched the cabinet. At last he got up from the sofa on which he had been lying, went over to it, and having unlocked it, touched some hidden spring. A triangular drawer passed slowly out. His fingers moved instinctively towards it, dipped in, and closed on something. It was a small Chinese box of black and gold-dust lacquer, elaborately wrought, the sides patterned with curved waves, and the silken cords hung with round crystals and tasselled in plaited metal threads. He opened it. Inside was a green paste, waxy in lustre, the odour curiously heavy and persistent.

He hesitated for some moments, with a strangely immobile smile upon his face. Then shivering, though the atmosphere of the room was terribly hot, he drew himself up and glanced at the clock. It was twenty minutes to twelve. He put the box back, shutting the cabinet doors as he did so, and went into his bedroom.

As midnight was striking bronze blows upon the dusky air, Dorian Gray, dressed commonly, and with a muffler wrapped round his throat, crept quietly out of his house. In Bond Street he found a hansom with a good horse. He hailed it and in a low voice gave the driver an address.

The man shook his head. "It is too far for me," he muttered.

"Here is a sovereign for you," said Dorian. "You shall have another if you drive fast."

"All right, sir," answered the man, "you will be there in an hour," and after his fare had got in he turned his horse round and drove rapidly towards the river.

CHAPTER

16

A cold rain began to fall, and the blurred street-lamps looked ghastly in the dripping mist. The public-houses were just closing, and dim men and women were clustering in broken groups round their doors. From some of the bars came the sound of horrible laughter. In others, drunkards brawled and screamed.

Lying back in the hansom, with his hat pulled over his forehead, Dorian Gray watched with listless eyes the sordid shame of the great city, and now and then he repeated to himself the words that Lord Henry had said to him on the first day they had met, "To cure the soul by means of the senses, and the senses by means of the soul." Yes, that was the secret. He had often tried it, and would try it again now. There were opium dens where one could buy oblivion, dens of horror where the memory of old sins could be destroyed by the madness of sins that were new.

The moon hung low in the sky like a yellow skull. From time to time a huge misshapen cloud stretched a long arm across and hid it. The gas-lamps grew fewer, and the streets more narrow and gloomy. Once the man lost his way and had to drive back half a mile. A steam rose from the horse as

it splashed up the puddles. The sidewindows of the hansom were clogged with a grey-flannel mist.

"To cure the soul by means of the senses, and the senses by means of the soul!" How the words rang in his ears! His soul, certainly, was sick to death. Was it true that the senses could cure it? Innocent blood had been spilled. What could atone for that? Ah! for that there was no atonement; but though forgiveness was impossible, forgetfulness was possible still, and he was determined to forget, to stamp the thing out, to crush it as one would crush the adder that had stung one. Indeed, what right had Basil to have spoken to him as he had done? Who had made him a judge over others? He had said things that were dreadful, horrible, not to be endured.

On and on plodded the hansom, going slower, it seemed to him, at each step. He thrust up the trap and called to the man to drive faster. The hideous hunger for opium began to gnaw at him. His throat burned and his delicate hands twitched nervously together. He struck at the horse madly with his stick. The driver laughed and whipped up. He laughed in answer, and the man was silent.

The way seemed interminable, and the streets like the black web of some sprawling spider. The monotony became unbearable, and as the mist thickened, he felt afraid.

Then they passed by lonely brickfields. The fog was lighter here, and he could see the strange, bottle-shaped kilns with their orange, fanlike tongues of fire. A dog barked as they went by, and far away in the darkness some wandering sea-gull screamed. The horse stumbled in a rut, then swerved aside and broke into a gallop.

After some time they left the clay road and rattled again over rough-paven streets. Most of the windows were dark, but now and then fantastic shadows were silhouetted against some lamplit blind. He watched them curiously. They moved like monstrous marionettes and made gestures like live things. He hated them. A dull rage was in his heart. As they turned a corner, a woman yelled something at them from an open door, and two men ran after the hansom for about a hundred yards. The driver beat at them with his whip.

It is said that passion makes one think in a circle. Certainly with hideous iteration the bitten lips of Dorian Gray shaped and reshaped those subtle words that dealt with soul and sense, till he

had found in them the full expression, as it were, of his mood, and justified, by intellectual approval, passions that without such justification would still have dominated his temper. From cell to cell of his brain crept the one thought; and the wild desire to live, most terrible of all man's appetites, quickened into force each trembling nerve and fibre. Ugliness that had once been hateful to him because it made things real, became dear to him now for that very reason. Ugliness was the one reality. The coarse brawl, the loathsome den, the crude violence of disordered life, the very vileness of thief and outcast, were more vivid, in their intense actuality of impression, than all the gracious shapes of art, the dreamy shadows of song. They were what he needed for forgetfulness. In three days he would be free.

Suddenly the man drew up with a jerk at the top of a dark lane. Over the low roofs and jagged chimney-stacks of the houses rose the black masts of ships. Wreaths of white mist clung like ghostly sails to the yards.

"Somewhere about here, sir, ain't it?" he asked huskily through the trap.

Dorian started and peered round. "This will do," he answered, and having got out hastily and given the driver the extra fare he had promised him, he walked quickly in the direction of the quay. Here and there a lantern gleamed at the stern of some huge merchantman. The light shook and splintered in the puddles. A red glare came from an outward-bound steamer that was coaling. The slimy pavement looked like a wet mackintosh.

He hurried on towards the left, glancing back now and then to see if he was being followed. In about seven or eight minutes he reached a small shabby house that was wedged in between two gaunt factories. In one of the top-windows stood a lamp. He stopped and gave a peculiar knock.

After a little time he heard steps in the passage and the chain being unhooked. The door opened quietly, and he went in without saying a word to the squat misshapen figure that flattened itself into the shadow as he passed. At the end of the hall hung a tattered green curtain that swayed and shook in the gusty wind which had followed him in from the street. He dragged it aside and entered

a long low room which looked as if it had once been a third-rate dancing-saloon. Shrill flaring gas-jets, dulled and distorted in the fly-blown mirrors that faced them, were ranged round the walls. Greasy reflectors of ribbed tin backed them, making quivering disks of light. The floor was covered with ochre-coloured sawdust, trampled here and there into mud, and stained with dark rings of spilled liquor. Some Malays were crouching by a little charcoal stove, playing with bone counters and showing their white teeth as they chattered. In one corner, with his head buried in his arms, a sailor sprawled over a table, and by the tawdrily painted bar that ran across one complete side stood two haggard women, mocking an old man who was brushing the sleeves of his coat with an expression of disgust. "He thinks he's got red ants on him," laughed one of them, as Dorian passed by. The man looked at her in terror and began to whimper.

At the end of the room there was a little staircase, leading to a darkened chamber. As Dorian hurried up its three rickety steps, the heavy odour of opium met him. He heaved a deep breath, and his nostrils quivered with pleasure. When he entered, a young man with smooth yellow hair, who was bending over a lamp lighting a long thin pipe, looked up at him and nodded in a hesitating manner.

"You here, Adrian?" muttered Dorian.

"Where else should I be?" he answered, listlessly. "None of the chaps will speak to me now."

"I thought you had left England."

"Darlington is not going to do anything. My brother paid the bill at last. George doesn't speak to me either . . . I don't care," he added with a sigh. "As long as one has this stuff, one doesn't want friends. I think I have had too many friends."

Dorian winced and looked round at the grotesque things that lay in such fantastic postures on the ragged mattresses. The twisted limbs, the gaping mouths, the staring lustreless eyes, fascinated him. He knew in what strange heavens they were suffering, and what dull hells were teaching them the secret of some new joy. They were better off than he was. He was prisoned in thought. Memory, like a horrible malady, was eating his soul away. From time to time he seemed to see the eyes of Basil Hallward looking at him. Yet he felt

he could not stay. The presence of Adrian Singleton troubled him. He wanted to be where no one would know who he was. He wanted to escape from himself.

"I am going on to the other place," he said after a pause.

"On the wharf?"

"Yes."

"That mad-cat is sure to be there. They won't have her in this place now."

Dorian shrugged his shoulders. "I am sick of women who love one. Women who hate one are much more interesting. Besides, the stuff is better."

"Much the same."

"I like it better. Come and have something to drink. I must have something."

"I don't want anything," murmured the young man.

"Never mind."

Adrian Singleton rose up wearily and followed Dorian to the bar. A half-caste, in a ragged turban and a shabby ulster, grinned a hideous greeting as he thrust a bottle of brandy and two tumblers in front of them. The women sidled up and began to chatter. Dorian turned his back on them and said something in a low voice to Adrian Singleton.

A crooked smile, like a Malay crease, writhed across the face of one of the women. "We are very proud to-night," she sneered.

"For God's sake don't talk to me," cried Dorian, stamping his foot on the ground. "What do you want? Money? Here it is. Don't ever talk to me again."

Two red sparks flashed for a moment in the woman's sodden eyes, then flickered out and left them dull and glazed. She tossed her head and raked the coins off the counter with greedy fingers. Her companion watched her enviously.

"It's no use," sighed Adrian Singleton. "I don't care to go back. What does it matter? I am quite happy here."

"You will write to me if you want anything, won't you?" said Dorian, after a pause.

"Perhaps."

"Good night, then."

"Good night," answered the young man, passing up the steps and wiping his parched mouth with a handkerchief.

Dorian walked to the door with a look of pain in his face. As he drew the curtain aside, a hideous laugh broke from the painted lips of the woman who had taken his money. "There goes the devil's bargain!" she hiccoughed, in a hoarse voice.

"Curse you!" he answered, "don't call me that."

She snapped her fingers. "Prince Charming is what you like to be called, ain't it?" she yelled after him.

The drowsy sailor leaped to his feet as she spoke, and looked wildly round. The sound of the shutting of the hall door fell on his ear. He rushed out as if in pursuit.

Dorian Gray hurried along the quay through the drizzling rain. His meeting with Adrian Singleton had strangely moved him, and he wondered if the ruin of that young life was really to be laid at his door, as Basil Hallward had said to him with such infamy of insult. He bit his lip, and for a few seconds his eyes grew sad. Yet, after all, what did it matter to him? One's days were too brief to take the burden of another's errors on one's shoulders. Each man lived his own life and paid his own price for living it. The only pity was one had to pay so often for a single fault. One had to pay over and over again, indeed. In her dealings with man, destiny never closed her accounts.

There are moments, psychologists tell us, when the passion for sin, or for what the world calls sin, so dominates a nature that every fibre of the body, as every cell of the brain, seems to be instinct with fearful impulses. Men and women at such moments lose the freedom of their will. They move to their terrible end as automatons move. Choice is taken from them, and conscience is either killed, or, if it lives at all, lives but to give rebellion its fascination and disobedience its charm. For all sins, as theologians weary not of reminding us, are sins of disobedience. When that high spirit, that morning star of evil, fell from heaven, it was as a rebel that he fell.

Callous, concentrated on evil, with stained mind, and soul hungry for rebellion, Dorian Gray hastened on, quickening his step as he went, but as he darted aside into a dim archway, that had served him often as a short cut to the ill-famed place where he was going,

he felt himself suddenly seized from behind, and before he had time to defend himself, he was thrust back against the wall, with a brutal hand round his throat.

He struggled madly for life, and by a terrible effort wrenched the tightening fingers away. In a second he heard the click of a revolver, and saw the gleam of a polished barrel, pointing straight at his head, and the dusky form of a short, thick-set man facing him.

"What do you want?" he gasped.

"Keep quiet," said the man. "If you stir, I shoot you."

"You are mad. What have I done to you?"

"You wrecked the life of Sibyl Vane," was the answer, "and Sibyl Vane was my sister. She killed herself. I know it. Her death is at your door. I swore I would kill you in return. For years I have sought you. I had no clue, no trace. The two people who could have described you were dead. I knew nothing of you but the pet name she used to call you. I heard it to-night by chance. Make your peace with God, for to-night you are going to die."

Dorian Gray grew sick with fear. "I never knew her," he stammered. "I never heard of her. You are mad."

"You had better confess your sin, for as sure as I am James Vane, you are going to die." There was a horrible moment. Dorian did not know what to say or do. "Down on your knees!" growled the man. "I give you one minute to make your peace—no more. I go on board to-night for India, and I must do my job first. One minute. That's all."

Dorian's arms fell to his side. Paralysed with terror, he did not know what to do. Suddenly a wild hope flashed across his brain. "Stop," he cried. "How long ago is it since your sister died? Quick, tell me!"

"Eighteen years," said the man. "Why do you ask me? What do years matter?"

"Eighteen years," laughed Dorian Gray, with a touch of triumph in his voice. "Eighteen years! Set me under the lamp and look at my face!"

James Vane hesitated for a moment, not understanding what was meant. Then he seized Dorian Gray and dragged him from the archway.

Dim and wavering as was the wind-blown light, yet it served to show him the hideous error, as it seemed, into which he had fallen, for the face of the man he had sought to kill had all the bloom of boyhood, all the unstained purity of youth. He seemed little more than a lad of twenty summers, hardly older, if older indeed at all, than his sister had been when they had parted so many years ago. It was obvious that this was not the man who had destroyed her life.

He loosened his hold and reeled back. "My God! my God!" he cried, "and I would have murdered you!"

Dorian Gray drew a long breath. "You have been on the brink of committing a terrible crime, my man," he said, looking at him sternly. "Let this be a warning to you not to take vengeance into your own hands."

"Forgive me, sir," muttered James Vane. "I was deceived. A chance word I heard in that damned den set me on the wrong track."

"You had better go home and put that pistol away, or you may get into trouble," said Dorian, turning on his heel and going slowly down the street.

James Vane stood on the pavement in horror. He was trembling from head to foot. After a little while, a black shadow that had been creeping along the dripping wall moved out into the light and came close to him with stealthy footsteps. He felt a hand laid on his arm and looked round with a start. It was one of the women who had been drinking at the bar.

"Why didn't you kill him?" she hissed out, putting haggard face quite close to his. "I knew you were following him when you rushed out from Daly's. You fool! You should have killed him. He has lots of money, and he's as bad as bad."

"He is not the man I am looking for," he answered, "and I want no man's money. I want a man's life. The man whose life I want must be nearly forty now. This one is little more than a boy. Thank God, I have not got his blood upon my hands."

The woman gave a bitter laugh. "Little more than a boy!" she sneered. "Why, man, it's nigh on eighteen years since Prince Charming made me what I am."

"You lie!" cried James Vane.

She raised her hand up to heaven. "Before God I am telling the truth," she cried.

"Before God?"

"Strike me dumb if it ain't so. He is the worst one that comes here. They say he has sold himself to the devil for a pretty face. It's nigh on eighteen years since I met him. He hasn't changed much since then. I have, though," she added, with a sickly leer.

"You swear this?"

"I swear it," came in hoarse echo from her flat mouth. "But don't give me away to him," she whined; "I am afraid of him. Let me have some money for my night's lodging."

He broke from her with an oath and rushed to the corner of the street, but Dorian Gray had disappeared. When he looked back, the woman had vanished also.

CHAPTER

17

A week later Dorian Gray was sitting in the conservatory at Selby Royal, talking to the pretty Duchess of Monmouth, who with her husband, a jaded-looking man of sixty, was amongst his guests. It was tea-time, and the mellow light of the huge, lace-covered lamp that stood on the table lit up the delicate china and hammered silver of the service at which the duchess was presiding. Her white hands were moving daintily among the cups, and her full red lips were smiling at something that Dorian had whispered to her. Lord Henry was lying back in a silk-draped wicker chair, looking at them. On a peach-coloured divan sat Lady Narborough, pretending to listen to the duke's description of the last Brazilian beetle that he had added to his collection. Three young men in elaborate smoking-suits were handing tea-cakes to some of the women. The house-party consisted of twelve people, and there were more expected to arrive on the next day.

"What are you two talking about?" said Lord Henry, strolling over to the table and putting his cup down. "I hope Dorian has told you about my plan for rechristening everything, Gladys. It is a delightful idea."

"But I don't want to be rechristened, Harry," rejoined the duchess, looking up at him with her wonderful eyes. "I am quite satisfied with my own name, and I am sure Mr. Gray should be satisfied with his."

"My dear Gladys, I would not alter either name for the world. They are both perfect. I was thinking chiefly of flowers. Yesterday I cut an orchid, for my button-hole. It was a marvellous spotted thing, as effective as the seven deadly sins. In a thoughtless moment I asked one of the gardeners what it was called. He told me it was a fine specimen of *Robinsoniana*, or something dreadful of that kind. It is a sad truth, but we have lost the faculty of giving lovely names to things. Names are everything. I never quarrel with actions. My one quarrel is with words. That is the reason I hate vulgar realism in literature. The man who could call a spade a spade should be compelled to use one. It is the only thing he is fit for."

"Then what should we call you, Harry?" she asked.

"His name is Prince Paradox," said Dorian.

"I recognize him in a flash," exclaimed the duchess.

"I won't hear of it," laughed Lord Henry, sinking into a chair. "From a label there is no escape! I refuse the title."

"Royalties may not abdicate," fell as a warning from pretty lips.

"You wish me to defend my throne, then?"

"Yes."

"I give the truths of to-morrow."

"I prefer the mistakes of to-day," she answered.

"You disarm me, Gladys," he cried, catching the wilfulness of her mood.

"Of your shield, Harry, not of your spear."

"I never tilt against beauty," he said, with a wave of his hand.

"That is your error, Harry, believe me. You value beauty far too much."

"How can you say that? I admit that I think that it is better to be beautiful than to be good. But on the other hand, no one is more ready than I am to acknowledge that it is better to be good than to be ugly."

"Ugliness is one of the seven deadly sins, then?" cried the duchess. "What becomes of your simile about the orchid?"

"Ugliness is one of the seven deadly virtues, Gladys. You, as a good Tory, must not underrate them. Beer, the Bible, and the seven deadly virtues have made our England what she is."

"You don't like your country, then?" she asked.

"I live in it."

"That you may censure it the better."

"Would you have me take the verdict of Europe on it?" he inquired.

"What do they say of us?"

"That Tartuffe has emigrated to England and opened a shop."

"Is that yours, Harry?"

"I give it to you."

"I could not use it. It is too true."

"You need not be afraid. Our countrymen never recognize a description."

"They are practical."

"They are more cunning than practical. When they make up their ledger, they balance stupidity by wealth, and vice by hypocrisy."

"Still, we have done great things."

"Great things have been thrust on us, Gladys."

"We have carried their burden."

"Only as far as the Stock Exchange."

She shook her head. "I believe in the race," she cried.

"It represents the survival of the pushing."

"It has development."

"Decay fascinates me more."

"What of art?" she asked.

"It is a malady."

"Love?"

"An illusion."

"Religion?"

"The fashionable substitute for belief."

"You are a sceptic."

"Never! Scepticism is the beginning of faith."

"What are you?"

"To define is to limit."

"Give me a clue."

"Threads snap. You would lose your way in the labyrinth."

"You bewilder me. Let us talk of some one else."

"Our host is a delightful topic. Years ago he was christened Prince Charming."

"Ah! don't remind me of that," cried Dorian Gray.

"Our host is rather horrid this evening," answered the duchess, colouring. "I believe he thinks that Monmouth married me on purely scientific principles as the best specimen he could find of a modern butterfly."

"Well, I hope he won't stick pins into you, Duchess," laughed Dorian.

"Oh! my maid does that already, Mr. Gray, when she is annoyed with me."

"And what does she get annoyed with you about, Duchess?"

"For the most trivial things, Mr. Gray, I assure you. Usually because I come in at ten minutes to nine and tell her that I must be dressed by half-past eight."

"How unreasonable of her! You should give her warning."

"I daren't, Mr. Gray. Why, she invents hats for me. You remember the one I wore at Lady Hilstone's garden-party? You don't, but it is nice of you to pretend that you do. Well, she made it out of nothing. All good hats are made out of nothing."

"Like all good reputations, Gladys," interrupted Lord Henry. "Every effect that one produces gives one an enemy. To be popular one must be a mediocrity."

"Not with women," said the duchess, shaking her head; "and women rule the world. I assure you we can't bear mediocrities. We women, as some one says, love with our ears, just as you men love with your eyes, if you ever love at all."

"It seems to me that we never do anything else," murmured Dorian.

"Ah! then, you never really love, Mr. Gray," answered the duchess with mock sadness.

"My dear Gladys!" cried Lord Henry. "How can you say that? Romance lives by repetition, and repetition converts an appetite into an art. Besides, each time that one loves is the only time one has ever loved. Difference of object does not alter singleness of passion.

It merely intensifies it. We can have in life but one great experience at best, and the secret of life is to reproduce that experience as often as possible."

"Even when one has been wounded by it, Harry?" asked the duchess after a pause.

"Especially when one has been wounded by it," answered Lord Henry.

The duchess turned and looked at Dorian Gray with a curious expression in her eyes. "What do you say to that, Mr. Gray?" she inquired.

Dorian hesitated for a moment. Then he threw his head back and laughed. "I always agree with Harry, Duchess."

"Even when he is wrong?"

"Harry is never wrong, Duchess."

"And does his philosophy make you happy?"

"I have never searched for happiness. Who wants happiness? I have searched for pleasure."

"And found it, Mr. Gray?"

"Often. Too often."

The duchess sighed. "I am searching for peace," she said, "and if I don't go and dress, I shall have none this evening."

"Let me get you some orchids, Duchess," cried Dorian, starting to his feet and walking down the conservatory.

"You are flirting disgracefully with him," said Lord Henry to his cousin. "You had better take care. He is very fascinating."

"If he were not, there would be no battle."

"Greek meets Greek, then?"

"I am on the side of the Trojans. They fought for a woman."

"They were defeated."

"There are worse things than capture," she answered.

"You gallop with a loose rein."

"Pace gives life," was the *riposte.*

"I shall write it in my diary to-night."

"What?"

"That a burnt child loves the fire."

"I am not even singed. My wings are untouched."

"You use them for everything, except flight."

"Courage has passed from men to women. It is a new experience for us."

"You have a rival."

"Who?"

He laughed. "Lady Narborough," he whispered. "She perfectly adores him."

"You fill me with apprehension. The appeal to antiquity is fatal to us who are romanticists."

"Romanticists! You have all the methods of science."

"Men have educated us."

"But not explained you."

"Describe us as a sex," was her challenge.

"Sphinxes without secrets."

She looked at him, smiling. "How long Mr. Gray is!" she said. "Let us go and help him. I have not yet told him the colour of my frock."

"Ah! you must suit your frock to his flowers, Gladys."

"That would be a premature surrender."

"Romantic art begins with its climax."

"I must keep an opportunity for retreat."

"In the Parthian manner?"*

"They found safety in the desert. I could not do that."

"Women are not always allowed a choice," he answered, but hardly had he finished the sentence before from the far end of the conservatory came a stifled groan, followed by the dull sound of a heavy fall. Everybody started up. The duchess stood motionless in horror. And with fear in his eyes, Lord Henry rushed through the flapping palms to find Dorian Gray lying face downwards on the tiled floor in a deathlike swoon.

He was carried at once into the blue drawing room and laid upon one of the sofas. After a short time, he came to himself and looked round with a dazed expression.

"What has happened?" he asked. "Oh! I remember. Am I safe here, Harry?" He began to tremble.

---

* The ancient Parthians had devised an offensive form a retreat by shooting arrows behind them on the advancing enemy.

“My dear Dorian,” answered Lord Henry, “you merely fainted. That was all. You must have overtired yourself. You had better not come down to dinner. I will take your place.”

“No, I will come down,” he said, struggling to his feet. “I would rather come down. I must not be alone.”

He went to his room and dressed. There was a wild recklessness of gaiety in his manner as he sat at table, but now and then a thrill of terror ran through him when he remembered that, pressed against the window of the conservatory, like a white handkerchief, he had seen the face of James Vane watching him.

CHAPTER

18

The next day he did not leave the house, and, indeed, spent most of the time in his own room, sick with a wild terror of dying, and yet indifferent to life itself. The consciousness of being hunted, snared, tracked down, had begun to dominate him. If the tapestry did but tremble in the wind, he shook. The dead leaves that were blown against the leaded panes seemed to him like his own wasted resolutions and wild regrets. When he closed his eyes, he saw again the sailor's face peering through the mist-stained glass, and horror seemed once more to lay its hand upon his heart.

But perhaps it had been only his fancy that had called vengeance out of the night and set the hideous shapes of punishment before him. Actual life was chaos, but there was something terribly logical in the imagination. It was the imagination that set remorse to dog the feet of sin. It was the imagination that made each crime bear its misshapen brood. In the common world of fact the wicked were not punished, nor the good rewarded. Success was given to the strong, failure thrust upon the weak. That was all. Besides, had any stranger been prowling round the house, he would have been seen by the servants or the keepers. Had any foot-marks been found on the flower-beds, the gardeners would have reported

it. Yes, it had been merely fancy. Sibyl Vane's brother had not come back to kill him. He had sailed away in his ship to founder in some winter sea. From him, at any rate, he was safe. Why, the man did not know who he was, could not know who he was. The mask of youth had saved him.

And yet if it had been merely an illusion, how terrible it was to think that conscience could raise such fearful phantoms, and give them visible form, and make them move before one! What sort of life would his be if, day and night, shadows of his crime were to peer at him from silent corners, to mock him from secret places, to whisper in his ear as he sat at the feast, to wake him with icy fingers as he lay asleep! As the thought crept through his brain, he grew pale with terror, and the air seemed to him to have become suddenly colder. Oh! in what a wild hour of madness he had killed his friend! How ghastly the mere memory of the scene! He saw it all again. Each hideous detail came back to him with added horror. Out of the black cave of time, terrible and swathed in scarlet, rose the image of his sin. When Lord Henry came in at six o'clock, he found him crying as one whose heart will break.

It was not till the third day that he ventured to go out. There was something in the clear, pine-scented air of that winter morning that seemed to bring him back his joyousness and his ardour for life. But it was not merely the physical conditions of environment that had caused the change. His own nature had revolted against the excess of anguish that had sought to maim and mar the perfection of its calm. With subtle and finely wrought temperaments it is always so. Their strong passions must either bruise or bend. They either slay the man, or themselves die. Shallow sorrows and shallow loves live on. The loves and sorrows that are great are destroyed by their own plenitude. Besides, he had convinced himself that he had been the victim of a terror-stricken imagination, and looked back now on his fears with something of pity and not a little of contempt.

After breakfast, he walked with the duchess for an hour in the garden and then drove across the park to join the shooting-party. The crisp frost lay like salt upon the grass. The sky was an inverted cup of blue metal. A thin film of ice bordered the flat, reed-grown lake.

At the corner of the pine-wood he caught sight of Sir Geoffrey Clouston, the duchess's brother, jerking two spent cartridges out of his gun. He jumped from the cart, and having told the groom to take the mare home, made his way towards his guest through the withered bracken and rough undergrowth.

"Have you had good sport, Geoffrey?" he asked.

"Not very good, Dorian. I think most of the birds have gone to the open. I dare say it will be better after lunch, when we get to new ground."

Dorian strolled along by his side. The keen aromatic air, the brown and red lights that glimmered in the wood, the hoarse cries of the beaters ringing out from time to time, and the sharp snaps of the guns that followed, fascinated him and filled him with a sense of delightful freedom. He was dominated by the carelessness of happiness, by the high indifference of joy.

Suddenly from a lumpy tussock of old grass some twenty yards in front of them, with black-tipped ears erect and long hinder limbs throwing it forward, started a hare. It bolted for a thicket of alders. Sir Geoffrey put his gun to his shoulder, but there was something in the animal's grace of movement that strangely charmed Dorian Gray, and he cried out at once, "Don't shoot it, Geoffrey. Let it live."

"What nonsense, Dorian!" laughed his companion, and as the hare bounded into the thicket, he fired. There were two cries heard, the cry of a hare in pain, which is dreadful, the cry of a man in agony, which is worse.

"Good heavens! I have hit a beater!" exclaimed Sir Geoffrey. "What an ass the man was to get in front of the guns! Stop shooting there!" he called out at the top of his voice. "A man is hurt."

The head-keeper came running up with a stick in his hand.

"Where, sir? Where is he?" he shouted. At the same time, the firing ceased along the line.

"Here," answered Sir Geoffrey angrily, hurrying towards the thicket. "Why on earth don't you keep your men back? Spoiled my shooting for the day."

Dorian watched them as they plunged into the alder-clump, brushing the lithe swinging branches aside. In a few moments they emerged, dragging a body after them into the sunlight. He turned

away in horror. It seemed to him that misfortune followed wherever he went. He heard Sir Geoffrey ask if the man was really dead, and the affirmative answer of the keeper. The wood seemed to him to have become suddenly alive with faces. There was the trampling of myriad feet and the low buzz of voices. A great copper-breasted pheasant came beating through the boughs overhead.

After a few moments—that were to him, in his perturbed state, like endless hours of pain—he felt a hand laid on his shoulder. He started and looked round.

"Dorian," said Lord Henry, "I had better tell them that the shooting is stopped for to-day. It would not look well to go on."

"I wish it were stopped for ever, Harry," he answered bitterly. "The whole thing is hideous and cruel. Is the man . . .?"

He could not finish the sentence.

"I am afraid so," rejoined Lord Henry. "He got the whole charge of shot in his chest. He must have died almost instantaneously. Come; let us go home."

They walked side by side in the direction of the avenue for nearly fifty yards without speaking. Then Dorian looked at Lord Henry and said, with a heavy sigh, "It is a bad omen, Harry, a very bad omen."

"What is?" asked Lord Henry. "Oh! this accident, I suppose. My dear fellow, it can't be helped. It was the man's own fault. Why did he get in front of the guns? Besides, it is nothing to us. It is rather awkward for Geoffrey, of course. It does not do to pepper beaters. It makes people think that one is a wild shot. And Geoffrey is not; he shoots very straight. But there is no use talking about the matter."

Dorian shook his head. "It is a bad omen, Harry. I feel as if something horrible were going to happen to some of us. To myself, perhaps," he added, passing his hand over his eyes, with a gesture of pain.

The elder man laughed. "The only horrible thing in the world is *ennui*, Dorian. That is the one sin for which there is no forgiveness. But we are not likely to suffer from it unless these fellows keep chattering about this thing at dinner. I must tell them that the subject is to be tabooed. As for omens, there is no such thing as an omen. Destiny does not send us heralds. She is too wise or too cruel for that. Besides, what on earth could happen to you, Dorian? You

have everything in the world that a man can want. There is no one who would not be delighted to change places with you."

"There is no one with whom I would not change places, Harry. Don't laugh like that. I am telling you the truth. The wretched peasant who has just died is better off than I am. I have no terror of death. It is the coming of death that terrifies me. Its monstrous wings seem to wheel in the leaden air around me. Good heavens! don't you see a man moving behind the trees there, watching me, waiting for me?"

Lord Henry looked in the direction in which the trembling gloved hand was pointing. "Yes," he said, smiling, "I see the gardener waiting for you. I suppose he wants to ask you what flowers you wish to have on the table to-night. How absurdly nervous you are, my dear fellow! You must come and see my doctor, when we get back to town."

Dorian heaved a sigh of relief as he saw the gardener approaching. The man touched his hat, glanced for a moment at Lord Henry in a hesitating manner, and then produced a letter, which he handed to his master. "Her Grace told me to wait for an answer," he murmured.

Dorian put the letter into his pocket. "Tell her Grace that I am coming in," he said, coldly. The man turned round and went rapidly in the direction of the house.

"How fond women are of doing dangerous things!" laughed Lord Henry. "It is one of the qualities in them that I admire most. A woman will flirt with anybody in the world as long as other people are looking on."

"How fond you are of saying dangerous things, Harry! In the present instance, you are quite astray. I like the duchess very much, but I don't love her."

"And the duchess loves you very much, but she likes you less, so you are excellently matched."

"You are talking scandal, Harry, and there is never any basis for scandal."

"The basis of every scandal is an immoral certainty," said Lord Henry, lighting a cigarette.

"You would sacrifice anybody, Harry, for the sake of an epigram."

"The world goes to the altar of its own accord," was the answer.

"I wish I could love," cried Dorian Gray with a deep note of pathos in his voice. "But I seem to have lost the passion and forgotten the desire. I am too much concentrated on myself. My own personality has become a burden to me. I want to escape, to go away, to forget. It was silly of me to come down here at all. I think I shall send a wire to Harvey to have the yacht got ready. On a yacht one is safe."

"Safe from what, Dorian? You are in some trouble. Why not tell me what it is? You know I would help you."

"I can't tell you, Harry," he answered sadly. "And I dare say it is only a fancy of mine. This unfortunate accident has upset me. I have a horrible presentiment that something of the kind may happen to me."

"What nonsense!"

"I hope it is, but I can't help feeling it. Ah! here is the duchess, looking like Artemis* in a tailor-made gown. You see we have come back, Duchess."

"I have heard all about it, Mr. Gray," she answered. "Poor Geoffrey is terribly upset. And it seems that you asked him not to shoot the hare. How curious!"

"Yes, it was very curious. I don't know what made me say it. Some whim, I suppose. It looked the loveliest of little live things. But I am sorry they told you about the man. It is a hideous subject."

"It is an annoying subject," broke in Lord Henry. "It has no psychological value at all. Now if Geoffrey had done the thing on purpose, how interesting he would be! I should like to know some one who had committed a real murder."

"How horrid of you, Harry!" cried the duchess. "Isn't it, Mr. Gray? Harry, Mr. Gray is ill again. He is going to faint."

Dorian drew himself up with an effort and smiled. "It is nothing, Duchess," he murmured; "my nerves are dreadfully out of order. That is all. I am afraid I walked too far this morning. I didn't hear what Harry said. Was it very bad? You must tell me some other time. I think I must go and lie down. You will excuse me, won't you?"

---

* A Greek goddess disguised as huntress.

They had reached the great flight of steps that led from the conservatory on to the terrace. As the glass door closed behind Dorian, Lord Henry turned and looked at the duchess with his slumberous eyes. "Are you very much in love with him?" he asked.

She did not answer for some time, but stood gazing at the landscape. "I wish I knew," she said at last.

He shook his head. "Knowledge would be fatal. It is the uncertainty that charms one. A mist makes things wonderful."

"One may lose one's way."

"All ways end at the same point, my dear Gladys."

"What is that?"

"Disillusion."

"It was my *debut* in life," she sighed.

"It came to you crowned."

"I am tired of strawberry leaves."

"They become you."

"Only in public."

"You would miss them," said Lord Henry.

"I will not part with a petal."

"Monmouth has ears."

"Old age is dull of hearing."

"Has he never been jealous?"

"I wish he had been."

He glanced about as if in search of something. "What are you looking for?" she inquired.

"The button from your foil," he answered. "You have dropped it."

She laughed. "I have still the mask."

"It makes your eyes lovelier," was his reply.

She laughed again. Her teeth showed like white seeds in a scarlet fruit.

Upstairs, in his own room, Dorian Gray was lying on a sofa, with terror in every tingling fibre of his body. Life had suddenly become too hideous a burden for him to bear. The dreadful death of the unlucky beater, shot in the thicket like a wild animal, had seemed to him to pre-figure death for himself also. He had nearly swooned at what Lord Henry had said in a chance mood of cynical jesting.

At five o'clock he rang his bell for his servant and gave him orders to pack his things for the night-express to town, and to have the brougham at the door by eight-thirty. He was determined not to sleep another night at Selby Royal. It was an ill-omened place. Death walked there in the sunlight. The grass of the forest had been spotted with blood.

Then he wrote a note to Lord Henry, telling him that he was going up to town to consult his doctor and asking him to entertain his guests in his absence. As he was putting it into the envelope, a knock came to the door, and his valet informed him that the head-keeper wished to see him. He frowned and bit his lip. "Send him in," he muttered, after some moments' hesitation.

As soon as the man entered, Dorian pulled his chequebook out of a drawer and spread it out before him.

"I suppose you have come about the unfortunate accident of this morning, Thornton?" he said, taking up a pen.

"Yes, sir," answered the gamekeeper.

"Was the poor fellow married? Had he any people dependent on him?" asked Dorian, looking bored. "If so, I should not like them to be left in want, and will send them any sum of money you may think necessary."

"We don't know who he is, sir. That is what I took the liberty of coming to you about."

"Don't know who he is?" said Dorian, listlessly. "What do you mean? Wasn't he one of your men?"

"No, sir. Never saw him before. Seems like a sailor, sir."

The pen dropped from Dorian Gray's hand, and he felt as if his heart had suddenly stopped beating. "A sailor?" he cried out. "Did you say a sailor?"

"Yes, sir. He looks as if he had been a sort of sailor; tattooed on both arms, and that kind of thing."

"Was there anything found on him?" said Dorian, leaning forward and looking at the man with startled eyes. "Anything that would tell his name?"

"Some money, sir—not much, and a six-shooter. There was no name of any kind. A decent-looking man, sir, but rough-like. A sort of sailor we think."

Dorian started to his feet. A terrible hope fluttered past him. He clutched at it madly. "Where is the body?" he exclaimed. "Quick! I must see it at once."

"It is in an empty stable in the Home Farm, sir. The folk don't like to have that sort of thing in their houses. They say a corpse brings bad luck."

"The Home Farm! Go there at once and meet me. Tell one of the grooms to bring my horse round. No. Never mind. I'll go to the stables myself. It will save time."

In less than a quarter of an hour, Dorian Gray was galloping down the long avenue as hard as he could go. The trees seemed to sweep past him in spectral procession, and wild shadows to fling themselves across his path. Once the mare swerved at a white gate-post and nearly threw him. He lashed her across the neck with his crop. She cleft the dusky air like an arrow. The stones flew from her hoofs.

At last he reached the Home Farm. Two men were loitering in the yard. He leaped from the saddle and threw the reins to one of them. In the farthest stable a light was glimmering. Something seemed to tell him that the body was there, and he hurried to the door and put his hand upon the latch.

There he paused for a moment, feeling that he was on the brink of a discovery that would either make or mar his life. Then he thrust the door open and entered.

On a heap of sacking in the far corner was lying the dead body of a man dressed in a coarse shirt and a pair of blue trousers. A spotted handkerchief had been placed over the face. A coarse candle, stuck in a bottle, sputtered beside it.

Dorian Gray shuddered. He felt that his could not be the hand to take the handkerchief away, and called out to one of the farm-servants to come to him.

"Take that thing off the face. I wish to see it," he said, clutching at the door-post for support.

When the farm-servant had done so, he stepped forward. A cry of joy broke from his lips. The man who had been shot in the thicket was James Vane.

He stood there for some minutes looking at the dead body. As he rode home, his eyes were full of tears, for he knew he was safe.

CHAPTER

19

"There is no use your telling me that you are going to be good," cried Lord Henry, dipping his white fingers into a red copper bowl filled with rose-water. "You are quite perfect. Pray, don't change."

Dorian Gray shook his head. "No, Harry, I have done too many dreadful things in my life. I am not going to do any more. I began my good actions yesterday."

"Where were you yesterday?"

"In the country, Harry. I was staying at a little inn by myself."

"My dear boy," said Lord Henry, smiling, "anybody can be good in the country. There are no temptations there. That is the reason why people who live out of town are so absolutely uncivilized. Civilization is not by any means an easy thing to attain to. There are only two ways by which man can reach it. One is by being cultured, the other by being corrupt. Country people have no opportunity of being either, so they stagnate."

"Culture and corruption," echoed Dorian. "I have known something of both. It seems terrible to me now that they should ever be found together. For I have a new ideal, Harry. I am going to alter. I think I have altered."

"You have not yet told me what your good action was. Or did you say you had done more than one?" asked his companion as he spilled into his plate a little crimson pyramid of seeded strawberries and, through a perforated, shell-shaped spoon, snowed white sugar upon them.

"I can tell you, Harry. It is not a story I could tell to any one else. I spared somebody. It sounds vain, but you understand what I mean. She was quite beautiful and wonderfully like Sibyl Vane. I think it was that which first attracted me to her. You remember Sibyl, don't you? How long ago that seems! Well, Hetty was not one of our own class, of course. She was simply a girl in a village. But I really loved her. I am quite sure that I loved her. All during this wonderful May that we have been having, I used to run down and see her two or three times a week. Yesterday she met me in a little orchard. The apple-blossoms kept tumbling down on her hair, and she was laughing. We were to have gone away together this morning at dawn. Suddenly I determined to leave her as flowerlike as I had found her."

"I should think the novelty of the emotion must have given you a thrill of real pleasure, Dorian," interrupted Lord Henry. "But I can finish your idyll for you. You gave her good advice and broke her heart. That was the beginning of your reformation."

"Harry, you are horrible! You mustn't say these dreadful things. Hetty's heart is not broken. Of course, she cried and all that. But there is no disgrace upon her. She can live, like Perdita, in her garden of mint and marigold."

"And weep over a faithless Florizel," said Lord Henry, laughing, as he leaned back in his chair. "My dear Dorian, you have the most curiously boyish moods. Do you think this girl will ever be really content now with any one of her own rank? I suppose she will be married some day to a rough carter or a grinning ploughman. Well, the fact of having met you, and loved you, will teach her to despise her husband, and she will be wretched. From a moral point of view, I cannot say that I think much of your great renunciation. Even as a beginning, it is poor. Besides, how do you know that Hetty isn't floating at the present moment in some starlit mill-pond, with lovely water-lilies round her, like Ophelia?"

"I can't bear this, Harry! You mock at everything, and then suggest the most serious tragedies. I am sorry I told you now. I don't care what you say to me. I know I was right in acting as I did. Poor Hetty! As I rode past the farm this morning, I saw her white face at the window, like a spray of jasmine. Don't let us talk about it any more, and don't try to persuade me that the first good action I have done for years, the first little bit of self-sacrifice I have ever known, is really a sort of sin. I want to be better. I am going to be better. Tell me something about yourself. What is going on in town? I have not been to the club for days."

"The people are still discussing poor Basil's disappearance."

"I should have thought they had got tired of that by this time," said Dorian, pouring himself out some wine and frowning slightly.

"My dear boy, they have only been talking about it for six weeks, and the British public are really not equal to the mental strain of having more than one topic every three months. They have been very fortunate lately, however. They have had my own divorce-case and Alan Campbell's suicide. Now they have got the mysterious disappearance of an artist. Scotland Yard still insists that the man in the grey ulster who left for Paris by the midnight train on the ninth of November was poor Basil, and the French police declare that Basil never arrived in Paris at all. I suppose in about a fortnight we shall be told that he has been seen in San Francisco. It is an odd thing, but every one who disappears is said to be seen at San Francisco. It must be a delightful city, and possess all the attractions of the next world."

"What do you think has happened to Basil?" asked Dorian, holding up his Burgundy against the light and wondering how it was that he could discuss the matter so calmly.

"I have not the slightest idea. If Basil chooses to hide himself, it is no business of mine. If he is dead, I don't want to think about him. Death is the only thing that ever terrifies me. I hate it."

"Why?" said the younger man wearily.

"Because," said Lord Henry, passing beneath his nostrils the gilt trellis of an open vinaigrette box, "one can survive everything nowadays except that. Death and vulgarity are the only two facts in the nineteenth century that one cannot explain away. Let us have our

coffee in the music room, Dorian. You must play Chopin to me. The man with whom my wife ran away played Chopin exquisitely. Poor Victoria! I was very fond of her. The house is rather lonely without her. Of course, married life is merely a habit, a bad habit. But then one regrets the loss even of one's worst habits. Perhaps one regrets them the most. They are such an essential part of one's personality."

Dorian said nothing, but rose from the table, and passing into the next room, sat down to the piano and let his fingers stray across the white and black ivory of the keys. After the coffee had been brought in, he stopped, and looking over at Lord Henry, said, "Harry, did it ever occur to you that Basil was murdered?"

Lord Henry yawned. "Basil was very popular, and always wore a Waterbury watch.* Why should he have been murdered? He was not clever enough to have enemies. Of course, he had a wonderful genius for painting. But a man can paint like Velasquez† and yet be as dull as possible. Basil was really rather dull. He only interested me once, and that was when he told me, years ago, that he had a wild adoration for you and that you were the dominant motive of his art."

"I was very fond of Basil," said Dorian with a note of sadness in his voice. "But don't people say that he was murdered?"

"Oh, some of the papers do. It does not seem to me to be at all probable. I know there are dreadful places in Paris, but Basil was not the sort of man to have gone to them. He had no curiosity. It was his chief defect."

"What would you say, Harry, if I told you that I had murdered Basil?" said the younger man. He watched him intently after he had spoken.

"I would say, my dear fellow, that you were posing for a character that doesn't suit you. All crime is vulgar, just as all vulgarity is crime. It is not in you, Dorian, to commit a murder. I am sorry if I hurt your vanity by saying so, but I assure you it is true. Crime belongs exclusively to the lower orders. I don't blame them in the smallest degree. I should fancy that crime was to them what art is to us, simply a method of procuring extraordinary sensations."

---

* A cheap American pocket watch, hardly worth stealing.
† Spanish painter Diego de Silva y Velasquez (1599-1660).

"A method of procuring sensations? Do you think, then, that a man who has once committed a murder could possibly do the same crime again? Don't tell me that."

"Oh! anything becomes a pleasure if one does it too often," cried Lord Henry, laughing. "That is one of the most important secrets of life. I should fancy, however, that murder is always a mistake. One should never do anything that one cannot talk about after dinner. But let us pass from poor Basil. I wish I could believe that he had come to such a really romantic end as you suggest, but I can't. I dare say he fell into the Seine off an omnibus and that the conductor hushed up the scandal. Yes: I should fancy that was his end. I see him lying now on his back under those dull-green waters, with the heavy barges floating over him and long weeds catching in his hair. Do you know, I don't think he would have done much more good work. During the last ten years his painting had gone off very much."

Dorian heaved a sigh, and Lord Henry strolled across the room and began to stroke the head of a curious Java parrot, a large, grey-plumaged bird with pink crest and tail, that was balancing itself upon a bamboo perch. As his pointed fingers touched it, it dropped the white scurf of crinkled lids over black, glasslike eyes and began to sway backwards and forwards.

"Yes," he continued, turning round and taking his handkerchief out of his pocket; "his painting had quite gone off. It seemed to me to have lost something. It had lost an ideal. When you and he ceased to be great friends, he ceased to be a great artist. What was it separated you? I suppose he bored you. If so, he never forgave you. It's a habit bores have. By the way, what has become of that wonderful portrait he did of you? I don't think I have ever seen it since he finished it. Oh! I remember your telling me years ago that you had sent it down to Selby, and that it had got mislaid or stolen on the way. You never got it back? What a pity! it was really a masterpiece. I remember I wanted to buy it. I wish I had now. It belonged to Basil's best period. Since then, his work was that curious mixture of bad painting and good intentions that always entitles a man to be called a representative British artist. Did you advertise for it? You should."

"I forget," said Dorian. "I suppose I did. But I never really liked it. I am sorry I sat for it. The memory of the thing is hateful to me. Why do you talk of it? It used to remind me of those curious lines in some play—*Hamlet*, I think—how do they run?—

"Like the painting of a sorrow,
A face without a heart."

Yes: that is what it was like."

Lord Henry laughed. "If a man treats life artistically, his brain is his heart," he answered, sinking into an armchair.

Dorian Gray shook his head and struck some soft chords on the piano. "'Like the painting of a sorrow,'" he repeated, "'a face without a heart.'"

The elder man lay back and looked at him with half-closed eyes. "By the way, Dorian," he said after a pause, "what does it profit a man if he gain the whole world and lose—how does the quotation run?—his own soul?"*

The music jarred, and Dorian Gray started and stared at his friend. "Why do you ask me that, Harry?"

"My dear fellow," said Lord Henry, elevating his eyebrows in surprise, "I asked you because I thought you might be able to give me an answer. That is all. I was going through the park last Sunday, and close by the Marble Arch there stood a little crowd of shabby-looking people listening to some vulgar street-preacher. As I passed by, I heard the man yelling out that question to his audience. It struck me as being rather dramatic. London is very rich in curious effects of that kind. A wet Sunday, an uncouth Christian in a mackintosh, a ring of sickly white faces under a broken roof of dripping umbrellas, and a wonderful phrase flung into the air by shrill hysterical lips—it was really very good in its way, quite a suggestion. I thought of telling the prophet that art had a soul, but that man had not. I am afraid, however, he would not have understood me."

"Don't, Harry. The soul is a terrible reality. It can be bought, and

* As in *Mark* 8: 36 and *Matthew* 16: 26.

sold, and bartered away. It can be poisoned, or made perfect. There is a soul in each one of us. I know it."

"Do you feel quite sure of that, Dorian?"

"Quite sure."

"Ah! then it must be an illusion. The things one feels absolutely certain about are never true. That is the fatality of faith, and the lesson of romance. How grave you are! Don't be so serious. What have you or I to do with the superstitions of our age? No: we have given up our belief in the soul. Play me something. Play me a nocturne, Dorian, and, as you play, tell me, in a low voice, how you have kept your youth. You must have some secret. I am only ten years older than you are, and I am wrinkled, and worn, and yellow. You are really wonderful, Dorian. You have never looked more charming than you do to-night. You remind me of the day I saw you first. You were rather cheeky, very shy, and absolutely extraordinary. You have changed, of course, but not in appearance. I wish you would tell me your secret. To get back my youth I would do anything in the world, except take exercise, get up early, or be respectable. Youth! There is nothing like it. It's absurd to talk of the ignorance of youth. The only people to whose opinions I listen now with any respect are people much younger than myself. They seem in front of me. Life has revealed to them her latest wonder. As for the aged, I always contradict the aged. I do it on principle. If you ask them their opinion on something that happened yesterday, they solemnly give you the opinions current in 1820, when people wore high stocks,* believed in everything, and knew absolutely nothing. How lovely that thing you are playing is! I wonder, did Chopin write it at Majorca, with the sea weeping round the villa and the salt spray dashing against the panes? It is marvellously romantic. What a blessing it is that there is one art left to us that is not imitative! Don't stop. I want music to-night. It seems to me that you are the young Apollo and that I am Marsyas listening to you.† I have sorrows, Dorian, of my own, that even you know nothing of. The tragedy of old age is not that

---

* Stiff neck-bands were fashionable for men in the early 19th century.

† Marsyas in Greek mythology was a Phrygian flute player who challenged Apollo for musical skills – and lost; thus symbolising the victory of the Greek over 'Phrygian mode'.

one is old, but that one is young. I am amazed sometimes at my own sincerity. Ah, Dorian, how happy you are! What an exquisite life you have had! You have drunk deeply of everything. You have crushed the grapes against your palate. Nothing has been hidden from you. And it has all been to you no more than the sound of music. It has not marred you. You are still the same."

"I am not the same, Harry."

"Yes, you are the same. I wonder what the rest of your life will be. Don't spoil it by renunciations. At present you are a perfect type. Don't make yourself incomplete. You are quite flawless now. You need not shake your head: you know you are. Besides, Dorian, don't deceive yourself. Life is not governed by will or intention. Life is a question of nerves, and fibres, and slowly built-up cells in which thought hides itself and passion has its dreams. You may fancy yourself safe and think yourself strong. But a chance tone of colour in a room or a morning sky, a particular perfume that you had once loved and that brings subtle memories with it, a line from a forgotten poem that you had come across again, a cadence from a piece of music that you had ceased to play—I tell you, Dorian, that it is on things like these that our lives depend. Browning writes about that somewhere; but our own senses will imagine them for us. There are moments when the odour of *lilas blanc** passes suddenly across me, and I have to live the strangest month of my life over again. I wish I could change places with you, Dorian. The world has cried out against us both, but it has always worshipped you. It always will worship you. You are the type of what the age is searching for, and what it is afraid it has found. I am so glad that you have never done anything, never carved a statue, or painted a picture, or produced anything outside of yourself! Life has been your art. You have set yourself to music. Your days are your sonnets."

Dorian rose up from the piano and passed his hand through his hair. "Yes, life has been exquisite," he murmured, "but I am not going to have the same life, Harry. And you must not say these extravagant things to me. You don't know everything about me. I

---

* (Fr.) White lilac.

think that if you did, even you would turn from me. You laugh. Don't laugh."

"Why have you stopped playing, Dorian? Go back and give me the nocturne over again. Look at that great, honey-coloured moon that hangs in the dusky air. She is waiting for you to charm her, and if you play she will come closer to the earth. You won't? Let us go to the club, then. It has been a charming evening, and we must end it charmingly. There is some one at White's who wants immensely to know you—young Lord Poole, Bournemouth's eldest son. He has already copied your neckties, and has begged me to introduce him to you. He is quite delightful and rather reminds me of you."

"I hope not," said Dorian with a sad look in his eyes. "But I am tired to-night, Harry. I shan't go to the club. It is nearly eleven, and I want to go to bed early."

"Do stay. You have never played so well as to-night. There was something in your touch that was wonderful. It had more expression than I had ever heard from it before."

"It is because I am going to be good," he answered, smiling. "I am a little changed already."

"You cannot change to me, Dorian," said Lord Henry. "You and I will always be friends."

"Yet you poisoned me with a book once. I should not forgive that. Harry, promise me that you will never lend that book to any one. It does harm."

"My dear boy, you are really beginning to moralize. You will soon be going about like the converted, and the revivalist, warning people against all the sins of which you have grown tired. You are much too delightful to do that. Besides, it is no use. You and I are what we are, and will be what we will be. As for being poisoned by a book, there is no such thing as that. Art has no influence upon action. It annihilates the desire to act. It is superbly sterile. The books that the world calls immoral are books that show the world its own shame. That is all. But we won't discuss literature. Come round to-morrow. I am going to ride at eleven. We might go together, and I will take you to lunch afterwards with Lady Branksome. She is a charming woman, and wants to consult you about some tapestries she is thinking of buying. Mind you come. Or shall we lunch with

our little duchess? She says she never sees you now. Perhaps you are tired of Gladys? I thought you would be. Her clever tongue gets on one's nerves. Well, in any case, be here at eleven."

"Must I really come, Harry?"

"Certainly. The park is quite lovely now. I don't think there have been such lilacs since the year I met you."

"Very well. I shall be here at eleven," said Dorian. "Good night, Harry." As he reached the door, he hesitated for a moment, as if he had something more to say. Then he sighed and went out.

CHAPTER

20

It was a lovely night, so warm that he threw his coat over his arm and did not even put his silk scarf round his throat. As he strolled home, smoking his cigarette, two young men in evening dress passed him. He heard one of them whisper to the other, "That is Dorian Gray." He remembered how pleased he used to be when he was pointed out, or stared at, or talked about. He was tired of hearing his own name now. Half the charm of the little village where he had been so often lately was that no one knew who he was. He had often told the girl whom he had lured to love him that he was poor, and she had believed him. He had told her once that he was wicked, and she had laughed at him and answered that wicked people were always very old and very ugly. What a laugh she had!—just like a thrush singing. And how pretty she had been in her cotton dresses and her large hats! She knew nothing, but she had everything that he had lost.

When he reached home, he found his servant waiting up for him. He sent him to bed, and threw himself down on the sofa in the library, and began to think over some of the things that Lord Henry had said to him.

Was it really true that one could never change? He felt a wild longing for the unstained purity of his boyhood—his

rose-white boyhood, as Lord Henry had once called it. He knew that he had tarnished himself, filled his mind with corruption and given horror to his fancy; that he had been an evil influence to others, and had experienced a terrible joy in being so; and that of the lives that had crossed his own, it had been the fairest and the most full of promise that he had brought to shame. But was it all irretrievable? Was there no hope for him?

Ah! in what a monstrous moment of pride and passion he had prayed that the portrait should bear the burden of his days, and he keep the unsullied splendour of eternal youth! All his failure had been due to that. Better for him that each sin of his life had brought its sure swift penalty along with it. There was purification in punishment. Not "Forgive us our sins" but "Smite us for our iniquities" should be the prayer of man to a most just God.

The curiously carved mirror that Lord Henry had given to him, so many years ago now, was standing on the table, and the white-limbed Cupids laughed round it as of old. He took it up, as he had done on that night of horror when he had first noted the change in the fatal picture, and with wild, tear-dimmed eyes looked into its polished shield. Once, some one who had terribly loved him had written to him a mad letter, ending with these idolatrous words: "The world is changed because you are made of ivory and gold. The curves of your lips rewrite history." The phrases came back to his memory, and he repeated them over and over to himself. Then he loathed his own beauty, and flinging the mirror on the floor, crushed it into silver splinters beneath his heel. It was his beauty that had ruined him, his beauty and the youth that he had prayed for. But for those two things, his life might have been free from stain. His beauty had been to him but a mask, his youth but a mockery. What was youth at best? A green, an unripe time, a time of shallow moods, and sickly thoughts. Why had he worn its livery? Youth had spoiled him.

It was better not to think of the past. Nothing could alter that. It was of himself, and of his own future, that he had to think. James Vane was hidden in a nameless grave in Selby churchyard. Alan Campbell had shot himself one night in his laboratory, but had not revealed the secret that he had been forced to know. The excitement,

such as it was, over Basil Hallward's disappearance would soon pass away. It was already waning. He was perfectly safe there. Nor, indeed, was it the death of Basil Hallward that weighed most upon his mind. It was the living death of his own soul that troubled him. Basil had painted the portrait that had marred his life. He could not forgive him that. It was the portrait that had done everything. Basil had said things to him that were unbearable, and that he had yet borne with patience. The murder had been simply the madness of a moment. As for Alan Campbell, his suicide had been his own act. He had chosen to do it. It was nothing to him.

A new life! That was what he wanted. That was what he was waiting for. Surely he had begun it already. He had spared one innocent thing, at any rate. He would never again tempt innocence. He would be good.

As he thought of Hetty Merton, he began to wonder if the portrait in the locked room had changed. Surely it was not still so horrible as it had been? Perhaps if his life became pure, he would be able to expel every sign of evil passion from the face. Perhaps the signs of evil had already gone away. He would go and look.

He took the lamp from the table and crept upstairs. As he unbarred the door, a smile of joy flitted across his strangely young-looking face and lingered for a moment about his lips. Yes, he would be good, and the hideous thing that he had hidden away would no longer be a terror to him. He felt as if the load had been lifted from him already.

He went in quietly, locking the door behind him, as was his custom, and dragged the purple hanging from the portrait. A cry of pain and indignation broke from him. He could see no change, save that in the eyes there was a look of cunning and in the mouth the curved wrinkle of the hypocrite. The thing was still loathsome—more loathsome, if possible, than before—and the scarlet dew that spotted the hand seemed brighter, and more like blood newly spilled. Then he trembled. Had it been merely vanity that had made him do his one good deed? Or the desire for a new sensation, as Lord Henry had hinted, with his mocking laugh? Or that passion to act a part that sometimes makes us do things finer than we are ourselves? Or, perhaps, all these? And why was the red stain larger than it had been?

It seemed to have crept like a horrible disease over the wrinkled fingers. There was blood on the painted feet, as though the thing had dripped—blood even on the hand that had not held the knife. Confess? Did it mean that he was to confess? To give himself up and be put to death? He laughed. He felt that the idea was monstrous. Besides, even if he did confess, who would believe him? There was no trace of the murdered man anywhere. Everything belonging to him had been destroyed. He himself had burned what had been below-stairs. The world would simply say that he was mad. They would shut him up if he persisted in his story . . . Yet it was his duty to confess, to suffer public shame, and to make public atonement. There was a God who called upon men to tell their sins to earth as well as to heaven. Nothing that he could do would cleanse him till he had told his own sin. His sin? He shrugged his shoulders. The death of Basil Hallward seemed very little to him. He was thinking of Hetty Merton. For it was an unjust mirror, this mirror of his soul that he was looking at. Vanity? Curiosity? Hypocrisy? Had there been nothing more in his renunciation than that? There had been something more. At least he thought so. But who could tell? . . . No. There had been nothing more. Through vanity he had spared her. In hypocrisy he had worn the mask of goodness. For curiosity's sake he had tried the denial of self. He recognized that now.

But this murder—was it to dog him all his life? Was he always to be burdened by his past? Was he really to confess? Never. There was only one bit of evidence left against him. The picture itself—that was evidence. He would destroy it. Why had he kept it so long? Once it had given him pleasure to watch it changing and growing old. Of late he had felt no such pleasure. It had kept him awake at night. When he had been away, he had been filled with terror lest other eyes should look upon it. It had brought melancholy across his passions. Its mere memory had marred many moments of joy. It had been like conscience to him. Yes, it had been conscience. He would destroy it.

He looked round and saw the knife that had stabbed Basil Hallward. He had cleaned it many times, till there was no stain left upon it. It was bright, and glistened. As it had killed the painter, so it would kill the painter's work, and all that that meant. It would kill

the past, and when that was dead, he would be free. It would kill this monstrous soul-life, and without its hideous warnings, he would be at peace. He seized the thing, and stabbed the picture with it.

There was a cry heard, and a crash. The cry was so horrible in its agony that the frightened servants woke and crept out of their rooms. Two gentlemen, who were passing in the square below, stopped and looked up at the great house. They walked on till they met a policeman and brought him back. The man rang the bell several times, but there was no answer. Except for a light in one of the top windows, the house was all dark. After a time, he went away and stood in an adjoining portico and watched.

"Whose house is that, Constable?" asked the elder of the two gentlemen.

"Mr. Dorian Gray's, sir," answered the policeman.

They looked at each other, as they walked away, and sneered. One of them was Sir Henry Ashton's uncle.

Inside, in the servants' part of the house, the half-clad domestics were talking in low whispers to each other. Old Mrs. Leaf was crying and wringing her hands. Francis was as pale as death.

After about a quarter of an hour, he got the coachman and one of the footmen and crept upstairs. They knocked, but there was no reply. They called out. Everything was still. Finally, after vainly trying to force the door, they got on the roof and dropped down on to the balcony. The windows yielded easily—their bolts were old.

When they entered, they found hanging upon the wall a splendid portrait of their master as they had last seen him, in all the wonder of his exquisite youth and beauty. Lying on the floor was a dead man, in evening dress, with a knife in his heart. He was withered, wrinkled, and loathsome of visage. It was not till they had examined the rings that they recognized who it was.

The Importance of Being Earnest

CHARACTERS

John Worthing, J.P.
Algernon Moncrieff
Rev. Canon Chasuble, D.D.

Cecily Cardew
Miss Prism, *(Governess)*

Lane, *(Manservant)*
Lady Bracknell
Hon. Gwendolen Fairfax
Merriman, *(Butler)*

THE SCENES OF THE PLAY

ACT I

Algernon Moncrieff's Flat in Half-Moon Street, W.

ACT II

The Garden at the Manor House, Woolton.

ACT III

Drawing-Room at the Manor House, Woolton.

TIME: The Present. PLACE: London

Act

1

SCENE—*Morning-room in* ALGERNON'S *flat in Half-Moon Street. The room is luxuriously and artistically furnished. The sound of a piano is heard in the adjoining room.* (LANE *is arranging afternoon tea on the table, and after the music has ceased,* ALGERNON *enters.*)

ALGERNON

Did you hear what I was playing, Lane?

LANE

I didn't think it polite to listen, sir.

ALGERNON

I'm sorry for that, for your sake. I don't play accurately—any one can play accurately—but I play with wonderful expression. As far as the piano is concerned, sentiment is my forte. I keep science for Life.

LANE

Yes, sir.

ALGERNON

And, speaking of the science of Life, have you got the cucumber sandwiches cut for Lady Bracknell?

LANE

Yes, sir. (*Hands them on a salver.*)

ALGERNON

(*Inspects them, takes two, and sits down on the sofa.*) Oh! . . . by the way, Lane, I see from your book that on Thursday night, when Lord Shoreman and Mr. Worthing were dining with me, eight bottles of champagne are entered as having been consumed.

LANE

Yes, sir; eight bottles and a pint.

ALGERNON

Why is it that at a bachelor's establishment the servants invariably drink the champagne? I ask merely for information.

LANE

I attribute it to the superior quality of the wine, sir. I have often observed that in married households the champagne is rarely of a first-rate brand.

ALGERNON

Good heavens! Is marriage so demoralising as that?

LANE

I believe it *is* a very pleasant state, sir. I have had very little experience of it myself up to the present. I have only been married once. That was in consequence of a misunderstanding between myself and a young person.

ALGERNON

(*Languidly.*) I don't know that I am much interested in your family life, Lane.

LANE

No, sir; it is not a very interesting subject. I never think of it myself.

ALGERNON

Very natural, I am sure. That will do, Lane, thank you.

LANE

Thank you, sir. (LANE *goes out.*)

ALGERNON

Lane's views on marriage seem somewhat lax. Really, if the lower orders don't set us a good example, what on earth is the

use of them? They seem, as a class, to have absolutely no sense of moral responsibility.

(*Enter* LANE.)

LANE

Mr. Ernest Worthing.

(*Enter* JACK. LANE *goes out.*)

ALGERNON

How are you, my dear Ernest? What brings you up to town?

JACK

Oh, pleasure, pleasure! What else should bring one anywhere? Eating as usual, I see, Algy!

ALGERNON

(*Stiffly.*) I believe it is customary in good society to take some slight refreshment at five o'clock. Where have you been since last Thursday?

JACK

(*Sitting down on the sofa.*) In the country.

ALGERNON

What on earth do you do there?

JACK

(*Pulling off his gloves.*) When one is in town one amuses oneself. When one is in the country one amuses other people. It is excessively boring.

ALGERNON

And who are the people you amuse?

JACK

(*Airily.*) Oh, neighbours, neighbours.

ALGERNON

Got nice neighbours in your part of Shropshire?

JACK

Perfectly horrid! Never speak to one of them.

ALGERNON

How immensely you must amuse them! (*Goes over and takes sandwich.*) By the way, Shropshire is your county, is it not?

JACK

Eh? Shropshire? Yes, of course. Hallo! Why all these cups? Why cucumber sandwiches? Why such reckless extravagance in one so young? Who is coming to tea?

ALGERNON

Oh! merely Aunt Augusta and Gwendolen.

JACK

How perfectly delightful!

ALGERNON

Yes, that is all very well; but I am afraid Aunt Augusta won't quite approve of your being here.

JACK

May I ask why?

ALGERNON

My dear fellow, the way you flirt with Gwendolen is perfectly disgraceful. It is almost as bad as the way Gwendolen flirts with you.

JACK

I am in love with Gwendolen. I have come up to town expressly to propose to her.

ALGERNON

I thought you had come up for pleasure? . . . I call that business.

JACK

How utterly unromantic you are!

ALGERNON

I really don't see anything romantic in proposing. It is very romantic to be in love. But there is nothing romantic about a definite proposal. Why, one may be accepted. One usually is, I believe. Then the excitement is all over. The very essence of romance is uncertainty. If ever I get married, I'll certainly try to forget the fact.

JACK

I have no doubt about that, dear Algy. The Divorce Court was specially invented for people whose memories are so curiously constituted.

ALGERNON

Oh! there is no use speculating on that subject. Divorces are made in Heaven—(JACK *puts out his hand to take a sandwich.* ALGERNON *at once interferes.*) Please don't touch the cucumber sandwiches. They are ordered specially for Aunt Augusta. (*Takes one and eats it.*)

JACK

Well, you have been eating them all the time.

ALGERNON

That is quite a different matter. She is my aunt. (*Takes plate from below.*) Have some bread and butter. The bread and butter is for Gwendolen. Gwendolen is devoted to bread and butter.

JACK

(*Advancing to table and helping himself.*) And very good bread and butter it is too.

ALGERNON

Well, my dear fellow, you need not eat as if you were going to eat it all. You behave as if you were married to her already. You are not married to her already, and I don't think you ever will be.

JACK

Why on earth do you say that?

ALGERNON

Well, in the first place girls never marry the men they flirt with. Girls don't think it right.

JACK

Oh, that is nonsense!

ALGERNON

It isn't. It is a great truth. It accounts for the extraordinary number of bachelors that one sees all over the place. In the second place, I don't give my consent.

JACK

Your consent!

ALGERNON

My dear fellow, Gwendolen is my first cousin. And before I allow you to marry her, you will have to clear up the whole question of Cecily. (*Rings bell.*)

JACK

Cecily! What on earth do you mean? What do you mean, Algy, by Cecily! I don't know any one of the name of Cecily.

(*Enter* LANE.)

ALGERNON

Bring me that cigarette case Mr. Worthing left in the smoking-room the last time he dined here.

LANE

Yes, sir. (LANE *goes out.*)

JACK

Do you mean to say you have had my cigarette case all this time? I wish to goodness you had let me know. I have been writing frantic letters to Scotland Yard about it. I was very nearly offering a large reward.

ALGERNON

Well, I wish you would offer one. I happen to be more than usually hard up.

JACK

There is no good offering a large reward now that the thing is found.

(*Enter* LANE *with the cigarette case on a salver.* ALGERNON *takes it at once.* LANE *goes out.*)

ALGERNON

I think that is rather mean of you, Ernest, I must say. (*Opens case and examines it.*) However, it makes no matter, for, now that I look at the inscription inside, I find that the thing isn't yours after all.

JACK

Of course it's mine. (*Moving to him.*) You have seen me with it a hundred times, and you have no right whatsoever to read what is written inside. It is a very ungentlemanly thing to read a private cigarette case.

ALGERNON

Oh! it is absurd to have a hard and fast rule about what one

should read and what one shouldn't. More than half of modern culture depends on what one shouldn't read.

JACK

I am quite aware of the fact, and I don't propose to discuss modern culture. It isn't the sort of thing one should talk of in private. I simply want my cigarette case back.

ALGERNON

Yes; but this isn't your cigarette case. This cigarette case is a present from some one of the name of Cecily, and you said you didn't know any one of that name.

JACK

Well, if you want to know, Cecily happens to be my aunt.

ALGERNON

Your aunt!

JACK

Yes. Charming old lady she is, too. Lives at Tunbridge Wells. Just give it back to me, Algy.

ALGERNON

(*Retreating to back of sofa.*) But why does she call herself little Cecily if she is your aunt and lives at Tunbridge Wells? (Reading.) 'From little Cecily with her fondest love.'

JACK

(*Moving to sofa and kneeling upon it.*) My dear fellow, what on earth is there in that? Some aunts are tall, some aunts are not tall. That is a matter that surely an aunt may be allowed to decide for herself. You seem to think that every aunt should be exactly like your aunt! That is absurd! For Heaven's sake give me back my cigarette case. (*Follows* ALGERNON *round the room.*)

ALGERNON

Yes. But why does your aunt call you her uncle? 'From little Cecily, with her fondest love to her dear Uncle Jack.' There is no objection, I admit, to an aunt being a small aunt, but why an aunt, no matter what her size may be, should call her own nephew her uncle, I can't quite make out. Besides, your name isn't Jack at all; it is Ernest.

JACK

It isn't Ernest; it's Jack.

ALGERNON

You have always told me it was Ernest. I have introduced you to every one as Ernest. You answer to the name of Ernest. You look as if your name was Ernest. You are the most earnest-looking person I ever saw in my life. It is perfectly absurd your saying that your name isn't Ernest. It's on your cards. Here is one of them. (*Taking it from case.*) 'Mr. Ernest Worthing, B. 4, The Albany.' I'll keep this as a proof that your name is Ernest if ever you attempt to deny it to me, or to Gwendolen, or to any one else. (*Puts the card in his pocket.*)

JACK

Well, my name is Ernest in town and Jack in the country, and the cigarette case was given to me in the country.

ALGERNON

Yes, but that does not account for the fact that your small Aunt Cecily, who lives at Tunbridge Wells, calls you her dear uncle. Come, old boy, you had much better have the thing out at once.

JACK

My dear Algy, you talk exactly as if you were a dentist. It is very vulgar to talk like a dentist when one isn't a dentist. It produces a false impression.

ALGERNON

Well, that is exactly what dentists always do. Now, go on! Tell me the whole thing. I may mention that I have always suspected you of being a confirmed and secret Bunburyist; and I am quite sure of it now.

JACK

Bunburyist? What on earth do you mean by a Bunburyist?

ALGERNON

I'll reveal to you the meaning of that incomparable expression as soon as you are kind enough to inform me why you are Ernest in town and Jack in the country.

JACK

Well, produce my cigarette case first.

ALGERNON

Here it is. (*Hands cigarette case.*) Now produce your explanation, and pray make it improbable. (*Sits on sofa.*)

JACK

My dear fellow, there is nothing improbable about my explanation at all. In fact it's perfectly ordinary. Old Mr. Thomas Cardew, who adopted me when I was a little boy, made me in his will guardian to his grand-daughter, Miss Cecily Cardew. Cecily, who addresses me as her uncle from motives of respect that you could not possibly appreciate, lives at my place in the country under the charge of her admirable governess, Miss Prism.

ALGERNON

Where is that place in the country, by the way?

JACK

That is nothing to you, dear boy. You are not going to be invited . . . I may tell you candidly that the place is not in Shropshire.

ALGERNON

I suspected that, my dear fellow! I have Bunburyed all over Shropshire on two separate occasions. Now, go on. Why are you Ernest in town and Jack in the country?

JACK

My dear Algy, I don't know whether you will be able to understand my real motives. You are hardly serious enough. When one is placed in the position of guardian, one has to adopt a very high moral tone on all subjects. It's one's duty to do so. And as a high moral tone can hardly be said to conduce very much to either one's health or one's happiness, in order to get up to town I have always pretended to have a younger brother of the name of Ernest, who lives in the Albany, and gets into the most dreadful scrapes. That, my dear Algy, is the whole truth pure and simple.

ALGERNON

The truth is rarely pure and never simple. Modern life would be very tedious if it were either, and modern literature a complete impossibility!

JACK

That wouldn't be at all a bad thing.

ALGERNON

Literary criticism is not your forte, my dear fellow. Don't try it. You should leave that to people who haven't been at a

University. They do it so well in the daily papers. What you really are is a Bunburyist. I was quite right in saying you were a Bunburyist. You are one of the most advanced Bunburyists I know.

JACK

What on earth do you mean?

ALGERNON

You have invented a very useful younger brother called Ernest, in order that you may be able to come up to town as often as you like. I have invented an invaluable permanent invalid called Bunbury, in order that I may be able to go down into the country whenever I choose. Bunbury is perfectly invaluable. If it wasn't for Bunbury's extraordinary bad health, for instance, I wouldn't be able to dine with you at Willis's to-night, for I have been really engaged to Aunt Augusta for more than a week.

JACK

I haven't asked you to dine with me anywhere to-night.

ALGERNON

I know. You are absurdly careless about sending out invitations. It is very foolish of you. Nothing annoys people so much as not receiving invitations.

JACK

You had much better dine with your Aunt Augusta.

ALGERNON

I haven't the smallest intention of doing anything of the kind. To begin with, I dined there on Monday, and once a week is quite enough to dine with one's own relations. In the second place, whenever I do dine there I am always treated as a member of the family, and sent down with either no woman at all, or two. In the third place, I know perfectly well whom she will place me next to, to-night. She will place me next Mary Farquhar, who always flirts with her own husband across the dinner-table. That is not very pleasant. Indeed, it is not even decent . . . and that sort of thing is enormously on the increase. The amount of women in London who flirt with their own husbands is perfectly scandalous. It looks so bad. It is simply washing one's clean linen in public. Besides, now that I know you to be a confirmed

Bunburyist I naturally want to talk to you about Bunburying. I want to tell you the rules.

JACK

I'm not a Bunburyist at all. If Gwendolen accepts me, I am going to kill my brother, indeed I think I'll kill him in any case. Cecily is a little too much interested in him. It is rather a bore. So I am going to get rid of Ernest. And I strongly advise you to do the same with Mr. . . . with your invalid friend who has the absurd name.

ALGERNON

Nothing will induce me to part with Bunbury, and if you ever get married, which seems to me extremely problematic, you will be very glad to know Bunbury. A man who marries without knowing Bunbury has a very tedious time of it.

JACK

That is nonsense. If I marry a charming girl like Gwendolen, and she is the only girl I ever saw in my life that I would marry, I certainly won't want to know Bunbury.

ALGERNON

Then your wife will. You don't seem to realise, that in married life three is company and two is none.

JACK

(*Sententiously.*) That, my dear young friend, is the theory that the corrupt French Drama has been propounding for the last fifty years.

ALGERNON

Yes; and that the happy English home has proved in half the time.

JACK

For heaven's sake, don't try to be cynical. It's perfectly easy to be cynical.

ALGERNON

My dear fellow, it isn't easy to be anything nowadays. There's such a lot of beastly competition about. (*The sound of an electric bell is heard.*) Ah! that must be Aunt Augusta. Only relatives, or creditors, ever ring in that Wagnerian manner. Now, if I get her out of the way for ten minutes, so that you can have an

opportunity for proposing to Gwendolen, may I dine with you to-night at Willis's?

JACK

I suppose so, if you want to.

ALGERNON

Yes, but you must be serious about it. I hate people who are not serious about meals. It is so shallow of them.

(*Enter* LANE.)

LANE

Lady Bracknell and Miss Fairfax. (ALGERNON *goes forward to meet them. Enter* LADY BRACKNELL *and* GWENDOLEN.)

LADY BRACKNELL

Good afternoon, dear Algernon, I hope you are behaving very well.

ALGERNON

I'm feeling very well, Aunt Augusta.

LADY BRACKNELL

That's not quite the same thing. In fact the two things rarely go together. (*Sees* JACK *and bows to him with icy coldness.*)

ALGERNON

(*To* GWENDOLEN.) Dear me, you are smart!

GWENDOLEN

I am always smart! Am I not, Mr. Worthing?

JACK

You're quite perfect, Miss Fairfax.

GWENDOLEN

Oh! I hope I am not that. It would leave no room for developments, and I intend to develop in *many directions.* (GWENDOLEN and JACK *sit down together in the corner.*)

LADY BRACKNELL

I'm sorry if we are a little late, Algernon, but I was obliged to call on dear Lady Harbury. I hadn't been there since her poor husband's death. I never saw a woman so altered; she looks quite twenty years younger. And now I'll have a cup of tea, and one of those nice cucumber sandwiches you promised me.

ALGERNON

Certainly, Aunt Augusta. (*Goes over to tea-table.*)

LADY BRACKNELL

Won't you come and sit here, Gwendolen?

GWENDOLEN

Thanks, mamma, I'm quite comfortable where I am.

ALGERNON

(*Picking up empty plate in horror.*) Good heavens! Lane! Why are there no cucumber sandwiches? I ordered them specially.

LANE

(*Gravely.*) There were no cucumbers in the market this morning, sir. I went down twice.

ALGERNON

No cucumbers!

LANE

No, sir. Not even for ready money.

ALGERNON

That will do, Lane, thank you.

LANE

Thank you, sir. (*Goes out.*)

ALGERNON

I am greatly distressed, Aunt Augusta, about there being no cucumbers, not even for ready money.

LADY BRACKNELL

It really makes no matter, Algernon. I had some crumpets with Lady Harbury, who seems to me to be living entirely for pleasure now.

ALGERNON

I hear her hair has turned quite gold from grief.

LADY BRACKNELL

It certainly has changed its colour. From what cause I, of course, cannot say. (ALGERNON *crosses and hands tea.*) Thank you. I've quite a treat for you to-night, Algernon. I am going to send you down with Mary Farquhar. She is such a nice woman, and so attentive to her husband. It's delightful to watch them.

ALGERNON

I am afraid, Aunt Augusta, I shall have to give up the pleasure of dining with you to-night after all.

LADY BRACKNELL

(*Frowning.*) I hope not, Algernon. It would put my table completely out. Your uncle would have to dine upstairs. Fortunately he is accustomed to that.

ALGERNON

It is a great bore, and, I need hardly say, a terrible disappointment to me, but the fact is I have just had a telegram to say that my poor friend Bunbury is very ill again. (*Exchanges glances with* JACK.) They seem to think I should be with him.

LADY BRACKNELL

It is very strange. This Mr. Bunbury seems to suffer from curiously bad health.

ALGERNON

Yes; poor Bunbury is a dreadful invalid.

LADY BRACKNELL

Well, I must say, Algernon, that I think it is high time that Mr. Bunbury made up his mind whether he was going to live or to die. This shilly-shallying with the question is absurd. Nor do I in any way approve of the modern sympathy with invalids. I consider it morbid. Illness of any kind is hardly a thing to be encouraged in others. Health is the primary duty of life. I am always telling that to your poor uncle, but he never seems to take much notice . . . as far as any improvement in his ailment goes. I should be much obliged if you would ask Mr. Bunbury, from me, to be kind enough not to have a relapse on Saturday, for I rely on you to arrange my music for me. It is my last reception, and one wants something that will encourage conversation, particularly at the end of the season when every one has practically said whatever they had to say, which, in most cases, was probably not much.

ALGERNON

I'll speak to Bunbury, Aunt Augusta, if he is still conscious, and I think I can promise you he'll be all right by Saturday. Of course the music is a great difficulty. You see, if one plays good music,

people don't listen, and if one plays bad music people don't talk. But I'll run over the programme I've drawn out, if you will kindly come into the next room for a moment.

LADY BRACKNELL

Thank you, Algernon. It is very thoughtful of you. (*Rising, and following* ALGERNON.) I'm sure the programme will be delightful, after a few expurgations. French songs I cannot possibly allow. People always seem to think that they are improper, and either look shocked, which is vulgar, or laugh, which is worse. But German sounds a thoroughly respectable language, and indeed, I believe is so. Gwendolen, you will accompany me.

GWENDOLEN

Certainly, mamma. (LADY BRACKNELL *and* ALGERNON *go into the music-room,* GWENDOLEN *remains behind.*)

JACK

Charming day it has been, Miss Fairfax.

GWENDOLEN

Pray don't talk to me about the weather, Mr. Worthing. Whenever people talk to me about the weather, I always feel quite certain that they mean something else. And that makes me so nervous.

JACK

I do mean something else.

GWENDOLEN

I thought so. In fact, I am never wrong.

JACK

And I would like to be allowed to take advantage of Lady Bracknell's temporary absence . . .

GWENDOLEN

I would certainly advise you to do so. Mamma has a way of coming back suddenly into a room that I have often had to speak to her about.

JACK

(*Nervously.*) Miss Fairfax, ever since I met you I have admired you more than any girl . . . I have ever met since . . . I met you.

GWENDOLEN

Yes, I am quite well aware of the fact. And I often wish that in public, at any rate, you had been more demonstrative. For

me you have always had an irresistible fascination. Even before I met you I was far from indifferent to you. (JACK *looks at her in amazement.*) We live, as I hope you know, Mr. Worthing, in an age of ideals. The fact is constantly mentioned in the more expensive monthly magazines, and has reached the provincial pulpits, I am told; and my ideal has always been to love some one of the name of Ernest. There is something in that name that inspires absolute confidence. The moment Algernon first mentioned to me that he had a friend called Ernest, I knew I was destined to love you.

JACK

You really love me, Gwendolen?

GWENDOLEN

Passionately!

JACK

Darling! You don't know how happy you've made me.

GWENDOLEN

My own Ernest!

JACK

But you don't really mean to say that you couldn't love me if my name wasn't Ernest?

GWENDOLEN

But your name is Ernest.

JACK

Yes, I know it is. But supposing it was something else? Do you mean to say you couldn't love me then?

GWENDOLEN

(*Glibly.*) Ah! that is clearly a metaphysical speculation, and like most metaphysical speculations has very little reference at all to the actual facts of real life, as we know them.

JACK

Personally, darling, to speak quite candidly, I don't much care about the name of Ernest . . . I don't think the name suits me at all.

GWENDOLEN

It suits you perfectly. It is a divine name. It has a music of its own. It produces vibrations.

JACK

Well, really, Gwendolen, I must say that I think there are lots of other much nicer names. I think Jack, for instance, a charming name.

GWENDOLEN

Jack? . . . No, there is very little music in the name Jack, if any at all, indeed. It does not thrill. It produces absolutely no vibrations . . . I have known several Jacks, and they all, without exception, were more than usually plain. Besides, Jack is a notorious domesticity for John! And I pity any woman who is married to a man called John. She would probably never be allowed to know the entrancing pleasure of a single moment's solitude. The only really safe name is Ernest.

JACK

Gwendolen, I must get christened at once—I mean we must get married at once. There is no time to be lost.

GWENDOLEN

Married, Mr. Worthing?

JACK

(*Astounded.*) Well . . . surely. You know that I love you, and you led me to believe, Miss Fairfax, that you were not absolutely indifferent to me.

GWENDOLEN

I adore you. But you haven't proposed to me yet. Nothing has been said at all about marriage. The subject has not even been touched on.

JACK

Well . . . may I propose to you now?

GWENDOLEN

I think it would be an admirable opportunity. And to spare you any possible disappointment, Mr. Worthing, I think it only fair to tell you quite frankly before-hand that I am fully determined to accept you.

JACK

Gwendolen!

GWENDOLEN

Yes, Mr. Worthing, what have you got to say to me?

Jack

You know what I have got to say to you.

Gwendolen

Yes, but you don't say it.

Jack

Gwendolen, will you marry me? (Goes on his knees.)

Gwendolen

Of course I will, darling. How long you have been about it! I am afraid you have had very little experience in how to propose.

Jack

My own one, I have never loved any one in the world but you.

Gwendolen

Yes, but men often propose for practice. I know my brother Gerald does. All my girl-friends tell me so. What wonderfully blue eyes you have, Ernest! They are quite, quite, blue. I hope you will always look at me just like that, especially when there are other people present.

(*Enter* Lady Bracknell.)

Lady Bracknell

Mr. Worthing! Rise, sir, from this semi-recumbent posture. It is most indecorous.

Gwendolen

Mamma! (*He tries to rise; she restrains him.*) I must beg you to retire. This is no place for you. Besides, Mr. Worthing has not quite finished yet.

Lady Bracknell

Finished what, may I ask?

Gwendolen

I am engaged to Mr. Worthing, mamma. (*They rise together.*)

Lady Bracknell

Pardon me, you are not engaged to any one. When you do become engaged to some one, I, or your father, should his health permit him, will inform you of the fact. An engagement should come on a young girl as a surprise, pleasant or unpleasant, as the case may be. It is hardly a matter that she could be allowed to arrange

for herself . . . And now I have a few questions to put to you, Mr. Worthing. While I am making these inquiries, you, Gwendolen, will wait for me below in the carriage.

GWENDOLEN

(*Reproachfully.*) Mamma!

LADY BRACKNELL

In the carriage, Gwendolen! (GWENDOLEN *goes to the door. She and Jack blow kisses to each other behind* LADY BRACKNELL'S *back.* LADY BRACKNELL *looks vaguely about as if she could not understand what the noise was. Finally turns round.*) Gwendolen, the carriage!

GWENDOLEN

Yes, mamma. (*Goes out, looking back at* JACK.)

LADY BRACKNELL

(*Sitting down.*) You can take a seat, Mr. Worthing. (*Looks in her pocket for note-book and pencil.*)

JACK

Thank you, Lady Bracknell, I prefer standing.

LADY BRACKNELL

(*Pencil and note-book in hand.*) I feel bound to tell you that you are not down on my list of eligible young men, although I have the same list as the dear Duchess of Bolton has. We work together, in fact. However, I am quite ready to enter your name, should your answers be what a really affectionate mother requires. Do you smoke?

JACK

Well, yes, I must admit I smoke.

LADY BRACKNELL

I am glad to hear it. A man should always have an occupation of some kind. There are far too many idle men in London as it is. How old are you?

JACK

Twenty-nine.

LADY BRACKNELL

A very good age to be married at. I have always been of opinion that a man who desires to get married should know either everything or nothing. Which do you know?

JACK

(*After some hesitation.*) I know nothing, Lady Bracknell.

LADY BRACKNELL

I am pleased to hear it. I do not approve of anything that tampers with natural ignorance. Ignorance is like a delicate exotic fruit; touch it and the bloom is gone. The whole theory of modern education is radically unsound. Fortunately in England, at any rate, education produces no effect whatsoever. If it did, it would prove a serious danger to the upper classes, and probably lead to acts of violence in Grosvenor Square. What is your income?

JACK

Between seven and eight thousand a year.

LADY BRACKNELL

(*Makes a note in her book.*) In land, or in investments?

JACK

In investments, chiefly.

LADY BRACKNELL

That is satisfactory. What between the duties expected of one during one's lifetime, and the duties exacted from one after one's death, land has ceased to be either a profit or a pleasure. It gives one position, and prevents one from keeping it up. That's all that can be said about land.

JACK

I have a country house with some land, of course, attached to it, about fifteen hundred acres, I believe; but I don't depend on that for my real income. In fact, as far as I can make out, the poachers are the only people who make anything out of it.

LADY BRACKNELL

A country house! How many bedrooms? Well, that point can be cleared up afterwards. You have a town house, I hope? A girl with a simple, unspoiled nature, like Gwendolen, could hardly be expected to reside in the country.

JACK

Well, I own a house in Belgrave Square, but it is let by the year to Lady Bloxham. Of course, I can get it back whenever I like, at six months' notice.

LADY BRACKNELL

Lady Bloxham? I don't know her.

JACK

Oh, she goes about very little. She is a lady considerably advanced in years.

LADY BRACKNELL

Ah, nowadays that is no guarantee of respectability of character. What number in Belgrave Square?

JACK

149.

LADY BRACKNELL

(*Shaking her head.*) The unfashionable side. I thought there was something. However, that could easily be altered.

JACK

Do you mean the fashion, or the side?

LADY BRACKNELL

(*Sternly.*) Both, if necessary, I presume. What are your politics?

JACK

Well, I am afraid I really have none. I am a Liberal Unionist.

LADY BRACKNELL

Oh, they count as Tories. They dine with us. Or come in the evening, at any rate. Now to minor matters. Are your parents living?

JACK

I have lost both my parents.

LADY BRACKNELL

To lose one parent, Mr. Worthing, may be regarded as a misfortune; to lose both looks like carelessness. Who was your father? He was evidently a man of some wealth. Was he born in what the Radical papers call the purple of commerce, or did he rise from the ranks of the aristocracy?

JACK

I am afraid I really don't know. The fact is, Lady Bracknell, I said I had lost my parents. It would be nearer the truth to say that my parents seem to have lost me . . . I don't actually know who I am by birth. I was . . . well, I was found.

LADY BRACKNELL

Found!

JACK

The late Mr. Thomas Cardew, an old gentleman of a very charitable and kindly disposition, found me, and gave me the name of Worthing, because he happened to have a first-class ticket for Worthing in his pocket at the time. Worthing is a place in Sussex. It is a seaside resort.

LADY BRACKNELL

Where did the charitable gentleman who had a first-class ticket for this seaside resort find you?

JACK

(*Gravely.*) In a hand-bag.

LADY BRACKNELL

A hand-bag?

JACK

(*Very seriously.*) Yes, Lady Bracknell. I was in a hand-bag—a somewhat large, black leather hand-bag, with handles to it—an ordinary hand-bag in fact.

LADY BRACKNELL

In what locality did this Mr. James, or Thomas, Cardew come across this ordinary hand-bag?

JACK

In the cloak-room at Victoria Station. It was given to him in mistake for his own.

LADY BRACKNELL

The cloak-room at Victoria Station?

JACK

Yes. The Brighton line.

LADY BRACKNELL

The line is immaterial. Mr. Worthing, I confess I feel somewhat bewildered by what you have just told me. To be born, or at any rate bred, in a hand-bag, whether it had handles or not, seems to me to display a contempt for the ordinary decencies of family life that reminds one of the worst excesses of the French Revolution. And I presume you know what that unfortunate movement led to? As for the particular locality in which the

hand-bag was found, a cloak-room at a railway station might serve to conceal a social indiscretion—has probably, indeed, been used for that purpose before now—but it could hardly be regarded as an assured basis for a recognised position in good society.

JACK

May I ask you then what you would advise me to do? I need hardly say I would do anything in the world to ensure Gwendolen's happiness.

LADY BRACKNELL

I would strongly advise you, Mr. Worthing, to try and acquire some relations as soon as possible, and to make a definite effort to produce at any rate one parent, of either sex, before the season is quite over.

JACK

Well, I don't see how I could possibly manage to do that. I can produce the hand-bag at any moment. It is in my dressing-room at home. I really think that should satisfy you, Lady Bracknell.

LADY BRACKNELL

Me, sir! What has it to do with me? You can hardly imagine that I and Lord Bracknell would dream of allowing our only daughter—a girl brought up with the utmost care—to marry into a cloak-room, and form an alliance with a parcel? Good morning, Mr. Worthing! (LADY BRACKNELL *sweeps out in majestic indignation.*)

JACK

Good morning! (ALGERNON, *from the other room, strikes up the Wedding March.* JACK *looks perfectly furious, and goes to the door.*) For goodness' sake don't play that ghastly tune, Algy. How idiotic you are! (*The music stops and* ALGERNON *enters cheerily.*)

ALGERNON

Didn't it go off all right, old boy? You don't mean to say Gwendolen refused you? I know it is a way she has. She is always refusing people. I think it is most ill-natured of her.

JACK

Oh, Gwendolen is as right as a trivet. As far as she is concerned, we are engaged. Her mother is perfectly unbearable. Never met

such a Gorgon . . . I don't really know what a Gorgon is like, but I am quite sure that Lady Bracknell is one. In any case, she is a monster, without being a myth, which is rather unfair . . . I beg your pardon, Algy, I suppose I shouldn't talk about your own aunt in that way before you.

ALGERNON

My dear boy, I love hearing my relations abused. It is the only thing that makes me put up with them at all. Relations are simply a tedious pack of people, who haven't got the remotest knowledge of how to live, nor the smallest instinct about when to die.

JACK

Oh, that is nonsense!

ALGERNON

It isn't!

JACK

Well, I won't argue about the matter. You always want to argue about things.

ALGERNON

That is exactly what things were originally made for.

JACK

Upon my word, if I thought that, I'd shoot myself . . . (*A pause.*) You don't think there is any chance of Gwendolen becoming like her mother in about a hundred and fifty years, do you, Algy?

ALGERNON

All women become like their mothers. That is their tragedy. No man does. That's his.

JACK

Is that clever?

ALGERNON

It is perfectly phrased! and quite as true as any observation in civilised life should be.

JACK

I am sick to death of cleverness. Everybody is clever nowadays. You can't go anywhere without meeting clever people. The thing has become an absolute public nuisance. I wish to goodness we had a few fools left.

ALGERNON

We have.

JACK

I should extremely like to meet them. What do they talk about?

ALGERNON

The fools? Oh! about the clever people, of course.

JACK

What fools!

ALGERNON

By the way, did you tell Gwendolen the truth about your being Ernest in town, and Jack in the country?

JACK

(*In a very patronising manner.*) My dear fellow, the truth isn't quite the sort of thing one tells to a nice, sweet, refined girl. What extraordinary ideas you have about the way to behave to a woman!

ALGERNON

The only way to behave to a woman is to make love to her, if she is pretty, and to some one else, if she is plain.

JACK

Oh, that is nonsense.

ALGERNON

What about your brother? What about the profligate Ernest?

JACK

Oh, before the end of the week I shall have got rid of him. I'll say he died in Paris of apoplexy. Lots of people die of apoplexy, quite suddenly, don't they?

ALGERNON

Yes, but it's hereditary, my dear fellow. It's a sort of thing that runs in families. You had much better say a severe chill.

JACK

You are sure a severe chill isn't hereditary, or anything of that kind?

ALGERNON

Of course it isn't!

JACK

Very well, then. My poor brother Ernest to carried off suddenly, in Paris, by a severe chill. That gets rid of him.

ALGERNON

But I thought you said that . . . Miss Cardew was a little too much interested in your poor brother Ernest? Won't she feel his loss a good deal?

JACK

Oh, that is all right. Cecily is not a silly romantic girl, I am glad to say. She has got a capital appetite, goes long walks, and pays no attention at all to her lessons.

ALGERNON

I would rather like to see Cecily.

JACK

I will take very good care you never do. She is excessively pretty, and she is only just eighteen.

ALGERNON

Have you told Gwendolen yet that you have an excessively pretty ward who is only just eighteen?

JACK

Oh! one doesn't blurt these things out to people. Cecily and Gwendolen are perfectly certain to be extremely great friends. I'll bet you anything you like that half an hour after they have met, they will be calling each other sister.

ALGERNON

Women only do that when they have called each other a lot of other things first. Now, my dear boy, if we want to get a good table at Willis's, we really must go and dress. Do you know it is nearly seven?

JACK

(*Irritably.*) Oh! It always is nearly seven.

ALGERNON

Well, I'm hungry.

JACK

I never knew you when you weren't . . .

ALGERNON

What shall we do after dinner? Go to a theatre?

JACK

Oh no! I loathe listening.

ALGERNON

Well, let us go to the Club?

JACK

Oh, no! I hate talking.

ALGERNON

Well, we might trot round to the Empire at ten?

JACK

Oh, no! I can't bear looking at things. It is so silly.

ALGERNON

Well, what shall we do?

JACK

Nothing!

ALGERNON

It is awfully hard work doing nothing. However, I don't mind hard work where there is no definite object of any kind.

(*Enter* LANE.)

LANE

Miss Fairfax.

(*Enter* GWENDOLEN. LANE *goes out.*)

ALGERNON

Gwendolen, upon my word!

GWENDOLEN

Algy, kindly turn your back. I have something very particular to say to Mr. Worthing.

ALGERNON

Really, Gwendolen, I don't think I can allow this at all.

GWENDOLEN

Algy, you always adopt a strictly immoral attitude towards life. You are not quite old enough to do that. (ALGERNON *retires to the fireplace.*)

JACK

My own darling!

GWENDOLEN

Ernest, we may never be married. From the expression on mamma's face I fear we never shall. Few parents nowadays pay any regard to what their children say to them. The old-fashioned respect for the young is fast dying out. Whatever influence I ever had over mamma, I lost at the age of three. But although she may prevent us from becoming man and wife, and I may marry some one else, and marry often, nothing that she can possibly do can alter my eternal devotion to you.

JACK

Dear Gwendolen!

GWENDOLEN

The story of your romantic origin, as related to me by mamma, with unpleasing comments, has naturally stirred the deeper fibres of my nature. Your Christian name has an irresistible fascination. The simplicity of your character makes you exquisitely incomprehensible to me. Your town address at the Albany I have. What is your address in the country?

JACK

The Manor House, Woolton, Hertfordshire. (ALGERNON, *who has been carefully listening, smiles to himself, and writes the address on his shirt-cuff. Then picks up the Railway Guide.*)

GWENDOLEN

There is a good postal service, I suppose? It may be necessary to do something desperate. That of course will require serious consideration. I will communicate with you daily.

JACK

My own one!

GWENDOLEN

How long do you remain in town?

JACK

Till Monday.

GWENDOLEN

Good! Algy, you may turn round now.

ALGERNON

Thanks, I've turned round already.

GWENDOLEN

You may also ring the bell.

JACK

You will let me see you to your carriage, my own darling?

GWENDOLEN

Certainly.

JACK

(*To* LANE, *who now enters.*) I will see Miss Fairfax out.

LANE

Yes, sir. (JACK *and* GWENDOLEN *go off.*) (LANE *presents several letters on a salver to* ALGERNON. *It is to be surmised that they are bills, as* ALGERNON, *after looking at the envelopes, tears them up.*)

ALGERNON

A glass of sherry, Lane.

LANE

Yes, sir.

ALGERNON

To-morrow, Lane, I'm going Bunburying.

LANE

Yes, sir.

ALGERNON

I shall probably not be back till Monday. You can put up my dress clothes, my smoking jacket, and all the Bunbury suits . . .

LANE

Yes, sir. (*Handing sherry.*)

ALGERNON

I hope to-morrow will be a fine day, Lane.

LANE

It never is, sir.

ALGERNON

Lane, you're a perfect pessimist.

LANE

I do my best to give satisfaction, sir.

(*Enter* JACK. LANE *goes off.*)

JACK

There's a sensible, intellectual girl! the only girl I ever cared for in my life. (ALGERNON *is laughing immoderately.*) What on earth are you so amused at?

ALGERNON

Oh, I'm a little anxious about poor Bunbury, that is all.

JACK

If you don't take care, your friend Bunbury will get you into a serious scrape some day.

ALGERNON

I love scrapes. They are the only things that are never serious.

JACK

Oh, that's nonsense, Algy. You never talk anything but nonsense.

ALGERNON

Nobody ever does. (JACK *looks indignantly at him, and leaves the room.* ALGERNON *lights a cigarette, reads his shirt-cuff, and smiles.*)

Act 2

SCENE—*Garden at the Manor House. A flight of grey stone steps leads up to the house. The garden, an old-fashioned one, full of roses. Time of year, July. Basket chairs, and a table covered with books, are set under a large yew-tree.*

(MISS PRISM *discovered seated at the table.*
CECILY *is at the back watering flowers.*)

MISS PRISM
(*Calling.*) Cecily, Cecily! Surely such a utilitarian occupation as the watering of flowers is rather Moulton's duty than yours? Especially at a moment when intellectual pleasures await you. Your German grammar is on the table. Pray open it at page fifteen. We will repeat yesterday's lesson.

CECILY
(*Coming over very slowly.*) But I don't like German. It isn't at all a becoming language. I know perfectly well that I look quite plain after my German lesson.

MISS PRISM
Child, you know how anxious your guardian is that you

should improve yourself in every way. He laid particular stress on your German, as he was leaving for town yesterday. Indeed, he always lays stress on your German when he is leaving for town.

CECILY

Dear Uncle Jack is so very serious! Sometimes he is so serious that I think he cannot be quite well.

MISS PRISM

(*Drawing herself up.*) Your guardian enjoys the best of health, and his gravity of demeanour is especially to be commended in one so comparatively young as he is. I know no one who has a higher sense of duty and responsibility.

CECILY

I suppose that is why he often looks a little bored when we three are together.

MISS PRISM

Cecily! I am surprised at you. Mr. Worthing has many troubles in his life. Idle merriment and triviality would be out of place in his conversation. You must remember his constant anxiety about that unfortunate young man his brother.

CECILY

I wish Uncle Jack would allow that unfortunate young man, his brother, to come down here sometimes. We might have a good influence over him, Miss Prism. I am sure you certainly would. You know German, and geology, and things of that kind influence a man very much. (CECILY *begins to write in her diary.*)

MISS PRISM

(*Shaking her head.*) I do not think that even I could produce any effect on a character that according to his own brother's admission is irretrievably weak and vacillating. Indeed I am not sure that I would desire to reclaim him. I am not in favour of this modern mania for turning bad people into good people at a moment's notice. As a man sows so let him reap. You must put away your diary, Cecily. I really don't see why you should keep a diary at all.

CECILY

I keep a diary in order to enter the wonderful secrets of my life. If I didn't write them down, I should probably forget all about them.

Miss Prism

Memory, my dear Cecily, is the diary that we all carry about with us.

Cecily

Yes, but it usually chronicles the things that have never happened, and couldn't possibly have happened. I believe that Memory is responsible for nearly all the three-volume novels that Mudie sends us.

Miss Prism

Do not speak slightingly of the three-volume novel, Cecily. I wrote one myself in earlier days.

Cecily

Did you really, Miss Prism? How wonderfully clever you are! I hope it did not end happily? I don't like novels that end happily. They depress me so much.

Miss Prism

The good ended happily, and the bad unhappily. That is what Fiction means.

Cecily

I suppose so. But it seems very unfair. And was your novel ever published?

Miss Prism

Alas! no. The manuscript unfortunately was abandoned. (Cecily *starts.*) I use the word in the sense of lost or mislaid. To your work, child, these speculations are profitless.

Cecily

(*Smiling.*) But I see dear Dr. Chasuble coming up through the garden.

Miss Prism

(*Rising and advancing.*) Dr. Chasuble! This is indeed a pleasure.

(*Enter* Canon Chasuble.)

Chasuble

And how are we this morning? Miss Prism, you are, I trust, well?

Cecily

Miss Prism has just been complaining of a slight headache. I

think it would do her so much good to have a short stroll with you in the Park, Dr. Chasuble.

MISS PRISM

Cecily, I have not mentioned anything about a headache.

CECILY

No, dear Miss Prism, I know that, but I felt instinctively that you had a headache. Indeed I was thinking about that, and not about my German lesson, when the Rector came in.

CHASUBLE

I hope, Cecily, you are not inattentive.

CECILY

Oh, I am afraid I am.

CHASUBLE

That is strange. Were I fortunate enough to be Miss Prism's pupil, I would hang upon her lips. (MISS PRISM *glares.*) I spoke metaphorically.—My metaphor was drawn from bees. Ahem! Mr. Worthing, I suppose, has not returned from town yet?

MISS PRISM

We do not expect him till Monday afternoon.

CHASUBLE

Ah yes, he usually likes to spend his Sunday in London. He is not one of those whose sole aim is enjoyment, as, by all accounts, that unfortunate young man his brother seems to be. But I must not disturb Egeria and her pupil any longer.

MISS PRISM

Egeria? My name is Lætitia, Doctor.

CHASUBLE

(*Bowing.*) A classical allusion merely, drawn from the Pagan authors. I shall see you both no doubt at Evensong?

MISS PRISM

I think, dear Doctor, I will have a stroll with you. I find I have a headache after all, and a walk might do it good.

CHASUBLE

With pleasure, Miss Prism, with pleasure. We might go as far as the schools and back.

MISS PRISM

That would be delightful. Cecily, you will read your Political

Economy in my absence. The chapter on the Fall of the Rupee you may omit. It is somewhat too sensational. Even these metallic problems have their melodramatic side.

(*Goes down the garden with* DR. CHASUBLE.)

CECILY

(*Picks up books and throws them back on table.*) Horrid Political Economy! Horrid Geography! Horrid, horrid German!

(*Enter* MERRIMAN *with a card on a salver.*)

MERRIMAN

Mr. Ernest Worthing has just driven over from the station. He has brought his luggage with him.

CECILY

(*Takes the card and reads it.*) 'Mr. Ernest Worthing, B. 4, The Albany, W.' Uncle Jack's brother! Did you tell him Mr. Worthing was in town?

MERRIMAN

Yes, Miss. He seemed very much disappointed. I mentioned that you and Miss Prism were in the garden. He said he was anxious to speak to you privately for a moment.

CECILY

Ask Mr. Ernest Worthing to come here. I suppose you had better talk to the housekeeper about a room for him.

MERRIMAN

Yes, Miss. (MERRIMAN *goes off.*)

CECILY

I have never met any really wicked person before. I feel rather frightened. I am so afraid he will look just like every one else.

(*Enter* ALGERNON, *very gay and debonnair.*)

He does!

ALGERNON

(*Raising his hat.*) You are my little cousin Cecily, I'm sure.

CECILY

You are under some strange mistake. I am not little. In fact, I believe I am more than usually tall for my age. (Algernon *is rather taken aback.*) But I am your cousin Cecily. You, I see from your card, are Uncle Jack's brother, my cousin Ernest, my wicked cousin Ernest.

ALGERNON

Oh! I am not really wicked at all, cousin Cecily. You mustn't think that I am wicked.

CECILY

If you are not, then you have certainly been deceiving us all in a very inexcusable manner. I hope you have not been leading a double life, pretending to be wicked and being really good all the time. That would be hypocrisy.

ALGERNON

(*Looks at her in amazement.*) Oh! Of course I have been rather reckless.

CECILY

I am glad to hear it.

ALGERNON

In fact, now you mention the subject, I have been very bad in my own small way.

CECILY

I don't think you should be so proud of that, though I am sure it must have been very pleasant.

ALGERNON

It is much pleasanter being here with you.

CECILY

I can't understand how you are here at all. Uncle Jack won't be back till Monday afternoon.

ALGERNON

That is a great disappointment. I am obliged to go up by the first train on Monday morning. I have a business appointment that I am anxious . . . to miss?

CECILY

Couldn't you miss it anywhere but in London?

ALGERNON

No: the appointment is in London.

CECILY

Well, I know, of course, how important it is not to keep a business engagement, if one wants to retain any sense of the beauty of life, but still I think you had better wait till Uncle Jack arrives. I know he wants to speak to you about your emigrating.

ALGERNON

About my what?

CECILY

Your emigrating. He has gone up to buy your outfit.

ALGERNON

I certainly wouldn't let Jack buy my outfit. He has no taste in neckties at all.

CECILY

I don't think you will require neckties. Uncle Jack is sending you to Australia.

ALGERNON

Australia! I'd sooner die.

CECILY

Well, he said at dinner on Wednesday night, that you would have to choose between this world, the next world, and Australia.

ALGERNON

Oh, well! The accounts I have received of Australia and the next world, are not particularly encouraging. This world is good enough for me, cousin Cecily.

CECILY

Yes, but are you good enough for it?

ALGERNON

I'm afraid I'm not that. That is why I want you to reform me. You might make that your mission, if you don't mind, cousin Cecily.

CECILY

I'm afraid I've no time, this afternoon.

ALGERNON

Well, would you mind my reforming myself this afternoon?

CECILY

It is rather Quixotic of you. But I think you should try.

ALGERNON

I will. I feel better already.

CECILY

You are looking a little worse.

ALGERNON

That is because I am hungry.

CECILY

How thoughtless of me. I should have remembered that when one is going to lead an entirely new life, one requires regular and wholesome meals. Won't you come in?

ALGERNON

Thank you. Might I have a buttonhole first? I never have any appetite unless I have a buttonhole first.

CECILY

A Marechal Niel? (*Picks up scissors.*)

ALGERNON

No, I'd sooner have a pink rose.

CECILY

Why? (*Cuts a flower.*)

ALGERNON

Because you are like a pink rose, Cousin Cecily.

CECILY

I don't think it can be right for you to talk to me like that. Miss Prism never says such things to me.

ALGERNON

Then Miss Prism is a short-sighted old lady. (CECILY *puts the rose in his buttonhole.*) You are the prettiest girl I ever saw.

CECILY

Miss Prism says that all good looks are a snare.

ALGERNON

They are a snare that every sensible man would like to be caught in.

CECILY

Oh, I don't think I would care to catch a sensible man. I shouldn't know what to talk to him about.

(*They pass into the house.* MISS PRISM *and* DR. CHASUBLE *return.*)

MISS PRISM

You are too much alone, dear Dr. Chasuble. You should get married. A misanthrope I can understand—a womanthrope, never!

CHASUBLE

(*With a scholar's shudder.*) Believe me, I do not deserve so neologistic a phrase. The precept as well as the practice of the Primitive Church was distinctly against matrimony.

MISS PRISM

(*Sententiously.*) That is obviously the reason why the Primitive Church has not lasted up to the present day. And you do not seem to realise, dear Doctor, that by persistently remaining single, a man converts himself into a permanent public temptation. Men should be more careful; this very celibacy leads weaker vessels astray.

CHASUBLE

But is a man not equally attractive when married?

MISS PRISM

No married man is ever attractive except to his wife.

CHASUBLE

And often, I've been told, not even to her.

MISS PRISM

That depends on the intellectual sympathies of the woman. Maturity can always be depended on. Ripeness can be trusted. Young women are green. (DR. CHASUBLE *starts.*) I spoke horticulturally. My metaphor was drawn from fruits. But where is Cecily?

CHASUBLE

Perhaps she followed us to the schools.

(*Enter* JACK *slowly from the back of the garden. He is dressed in the deepest mourning, with crape hatband and black gloves.*)

MISS PRISM

Mr. Worthing!

CHASUBLE

Mr. Worthing?

MISS PRISM

This is indeed a surprise. We did not look for you till Monday afternoon.

JACK

(*Shakes* MISS PRISM'S *hand in a tragic manner.*) I have returned sooner than I expected. Dr. Chasuble, I hope you are well?

CHASUBLE

Dear Mr. Worthing, I trust this garb of woe does not betoken some terrible calamity?

JACK

My brother.

MISS PRISM

More shameful debts and extravagance?

CHASUBLE

Still leading his life of pleasure?

JACK

(*Shaking his head.*) Dead!

CHASUBLE

Your brother Ernest dead?

JACK

Quite dead.

MISS PRISM

What a lesson for him! I trust he will profit by it.

CHASUBLE

Mr. Worthing, I offer you my sincere condolence. You have at least the consolation of knowing that you were always the most generous and forgiving of brothers.

JACK

Poor Ernest! He had many faults, but it is a sad, sad blow.

CHASUBLE

Very sad indeed. Were you with him at the end?

JACK

No. He died abroad; in Paris, in fact. I had a telegram last night from the manager of the Grand Hotel.

CHASUBLE

Was the cause of death mentioned?

JACK

A severe chill, it seems.

MISS PRISM

As a man sows, so shall he reap.

CHASUBLE

(*Raising his hand.*) Charity, dear Miss Prism, charity! None of us are perfect. I myself am peculiarly susceptible to draughts. Will the interment take place here?

JACK

No. He seems to have expressed a desire to be buried in Paris.

CHASUBLE

In Paris! (*Shakes his head.*) I fear that hardly points to any very serious state of mind at the last. You would no doubt wish me to make some slight allusion to this tragic domestic affliction next Sunday. (JACK *presses his hand convulsively.*) My sermon on the meaning of the manna in the wilderness can be adapted to almost any occasion, joyful, or, as in the present case, distressing. (*All sigh.*) I have preached it at harvest celebrations, christenings, confirmations, on days of humiliation and festal days. The last time I delivered it was in the Cathedral, as a charity sermon on behalf of the Society for the Prevention of Discontent among the Upper Orders. The Bishop, who was present, was much struck by some of the analogies I drew.

JACK

Ah! that reminds me, you mentioned christenings I think, Dr. Chasuble? I suppose you know how to christen all right? (DR. CHASUBLE *looks astounded.*) I mean, of course, you are continually christening, aren't you?

MISS PRISM

It is, I regret to say, one of the Rector's most constant duties in this parish. I have often spoken to the poorer classes on the subject. But they don't seem to know what thrift is.

CHASUBLE

But is there any particular infant in whom you are interested, Mr. Worthing? Your brother was, I believe, unmarried, was he not?

JACK

Oh yes.

MISS PRISM

(*Bitterly.*) People who live entirely for pleasure usually are.

JACK

But it is not for any child, dear Doctor. I am very fond of children. No! the fact is, I would like to be christened myself, this afternoon, if you have nothing better to do.

CHASUBLE

But surely, Mr. Worthing, you have been christened already?

JACK

I don't remember anything about it.

CHASUBLE

But have you any grave doubts on the subject?

JACK

I certainly intend to have. Of course I don't know if the thing would bother you in any way, or if you think I am a little too old now.

CHASUBLE

Not at all. The sprinkling, and, indeed, the immersion of adults is a perfectly canonical practice.

JACK

Immersion!

CHASUBLE

You need have no apprehensions. Sprinkling is all that is necessary, or indeed I think advisable. Our weather is so changeable. At what hour would you wish the ceremony performed?

JACK

Oh, I might trot round about five if that would suit you.

CHASUBLE

Perfectly, perfectly! In fact I have two similar ceremonies to perform at that time. A case of twins that occurred recently in one of the outlying cottages on your own estate. Poor Jenkins the carter, a most hard-working man.

JACK

Oh! I don't see much fun in being christened along with other babies. It would be childish. Would half-past five do?

CHASUBLE

Admirably! Admirably! (*Takes out watch.*) And now, dear Mr. Worthing, I will not intrude any longer into a house of sorrow. I would merely beg you not to be too much bowed down by grief. What seem to us bitter trials are often blessings in disguise.

MISS PRISM

This seems to me a blessing of an extremely obvious kind.

(*Enter* CECILY *from the house.*)

CECILY

Uncle Jack! Oh, I am pleased to see you back. But what horrid clothes you have got on! Do go and change them.

MISS PRISM

Cecily!

CHASUBLE

My child! my child! (CECILY *goes towards* JACK*; he kisses her brow in a melancholy manner.*)

CECILY

What is the matter, Uncle Jack? Do look happy! You look as if you had toothache, and I have got such a surprise for you. Who do you think is in the dining-room? Your brother!

JACK

Who?

CECILY

Your brother Ernest. He arrived about half an hour ago.

JACK

What nonsense! I haven't got a brother.

CECILY

Oh, don't say that. However badly he may have behaved to you in the past he is still your brother. You couldn't be so heartless as to disown him. I'll tell him to come out. And you will shake hands with him, won't you, Uncle Jack? (*Runs back into the house.*)

CHASUBLE

These are very joyful tidings.

MISS PRISM

After we had all been resigned to his loss, his sudden return seems to me peculiarly distressing.

JACK

My brother is in the dining-room? I don't know what it all means. I think it is perfectly absurd.

(*Enter* ALGERNON *and* CECILY *hand in hand. They come slowly up to* JACK.)

JACK

Good heavens! (*Motions* ALGERNON *away.*)

ALGERNON

Brother John, I have come down from town to tell you that I am very sorry for all the trouble I have given you, and that I intend to lead a better life in the future. (JACK *glares at him and does not take his hand.*)

CECILY

Uncle Jack, you are not going to refuse your own brother's hand?

JACK

Nothing will induce me to take his hand. I think his coming down here disgraceful. He knows perfectly well why.

CECILY

Uncle Jack, do be nice. There is some good in every one. Ernest has just been telling me about his poor invalid friend Mr. Bunbury whom he goes to visit so often. And surely there must be much good in one who is kind to an invalid, and leaves the pleasures of London to sit by a bed of pain.

JACK

Oh! he has been talking about Bunbury, has he?

CECILY

Yes, he has told me all about poor Mr. Bunbury, and his terrible state of health.

JACK

Bunbury! Well, I won't have him talk to you about Bunbury or about anything else. It is enough to drive one perfectly frantic.

ALGERNON

Of course I admit that the faults were all on my side. But I must say that I think that Brother John's coldness to me is peculiarly painful. I expected a more enthusiastic welcome, especially considering it is the first time I have come here.

CECILY

Uncle Jack, if you don't shake hands with Ernest I will never forgive you.

JACK

Never forgive me?

CECILY

Never, never, never!

JACK

Well, this is the last time I shall ever do it. (*Shakes with* ALGERNON *and glares.*)

CHASUBLE

It's pleasant, is it not, to see so perfect a reconciliation? I think we might leave the two brothers together.

MISS PRISM

Cecily, you will come with us.

CECILY

Certainly, Miss Prism. My little task of reconciliation is over.

CHASUBLE

You have done a beautiful action to-day, dear child.

MISS PRISM

We must not be premature in our judgments.

CECILY

I feel very happy. (*They all go off except* JACK *and* ALGERNON.)

JACK

You young scoundrel, Algy, you must get out of this place as soon as possible. I don't allow any Bunburying here.

(*Enter* MERRIMAN.)

MERRIMAN

I have put Mr. Ernest's things in the room next to yours, sir. I suppose that is all right?

JACK

What?

MERRIMAN

Mr. Ernest's luggage, sir. I have unpacked it and put it in the room next to your own.

JACK

His luggage?

MERRIMAN

Yes, sir. Three portmanteaus, a dressing-case, two hat-boxes, and a large luncheon-basket.

ALGERNON

I am afraid I can't stay more than a week this time.

JACK

Merriman, order the dog-cart at once. Mr. Ernest has been suddenly called back to town.

MERRIMAN

Yes, sir. (*Goes back into the house.*)

ALGERNON

What a fearful liar you are, Jack. I have not been called back to town at all.

JACK

Yes, you have.

ALGERNON

I haven't heard any one call me.

JACK

Your duty as a gentleman calls you back.

ALGERNON

My duty as a gentleman has never interfered with my pleasures in the smallest degree.

JACK

I can quite understand that.

ALGERNON

Well, Cecily is a darling.

JACK

You are not to talk of Miss Cardew like that. I don't like it.

ALGERNON

Well, I don't like your clothes. You look perfectly ridiculous in

them. Why on earth don't you go up and change? It is perfectly childish to be in deep mourning for a man who is actually staying for a whole week with you in your house as a guest. I call it grotesque.

JACK

You are certainly not staying with me for a whole week as a guest or anything else. You have got to leave . . . by the four-five train.

ALGERNON

I certainly won't leave you so long as you are in mourning. It would be most unfriendly. If I were in mourning you would stay with me, I suppose. I should think it very unkind if you didn't.

JACK

Well, will you go if I change my clothes?

ALGERNON

Yes, if you are not too long. I never saw anybody take so long to dress, and with such little result.

JACK

Well, at any rate, that is better than being always over-dressed as you are.

ALGERNON

If I am occasionally a little over-dressed, I make up for it by being always immensely over-educated.

JACK

Your vanity is ridiculous, your conduct an outrage, and your presence in my garden utterly absurd. However, you have got to catch the four-five, and I hope you will have a pleasant journey back to town. This Bunburying, as you call it, has not been a great success for you. (*Goes into the house.*)

ALGERNON

I think it has been a great success. I'm in love with Cecily, and that is everything. (*Enter* CECILY *at the back of the garden. She picks up the can and begins to water the flowers.*) But I must see her before I go, and make arrangements for another Bunbury. Ah, there she is.

CECILY

Oh, I merely came back to water the roses. I thought you were with Uncle Jack.

Algernon

He's gone to order the dog-cart for me.

Cecily

Oh, is he going to take you for a nice drive?

Algernon

He's going to send me away.

Cecily

Then have we got to part?

Algernon

I am afraid so. It's a very painful parting.

Cecily

It is always painful to part from people whom one has known for a very brief space of time. The absence of old friends one can endure with equanimity. But even a momentary separation from anyone to whom one has just been introduced is almost unbearable.

Algernon

Thank you.

(*Enter* Merriman.)

Merriman

The dog-cart is at the door, sir. (Algernon *looks appealingly at* Cecily.)

Cecily

It can wait, Merriman for . . . five minutes.

Merriman

Yes, Miss. (*Exit* Merriman.)

Algernon

I hope, Cecily, I shall not offend you if I state quite frankly and openly that you seem to me to be in every way the visible personification of absolute perfection.

Cecily

I think your frankness does you great credit, Ernest. If you will allow me, I will copy your remarks into my diary. (*Goes over to table and begins writing in diary.*)

ALGERNON

Do you really keep a diary? I'd give anything to look at it. May I?

CECILY

Oh no. (*Puts her hand over it.*) You see, it is simply a very young girl's record of her own thoughts and impressions, and consequently meant for publication. When it appears in volume form I hope you will order a copy. But pray, Ernest, don't stop. I delight in taking down from dictation. I have reached 'absolute perfection'. You can go on. I am quite ready for more.

ALGERNON

(*Somewhat taken aback.*) Ahem! Ahem!

CECILY

Oh, don't cough, Ernest. When one is dictating one should speak fluently and not cough. Besides, I don't know how to spell a cough. (*Writes as* ALGERNON *speaks.*)

ALGERNON

(*Speaking very rapidly.*) Cecily, ever since I first looked upon your wonderful and incomparable beauty, I have dared to love you wildly, passionately, devotedly, hopelessly.

CECILY

I don't think that you should tell me that you love me wildly, passionately, devotedly, hopelessly. Hopelessly doesn't seem to make much sense, does it?

ALGERNON

Cecily!

(*Enter* MERRIMAN.)

MERRIMAN

The dog-cart is waiting, sir.

ALGERNON

Tell it to come round next week, at the same hour.

MERRIMAN

(*Looks at* CECILY, *who makes no sign.*) Yes, sir.

(MERRIMAN *retires.*)

CECILY

Uncle Jack would be very much annoyed if he knew you were staying on till next week, at the same hour.

ALGERNON

Oh, I don't care about Jack. I don't care for anybody in the whole world but you. I love you, Cecily. You will marry me, won't you?

CECILY

You silly boy! Of course. Why, we have been engaged for the last three months.

ALGERNON

For the last three months?

CECILY

Yes, it will be exactly three months on Thursday.

ALGERNON

But how did we become engaged?

CECILY

Well, ever since dear Uncle Jack first confessed to us that he had a younger brother who was very wicked and bad, you of course have formed the chief topic of conversation between myself and Miss Prism. And of course a man who is much talked about is always very attractive. One feels there must be something in him, after all. I daresay it was foolish of me, but I fell in love with you, Ernest.

ALGERNON

Darling! And when was the engagement actually settled?

CECILY

On the 14th of February last. Worn out by your entire ignorance of my existence, I determined to end the matter one way or the other, and after a long struggle with myself I accepted you under this dear old tree here. The next day I bought this little ring in your name, and this is the little bangle with the true lover's knot I promised you always to wear.

ALGERNON

Did I give you this? It's very pretty, isn't it?

CECILY

Yes, you've wonderfully good taste, Ernest. It's the excuse I've always given for your leading such a bad life. And this is the box

in which I keep all your dear letters. (*Kneels at table, opens box, and produces letters tied up with blue ribbon.*)

ALGERNON

My letters! But, my own sweet Cecily, I have never written you any letters.

CECILY

You need hardly remind me of that, Ernest. I remember only too well that I was forced to write your letters for you. I wrote always three times a week, and sometimes oftener.

ALGERNON

Oh, do let me read them, Cecily?

CECILY

Oh, I couldn't possibly. They would make you far too conceited. (*Replaces box.*) The three you wrote me after I had broken off the engagement are so beautiful, and so badly spelled, that even now I can hardly read them without crying a little.

ALGERNON

But was our engagement ever broken off?

CECILY

Of course it was. On the 22nd of last March. You can see the entry if you like. (*Shows diary.*) 'To-day I broke off my engagement with Ernest. I feel it is better to do so. The weather still continues charming.'

ALGERNON

But why on earth did you break it off? What had I done? I had done nothing at all. Cecily, I am very much hurt indeed to hear you broke it off. Particularly when the weather was so charming.

CECILY

It would hardly have been a really serious engagement if it hadn't been broken off at least once. But I forgave you before the week was out.

ALGERNON

(Crossing to her, and kneeling.) What a perfect angel you are, Cecily.

CECILY

You dear romantic boy. (*He kisses her, she puts her fingers through his hair.*) I hope your hair curls naturally, does it?

ALGERNON

Yes, darling, with a little help from others.

CECILY

I am so glad.

ALGERNON

You'll never break off our engagement again, Cecily?

CECILY

I don't think I could break it off now that I have actually met you. Besides, of course, there is the question of your name.

ALGERNON

Yes, of course. (*Nervously.*)

CECILY

You must not laugh at me, darling, but it had always been a girlish dream of mine to love some one whose name was Ernest. (ALGERNON *rises*, CECILY *also.*) There is something in that name that seems to inspire absolute confidence. I pity any poor married woman whose husband is not called Ernest.

ALGERNON

But, my dear child, do you mean to say you could not love me if I had some other name?

CECILY

But what name?

ALGERNON

Oh, any name you like—Algernon—for instance . . .

CECILY

But I don't like the name of Algernon.

ALGERNON

Well, my own dear, sweet, loving little darling, I really can't see why you should object to the name of Algernon. It is not at all a bad name. In fact, it is rather an aristocratic name. Half of the chaps who get into the Bankruptcy Court are called Algernon. But seriously, Cecily . . . (*Moving to her*) . . . if my name was Algy, couldn't you love me?

CECILY

(*Rising.*) I might respect you, Ernest, I might admire your character, but I fear that I should not be able to give you my undivided attention.

Algernon

Ahem! Cecily! (*Picking up hat.*) Your Rector here is, I suppose, thoroughly experienced in the practice of all the rites and ceremonials of the Church?

Cecily

Oh, yes. Dr. Chasuble is a most learned man. He has never written a single book, so you can imagine how much he knows.

Algernon

I must see him at once on a most important christening—I mean on most important business.

Cecily

Oh!

Algernon

I shan't be away more than half an hour.

Cecily

Considering that we have been engaged since February the 14th, and that I only met you to-day for the first time, I think it is rather hard that you should leave me for so long a period as half an hour. Couldn't you make it twenty minutes?

Algernon

I'll be back in no time. (*Kisses her and rushes down the garden.*)

Cecily

What an impetuous boy he is! I like his hair so much. I must enter his proposal in my diary.

(*Enter* Merriman.)

Merriman

A Miss Fairfax has just called to see Mr. Worthing. On very important business, Miss Fairfax states.

Cecily

Isn't Mr. Worthing in his library?

Merriman

Mr. Worthing went over in the direction of the Rectory some time ago.

Cecily

Pray ask the lady to come out here; Mr. Worthing is sure to be back soon. And you can bring tea.

Merriman

Yes, Miss. (*Goes out.*)

Cecily

Miss Fairfax! I suppose one of the many good elderly women who are associated with Uncle Jack in some of his philanthropic work in London. I don't quite like women who are interested in philanthropic work. I think it is so forward of them.

(*Enter* Merriman.)

Merriman

Miss Fairfax.

(*Enter* Gwendolen.) (*Exit* Merriman.)

Cecily

(*Advancing to meet her.*) Pray let me introduce myself to you. My name is Cecily Cardew.

Gwendolen

Cecily Cardew? (*Moving to her and shaking hands.*) What a very sweet name! Something tells me that we are going to be great friends. I like you already more than I can say. My first impressions of people are never wrong.

Cecily

How nice of you to like me so much after we have known each other such a comparatively short time. Pray sit down.

Gwendolen

(*Still standing up.*) I may call you Cecily, may I not?

Cecily

With pleasure!

Gwendolen

And you will always call me Gwendolen, won't you?

Cecily

If you wish.

GWENDOLEN

Then that is all quite settled, is it not?

CECILY

I hope so. (*A pause. They both sit down together.*)

GWENDOLEN

Perhaps this might be a favourable opportunity for my mentioning who I am. My father is Lord Bracknell. You have never heard of papa, I suppose?

CECILY

I don't think so.

GWENDOLEN

Outside the family circle, papa, I am glad to say, is entirely unknown. I think that is quite as it should be. The home seems to me to be the proper sphere for the man. And certainly once a man begins to neglect his domestic duties he becomes painfully effeminate, does he not? And I don't like that. It makes men so very attractive. Cecily, mamma, whose views on education are remarkably strict, has brought me up to be extremely short-sighted; it is part of her system; so do you mind my looking at you through my glasses?

CECILY

Oh! not at all, Gwendolen. I am very fond of being looked at.

GWENDOLEN

(*After examining* CECILY *carefully through a lorgnette.*) You are here on a short visit, I suppose.

CECILY

Oh no! I live here.

GWENDOLEN

(*Severely.*) Really? Your mother, no doubt, or some female relative of advanced years, resides here also?

CECILY

Oh no! I have no mother, nor, in fact, any relations.

GWENDOLEN

Indeed?

CECILY

My dear guardian, with the assistance of Miss Prism, has the arduous task of looking after me.

GWENDOLEN

Your guardian?

CECILY

Yes, I am Mr. Worthing's ward.

GWENDOLEN

Oh! It is strange he never mentioned to me that he had a ward. How secretive of him! He grows more interesting hourly. I am not sure, however, that the news inspires me with feelings of unmixed delight. (*Rising and going to her.*) I am very fond of you, Cecily; I have liked you ever since I met you! But I am bound to state that now that I know that you are Mr. Worthing's ward, I cannot help expressing a wish you were—well, just a little older than you seem to be—and not quite so very alluring in appearance. In fact, if I may speak candidly—Cecily. Pray do! I think that whenever one has anything unpleasant to say, one should always be quite candid.

GWENDOLEN

Well, to speak with perfect candour, Cecily, I wish that you were fully forty-two, and more than usually plain for your age. Ernest has a strong upright nature. He is the very soul of truth and honour. Disloyalty would be as impossible to him as deception. But even men of the noblest possible moral character are extremely susceptible to the influence of the physical charms of others. Modern, no less than Ancient History, supplies us with many most painful examples of what I refer to. If it were not so, indeed, History would be quite unreadable.

CECILY

I beg your pardon, Gwendolen, did you say Ernest?

GWENDOLEN

Yes.

CECILY

Oh, but it is not Mr. Ernest Worthing who is my guardian. It is his brother—his elder brother.

GWENDOLEN

(*Sitting down again.*) Ernest never mentioned to me that he had a brother.

CECILY

I am sorry to say they have not been on good terms for a long time.

GWENDOLEN

Ah! that accounts for it. And now that I think of it I have never heard any man mention his brother. The subject seems distasteful to most men. Cecily, you have lifted a load from my mind. I was growing almost anxious. It would have been terrible if any cloud had come across a friendship like ours, would it not? Of course you are quite, quite sure that it is not Mr. Ernest Worthing who is your guardian?

CECILY

Quite sure. (*A pause.*) In fact, I am going to be his.

GWENDOLEN

(*Inquiringly.*) I beg your pardon?

CECILY

(*Rather shy and confidingly.*) Dearest Gwendolen, there is no reason why I should make a secret of it to you. Our little county newspaper is sure to chronicle the fact next week. Mr. Ernest Worthing and I are engaged to be married.

GWENDOLEN

(*Quite politely, rising.*) My darling Cecily, I think there must be some slight error. Mr. Ernest Worthing is engaged to me. The announcement will appear in the *Morning Post* on Saturday at the latest.

CECILY

(*Very politely, rising.*) I am afraid you must be under some misconception. Ernest proposed to me exactly ten minutes ago. (*Shows diary.*)

GWENDOLEN

(*Examines diary through her lorgnettte carefully.*) It is certainly very curious, for he asked me to be his wife yesterday afternoon at 5.30. If you would care to verify the incident, pray do so. (*Produces diary of her own.*) I never travel without my diary. One should always have something sensational to read in the train. I am so sorry, dear Cecily, if it is any disappointment to you, but I am afraid I have the prior claim.

CECILY

It would distress me more than I can tell you, dear Gwendolen, if it caused you any mental or physical anguish, but I feel bound to point out that since Ernest proposed to you he clearly has changed his mind.

GWENDOLEN

(*Meditatively.*) If the poor fellow has been entrapped into any foolish promise I shall consider it my duty to rescue him at once, and with a firm hand.

CECILY

(*Thoughtfully and sadly.*) Whatever unfortunate entanglement my dear boy may have got into, I will never reproach him with it after we are married.

GWENDOLEN

Do you allude to me, Miss Cardew, as an entanglement? You are presumptuous. On an occasion of this kind it becomes more than a moral duty to speak one's mind. It becomes a pleasure.

CECILY

Do you suggest, Miss Fairfax, that I entrapped Ernest into an engagement? How dare you? This is no time for wearing the shallow mask of manners. When I see a spade I call it a spade.

GWENDOLEN

(*Satirically.*) I am glad to say that I have never seen a spade. It is obvious that our social spheres have been widely different.

(*Enter* MERRIMAN, *followed by the footman.*
He carries a salver, table cloth, and plate stand.
CECILY *is about to retort. The presence of the servants exercises*
a restraining influence, under which both girls chafe.)

MERRIMAN

Shall I lay tea here as usual, Miss?

CECILY

(*Sternly, in a calm voice.*) Yes, as usual. (MERRIMAN *begins to clear table and lay cloth. A long pause.* CECILY *and* GWENDOLEN *glare at each other.*)

GWENDOLEN

Are there many interesting walks in the vicinity, Miss Cardew?

CECILY

Oh! yes! a great many. From the top of one of the hills quite close one can see five counties.

GWENDOLEN

Five counties! I don't think I should like that; I hate crowds.

CECILY

(*Sweetly.*) I suppose that is why you live in town? (GWENDOLEN *bites her lip, and beats her foot nervously with her parasol.*)

GWENDOLEN

(*Looking round.*) Quite a well-kept garden this is, Miss Cardew.

CECILY

So glad you like it, Miss Fairfax.

GWENDOLEN

I had no idea there were any flowers in the country.

CECILY

Oh, flowers are as common here, Miss Fairfax, as people are in London.

GWENDOLEN

Personally I cannot understand how anybody manages to exist in the country, if anybody who is anybody does. The country always bores me to death.

CECILY

Ah! This is what the newspapers call agricultural depression, is it not? I believe the aristocracy are suffering very much from it just at present. It is almost an epidemic amongst them, I have been told. May I offer you some tea, Miss Fairfax?

GWENDOLEN

(*With elaborate politeness.*) Thank you. (*Aside.*) Detestable girl! But I require tea!

CECILY

(*Sweetly.*) Sugar?

GWENDOLEN

(*Superciliously.*) No, thank you. Sugar is not fashionable any more. (CECILY *looks angrily at her, takes up the tongs and puts four lumps of sugar into the cup.*)

CECILY

(*Severely.*) Cake or bread and butter?

GWENDOLEN

(*In a bored manner.*) Bread and butter, please. Cake is rarely seen at the best houses nowadays.

CECILY

(*Cuts a very large slice of cake, and puts it on the tray.*) Hand that to Miss Fairfax. (MERRIMAN *does so, and goes out with footman.* GWENDOLEN *drinks the tea and makes a grimace. Puts down cup at once, reaches out her hand to the bread and butter, looks at it, and finds it is cake. Rises in indignation.*)

GWENDOLEN

You have filled my tea with lumps of sugar, and though I asked most distinctly for bread and butter, you have given me cake. I am known for the gentleness of my disposition, and the extraordinary sweetness of my nature, but I warn you, Miss Cardew, you may go too far.

CECILY

(*Rising.*) To save my poor, innocent, trusting boy from the machinations of any other girl there are no lengths to which I would not go.

GWENDOLEN

From the moment I saw you I distrusted you. I felt that you were false and deceitful. I am never deceived in such matters. My first impressions of people are invariably right.

CECILY

It seems to me, Miss Fairfax, that I am trespassing on your valuable time. No doubt you have many other calls of a similar character to make in the neighbourhood.

(*Enter* JACK.)

GWENDOLEN

(*Catching sight of him.*) Ernest! My own Ernest!

JACK

Gwendolen! Darling! (*Offers to kiss her.*)

GWENDOLEN

(Draws back.) A moment! May I ask if you are engaged to be married to this young lady? (*Points to* CECILY.)

JACK

(*Laughing.*) To dear little Cecily! Of course not! What could have put such an idea into your pretty little head?

GWENDOLEN

Thank you. You may! (*Offers her cheek.*)

CECILY

(*Very sweetly.*) I knew there must be some misunderstanding, Miss Fairfax. The gentleman whose arm is at present round your waist is my guardian, Mr. John Worthing.

GWENDOLEN

I beg your pardon?

CECILY

This is Uncle Jack.

GWENDOLEN

(*Receding.*) Jack! Oh!

(*Enter* ALGERNON.)

CECILY

Here is Ernest.

ALGERNON

(*Goes straight over to* CECILY *without noticing any one else.*) My own love! (*Offers to kiss her.*)

CECILY

(*Drawing back.*) A moment, Ernest! May I ask you—are you engaged to be married to this young lady?

ALGERNON

(*Looking round.*) To what young lady? Good heavens! Gwendolen!

CECILY

Yes! to good heavens, Gwendolen, I mean to Gwendolen.

ALGERNON

(*Laughing.*) Of course not! What could have put such an idea into your pretty little head?

CECILY

Thank you. (*Presenting her cheek to be kissed.*) You may. (ALGERNON *kisses her.*)

GWENDOLEN

I felt there was some slight error, Miss Cardew. The gentleman who is now embracing you is my cousin, Mr. Algernon Moncrieff.

CECILY

(*Breaking away from* ALGERNON.) Algernon Moncrieff! Oh! (*The two girls move towards each other and put their arms round each other's waists as if for protection.*)

CECILY

Are you called Algernon?

ALGERNON

I cannot deny it.

CECILY

Oh!

GWENDOLEN

Is your name really John?

JACK

(*Standing rather proudly.*) I could deny it if I liked. I could deny anything if I liked. But my name certainly is John. It has been John for years.

CECILY

(*To* GWENDOLEN.) A gross deception has been practised on both of us.

GWENDOLEN

My poor wounded Cecily!

CECILY

My sweet wronged Gwendolen!

GWENDOLEN

(*Slowly and seriously.*) You will call me sister, will you not? (*They embrace.* JACK *and* ALGERNON *groan and walk up and down.*)

CECILY

(*Rather brightly.*) There is just one question I would like to be allowed to ask my guardian.

GWENDOLEN

An admirable idea! Mr. Worthing, there is just one question I would like to be permitted to put to you. Where is your brother Ernest? We are both engaged to be married to your brother

Ernest, so it is a matter of some importance to us to know where your brother Ernest is at present.

JACK

(*Slowly and hesitatingly.*) Gwendolen—Cecily—it is very painful for me to be forced to speak the truth. It is the first time in my life that I have ever been reduced to such a painful position, and I am really quite inexperienced in doing anything of the kind. However, I will tell you quite frankly that I have no brother Ernest. I have no brother at all. I never had a brother in my life, and I certainly have not the smallest intention of ever having one in the future.

CECILY

(*Surprised.*) No brother at all?

JACK

(*Cheerily.*) None!

GWENDOLEN

(*Severely.*) Had you never a brother of any kind?

JACK

(*Pleasantly.*) Never. Not even of any kind.

GWENDOLEN

I am afraid it is quite clear, Cecily, that neither of us is engaged to be married to any one.

CECILY

It is not a very pleasant position for a young girl suddenly to find herself in. Is it?

GWENDOLEN

Let us go into the house. They will hardly venture to come after us there.

CECILY

No, men are so cowardly, aren't they? (*They retire into the house with scornful looks.*)

JACK

This ghastly state of things is what you call Bunburying, I suppose?

ALGERNON

Yes, and a perfectly wonderful Bunbury it is. The most wonderful Bunbury I have ever had in my life.

JACK

Well, you've no right whatsoever to Bunbury here.

ALGERNON

That is absurd. One has a right to Bunbury anywhere one chooses. Every serious Bunburyist knows that.

JACK

Serious Bunburyist! Good heavens!

ALGERNON

Well, one must be serious about something, if one wants to have any amusement in life. I happen to be serious about Bunburying. What on earth you are serious about I haven't got the remotest idea. About everything, I should fancy. You have such an absolutely trivial nature.

JACK

Well, the only small satisfaction I have in the whole of this wretched business is that your friend Bunbury is quite exploded. You won't be able to run down to the country quite so often as you used to do, dear Algy. And a very good thing too.

ALGERNON

Your brother is a little off colour, isn't he, dear Jack? You won't be able to disappear to London quite so frequently as your wicked custom was. And not a bad thing either.

JACK

As for your conduct towards Miss Cardew, I must say that your taking in a sweet, simple, innocent girl like that is quite inexcusable. To say nothing of the fact that she is my ward.

ALGERNON

I can see no possible defence at all for your deceiving a brilliant, clever, thoroughly experienced young lady like Miss Fairfax. To say nothing of the fact that she is my cousin.

JACK

I wanted to be engaged to Gwendolen, that is all. I love her.

ALGERNON

Well, I simply wanted to be engaged to Cecily. I adore her.

JACK

There is certainly no chance of your marrying Miss Cardew.

ALGERNON

I don't think there is much likelihood, Jack, of you and Miss Fairfax being united.

JACK

Well, that is no business of yours.

ALGERNON

If it was my business, I wouldn't talk about it. (*Begins to eat muffins.*) It is very vulgar to talk about one's business. Only people like stock-brokers do that, and then merely at dinner parties.

JACK

How can you sit there, calmly eating muffins when we are in this horrible trouble, I can't make out. You seem to me to be perfectly heartless.

ALGERNON

Well, I can't eat muffins in an agitated manner. The butter would probably get on my cuffs. One should always eat muffins quite calmly. It is the only way to eat them.

JACK

I say it's perfectly heartless your eating muffins at all, under the circumstances.

ALGERNON

When I am in trouble, eating is the only thing that consoles me. Indeed, when I am in really great trouble, as any one who knows me intimately will tell you, I refuse everything except food and drink. At the present moment I am eating muffins because I am unhappy. Besides, I am particularly fond of muffins. (*Rising.*)

JACK

(*Rising.*) Well, that is no reason why you should eat them all in that greedy way. (*Takes muffins from* ALGERNON.)

ALGERNON

(*Offering tea-cake.*) I wish you would have tea-cake instead. I don't like tea-cake.

JACK

Good heavens! I suppose a man may eat his own muffins in his own garden.

ALGERNON

But you have just said it was perfectly heartless to eat muffins.

JACK

I said it was perfectly heartless of you, under the circumstances. That is a very different thing.

ALGERNON

That may be. But the muffins are the same. (*He seizes the muffin-dish from* JACK.)

JACK

Algy, I wish to goodness you would go.

ALGERNON

You can't possibly ask me to go without having some dinner. It's absurd. I never go without my dinner. No one ever does, except vegetarians and people like that. Besides I have just made arrangements with Dr. Chasuble to be christened at a quarter to six under the name of Ernest.

JACK

My dear fellow, the sooner you give up that nonsense the better. I made arrangements this morning with Dr. Chasuble to be christened myself at 5.30, and I naturally will take the name of Ernest. Gwendolen would wish it. We can't both be christened Ernest. It's absurd. Besides, I have a perfect right to be christened if I like. There is no evidence at all that I have ever been christened by anybody. I should think it extremely probable I never was, and so does Dr. Chasuble. It is entirely different in your case. You have been christened already.

ALGERNON

Yes, but I have not been christened for years.

JACK

Yes, but you have been christened. That is the important thing.

ALGERNON

Quite so. So I know my constitution can stand it. If you are not quite sure about your ever having been christened, I must say I think it rather dangerous your venturing on it now. It might make you very unwell. You can hardly have forgotten that some one very closely connected with you was very nearly carried off this week in Paris by a severe chill.

JACK

Yes, but you said yourself that a severe chill was not hereditary.

ALGERNON

It usen't to be, I know—but I daresay it is now. Science is always making wonderful improvements in things.

JACK

(*Picking up the muffin-dish.*) Oh, that is nonsense; you are always talking nonsense.

ALGERNON

Jack, you are at the muffins again! I wish you wouldn't. There are only two left. (*Takes them.*) I told you I was particularly fond of muffins.

JACK

But I hate tea-cake.

ALGERNON

Why on earth then do you allow tea-cake to be served up for your guests? What ideas you have of hospitality!

JACK

Algernon! I have already told you to go. I don't want you here. Why don't you go!

ALGERNON

I haven't quite finished my tea yet! and there is still one muffin left. (JACK *groans, and sinks into a chair.* ALGERNON *still continues eating.*)

Act 3

SCENE—*Morning-room at the Manor House.* GWENDOLEN *and* CECILY *are at the window, looking out into the garden.*

GWENDOLEN

The fact that they did not follow us at once into the house, as any one else would have done, seems to me to show that they have some sense of shame left.

CECILY

They have been eating muffins. That looks like repentance.

GWENDOLEN

(*After a pause.*) They don't seem to notice us at all. Couldn't you cough?

CECILY

But I haven't got a cough.

GWENDOLEN

They're looking at us. What effrontery!

CECILY

They're approaching. That's very forward of them.

GWENDOLEN

Let us preserve a dignified silence.

CECILY

Certainly. It's the only thing to do now.

(*Enter* JACK *followed by* ALGERNON. *They whistle some dreadful popular air from a British Opera.*)

GWENDOLEN

This dignified silence seems to produce an unpleasant effect.

CECILY

A most distasteful one.

GWENDOLEN

But we will not be the first to speak.

CECILY

Certainly not.

GWENDOLEN

Mr. Worthing, I have something very particular to ask you. Much depends on your reply.

CECILY

Gwendolen, your common sense is invaluable. Mr. Moncrieff, kindly answer me the following question. Why did you pretend to be my guardian's brother?

ALGERNON

In order that I might have an opportunity of meeting you.

CECILY

(*To* GWENDOLEN.) That certainly seems a satisfactory explanation, does it not?

GWENDOLEN

Yes, dear, if you can believe him.

CECILY

I don't. But that does not affect the wonderful beauty of his answer.

GWENDOLEN

True. In matters of grave importance, style, not sincerity is the vital thing. Mr. Worthing, what explanation can you offer to me for pretending to have a brother? Was it in order that you might

have an opportunity of coming up to town to see me as often as possible?

JACK

Can you doubt it, Miss Fairfax?

GWENDOLEN

I have the gravest doubts upon the subject. But I intend to crush them. This is not the moment for German scepticism. (*Moving to* CECILY.) Their explanations appear to be quite satisfactory, especially Mr. Worthing's. That seems to me to have the stamp of truth upon it.

CECILY

I am more than content with what Mr. Moncrieff said. His voice alone inspires one with absolute credulity.

GWENDOLEN

Then you think we should forgive them?

CECILY

Yes. I mean no.

GWENDOLEN

True! I had forgotten. There are principles at stake that one cannot surrender. Which of us should tell them? The task is not a pleasant one.

CECILY

Could we not both speak at the same time?

GWENDOLEN

An excellent idea! I nearly always speak at the same time as other people. Will you take the time from me?

CECILY

Certainly. (GWENDOLEN *beats time with uplifted finger.*)

GWENDOLEN and CECILY (*Speaking together.*) Your Christian names are still an insuperable barrier. That is all!

JACK and ALGERNON (Speaking together.) Our Christian names! Is that all? But we are going to be christened this afternoon.

GWENDOLEN

(*To* JACK.) For my sake you are prepared to do this terrible thing?

JACK

I am.

CECILY

(*To* ALGERNON.) To please me you are ready to face this fearful ordeal?

ALGERNON

I am!

GWENDOLEN

How absurd to talk of the equality of the sexes! Where questions of self-sacrifice are concerned, men are infinitely beyond us.

JACK

We are. (*Clasps hands with* ALGERNON.)

CECILY

They have moments of physical courage of which we women know absolutely nothing.

GWENDOLEN

(*To* JACK.) Darling!

ALGERNON

(*To* CECILY.) Darling! (*They fall into each other's arms.*)

(*Enter* MERRIMAN. *When he enters he coughs loudly, seeing the situation.*)

MERRIMAN

Ahem! Ahem! Lady Bracknell!

JACK

Good heavens!

(*Enter* LADY BRACKNELL. *The couples separate in alarm. Exit* MERRIMAN.)

LADY BRACKNELL

Gwendolen! What does this mean?

GWENDOLEN

Merely that I am engaged to be married to Mr. Worthing, mamma.

LADY BRACKNELL

Come here. Sit down. Sit down immediately. Hesitation of any kind is a sign of mental decay in the young, of physical weakness

in the old. (*Turns to* JACK.) Apprised, sir, of my daughter's sudden flight by her trusty maid, whose confidence I purchased by means of a small coin, I followed her at once by a luggage train. Her unhappy father is, I am glad to say, under the impression that she is attending a more than usually lengthy lecture by the University Extension Scheme on the Influence of a permanent income on Thought. I do not propose to undeceive him. Indeed I have never undeceived him on any question. I would consider it wrong. But of course, you will clearly understand that all communication between yourself and my daughter must cease immediately from this moment. On this point, as indeed on all points, I am firm.

JACK

I am engaged to be married to Gwendolen Lady Bracknell!

LADY BRACKNELL

You are nothing of the kind, sir. And now, as regards Algernon! . . . Algernon!

ALGERNON

Yes, Aunt Augusta.

LADY BRACKNELL

May I ask if it is in this house that your invalid friend Mr. Bunbury resides?

ALGERNON

(*Stammering.*) Oh! No! Bunbury doesn't live here. Bunbury is somewhere else at present. In fact, Bunbury is dead.

LADY BRACKNELL

Dead! When did Mr. Bunbury die? His death must have been extremely sudden.

ALGERNON

(*Airily.*) Oh! I killed Bunbury this afternoon. I mean poor Bunbury died this afternoon.

LADY BRACKNELL

What did he die of?

ALGERNON

Bunbury? Oh, he was quite exploded.

LADY BRACKNELL

Exploded! Was he the victim of a revolutionary outrage? I was

not aware that Mr. Bunbury was interested in social legislation. If so, he is well punished for his morbidity.

ALGERNON

My dear Aunt Augusta, I mean he was found out! The doctors found out that Bunbury could not live, that is what I mean—so Bunbury died.

LADY BRACKNELL

He seems to have had great confidence in the opinion of his physicians. I am glad, however, that he made up his mind at the last to some definite course of action, and acted under proper medical advice. And now that we have finally got rid of this Mr. Bunbury, may I ask, Mr. Worthing, who is that young person whose hand my nephew Algernon is now holding in what seems to me a peculiarly unnecessary manner?

JACK

That lady is Miss Cecily Cardew, my ward. (LADY BRACKNELL *bows coldly to* CECILY.)

ALGERNON

I am engaged to be married to Cecily, Aunt Augusta.

LADY BRACKNELL

I beg your pardon?

CECILY

Mr. Moncrieff and I are engaged to be married, Lady Bracknell.

LADY BRACKNELL

(*With a shiver, crossing to the sofa and sitting down.*) I do not know whether there is anything peculiarly exciting in the air of this particular part of Hertfordshire, but the number of engagements that go on seems to me considerably above the proper average that statistics have laid down for our guidance. I think some preliminary inquiry on my part would not be out of place. Mr. Worthing, is Miss Cardew at all connected with any of the larger railway stations in London? I merely desire information. Until yesterday I had no idea that there were any families or persons whose origin was a Terminus. (JACK *looks perfectly furious, but restrains himself.*)

JACK

(*In a clear, cold voice.*) Miss Cardew is the grand-daughter of the

late Mr. Thomas Cardew of 149 Belgrave Square, S.W.; Gervase Park, Dorking, Surrey; and the Sporran, Fifeshire, N.B.

LADY BRACKNELL

That sounds not unsatisfactory. Three addresses always inspire confidence, even in tradesmen. But what proof have I of their authenticity?

JACK

I have carefully preserved the Court Guides of the period. They are open to your inspection, Lady Bracknell.

LADY BRACKNELL

(*Grimly.*) I have known strange errors in that publication.

JACK

Miss Cardew's family solicitors are Messrs. Markby, Markby, and Markby.

LADY BRACKNELL

Markby, Markby, and Markby? A firm of the very highest position in their profession. Indeed I am told that one of the Mr. Markby's is occasionally to be seen at dinner parties. So far I am satisfied.

JACK

(*Very irritably.*) How extremely kind of you, Lady Bracknell! I have also in my possession, you will be pleased to hear, certificates of Miss Cardew's birth, baptism, whooping cough, registration, vaccination, confirmation, and the measles; both the German and the English variety.

LADY BRACKNELL

Ah! A life crowded with incident, I see; though perhaps somewhat too exciting for a young girl. I am not myself in favour of premature experiences. (*Rises, looks at her watch.*) Gwendolen! the time approaches for our departure. We have not a moment to lose. As a matter of form, Mr. Worthing, I had better ask you if Miss Cardew has any little fortune?

JACK

Oh! about a hundred and thirty thousand pounds in the Funds. That is all. Goodbye, Lady Bracknell. So pleased to have seen you.

LADY BRACKNELL

(*Sitting down again.*) A moment, Mr. Worthing. A hundred and

thirty thousand pounds! And in the Funds! Miss Cardew seems to me a most attractive young lady, now that I look at her. Few girls of the present day have any really solid qualities, any of the qualities that last, and improve with time. We live, I regret to say, in an age of surfaces. (*To* CECILY.) Come over here, dear. (CECILY *goes across.*) Pretty child! your dress is sadly simple, and your hair seems almost as Nature might have left it. But we can soon alter all that. A thoroughly experienced French maid produces a really marvellous result in a very brief space of time. I remember recommending one to young Lady Lancing, and after three months her own husband did not know her.

JACK

And after six months nobody knew her.

LADY BRACKNELL

(*Glares at* JACK *for a few moments. Then bends, with a practised smile, to* CECILY.) Kindly turn round, sweet child. (CECILY *turns completely round.*) No, the side view is what I want. (CECILY *presents her profile.*) Yes, quite as I expected. There are distinct social possibilities in your profile. The two weak points in our age are its want of principle and its want of profile. The chin a little higher, dear. Style largely depends on the way the chin is worn. They are worn very high, just at present. Algernon!

ALGERNON

Yes, Aunt Augusta!

LADY BRACKNELL

There are distinct social possibilities in Miss Cardew's profile.

ALGERNON

Cecily is the sweetest, dearest, prettiest girl in the whole world. And I don't care twopence about social possibilities.

LADY BRACKNELL

Never speak disrespectfully of Society, Algernon. Only people who can't get into it do that. (*To* CECILY.) Dear child, of course you know that Algernon has nothing but his debts to depend upon. But I do not approve of mercenary marriages. When I married Lord Bracknell I had no fortune of any kind. But I never dreamed for a moment of allowing that to stand in my way. Well, I suppose I must give my consent.

ALGERNON

Thank you, Aunt Augusta.

LADY BRACKNELL

Cecily, you may kiss me!

CECILY

(*Kisses her.*) Thank you, Lady Bracknell.

LADY BRACKNELL

You may also address me as Aunt Augusta for the future.

CECILY

Thank you, Aunt Augusta.

LADY BRACKNELL

The marriage, I think, had better take place quite soon.

ALGERNON

Thank you, Aunt Augusta.

CECILY

Thank you, Aunt Augusta.

LADY BRACKNELL

To speak frankly, I am not in favour of long engagements. They give people the opportunity of finding out each other's character before marriage, which I think is never advisable.

JACK

I beg your pardon for interrupting you, Lady Bracknell, but this engagement is quite out of the question. I am Miss Cardew's guardian, and she cannot marry without my consent until she comes of age. That consent I absolutely decline to give.

LADY BRACKNELL

Upon what grounds may I ask? Algernon is an extremely, I may almost say an ostentatiously, eligible young man. He has nothing, but he looks everything. What more can one desire?

JACK

It pains me very much to have to speak frankly to you, Lady Bracknell, about your nephew, but the fact is that I do not approve at all of his moral character. I suspect him of being untruthful. (ALGERNON *and* CECILY *look at him in indignant amazement.*)

LADY BRACKNELL

Untruthful! My nephew Algernon? Impossible! He is an Oxonian.

JACK

I fear there can be no possible doubt about the matter. This afternoon during my temporary absence in London on an important question of romance, he obtained admission to my house by means of the false pretence of being my brother. Under an assumed name he drank, I've just been informed by my butler, an entire pint bottle of my Perrier-Jouet, Brut, '89; wine I was specially reserving for myself. Continuing his disgraceful deception, he succeeded in the course of the afternoon in alienating the affections of my only ward. He subsequently stayed to tea, and devoured every single muffin. And what makes his conduct all the more heartless is, that he was perfectly well aware from the first that I have no brother, that I never had a brother, and that I don't intend to have a brother, not even of any kind. I distinctly told him so myself yesterday afternoon.

LADY BRACKNELL

Ahem! Mr. Worthing, after careful consideration I have decided entirely to overlook my nephew's conduct to you.

JACK

That is very generous of you, Lady Bracknell. My own decision, however, is unalterable. I decline to give my consent.

LADY BRACKNELL

(*To* CECILY.) Come here, sweet child. (CECILY *goes over.*) How old are you, dear?

CECILY

Well, I am really only eighteen, but I always admit to twenty when I go to evening parties.

LADY BRACKNELL

You are perfectly right in making some slight alteration. Indeed, no woman should ever be quite accurate about her age. It looks so calculating . . . (*In a meditative manner.*) Eighteen, but admitting to twenty at evening parties. Well, it will not be very long before you are of age and free from the restraints of tutelage. So I don't think your guardian's consent is, after all, a matter of any importance.

JACK

Pray excuse me, Lady Bracknell, for interrupting you again,

but it is only fair to tell you that according to the terms of her grandfather's will Miss Cardew does not come legally of age till she is thirty-five.

LADY BRACKNELL

That does not seem to me to be a grave objection. Thirty-five is a very attractive age. London society is full of women of the very highest birth who have, of their own free choice, remained thirty-five for years. Lady Dumbleton is an instance in point. To my own knowledge she has been thirty-five ever since she arrived at the age of forty, which was many years ago now. I see no reason why our dear Cecily should not be even still more attractive at the age you mention than she is at present. There will be a large accumulation of property.

CECILY

Algy, could you wait for me till I was thirty-five?

ALGERNON

Of course I could, Cecily. You know I could.

CECILY

Yes, I felt it instinctively, but I couldn't wait all that time. I hate waiting even five minutes for anybody. It always makes me rather cross. I am not punctual myself, I know, but I do like punctuality in others, and waiting, even to be married, is quite out of the question.

ALGERNON

Then what is to be done, Cecily?

CECILY

I don't know, Mr. Moncrieff.

LADY BRACKNELL

My dear Mr. Worthing, as Miss Cardew states positively that she cannot wait till she is thirty-five—a remark which I am bound to say seems to me to show a somewhat impatient nature—I would beg of you to reconsider your decision.

JACK

But my dear Lady Bracknell, the matter is entirely in your own hands. The moment you consent to my marriage with Gwendolen, I will most gladly allow your nephew to form an alliance with my ward.

LADY BRACKNELL

(*Rising and drawing herself up.*) You must be quite aware that what you propose is out of the question.

JACK

Then a passionate celibacy is all that any of us can look forward to.

LADY BRACKNELL

That is not the destiny I propose for Gwendolen. Algernon, of course, can choose for himself. (*Pulls out her watch.*) Come, dear, (GWENDOLEN *rises*) we have already missed five, if not six, trains. To miss any more might expose us to comment on the platform.

(*Enter* DR. CHASUBLE.)

CHASUBLE

Everything is quite ready for the christenings.

LADY BRACKNELL

The christenings, sir! Is not that somewhat premature?

CHASUBLE

(*Looking rather puzzled, and pointing to* JACK *and* ALGERNON.) Both these gentlemen have expressed a desire for immediate baptism.

LADY BRACKNELL

At their age? The idea is grotesque and irreligious! Algernon, I forbid you to be baptized. I will not hear of such excesses. Lord Bracknell would be highly displeased if he learned that that was the way in which you wasted your time and money.

CHASUBLE

Am I to understand then that there are to be no christenings at all this afternoon?

JACK

I don't think that, as things are now, it would be of much practical value to either of us, Dr. Chasuble.

CHASUBLE

I am grieved to hear such sentiments from you, Mr. Worthing. They savour of the heretical views of the Anabaptists, views that I have completely refuted in four of my unpublished sermons. However, as your present mood seems to be one peculiarly secular, I will return to the church at once. Indeed, I have just

been informed by the pew-opener that for the last hour and a half Miss Prism has been waiting for me in the vestry.

LADY BRACKNELL

(*Starting.*) Miss Prism! Did I hear you mention a Miss Prism?

CHASUBLE

Yes, Lady Bracknell. I am on my way to join her.

LADY BRACKNELL

Pray allow me to detain you for a moment. This matter may prove to be one of vital importance to Lord Bracknell and myself. Is this Miss Prism a female of repellent aspect, remotely connected with education?

CHASUBLE

(*Somewhat indignantly.*) She is the most cultivated of ladies, and the very picture of respectability.

LADY BRACKNELL

It is obviously the same person. May I ask what position she holds in your household?

CHASUBLE

(*Severely.*) I am a celibate, madam.

JACK

(*Interposing.*) Miss Prism, Lady Bracknell, has been for the last three years Miss Cardew's esteemed governess and valued companion.

LADY BRACKNELL

In spite of what I hear of her, I must see her at once. Let her be sent for.

CHASUBLE

(*Looking off.*) She approaches; she is nigh.

(*Enter* MISS PRISM *hurriedly.*)

MISS PRISM

I was told you expected me in the vestry, dear Canon. I have been waiting for you there for an hour and three-quarters. (*Catches sight of* LADY BRACKNELL, *who has fixed her with a stony glare.* MISS PRISM *grows pale and quails. She looks anxiously round as if desirous to escape.*)

Lady Bracknell

(*In a severe, judicial voice.*) Prism! (Miss Prism *bows her head in shame.*) Come here, Prism! (Miss Prism *approaches in a humble manner.*) Prism! Where is that baby? (*General consternation. The Canon starts back in horror.* Algernon *and* Jack *pretend to be anxious to shield* Cecily *and* Gwendolen *from hearing the details of a terrible public scandal.*) Twenty-eight years ago, Prism, you left Lord Bracknell's house, Number 104, Upper Grosvenor Street, in charge of a perambulator that contained a baby of the male sex. You never returned. A few weeks later, through the elaborate investigations of the Metropolitan police, the perambulator was discovered at midnight, standing by itself in a remote corner of Bayswater. It contained the manuscript of a three-volume novel of more than usually revolting sentimentality. (Miss Prism *starts in involuntary indignation.*) But the baby was not there! (*Every one looks at* Miss Prism.) Prism! Where is that baby? (*A pause.*)

Miss Prism

Lady Bracknell, I admit with shame that I do not know. I only wish I did. The plain facts of the case are these. On the morning of the day you mention, a day that is for ever branded on my memory, I prepared as usual to take the baby out in its perambulator. I had also with me a somewhat old, but capacious hand-bag in which I had intended to place the manuscript of a work of fiction that I had written during my few unoccupied hours. In a moment of mental abstraction, for which I never can forgive myself, I deposited the manuscript in the basinette, and placed the baby in the hand-bag.

Jack

(*Who has been listening attentively.*) But where did you deposit the hand-bag?

Miss Prism

Do not ask me, Mr. Worthing.

Jack

Miss Prism, this is a matter of no small importance to me. I insist on knowing where you deposited the hand-bag that contained that infant.

MISS PRISM

I left it in the cloak-room of one of the larger railway stations in London.

Jack

What railway station?

MISS PRISM

(*Quite crushed.*) Victoria. The Brighton line. (*Sinks into a chair.*)

JACK

I must retire to my room for a moment. Gwendolen, wait here for me.

GWENDOLEN

If you are not too long, I will wait here for you all my life.

(*Exit* JACK *in great excitement.*)

CHASUBLE

What do you think this means, Lady Bracknell?

LADY BRACKNELL

I dare not even suspect, Dr. Chasuble. I need hardly tell you that in families of high position strange coincidences are not supposed to occur. They are hardly considered the thing. (*Noises heard overhead as if some one was throwing trunks about. Every one looks up.*)

CECILY

Uncle Jack seems strangely agitated.

CHASUBLE

Your guardian has a very emotional nature.

LADY BRACKNELL

This noise is extremely unpleasant. It sounds as if he was having an argument. I dislike arguments of any kind. They are always vulgar, and often convincing.

CHASUBLE

(*Looking up.*) It has stopped now. (*The noise is redoubled.*)

LADY BRACKNELL

I wish he would arrive at some conclusion.

GWENDOLEN

This suspense is terrible. I hope it will last.

(*Enter* JACK *with a hand-bag of black leather in his hand.*)

JACK

(*Rushing over to* MISS PRISM.) Is this the hand-bag, Miss Prism? Examine it carefully before you speak. The happiness of more than one life depends on your answer.

MISS PRISM

(*Calmly.*) It seems to be mine. Yes, here is the injury it received through the upsetting of a Gower Street omnibus in younger and happier days. Here is the stain on the lining caused by the explosion of a temperance beverage, an incident that occurred at Leamington. And here, on the lock, are my initials. I had forgotten that in an extravagant mood I had had them placed there. The bag is undoubtedly mine. I am delighted to have it so unexpectedly restored to me. It has been a great inconvenience being without it all these years.

JACK

(*In a pathetic voice.*) Miss Prism, more is restored to you than this hand-bag. I was the baby you placed in it.

MISS PRISM

(*Amazed.*) You?

JACK

(*Embracing her.*) Yes . . . mother!

MISS PRISM

(*Recoiling in indignant astonishment.*) Mr. Worthing! I am unmarried!

JACK

Unmarried! I do not deny that is a serious blow. But after all, who has the right to cast a stone against one who has suffered? Cannot repentance wipe out an act of folly? Why should there be one law for men, and another for women? Mother, I forgive you. (*Tries to embrace her again.*)

MISS PRISM

(*Still more indignant.*) Mr. Worthing, there is some error. (*Pointing to* LADY BRACKNELL.) There is the lady who can tell you who you really are.

JACK

(*After a pause.*) Lady Bracknell, I hate to seem inquisitive, but would you kindly inform me who I am?

LADY BRACKNELL

I am afraid that the news I have to give you will not altogether please you. You are the son of my poor sister, Mrs. Moncrieff, and consequently Algernon's elder brother.

JACK

Algy's elder brother! Then I have a brother after all. I knew I had a brother! I always said I had a brother! Cecily,—how could you have ever doubted that I had a brother? (*Seizes hold of* ALGERNON.) Dr. Chasuble, my unfortunate brother. Miss Prism, my unfortunate brother. Gwendolen, my unfortunate brother. Algy, you young scoundrel, you will have to treat me with more respect in the future. You have never behaved to me like a brother in all your life.

ALGERNON

Well, not till to-day, old boy, I admit. I did my best, however, though I was out of practice. (*Shakes hands.*)

GWENDOLEN

(*To* JACK.) My own! But what own are you? What is your Christian name, now that you have become some one else?

JACK

Good heavens! . . . I had quite forgotten that point. Your decision on the subject of my name is irrevocable, I suppose?

GWENDOLEN

I never change, except in my affections.

CECILY

What a noble nature you have, Gwendolen!

JACK

Then the question had better be cleared up at once. Aunt Augusta, a moment. At the time when Miss Prism left me in the hand-bag, had I been christened already?

LADY BRACKNELL

Every luxury that money could buy, including christening, had been lavished on you by your fond and doting parents.

JACK

Then I was christened! That is settled. Now, what name was I given? Let me know the worst.

LADY BRACKNELL

Being the eldest son you were naturally christened after your father.

JACK

(*Irritably.*) Yes, but what was my father's Christian name?

LADY BRACKNELL

(*Meditatively.*) I cannot at the present moment recall what the General's Christian name was. But I have no doubt he had one. He was eccentric, I admit. But only in later years. And that was the result of the Indian climate, and marriage, and indigestion, and other things of that kind.

JACK

Algy! Can't you recollect what our father's Christian name was?

ALGERNON

My dear boy, we were never even on speaking terms. He died before I was a year old.

JACK

His name would appear in the Army Lists of the period, I suppose, Aunt Augusta?

LADY BRACKNELL

The General was essentially a man of peace, except in his domestic life. But I have no doubt his name would appear in any military directory.

JACK

The Army Lists of the last forty years are here. These delightful records should have been my constant study. (*Rushes to bookcase and tears the books out.*) M. Generals . . . Mallam, Maxbohm, Magley, what ghastly names they have—Markby, Migsby, Mobbs, Moncrieff! Lieutenant 1840, Captain, Lieutenant-Colonel, Colonel, General 1869, Christian names, Ernest John. (*Puts book very quietly down and speaks quite calmly.*) I always told you, Gwendolen, my name was Ernest, didn't I? Well, it is Ernest after all. I mean it naturally is Ernest.

LADY BRACKNELL

Yes, I remember now that the General was called Ernest, I knew I had some particular reason for disliking the name.

GWENDOLEN

Ernest! My own Ernest! I felt from the first that you could have no other name!

JACK

Gwendolen, it is a terrible thing for a man to find out suddenly that all his life he has been speaking nothing but the truth. Can you forgive me?

GWENDOLEN

I can. For I feel that you are sure to change.

JACK

My own one!

CHASUBLE

(*To* MISS PRISM.) Lætitia! (*Embraces her*)

MISS PRISM

(*Enthusiastically.*) Frederick! At last!

ALGERNON

Cecily! (*Embraces her.*) At last!

JACK

Gwendolen! (*Embraces her.*) At last!

LADY BRACKNELL

My nephew, you seem to be displaying signs of triviality.

JACK

On the contrary, Aunt Augusta, I've now realised for the first time in my life the vital Importance of Being Earnest.

TABLEAU